THE DEVOURERS

Del Rey | New York

THE DEVOURERS

Indra Das

Published in the United States by Del Rey, an imprint of Random House, a division of Penguin Random House LLC, New York.

DEL REY and the HOUSE colophon are registered trademarks of Penguin Random House LLC.

Originally published in India, Pakistan, Sri Lanka, and Nepal by Penguin Books India Pvt. Ltd., a member of The Penguin Group, in 2015.

LIBRARY OF CONGRESS CATALOGING-IN-PUBLICATION DATA

Names: Das, Indra, author.
Title: The devourers / Indra Das.
Description: New York : Del Rey, 2016.
Identifiers: LCCN 2016008016 (print) | LCCN 2016018405 (ebook) |
ISBN 9781101967515 (hardback) | ISBN 9781101967522 (ebook)
Subjects: LCSH: College teachers—Fiction. | Shapeshifting—Fiction. |
Mogul Empire—Fiction. | India—Fiction. | BISAC: FICTION / Literary. |
FICTION / Fantasy / Historical. | GSAFD: Fantasy fiction.
Classification: LCC PR9499.4.D3525 D48 2016 (print) |
LCC PR9499.4.D3525 (ebook) | DDC 823/.92—dc23
LC record available at https://lccn.loc.gov/2016008016

Printed in the United States of America on acid-free paper.

randomhousebooks.com

2 4 6 8 9 7 5 3 1

First U.S. Edition

Book design by Virginia Norey

To my parents, who've waited patiently
to hold their son's first book in their hands

The roaring of lions, the howling of wolves,
the raging of the stormy sea, and the destructive sword,
are portions of eternity too great for the eye of man.

—WILLIAM BLAKE,
The Marriage of Heaven and Hell

Contents

Part One

❧

HUNTING GROUND

1

My part in this story began the winter before winters started getting warmer, on a full-moon night so bright you could see your own shadow on an unlit rooftop. It was under that moon—slightly smudged by December mist clinging to the streets of Kolkata—that I met a man who told me he was half werewolf. He said this to me as if it were no different from being half Bengali, half Punjabi, half Parsi. Half werewolf under a full moon. Not the most subtle kind of irony, but a necessary one, if I'm to value the veracity of my recollections.

To set the stage, I must tell you where I was.

Think of a field breathing the cool of nighttime into the soles of your shoes. A large tent in front of you   cloth, canvas, and bamboo— lit from within. Electric lamps surrounding a wooden stage that creaks under the bare feet of bright-robed minstrels. This tent is where the rural bards of Bengal, the bauls, gather every winter to make music for city people. It's raw music, at times both shrill and hoarse, stained with hashish smoke and the self-proclaimed madness of their sect. A celebration of what's been lost, under the vigil of orange-eyed streetlights.

I am there, that night.

Outside in the cold, in Shaktigarh Math, a city park. I watch the bauls and their audience through the fabric of the tent. Shadows flit across as they clap and cheer. The crowd extends outside, faces lit by cigarettes and spliffs. Hand-rolled cigarette between my fingers, grass under my shoes. A stranger walks up and stands beside me. The street dogs are gathering by the field, their eyes hungry. It's one in the morning.

"Afraid to go inside?" the stranger asks. "They may be mad, but they won't bite."

He's talking about the bauls. I laugh dutifully. I'm afraid he wants a smoke, having seen my tin of cigarettes. I don't want to share; I rolled them very carefully. I tell him I prefer the night air to the tent, not thinking to bring up the fact that there's no smoking allowed within. I ask what he's doing outside.

"The music's a little too shrill for my ears. I can appreciate it just fine from here." His voice is gentle, his words unhurried.

He takes out his own hash joint. I glance sideways at him as he lights up. The flame illuminates a slender face, its glow running along hairless skin and brushing against the lines of shadow that hug his high cheekbones. I'm disarmed by his androgynous beauty before he even tells his secret.

"I'm a werewolf," he says. Smoke flares out of his mouth in curls that wreathe his long black hair, giving him silver-blue locks for a passing second. I don't see him throw away the match, but his foot moves to rub it into the soil. He's wearing wicker sandals. Dark flecks of dirt hide under unclipped nails on the ends of his long toes. Apparently the cold doesn't bother him enough for socks or shoes.

Now, I wish I could tell you this man looks wolfish, that he has a hint of green glinting in his eyes, that his eyebrows meet right above his nose, that his palms have a scattering of hair that tickles my own palms as we shake hands, that his sideburns are thick and shaggy and silvered as the bark of a snow-dusted birch at gray dawn. But I'm not here to make things up.

"Need a light?" he asks, and I'm startled to find a new flame between his fingers, the hiss of the struck match reaching my ears like an afterthought. Afraid that I've been caught staring at his dirty toes and beautiful face, I nod, even though there's a lighter in my breast pocket. He touches the flame to my cigarette.

"You heard right," he says, tossing the match. "Well, I'm actually half werewolf. But you heard right."

"I didn't ask if I'd heard right."

"You were thinking it, though," he says with a smile.

"I wasn't, actually. I can hear just fine," I assure him. He keeps smiling. I get embarrassed.

"Thanks for the light," I say with a cough. My lungs burn from too enthusiastic a first drag. "I suppose I shouldn't be boasting about my hearing. Wolves have great hearing, right?"

"I'm not a wolf. And yes, they do."

"There aren't any wolves near Kolkata. Are there? They're probably extinct in India."

"Just because you don't see them doesn't mean they're not there," he says. I observe that his fingernails are as long as his toenails, and as dirty. Little black sickles hiding under them. I nod, light-headed from the nicotine rush.

"I've seen jackals on the golf greens at Tolly Club."

He doesn't say anything. I feel compelled to keep talking.

"My parents have a house. Like a weekend getaway. Outside the city, in Baniban. The caretakers there used to scare me when I was a boy, with stories about wildcats from the woods stealing their chickens. Now that you mention it, there might have been a wolf visit. I never really believed any of those stories. They scared me, though. I never even saw any of those animals. Except a snake, once." A true story. I still remember the gray coils of the serpent lying there by the flowerpots; it had been beaten to death by the help. They said it was venomous, though I certainly couldn't tell.

"You're not afraid of talking to strangers. I like that," he says, swaying slightly now to the rising call of the bauls' voices.

I feel shy now, which is absurd. "What's your other half, then? Human? Aren't all werewolves half human?" I ask him.

He picks a bit of tobacco out of his teeth, which I don't think I've ever seen a smoker actually do. Spittle clicks between his fingertips and his tongue. "Family history can be a tedious business. Though *family* isn't quite the right word."

And that's all he says. For someone who clearly wants to talk to me, he says very little.

"When did you find out you were a . . . a half werewolf?"

He shrugs. "I've been one all my life. Before we were called were-wolves, really."

"What's it like?" I ask, the questions flowing from my smoke-soured mouth. I can't think of anything more awkward at this moment than standing beside this man and not responding to what he's just said to me.

"You've seen the movies. I am master of my fortune. The moon is my mistress."

"And cliché is your cabaret?" I ask. Intoxicated disbelief dulls me into self-deprecation. I analyze my words, which seem nonsensical. I look around, checking to make sure the others standing around us in the field are still there, to run my eyes over the streaks of their shadows. The rhythm of the music snarls to the throb of light and shadow behind the walls of the tent.

He doesn't growl at me. "Are you an English professor, by any chance?"

"No. But close. I *am* a professor. Of history, actually. Started teaching a couple of years ago."

His shapely eyebrows rise. "History? Tales. The weaving of words. A favorite discipline of mine. I congratulate you on your choice of profession, young though you seem for such an endeavor. To tell stories of the past to children who walk into the future is a task both noble and taxing." I feel a mix of resentment and pleasure from being called young by someone who looks younger than me.

"Well, they're not exactly children, they're college students—"

"If only we had better storytellers, perhaps they would learn more willingly from the past," he says.

"Maybe."

"Am I speaking in clichés again, Professor?"

A white kitten, its wide eyes rimmed with rheum, looks up at me as it crawls around us. It starts at the violent sound of sticks shattering against each other. I see children mock-fighting with surprising malice nearby, their screams jarring and bodies lithe against the mist. The kitten stumbles and uses my ankle as cover. The street dogs skirt the edges of the field, pack instinct glittering in their eyes as they surround us. Muzzles peel back in tentative grimaces. Their teeth look yellow under the streetlights. They watch the kitten.

"You like cats?" the stranger asks, looking at the kitten, which gingerly licks my fingers with a dry and scratchy tongue as I pick it up. Its little heart putters against my palm. I can feel its warm body shaking.

Ash flutters from my cigarette as I tap it, brief lives twinkling and fading to gray by our feet. I take care not to burn the kitten.

"Let me guess," I say. "I've had the blood of the wolf within me all along. You've come to initiate me into the ways of our tribe, to run with my brothers and sisters to the lunar ebb and flow. I'm the chosen one. The savior of our people. And the time of our uprising has come. We're going to rule the world," I say, my sarcasm blunted by how serious I sound. I surprise myself with the eagerness with which I tell this story of possibilities to the stranger. The dogs have come closer, ignoring even the threat of so many humans to get closer to the kitten in my hands.

The stranger grins at me. It's the first time he seems animalistic.

"I want to tell you a story. Let's go inside."

"Won't it hurt your ears?"

He takes one deep drag before licking the burnt-out roach and making it disappear into one of his pockets. I realize that my cigarette has whittled away to the end, its heat tickling my cold fingers.

The stranger strides toward the tent, through the scattered people smoking, past the food stalls with their cheaply wired fluorescents ticking to the patter of night insects. The sizzle of batter in oil and babble of voices only aggravates the sense that I am treading on the tune the bauls are playing—everything here seems to be part of their music, as if the field itself were one stage, and all of us musicians. I toss the cigarette butt and follow the stranger. The dogs begin to follow as well, but stop. I can see more of them running around the field. Repositioning. I hold the kitten close to my chest and go inside.

The tent is a different universe. The hot smell of electric lamps tempered by the chill, the sweaty damp of the crowd, the claustrophobic buzz of being inside an enclosed fire hazard. Minstrels' feet thump on the stage like drumbeats, twins to the sharper pulse of their dugi drums and tremulous drone of the one-stringed ektara. Their saffron robes are ribbons of sound, twirling around their bark-burnt bodies as they dance, their madness set aflame by their own music.

My ears itch. Their voices are very loud. The stranger doesn't even grimace. Some of the spectators squat on the ground, some sit on folding chairs set in haphazard rows. We sit at the back of the tent. I can feel the cold metal of the chair through my pants.

The kitten compresses itself into a ball in my lap, its trembling eased somewhat. Its head darts to and fro. The stranger is looking at the bauls, swaying his head, tapping his feet, curling his toes.

"The story?" I ask.

"Listen. Don't say anything. I'm going to tell you a story."

"I know, I just said—"

He hisses, startling me into silence. The kitten almost leaps out of my lap. I clench my fingers around it, stroking its fur.

"Listen," he repeats. He is not looking at me. "I am going to tell you a story, and it is true. To set the stage, I must tell you where I was." His words wind their way through the overwhelming sound of the music, which seems to rise with each passing second. The light inside the tent is gauzy. The interior moves in slow arcs as dizziness sets in. I close my eyes. Darkness, touched with blossoms of light beyond my eyelids. His voice, soothing, guiding me as the dark becomes deeper.

The kitten is purring, vibrating against my hands. I can hear the scrabble of swift paws outside the tent, the anxious snarls of the dogs.

It is very dark as the stranger tells the story.

To set the stage, I must tell you where I was, *he says.*

It is very dark. I listen.

Think of a field. A swamp, rather. This is a long time ago. Kolkata. Calcutta, or what will be Calcutta. Maybe it is this very field, this very ground. It is different then, overgrown and marshy, the hum and tickle of insects like a grainy blanket over this winter night. It is cloudy, the moonlight diffuse as it sparkles on the stretches of water hiding under the reeds. The darkness is oppressive. There is no blush of electricity on the horizon, no vast cities for the sky to reflect. Somewhere beyond the dark, there are three villages: Kalikata, Sutanati, Gobindapur. They belong to the British East India Company. They are building a fort known as William. Things are changing, a new century nears. It will be the eighteenth, by the Christian calendar.

The campfire is an oasis of light. The bauls gather around, flames glistening on their dark swamp-damp skins, twinkling in their beards. They sing to ward off the encroaching darkness, their words lifting with the wood sparks toward the stars. They sing, unheeding of signatures on paper, of land exchanges and politics, of the white traders and their tensions with the Nawab and the Mughal Empire. Here in the firelight, they make music and tell stories to one another. To the land. To Bengal. To Hindustan, which does not belong to them, nor to the British, nor the Mughals. They know there are things in the wilderness that neither Mughal nor white man has in his documents of ownership. Things to be found in stories. Then again, they also claim to be mad.

I watch the bauls. I can see the others in the gloom, crouched amid the reeds, circling slowly. More approach from afar, their claws sinking into the mud. I can hear them, though. The rustle of their spined fur, the twisting of rushes against their backs.

A howl slices the dark. The bauls falter but continue singing, holding tight to their instruments and gnarled staves. I can hear the mosquitoes whining around them, alighting on knuckles popping against skin, gorging, dying in the heat of the fire. There is a young woman amid this group of traveling bauls. She looks out into the darkness, the words of their song dissolving on her tongue. Her hair is so black, it melts into the night. I remember the taste of her lips, moist but cool from the night air. She keeps her eyes beyond the borders of the fire, searching a wilderness stirred into sentience by the noises of insect and animal, cricket and cockroach, moth and mosquito, snake and mongoose, fox and field rat, jackal and wildcat. Her bright patchwork cloak is wrapped tight around her body, marking her out. She is tired, short, and unarmed, and stands no chance of surviving the attack. Not that the others do, either. I can smell her terror like sweat against the gritty spice of wood smoke. The wet soil of the marsh is cold between my toes. The insects catch in my fur, wrestling it, tickling like the reeds and plants around me.

The woman knows we are here, beyond their firelight. She knows because I told her myself, as a young man with long hair and kind eyes, tiger pelt on my back. *Your party will never reach Sutanati and the banks of the river. You are being hunted. You have a day to run away, for we are patient, and draw out the hunt for pleasure and sport,* I said to her in her sleep, while my own kin were unaware. I am a shape-shifter, after all, and not without my abilities.

She heard me, and saw me, though she slept while I whispered in her ear. She smelled my musk of swamp and blood, shit and piss and rank fur, hair and smooth human skin. She saw the lamps of my green eyes, and the pools of my brown eyes. I saw her face twitch as I spoke. She smelled of the stale sweat of travel, of the rich green of sleeping on grass, of the slick of oil on her lips from the roti and sabzi she had eaten before sleeping. I kissed her once. A chill ran across my neck as I did, because she reminded me so much of someone gone.

I look in the stranger's eyes to see if they are still brown. "I don't feel well," *I say.* Shhhh. *The susurrus of reeds in the breeze. The music of the bauls is unearthly now, their howls and shrieks like banshee wails. The lights are swaying, cutting white trails in the air. The kitten is coiled in my lap. The scrabble of paws, outside.*

The stranger shakes his head. You don't interrupt the storyteller, *he says with a gentle smile. I can feel the swamp outside, the city gone, the beasts gathering for the hunt in the misty wilderness. My fingers tighten around the kitten. The tent is an oasis of light, hot smell of electric lamps. Wood smoke. Wilderness encroaches.*

Close your eyes.

She heard me in her sleep, this baul woman with dirt in her hair, her lips sticky with just a little oil. It is clear that she remembers my warning, but she has not run away. Perhaps one of the bauls is her father, or mother, or sibling, or friend, or lover. It does not matter. She will not leave them behind. She begins to sing with them now, her scared voice strained. She remembers my smell, senses it now beyond the fire, in the tangle of the dark.

More of us come from the horizons. The scent of cow's blood, a slaughter on their muzzles. They have eaten. But their hunt is not over. Their eyes weave trails as they run, leaping fireflies tracking their loping gait. They flank the group of humans, cutting off escape.

The full moon watches through the clouds, eager for massacre. With a bark of exhaled air, the clatter of tusk on fang, we spring. The bauls' song is loud, and beautiful in its imperfection. It is their last. I run with my pack. My tribe. The bauls are surrounded. They sing till the very last moment.

The first kill is silent as our running, a glistening whisper of crimson in the air. The last is louder than the baying of a wolf, and rings like the bauls' mad song across the marshes of what is not yet Kolkata. I can hear the howl as I run with this human in my arms, into the darkness, away from the shadows of slaughter. The howl curdles into a roar, enveloping the scream of the last dying minstrel.

But she is alive, against me, shivering against my dew-dappled fur. She is alive.

I open my eyes. The tent is still here. The city is outside. Mosquitoes feast on my neck and arms, leaving welts.

"You can guess the rest, I'm sure," he says.

I wipe a sheen of sweat from my neck, shaking my head. "I think I got a bit much of your smoke," I mumble. But I know whatever just happened wasn't me getting a contact high. I feel like I've just woken from the most vivid dream I've ever had. "Don't tell me, you run away with this baul girl and live happily ever after. Never mind that you kidnapped her, and got her family and friends killed in front of her."

"Happily ever after," he says. "Isn't that ironic, considering I'm sitting right here, right now."

"Immortality is a side effect of lycanthropy, is it?" I ask. Remembering the kitten, I give it some more attention. It mewls, eyes narrowing to sleepy slits.

"Please, Professor. A lycanthrope is a person who mistakenly believes they can turn into a wolf. I'm not a person, I don't turn into a wolf, and I'm not ill. What I am has no basis in science or medicine."

"My mistake. You didn't answer my question, though. Are you saying you're immortal?"

His shoulders twitch. A silent laugh, perhaps. "Take what you will from my story. I never said that I was the hunter in the tale. It could have been one of my ancestors. A story passed down."

"I closed my eyes and I saw it. I smelled it. I don't even believe you, and I felt it. I felt it." I shake my head. "Are you a hypnotist?"

"I happen to be a good storyteller."

"Modest," I mutter, and shake my head. "So you're rationalizing after telling me you're a werewolf."

"Half werewolf. And, Professor, I am merely showing you the benefits of rationalizing a story. There are none. Stories are fiction. Made up."

"You told me that story was true," I remark, feeling smug.

"It is."

Even as he says this, I see the look in his eyes and know that his heart has been broken by someone with black hair that melted into night, someone whose crippling revulsion toward him, whose grease-stained kiss, still linger in his mind. I give him a moment of silence, surprised by this realization, as mundane as it is. After all, whose heart hasn't been broken by someone? He seems suddenly too old to look so young, with his smooth face and lush, long hair (touched though it is by the occasional strand of gray). We share a long silence for the first time. It disturbs me, the ease with which I feel sad for him after he's told me a story steeped in carnage, not to mention a rather romantic outlook on kissing people in their sleep.

"What happens afterward?" I venture, too curious not to ask.

"You're not a professor of literature, but you are a professor of history. History has all the stories. Make it up. Guess. A variation on the tragedy, I suppose. The woman is neither immortal, nor willing to forgive her kidnapper, this rakshasa, this monster. He leaves her in the village of Kalikata, or at the banks of the Hooghly at Sutanati, where her fellow travelers were bound." He pauses, taking a deep breath. He continues.

"Or even if he charms her with a shape-shifter's magic and they wander off and get married, she dies and he lives on to survive and tell his story to a random wayfarer centuries later. Either way, he is alone. His pack is not forgiving of intermingling with humans, nor sabotaging a hunt, making him an exile from his own kind. They can smell his betrayal from a mile away."

"This isn't too far from a story about a chosen one rising to lead his tribe to salvation, is it? Lone exile, wandering into the future, unable to die, shifting between shapes, all that."

He nods. "I'm just giving you some options. But I knew you had it in you, Professor. You can tell someone the rest of the story. Or tell it to yourself. Romance, fantasy, horror, realism, moralistic fable, history, lies, truth. It's all there for you. Pick and choose, my friend."

"You're the first Indian werewolf I've ever heard of."

"*Werewolf* is one word. A European one. We've been called many, many things. You can call me anything you like. The shape-shifter is a common thing in the end, and our stories are told here as everywhere else."

"And yet you used the European word," I say.

He nods. "You've got me there." I see him shift a bit in his chair, and wonder if I've made him uncomfortable.

"So if shape-shifters are so common, how come nobody knows about you?" I ask.

"Everybody knows about us. Most of them just don't believe that we're real anymore."

"Why don't you tell them you are?"

"Maybe in this day and age we just want to be left alone."

"And occasionally tell a story to a random wayfarer?"

"Exactly."

The kitten squeals and leaps out of my lap. The stranger has caught the animal before I can even react.

"Once everyone leaves, the dogs outside will chase this kitten down and tear it to pieces. For sport," he says, running his long fingers through the little creature's dirty fur. "'And humans have the arrogance to say they're the only animals capable of cruelty."

"Humans?" I try to laugh. "You're generalizing just a bit."

"Apologies." He looks at me. The crowd bursts into applause as the bauls finish. Chairs clatter against one another as several spectators stand, some drunk. I didn't even notice that the song had ended. The stranger speaks despite the cacophony, and his voice is clear enough that I can hear him. "You know what distinguishes us from the dogs out there?" he asks me. I nod, despite myself. I want to give him a laundry list of things, but I don't.

"We can tell stories," I say instead.

"Well done, Professor. Perhaps my story did not fall on deaf ears after all." I say nothing. He gets up, surprising me. "Wait." I raise my voice. "Where are you going?" I ask.

"I'm going to walk away with this kitten, of course. The dogs won't come near me. I like dogs, myself, but they can be a tad cruel sometimes. So can cats. So can we all. Anyway, that ragtag pack outside won't come near me. I'll feed this little thing till it has the strength to survive, and I'll let it come and go as it pleases after that."

"Ever the compassionate werewolf, are you?"

He shrugs, looking weary. "Come now. A moment of compassion every two centuries hardly makes one compassionate, does it? You don't want to hear about the things I've done in your and other lifetimes. But there it is. Just today, I saw two dogs—they were licking each other, lapping at each other's muzzles as if they loved each other with every cell in their bodies. Did they? Or was it just two animals sniffing out compatible genes? When two humans kiss, isn't it the same thing, deep down? I don't know. It was a moment I found worthy of keeping in my memory, and telling someone. I have done so. I thank you for lending a willing ear. I'm going now, Professor."

I don't know what to say. He gets up to leave. "Walk with me, if you like," he adds.

As if this has been his plan all along, or mine, I get up and follow him. So we leave, together. The dogs trail us at the edges of my vision, eager for the fragile prey curled up in the stranger's arms.

2

In the warren of narrow roads beyond Shaktigarh Math, we lose the sounds and music of the mela. They're replaced by the tick of claws on asphalt and concrete eroded by rain. I've always been afraid of street dogs at night, but they keep away, don't even bark. As if they smell something strange in the air. They watch us, ears pricked, silent Anubis-faced sentinels on the deserted street corners of Jadavpur. The rows of blanketed bodies on the footpaths give the streets the feeling of an open tomb. The dogs uncaring guardians to these sleeping humans who share their nocturnal territory, this electric-lit kingdom lined with the twinkle of broken glass, shadows etched across stucco and worn paint, walls glyphed with graffiti in Bengali, Hindi, English.

The stranger holds the kitten to his chest. Madonna and child. His hair catching light to halo his head. We pass a rickshaw parked by a piss-streaked wall, field rats huddling around its wheels, its puller wrapped in a shawl under the canopy. Beyond the corridor of the road, the flare of passing headlights pales the stranger's face for a moment.

"Do you want to hear more?" the stranger asks. I can't tell if he's hesitant or just being soft-spoken. His face stippled with the shadows of leaves, sandals slapping the road.

"Yes. Finish the story."

"Maybe someday. Tonight you deserve another one, for being such a good listener."

"If you like," I say.

"You know now. What to do," he tells me. I do. I close my eyes.

"Keep your eyes half open. As if meditating," he says. I let some light under my lids. I can smell the stranger now, as if his storytelling has worked him into a sweat. A smell that on anyone else would make me hold my breath. On him it feels alluring, like the smell of my own sweat on summer nights, sublimating on skin flushed with arousal, pooling in my armpits.

"Tell me if I'm about to trip over something," I tell him.

"What do you see when you think of a werewolf?" he asks me.

"I . . ."

"Don't answer, just think."

Something takes hold of me—the cold night air and the smell of the stranger making me feel faint. That stupor, like in the tent at the mela. I realize I want it. I think of what he's asked me to think. Of man and wolf, man and animal, man and woman and animal, twisted together, fur and bones and flesh and claws and teeth, glowing eyes and arched spines, human skin peeling and tearing to spill out flea-bitten fur, a mass of memories from literature and film and myth and art.

"You know, of course, of the men that lived far, far from here and now, wearing dead wolves and bears on their backs as they fought and killed."

His presence beside me is a bonfire, infecting the wash of street-lights with its warmth, even the mist becoming smoke.

"And here where we stand, long before India, before its empires and kingdoms, there were human tribes who identified with dogs and wolves, with wild animals. And there were, and still are, tribes who are not human, who identify with humans in similar ways. Who take the shape of humans, just as humans took the shape of animals by wearing skins."

The vestigial coat of my animal fur rises up, pathetic prickles under my cotton and wool clothes. I want to say something but can barely speak. His hand brushes my shoulder, and the contact courses through my entire arm. "It's all right," he says. "Now listen to me."

I walk forward half blind, guided by the sound of his voice. The lapping of tongues, clicking of fangs behind us. The minute vibration of the kitten's chest. I become aware of how cold it is again. *The stranger speaks, or chants, and it sounds like English.* But his accent seems different now, more guttural. I can almost hear other tongues behind his voice, like the overlapping tones of a throat singer's song.

I hear the panting, the claws, behind and around us. Even as I walk, I dream, of something next to me in the stranger's place, massive and hunched, rippling like the wind made flesh. Something neither human nor animal, bristling with an energy that I can only describe as elemental. I feel its heat, smell its pungent musk of blood-spiced piss and shit and mud-caked hair, feel it ready to lope out of this distant corner of my vision, on sinewy legs covered in fur, shimmering under streetlights eclipsed by its size. Those very streetlights become rows of high torches rippling with fire, a path for us two, human and non-human, leading into the well of a night long past, leading backward into the stinking dark of fermented history.

The stranger speaks, or chants, and it sounds like English.

The Úlfhéðinn pants like the beast he is not, like the dead wolf he wears on his broad back. Spittle flies from his froth-flecked lips, and his breath pours steaming on the cold air. Blood-rimmed pupils full and black, he stares at me. I am the beast he sees in himself, hot and rank and vast, bear and wolf and man. I am his doppelgänger, grown huge on the nourishment of his faith. His spear is held high and trembling, his shield streaked with spit where he has bitten it in frenzy, his boots stamping the frozen ground. My claw is firm, sunken in the soil. I am ready. He kicks the ground and runs to me.

It has been months since I've eaten of human, but I am not afraid. I am like Fenrir before Týr, come to bite the war god's hand, or to swallow the All-father himself. I am kveldulf, the evening-wolf come sunset. I see him, human beneath his bloodlust and dye. I am more than human. My howl drowns out his cry.

But he, too, is fearless. His spear slams into my head, the shaft quivering from the impact. His aim is perfect, his movements quick, and his arm strong. He leaps toward me as I slow down. There is a rain drizzling upon the earth and my naked fur and it is blood. It comes from the fresh hole beneath my blinded left eye, stanched only by the weapon that made it. The Úlfhéðinn pounces. The metal edge of his shield crashes into my face, cracking the bridge of my muzzle and shattering my curved fangs. He throws the shield to the ground and jumps onto me, gripping his spear. I look up at him in crippling disbelief, this human perched on my great form, and under the fanged crown of dead wolf's gums I see him turned. He is no shape-changer, and yet he has become a god in that moment. He has struck down Fenrir.

And then, I am afraid.

It is a terrible thing to be afraid in this shape, to hear my deafening howl twisted to a withering whine as the Úlfhéðinn throws his human cry up to the stars. His boots on my shoulders, he drives his weapon deeper into my head. Each turn of the broad spearhead widens a split running from the crack beneath my eye.

I am awakened by panic. I will die if I do nothing. I embrace him. My talons are too sharp for his unarmored sides, gouging deep lines across the seamed muscle of his torso. He tumbles against me, drenching me with his wounds. I rip him open and fling him off. Mouth mad and red, he gives me one last bloody roar of defiance. I return the cry tenfold and lunge.

His skull cracks beneath my tusks. Scarred hands spasm around the spear still in me, slide off the wet wood. I shake my wounded head, snapping his neck. The sound rings loud in the silenced forest. Limp, he falls from my mouth. The frozen ground melts to dark mud under the Úlfhéðinn's broken body. It is done.

I pull the spear from beneath my useless eye, opening the cleave in my skull. It spatters and hisses into the muddy snow. Seeking the rich scents of my prey's flesh and soul, I crawl on all fours to his corpse, touching my teeth to his stomach. A desperate hunger seizes my shuddering body and I devour him.

He has nearly taken my life, and now he returns it to me with each bite I take of him, burning in my gut like the flesh of some prophet imbued with divine flame. I feel as if I am eating of my own people, of the carcass of a shape-changer. Above the trees, the night sky is hung with the glowing banners of the Úlfhéðinn's gods. I eat of him as if he is my last supper. With his bones I go down into the cold hard earth, burrowing deep into the frost, my hide crisped with blood and water.

Night ends and I am still alive. I burst from the frozen grave I buried myself in, now turned to wet womb from my heat. Sunlight washes

over my skin, now without fur. Bitter winter cuts me despite dawn's
light. I am smaller, weaker, though still stronger than any human. The
gleam of starlight as only my second self can see it vanishes to give way
to the unsubtle glare of man's morning. I am more than human, but
less than my second self.

But today I am grateful for the dead man, who lies at my feet, and
lingers in my changed veins. I look at my arms, at the rest of my small,
pale shape, with its thickets of undergrown hair, and I bend low to the
frozen crimson mirror of my prey's blood. In its dark surface, I can see
my sunlit face, and it is now the face of the Úlfhéðinn, this man who
now lives in me. There is a new scar on his face, knotted and thick,
running down his cheek from just below the right eye, which is now
milky and gray. I bid farewell to my previous self.

I touch the slick of red ice, touch his crusted entrails, and kiss my
fingers; touch my forehead, my chest, my genitals. Here I fell by my
pride, and here I was remade by my prey.

I open my eyes.

I look at my small brown hands, smooth and lacking in scar tissue,
and I wonder who I am. Then I see the stranger next to me smoking a
cigarette, and know I am not him. His lips are rouged with new color.
I look at him, gaunt and tall, skin brown like mine, hair black, and I'm
amazed that I know this man now. I wonder where he's from—whether
born of some arcane violence in the depths of ancient Scandinavia, or
slid squalling into the hands of doctors in a hospital in India mere
decades ago, like me. I wonder at the fact that I'm even considering the
former.

He laughs, whether reading my mind I can't tell. "Welcome back,"
he says, a lick of smoke escaping his teeth. His fingers are stained with
the new red on his lips as well. I see a dead rat by his feet, neatly slit
open, though it could be lipstick on the stranger's mouth.

We're still near Jadavpur. This is real. But we've walked quite a bit.
No longer in the honeycomb of alleys around Shaktigarh Math, we
stand instead at the wider avenue of Prince Anwarshah Road. The
street is lined with shuttered shops and silent vehicles.

"If I didn't trust you, I'd swear you've drugged me somehow," I tell him.

"It's probably unwise to trust me, so you can swear all you like."

"You're admitting you're untrustworthy?" I ask.

"You just met me. Surely telling you a story or two isn't enough to gain someone's trust. You have to earn that, yes?"

"Telling a story or two. You've a way with understatement." I cough out a bit of laughter, bending down to grasp my knees. I feel incredibly tired. "God, I feel so hungry. Like I'm starving."

"Yes," he agrees, and lets out a piercing whistle.

A taxi stops beside us. The stranger tosses the remaining shred of his cigarette.

The driver tells us in Hindi that it'll be twenty rupees extra this late.

"Come on. Let's get you something to eat. My treat," the stranger tells me, holding open the cab door.

"That's really not necessary," I tell him as my stomach growls. But I get into the taxi all the same, slumping into the backseat like a drunken teenager. The stranger follows. The car's humid with the rubbery reek of sweat and upholstery. A string of browned lemons and chilies hanging from the rearview mirror twists in the air, charming the car with luck. The taxi pulls out past the row of off-duty cabs lining the front of South City Mall and its transparent façade, now dark, the hidden metal slashes of stilled escalator steps inside throwing weak reflections from the ambient streetlight. Dimmed billboards smile down on us with the giant faces of smiling models and Bollywood stars.

I slip in and out of a doze as the taxi moves through Kolkata by night. An empty city, populated only with the bulbous yellow beetle-shapes of Ambassador taxis and the roaring, painted monsters of supply lorries, their spattered mudflaps and rear bumpers decorated with crude faces of tusked demons and red English lettering in careful brushstrokes, warning of DANGER and imploring their fellow denizens of the road to BLOW HORN PLEASE as their shaking exhaust pipes belch clouds of dark smoke. Light filters through the car windows and slides across the stranger's face, which flashes with waking red when a car or truck stops next to us while indicating.

When we stop, it is on Ballygunge Circular Road, by Sharma's, one of the few all-night roadside dhabas that service the nocturnals of Kolkata. I have no idea whether the stranger pays the taxi driver his extra twenty rupees. Like a temple, Sharma's has drawn a flock to its open storefront, which breathes out air thick with the smell of scorched meat and live bodies. With the stranger next to me, it feels like a watering spot, an oasis for human animals to gather at night, ravenous and thirsty, from late-night lorry drivers and laborers to students and wealthy young clubbers. Women remain under-represented, some nervous and others uncaring amid the crush of eating men. The footpath and road in front of Sharma's is cluttered with double-parked cars, patrons eating inside them to avoid the crowd in the dhaba, their windshields occasionally spotted with bird shit from the trees above.

We sit at one of the tables inside, hard bench under our buttocks. We don't wait long for a tin tray of butter masala chicken, its gravy neon orange with a floating layer of oil. Ravenous, I dip my naan in the slop and eat the whole tray, feeding a hunger so strong it makes my belly hurt. The stranger doesn't eat, watching the patrons around us, face calm under the sleepless fluorescents, their light replicated by tiled walls marked with azure Pepsi ads. We don't talk much, but the silence feels earned after the past few hours that we've spent together. I feel a comfort from his presence as he taps his long fingers against his glass of hot chai, opaque with milk. A comfort, even though he looks at me like I'm a pet, scarfing up the food he's just poured into my dish.

"Mr. Half Werewolf. Mr. H. Werewolf. If you had to, out of all these people, which one would you pick to eat?" I ask, my lips and brain sloppy with sudden late-night nutrition. He just smiles, though he does look through the crowd as if considering the question. His gaze lands back on me. I can't tell whether that's deliberate.

And then I'm done eating, and this long night is over. So abrupt I can barely believe it, standing once again in the chill of the open air, stomach taut with food. It's dawn, but still dark. My companion lights another joint. I realize the kitten is gone, and am disappointed. I don't ask what happened to it.

"Thank you for the meal," I say.

"You're welcome. Now go home, Professor. It's late, and you've listened enough," he says.

"I don't know about that. Will I see you again?" I ask.

"I don't know. Would you like to see me again?"

"Yes. I want to hear the end of the first story."

He closes his eyes and takes a deep drag. His lips are still ruddy from whatever it was that he put on them while I was in his storytelling trance, despite being washed in milky tea. "You and your endings, Professor. They'll be the end of *you*, someday."

"You started it," I say.

"And I'm still living it," he says, and wipes his mouth. "Tomorrow. Oly Pub. Five thirty."

"I'll be there."

We walk over to a parked taxi nearby. The driver looks at us suspiciously and demands an extra fifty rupees this time.

"The price is going up, I see," I tell the stranger. "Can't you hypnotize him into not charging me extra?"

The stranger says nothing, and I'm embarrassed. "Do you want to share the cab? I'm heading toward Jodhpur Park. Where do you live?"

The stranger hitches with a silent laugh. "That's all right. Get home safely, Professor."

"Thank you. For the stories," I say, opening the taxi door and getting in.

The stranger smiles his red smile and walks away, sleeping kitten cradled in one arm, joint in the other hand. I almost don't notice this. I could have sworn the kitten was gone. I feel very far from the present. As the taxi rolls down Ballygunge Circular Road and its overhanging canopy of trees, past the yellow walls of the army base, I look back and lose sight of the stranger. Heart thundering, I wait to get home. Ever-present, the dogs watch from the sides of the road, their eyes throwing back the headlights.

Part Two

KVELDULF

1

A new day. I take the metro, emerge at Park Street station, and walk down the street to Oly. Park Street is the Times Square of Kolkata. Any devout Kolkatan will tell you this. That doesn't mean it's anything like Times Square, of course. But for a quiet man like me, it's enough. It's not as if I have a lot of friends to go bar-hopping and dancing with, or anything like that. So if you haven't been there already, imagine a wide street (well, compared with the usually narrow streets of this city), adorned with restaurants and stores and coffee shops and stalls and bars that have barnacled the smog-stained remnants of colonial British architecture. Add more recent buildings that stand shoulder-to-shoulder with these reformed mansions, and fill the whole place with people. That's one thing Park Street does have equal to Times Square—people. On the street walking side by side with passing cars, on the pavement rubbing shoulders like the buildings around them. They're everywhere, as you would expect in one of the most densely populated areas of the planet.

I am there, on Sunday, in the twilight that forms between the buildings of cities when the sun is too low to shine directly on the asphalt. The streetlights have come alive, but day still clings on. I've lived here so long, but meeting someone who claims to be more than human makes me see everything differently, like at the dhaba last night. My eyes linger on every street dog, curled by the passing feet of pedestrians or exploring the footpaths, so different from their predatory nocturnal incarnations. But more than the dogs, it's the people, the city that suddenly seems strange, yet not strange enough. Everything feels like a comedown from a trip, an intense high—so much so that it's physical, a headache growing behind my skull and promising to break at the notes of the stranger's voice.

I keep to the footpath, avoid the streaks of odorous water and garbage clotting the gutters. Steamy food-shacks offer passing clouds of warmth from winter's chill, the heat of open-air cooking trapped under blue plastic tarpaulins stretched over the sidewalks to shelter their customers. I pass hawkers selling snacks, sachets of supari, cigarettes, perfumes and colognes, pirated movies, discounted books and magazines, condoms both imported and not—all operating right beside less ephemeral retail outlets and eateries with glass walls that look into different worlds.

Everywhere, the behavior of our different packs and clans and tribes on display. Beggars hover close to the transparency of storefront windows in the hope of absorbing some of the opulence within. I pass the well-lit glitz that hovers around the entrance to Park Hotel and its fashionable discos and restaurants, edging by young men and women emerging from chauffeured cars, bodies musked with cologne. I'm careful not to touch any of the girls by accident (I hesitate to call them women), as I don't want to attract the ire of their well-groomed male companions. A pimp, probably on the lookout for hotel patrons, asks me in flamboyant English if I'd like to spend the night with a college girl, and I shake my head and keep walking. Not too far from there, I reach the popular refuge of the firmly middle classes, Oly Pub. It looks plain and weathered next to the higher-profile stretch of pavement real estate by the hotel, though the building does hint at a faded grandeur. I make a quick supper of a chicken and egg roll at Kusum's Rolls and Kebabs right next door, and head into the pub.

I nod to the doorman who probably recognizes me, and duck into the fluorescent-lit gloom. I go upstairs to the windowless sanctum of the air-conditioned section, hoping that the stranger will also go there. A cigarette haze hangs over the Formica tables, as if the winter mist has followed me inside.

I search the faces in the room till a waiter gives me a grumpy glance, pointing out the fact that I'm standing in the middle of the carpeted thoroughfare without saying a word. The stranger isn't here. My aching head feels heavier at his absence. Though it's still light out, Oly is already crowded. I find a table in the corner and order a whiskey double with water, hoping it will calm the headache. The same waiter brings me the drink and takes a while doing it. I bide my time, sipping my watered whiskey and nibbling at the pile of dirty-yellow daalmoot in the little plastic plate by my glass, feeling more and more guilty for taking up an entire table all by myself while the pub fills up.

But he does show up.

He appears by my table without warning, half an hour later. It looks like he's wearing the same flimsy kurta and worn jeans he wore yesterday, and his hair tumbles down to his shoulders again, the ponytail he left with last night abandoned. He's carrying a dusty blue-and-black JanSport backpack that makes him look younger. Like one of my students, except for those quivers of gray in his hair.

"Professor. I trust you weren't waiting long?" He takes off the backpack and slides it under the table with one foot. He's still wearing those sandals.

"Oh no. I was just, you know," I say.

"Waiting?"

"Yes. No, I mean, it hasn't been that long. Please, sit. Thanks for coming."

He pulls up the chair opposite and sits down. I blush, and am thankful for the smoke and dim lighting. I get the feeling that he knows I've been waiting a long time and likes it. Nervous sipping has almost emptied my glass of whiskey, so I feel tipsy and inclined to forgive him. I'm just glad that he actually showed up, and more grateful than I feel comfortable being. The sound of his voice is an uncanny placebo for the throb behind my eyes.

"Would you like a drink?" I ask.

He nods and waves his arm. To my amazement, the waiter shows up immediately. He isn't any less grumpy, but I've never been able to make a waiter at Oly Pub show up in fewer than five minutes. The stranger orders two whiskey doubles. I feel flattered, both by his taking the liberty to order me another and by his appropriation of my choice for his own drink. I have to stop myself from thanking him again.

"The haunt of heroes," he says, leaning back and looking around. I assume he's referring to the pub's original—now truncated—name, Olympia.

I wonder how to respond. The stranger folds his hands on the table and looks straight at me, making eye contact. I have no idea what to say to him, what we're going to talk about, how to start a conversation with him, why in hell I even wanted to meet him again.

"Did you keep the kitten?" I ask him.

"I ate it."

I stare at him.

"A poor joke. Forgive me and pull down your eyebrows. The kitten's safe, with a saucer of milk all her own. She's taken quite a liking to me. Or perhaps just to not being terrorized by stray dogs."

"I'm glad you kept her."

"So here we are, and you still haven't told me your name."

"Oh. I'm sorry. I'm Alok. Alok Mukherjee."

"I'm very pleased to meet you, Alok," he says and licks his teeth. There's something fidgety about him today, not like the calm of that old half werewolf I met yesterday.

"What's your name?" I ask, after waiting awkwardly.

"Professor—you don't mind if I still call you Professor, I hope—my name hardly matters."

"Why's that?"

"You *haven't* been listening." The refusal to play his part in this human ritual disturbs me. The waiter appears with his bottle of Royal Stag, a glass, and his bronze peg measure, and pours us both doubles. I wait.

"What should I call you, then?" I ask the stranger once the waiter's gone. The rims of our glasses meet sharply.

"You can call me anything you want. Anything at all."

I find this an unwieldy suggestion. "Are you still saying you're part werewolf?"

"Isn't that why you wanted to meet me again? To find out more? Alok," he lilts. "What do you want to know?"

"I—I don't know."

"I'm aware of that. I'm asking what you do want to know."

"I know what you're asking," I tell him, irritated. For all his effort to project immortal wisdom, there's something childish about his way of engaging with me. I look into my glass. "You're interesting. That's why I—" I clear my throat. "That's why I agreed to meet you again."

"How kind," he says.

"I want you to finish the story you started yesterday."

"Ah. Professor." He leans forward, placing his elbows on the table.

"You're clearly an intelligent man. I want you to know that. I'm not trying to best your intellect with an elaborate prank here."

"That's good, I guess. You don't have to keep calling me Professor."

He smiles. "I find you interesting, too, though you might not believe it. We're not the same at all. We're not even close to the same age. But if we're to talk like adults, you're going to have to take a leap of faith that quite frankly isn't possible for a human being in this day and age, not one in your social and environmental circumstances."

"You're telling me I'm going to have to believe whatever you say," I say.

"You don't have to believe me. But you're going to have to act like you do. For the sake of this play we've both walked into. You agreed to be in it, yesterday night. If you abide by that agreement, we can talk."

"And why do you think I'll do that?" I ask.

"Because you followed me out of the mela. Because you came here today," he says.

I nod slowly, unable to refute that. "Okay. Why are you here, then?"

The stranger takes a drink. "Yesterday I told you stories. You called it hypnotism. Say it is that. Say I'm hypnotizing you. That it's an illusion. A magician still needs an audience, doesn't he."

"If you're that good a magician, why find one person in a crowd. Why not charge people, fill an auditorium."

"Because that would be tawdry. Sometimes intimacy is the only way real magic works."

"Intimacy," I say, and rub my forehead. "I don't know your name."

"Get out of here, then," he says. I look up. "You're not my prisoner,

Professor Mukherjee, and don't pretend that you are. Leave, if you think the only way to achieve intimacy is dry custom, the exchange of facts and labels, names and professions. Intimacy lies in the body and the soul, in scent, in touch and taste and sound. A man whose name you don't know can tell you a tale to move you to tears, just by filling and emptying his lungs, by moving his tongue and lips, his fingers. Even after, you might never know him."

His voice doesn't rise. But I feel my heart beat faster, my headache thumping with it. I look at my unsteady hands, relish the whining note of my headache.

"Tell me something. Are you going to ask me for money after the evening's done?" I ask.

"No. I'm not a hawker."

I put the glass of whiskey and melting ice against my forehead.

"Magicians don't work for free."

"Metaphors only go so far. I'm not a magician, either. Just tell me, Alok. Do you want to hear more? You wanted to, last night. Do you still want to?"

I close my eyes, feel moisture trickling off the glass and down my head. I nod.

"You're more open-minded than most historians, then?" he asks. I open my eyes.

"Again with the generalizations. I'm not even sure where you got that one from."

"Very well. For one thing, I'm not going to finish the story I told you yesterday."

"Why not?" I ask.

"Because it's not important right now. It did what it was supposed to, and it'll come back when and if it needs to."

His face goes vacant as he looks at one of the resident rats of this dank Olympia. It scampers between the tables, darting over the crimson carpet and looking for crumbs to scavenge, unafraid of the many human feet around it. I remember the dead rat by the stranger's feet last night. The stranger looks young again, unlike yesterday night after he finished the stories. The unruly hair, the smirk. The familiar combo of jeans and kurta. For a second I think that maybe he actually is one of my students, playing an elaborate joke to humiliate me once it gets out on campus. That I've somehow failed to notice him in my classes, or failed him, and this is some kind of revenge.

"What *did* you do to me yesterday?" I ask, if just to stifle this thought.

"What you saw or felt has its provenance in your own head."

"It's absurd that you would even say that, after introducing yourself in the way you did. And it's not like I've never been told a story before. I felt something else. Like—" I stumble on the word, but force it out. "Like magic. Like you said."

He waits, as if for me to make a point.

"I've honestly never felt anything like it in my life. It felt like you shared a bit of lost time with me, shared the memories of something that can't—shouldn't—exist, like you had it hidden under that kurta of yours and just, I don't know, gave it to me."

A flash of teeth. "How eloquent."

"You're being facetious, but it's true. The more I think about it, the more I feel that you did something impossible yesterday night. If it's a trick, it's one I've never seen or heard of before."

He is silent for a moment.

"Well, Professor, I'm glad you liked my 'trick.' I have something to give you," he tells me.

He takes a gulp of his drink and pulls a large, mustard-yellow manila envelope out of his backpack. He places it on the table. I notice that his glass is almost empty already.

"You want to know more. Here is something more," he tells me, one hand on the envelope.

"What is this?"

"This is history. History most people—humans—aren't aware of, in particular. As a professor of history, I thought you might appreciate that."

"Can I open it?"

"Of course. I brought it here for you." He removes his hand from the envelope. I take it and open the flap to look inside. It's a plain black hardbound notebook, filled with slanted handwriting. Black ink and the smudged gray of pencils. From the first to the last, the pages (which have no lines on which to write, though the penmanship is straight and true) are crammed full. I catch fragments, written in English. In the middle, I find the skeleton of a leaf, which wisps out to float to my lap. I pick it up and put it back in the notebook.

"You want me to read this?" I ask.

"Yes. Take it with you," he says.

"What is it?"

"I suppose you could call it a journal, from another time. A voice from the past."

"Whose voice?" I ask.

"You'll find out when you read it."

"This is because you say you've—because you've lived a long time. That's why you have access to this?"

"Yes," he agrees.

"This doesn't look very old."

He smiles. "Very observant. I translated them from the original source. I doubt you can read the languages the source contains. Either way, I can't just go around giving historical artifacts to strangers, can I?"

I've tended to think of him as the stranger. I *am* a stranger to him. But I can't shake the feeling that he somehow already knows more about me from two conversations than many of my alleged friends do. Even family, why not. More than I could ever hope to know about him.

"You're a translator? Is that your job?" I ask him.

"I translated what's in that notebook you're holding. That doesn't make me a full-time translator."

"So I take your word that this notebook contains a journal from another time. Because, for some reason, you took up translating as a hobby."

"Lord above. You don't have to take my word for anything. Just pretend if it's easier. Read what I've given you and see what you think. Decide for yourself. No humans—well, that's not true. Very few humans have read what you're going to in those pages. This is just a part of what I can give you. There's more."

"So why are you giving me this?"

"I want to hire you. To transcribe these documents, type them out."

"But I'm not a transcriber. I just teach history. I write essays. Nothing like this. You should get a professional."

"Do I look like I want a professional? You're a student and teacher of history, Alok. That is enough. I'm giving you an opportunity that very few historians could even dream of. It's a simple request. Type out what you read. That's all. I'll pay you."

"And the sources? Do I get to see them? The actual historical documents. Surely you realize that if you actually have such things, I'd be very interested in seeing them, rather than this. I am a historian, after all. What period is this from? My specialization is late modern, colonial India mainly, but obviously, I'd be interested in any kind of text from the past."

"You might well see the original texts. If you prove yourself interested enough. Worthy of it. Just read the translation first. It might tell you a little more about what you want to know about what I am."

"A werewolf," I say, to pin him down a bit.

He licks the rim of his glass. I clench my jaw and look away, catching a glimpse of his tongue sliding wet from between his lips.

"Half," he says. He drains the last of his drink. I have much of my glass still left, despite drinking fast to keep up with him. He hasn't denied what he claimed yesterday, but he hasn't been embracing it, either. And now he's hired me to do a job. It feels odd, even mundane. But I can hardly forget what he's proven himself capable of. The thought of historical journals describing werewolves in the past does excite me, coming from this particular man.

"I'll do it," I say, and take too large a gulp of whiskey.

He wipes his mouth with the back of his hand. "Good," he says, and tosses some hundred-rupee notes on the table. Enough for both our drinks and tip. The opposite of demanding payment from me.

"You're leaving?" I ask.

"We will meet again," he says, snatching the backpack from under the table and slinging it onto his shoulders.

"Right. But. Where will we meet again?" I ask before he can hurry off.

He gets up and stops, looking distracted by my question.

"Do you have a phone number or an email address? Some way we can get in touch?" I suggest, to help things along.

"No. But I will see you again. Goodbye, Professor Alok Mukherjee. Thank you for accepting this task."

He walks away so quickly that I'd assume that he has an emergency to get to, if not for his calm. I don't have the time to ask how he's going to get in touch with me. I suppose I can call out before he disappears through the new patrons standing and waiting by the stairwell door for tables. But I don't.

I feel both excited and disappointed. I had expected more. To be hypnotized again like last night, away and out of my current body in this present. The headache remains.

Perhaps what he's given me will do as a substitute, for now. I double-check the pages of his notebook, to make sure that they actually have words on them, that they're not just a bunch of scribbles on paper. There is a line of poetry written on the inside of the front cover in pencil, small but visible. It's Blake, though I've forgotten what it's from. Seeing it reassures me. I feel drunk. Confident despite it all that I will see him again, just like he said. I shake my head and look around, to see if anyone has noticed what's transpired. But nothing has transpired, nothing that can be seen by anyone other than me. No one is looking at me. I have a whiskey to finish, alone. I start reading.

Part Three

THE FIRST SCROLL
(For Cyrah)

First Fragment[*]
This new parchment I write on is fresh skin:

Taken from the back of a boy we found wandering alone near the dusty walls of Lahore, weeks after we crossed the borders of the Mughal Empire and days after we swam across the silt-clouded waters of the Indus. I took the child by his warm brown arm and spoke into his ear in Punjabi, asking him, "Where are your parents?" and he answered in a wet voice, "They have sickened and died," and I slipped my thumbs under the curve of his jaw to feel him live before I bent his neck and broke it so he cried no longer (some have said I take to pity too easily). I hold him now in my hands, his skin toughened under the sun of his empire that forgot him and over the smoke of our campfires burning earth-fed wood.

Not a league from the child's killing we found his mother lying on the ground, clothed in flies. There was a newborn babe clutched in her arms snaked in purple umbilicus. The woman's thighs were scabbed in the sun-dried crust of the infant's birth, her stomach still flaccid from its expelled weight. The babe sucked at her cold nipple. It hurt me to see the bravery of this female, striving to feed her offspring moments before her death. I did not tell my companions my thoughts. I lingered a moment longer, to bless the female and her babe with remembrance.

---

[*] The stranger divides the translation into two fragments, which I assume are pieces of the original scroll mentioned within the text. His handwritten text has no real divisions, though I've remained faithful to his paragraph and line breaks. I attempted some formatting of my own by dividing the two fragments further into sections where it seemed appropriate.

How many times have I witnessed such sights across the centuries, and willfully ignored them?

Makedon dashed that cherub's head with a rock. A small mercy that he did not play with it. Gévaudan stared at the pitiful sight with a grimace of disdain. We did not eat of mother or infant, for our fardels* were full at the time, and we were in no mood to scavenge like wild dogs, having trekked long to reach Lahore. We went on, to let them rot or become food for lesser creatures than us. I sought some comfort on her behalf, for the fact that her older son lived on in some way inside us, in the weird metabolisms of our shifting selves, in our dreams of his young life.

I test the scroll I made from him here, this dried skin to clothe the flesh of a story, or many. It holds under the bone of the nib.

In Mumtazabad:†

I saw you. You of human men and women, you of one self and one soul. I cannot tell you that you shone out to me first. There were many men and women and children who kindled my appetites in Mumtazabad, where the workmen dwell and the travelers in Shah Jahan's empire may rest in caravanserais and barter in bazaars. I saw them everywhere, these virgins and sodomites, scented with dusty sweat and the stains of their exploits. Men with gray eyes and drought-cracked lips who prostrate themselves to their Allah, unaware of wolf-ish eyes that fall upon their upraised buttocks. Peasants male and female, naked but for plain loincloths grown damp, dark skin glazed with sweat from their toil, even in winter's chill. Noblemen lounging in shaded palanquins, mouths red with chewed betel, their salwars

---

* Archaic term for a bag or bundle.
† A town built during Mughal emperor Shah Jahan's reign to house the large number of workers building the Taj Mahal. Later it was also called Taj Ganji.

and breeches threaded with winter sun. Noblewomen in peshwaz robes, muslin waves that ripple like curtains at their windows, their veils brushing lips only glimpsed through fabric, powdered talc clinging like frosts on the downy slopes of their cheeks. So many succulent lives, churning with diverse energies, waiting to be tasted.

Yet I chose you. The sun was at its zenith when we entered the caravanserai, walking behind the odorous camels of a traveling merchant, and as the bleating animals parted and we came into the open courtyard, I saw you leaning against a pillar playing with your oiled curls, mouth sliced by the shadow of your nose. You looked at me, stared at me and my companions clad in strange furs and tunics so foreign, and your eyes seemed to me like no eyes I had ever seen north of the Indus. Yes, you looked at me and I wished you were not human, that I could cleave your soul in two and watch your second self emerge, a beast as lovely as your first.

I walked up to you and you stared still, chipped nails grasping those curls and twining them 'round your fingers. Your eyes, planets of shallow sea shaded by your unpowdered brow, eluding all colors, so gray and blue that they ceased to be either and seemed to me green, as the eyes of our second selves often are.

"What do you want, foreigner?" you asked me.

"As a foreigner, I want to talk to one who isn't foreign to this land," I said, and relished the surprise on your face as I spoke back to you in Pashto. But even as surprise sweetened your expression, you did not avert your gaze.

"Then keep moving. I wasn't born here but in Persia, and some here might think me a foreigner, though my mother brought me here in her arms when I was little."

"Would you believe it if I told you that I can't remember where I was born?" I asked you.

"I would not."

"Fairly answered. Still, it's true. That would make me a foreigner the world over, wouldn't it?"

"It would."

"Then it matters little where I am and where you are, because wherever I might meet you, I'll still be a foreigner and you less so."

"A feeble argument based on an impossibility," you said, fiddling with your hair again. You looked around, peering behind me.

"Where are your foreign friends, then? We don't often see men so heathen in appearance, no one can tell which part of the world they're from or what gods they hold true. And such devilish-looking folk even less so."

"Each of us is from a different place, and many places. I apologize, my lady, for our raiment, which is made from wild beasts and might lend us a disposition similar to them."

"I'm not so easily offended. There are more frightening men than you and your companions here in this sinkhole of a bazaar, not to mention this empire, despite your looks."

"You might be surprised," I said, and you seemed off-put by what seemed like a boast, but was merely the truth.

"So where have your friends gone?" you asked.

"To wash themselves in the baths."

"And you alone among them thinks keeping the stink of travel on you is attractive?"

"Your tongue is sharp. You might be thankful that I don't follow the customs of man in treating his woman."

"I'm not so easily thankful, either, traveler. If I offend you, take your leave."

"Like you, I'm not so easily offended, my lady."

"And you shouldn't be, looking like you do. It's sensible that you should look like a beast, if you don't follow the customs of man as you claim. Where are you from?"

"I don't remember. And I have ranged far and wide since that unremembered birth. But I came here with my companions from the gates of a city called Nürnberg. From another empire, like this one, but for the people of Europe, known sometimes as the Holy Roman Empire."

The mask of your wariness seemed to slip a little. "You've traveled far for one with no camels or horses. You must be very tired."

"I've had enough rest. Tell me, why is a young woman sitting here alone in the middle of a caravanserai? Why is your husband or suitor right now not at my neck with a blade for talking with you?"

"I let whatever suitors come my way pay for my travels, after which they slip from my sight and are never seen again," you said.

"And if you are not wed, why are you not in the company of other women, and covered? Surely you are Muslim, if you are from Persia," I said.

"Muslim I may be, yes, but I've no husband, nor family, nor home to stay in. My modesty matters little to anyone—I've as little need for covering myself as any Hindu commoner you see on the streets."

"That is unusual."

"Is it? Would that I were lucky enough for the privilege of purdah. Sounds like paradise to me. If you like, you can call Shah Jahan's guards to drag me to the nearest harem for your pleasure. Perhaps that would suit the eyes of a white man better than seeing a Muslim woman uncovered?"

"I'm merely curious, my lady. Even with the vast knowledge I've gathered of your kind and its various peoples, I sometimes get con-fused."

"My kind."

"Khr—that is, humans," I told you, strangely unafraid of revealing myself.

"It's told white men are arrogant, but this is new," you said, puzzled.

"And where are you traveling?" I asked.

"Your fellow white men land on our shores to the west, and now to the east as well. Perhaps they'll have work, or ships to carry me to other lands," you said.

"See the worlds."

"The world. Yes," you said.

"A strange inclination, for one of your position and sex."

"Is it?"

"So I supposed. My friends will return soon, and we'll be leaving here, once I've washed myself also at the bathhouse."

"Then what is it you want, if you're not staying? Get to it."

"These are gold coins from Europe, and more currency from this empire," I said, and gave you two crowns from a dead Frenchman's pocket, two silver rupiyas, and two golden mohurs.

"What do you want for this, if not to lie with me?" you asked.

"I want a lock of your hair."

"Why?"

"A jewel, if you will, for me to wear around my neck for the rest of my journey. This is a town of bazaars, and you offer your body, for a night or a span of noon, to travelers who yearn for the company of women. I ask for a minute portion of your body to keep for my own forever, rather than the whole for an hour."

"You want only bits of my hair for these coins?"

"I swear it."

"It's done," you said, and pulled a cascade of curls from behind your ear, and before I could offer you my Pesh-kabz,* you took a thin thread of hairs and placed it between your teeth, and with a wrench of your neck you severed three inches from yourself, deft as a seamstress dividing the string. Quick in my shadow, so no one would see. Your teeth were sharp stones dulled by civilization. You tied the lock into a circle and gave it to me, a knot of yourself in my hand, damp still from your strong bite. In my hand, your dead self, your spit, your skin, for a few coins in yours.

"One question, foreigner. How do you speak my language so well?" you asked.

"A dead man taught me, after I ate him, just as the Christ taught his disciples the love of their God after they ate him."

"You're a strange people, you white folk. But your dead man taught you well."

"Yes. He had little else to do, once he was in my stomach. I thank him every day for making my travels through your land easier."

"And I thank you for the coins. Farewell, foreigner," you said and walked away, unaware of the value of our transaction, unaware that I held you in my hand as a wolf holds a crippled hare under its great paw.

---

* A type of dagger originating in the region now known as Iran, in the seventeenth century.

A hunt:

A man, his face whittled by starvation to woody gnarl of cheekbones and sticky pebbles of teeth, jaundiced marble of bloodshot eyes, lean body wrapped in moldering cloth and goatskin.

He was not attractive prey, no. But we were hungry, and he was enough. He walked by the shore of the Yamuna, breathing heavy with sorrow of some sort, leaving a trail of oily scent. His stave of hacked branch etched little holes in the fragrant mud, which also reproduced in all their divine symmetry the impression of his feet across time.

We followed these tracks from afar, I slicing the water, my companions slouching across the land as shifting hills in the dusk, their fur the whispering thatches of coarse grass. It was too dark for this man to see us, so we let the wind rattle through our great throats and teeth, let him run in fear so that we had some mild sport at least. But still it was no effort.

He saw dancing lamps flare in those hills in the distance and realized some immense reckoning had come upon him, and he said words of prayer loud in the evening, tripping and smearing his knees with the soft ground. He ran straight into my jaws as I leaped from the water, drenching him in a final blessed rain before his death. He fed the water and the mud a deep and rich red of holy dread. I drank, the meat and bone between my fangs, the soul trapped, making my entire second self bristle in waves.

A meal:

Enough of the past.

Now here we sit, for all the world like three men camped under the starlit sky. Between us is another man, human to the bone and dead. We light our gathering with the dead man's soul. The moon is bright enough by far, but it pleases Makedon to show his mastery over ritual.

He spits in the wounds, anointing the litany of red trenches left on face, throat, chest, and sides by the fangs of our second selves. He cuts the body open from cock to throat with his dagger. The heat of the soul, condensing in cold air. He speaks our words until pale flame dances on the Hindu's violet insides as if he were a split skin-sack of kindling.

"Rise, Will o' the wisp," Makedon says, blowing on the false smoke of steam rising from the fresh kill, like a man coaxing fire from wood, "and name yourself chir batti instead, for in this empire no man, woman, or corpse is called Will. Be gone, Saxon tongue!"

With that he pries the corpse's creaking jaw open and cuts the still-slippery tongue from the mouth with his blade. He eats it raw.* Beside me, pale Gévaudan sticks his thin-fingered hands through the corpse fire and touches his face, rubs his hands. I do the same. The corpse light feels like nothing to the touch, but its glow calms me, reminding me of the burning of northern night skies many lifetimes in my past.

We sit on our haunches and take from our prey with bare hands. Soft iron from the man's liver sits on my tongue, fatty with some sickness engendered by poverty. From the smoking rupture of his gut, I taste the dregs of his last meal—sun-boiled berries scrounged from a seller's basket in nearby Mumtazabad. He was a thief, and a desperate one. Gévaudan digs the rest of the shit out of the stomach and throws it on the ground, cutting out the emptied tripe. Makedon takes the kidneys and guts, and slices out the rest of the sweetmeats for us to share. Under his blade, the precious bounty of the heart flowers into thick wet petals. These I covet eagerly.

---

* A hunt, followed by a meal consisting of a human being, and an insistence that they are not quite human; the narrator and his companions clearly share my dear stranger's delusions/predilections. If this wasn't in fact written by my stranger, perhaps this journal or tale, whatever it may be, is where he gets his ideas from? I'm assuming one needs to be more than human to survive eating raw human flesh like this; that can't be very safe. It's not my area of expertise, but there are, however, various examples of ritualistic cannibalism among human cultures all along the historical record.

We share the pieces of his life as his stories evaporate, his ghost fire invisible to his fellow humans who toil for the emperor of this land. When the flame has waned, his organs have been eaten, and we are satiated, we begin cutting up the rest of his body to store in our fardels, each using our favorite blades, gathered from across the world. As we work, humans in the distance work as well, across the river. I must describe the ingenuity of their endeavor, which we see clear by the moon's light:

An earthen ramp leads to a construction pit, miles of damp ground flattened by feet, the ruts left by cart-wheels smoothed by ox hooves and the callused, soiled soles of the humans. The pit holds an unfinished palace.* From the distance, its incomplete minarets lie under moon and star-bitten clouds like the fresh-hatched eggs of a roc,† the pit an abandoned nest swarming with ants—the thousand bodies of toiling workmen marble dusted and sweaty, glistening in torchlight. But this giant nest of stone and mineral gathered from across the empire is raised not to shelter the thousands that build it, but to place on the skin of the world a memorial to one human's mate.

From the incense-sweetened balconies of his great citadel at Ak-barabad, it is the emperor Shah Jahan who waits for this place, his miracle, to be born. Perhaps he lets tears of shame slip down his cheeks, thinking of the many hands that build his dead wife's tomb, none of them his own. Perhaps he paces in impatience, thinking these men and elephants and oxen too slow. Perhaps he does not care, wanting only to hold his beautiful Mumtaz Mahal, who held fourteen imperial whelps in her womb for him, just one more time. Perhaps he would give his entire empire, give the power to have this wonder built at the snap of his fingers, just to feel her lips on his again. Or perhaps it matters little, and she is just one of his many wives. It makes me

---

* From the description that follows, this is the construction site of the Taj Mahal, placing the time of these events anywhere between A.D. 1632 and 1653, the period it was being built. Probably somewhere in the middle (1640s) going by the degree of completion. Shah Jahan ruled the Mughal Empire until 1658.

† The roc or rukh, a mythical giant bird of prey. It's interesting to note that the narrator and his companions have recently completed a trek across the region of the Middle East. The myth of the roc has possible Arabic roots, but also resembles the powerful Garuda, from Hindu and Buddhist mythology.

wonder what secrets his body would hold; how his life would taste guttering between the jaws of my second self.

This man we have just eaten of, whose remains we dismember, he is no Shah Jahan, emperor of Mughals. He is an insignificant wastrel, but he, too, had love in his heart. My companions tasted it, but barely lingered on it. For centuries they have consumed men and women and children, and they find these opiates of emotion pleasing but unremarkable. Mere marinade for our carrion. Though I don't know Gévaudan's age, he smells young. Makedon has much time behind him. He hails from the lands that lay claim to one of the earliest kings of our kind. But I find it ever strange that we ignore these storms within our prey's bodies, simply because we ourselves have forsaken such things.

Watching the emperor's workmen from afar, we sit in the darkness. We have shattered our prey's bones, and sown the dust and shards into the earth for birds and worms to make their meal once the sun rises. The remains of the man are salted and stored in our fardels for later.

I have seen many things with my companions when crossing Eurasia, the ways and works of this manifold race we feed on, in all its diversity. Perhaps I will write one day of all these things. The luxury and poverty of nobility and peasantry in the Holy Roman Empire, all sharing their shit and piss and food within the stone cages of cities— hubristic pomp of the elder empires of Roman Caesars and dire morality of the squabbling Christ followers, trickling intermingled into the stones of monasteries and cathedrals, verminous shrines of holy art left by an age since passed. Fishermen roaming the shores of the Black Sea, eating their catch under the open sky with callused hands, ever watching a horizon crowned with the sails of Moorish pirate ships, beach fires marking the watered edge of the Ottoman Empire, leagues from the sultan's seat in that glittering city which the Turks call Kostantiniyye and I once knew as Byzantium. The hard-won lives of nomadic badawi as they herd their animals and villages across badlands, springing forth the lights of fleeting tent cities in desert darkness; the valor of the warrior Pashtuns riding their horses in the sand seas and bladed mountains of the Khorasan, their scimitars hammered Damascus steel, razor-sharp against even the tough hide of our second selves.

But it is always the strange intimacies of humans, differently expressed yet prevalent across all their empires and lands, observed in the darkest hours of night, that stick with me and stir my appetites in unexpected ways.

A conversation, as if between two men:

Makedon watches me scratch wetted bone nib over parchment on my lap. "Let us talk, like two men," he says. I nod. "What exactly is it that you're scribbling on that scroll? An epic to make of us three great heroes, demigods to the hapless humanity we crush between our jaws—our shifting selves twinned deities to the Apollonian and the Dionysian impulses of the khrissal,* who remains forever stranded between the two?" he says to me.

"I'd say the more accurate precursor for my journals isn't your Homer but Columbus, writing in curiosity on the shores of new worlds across the Atlantic."

"Is that right? I suppose that's fair. Columbus didn't eat the peoples of those ancient worlds, but he and his imperium have treated them as well as cattle and fowl for the cooking fire."

"What's that to do with anything, Makedon?"

"I know how you silently worship our prey. No doubt it's in that scroll of yours. I mention the expeditions of your professed antecedent Christophorus Columbus not because he was exceptional among humanity in the practice of cruelty. I mention them, because all of his

---

* Not a word that I could find in any mythology or dictionary I looked at. It appears to be a term used by these predatory "false" men for their quarry: humans. Curiously, despite this shared word and other shared language (*ghost fire*), they seem to hail from different parts of the world and have different cultural influences.

race, which you so admire while devouring, treat themselves just about as well as we treat them."

"There is a difference between cruelty and killing. You, I've seen, don't much separate the two. I don't think a wolf killing a lamb exercises cruelty. I don't see myself as treating khrissals poorly, though I eat of them for sustenance."

"You've never seen a wolf play with a still-living lamb bleating its blood across the snow, then. Khrissals are not the beautiful, intelligent lambs you see, nor are we impossibly noble wolves. No, khrissals are fierce, wombed, cock-slung spiders—yes, spiders, spewing the filth of excess thought across the earth in the glutinous webs of civilizations that scrabble for space to weave their own webs over those of their brethren. They have a fire in them, I'll give them that; no other animal has it, this Promethean fire. And I will forever cherish the taste of that fire dancing on my tongue. Oh yes, there is no substitute. But it is ultimately a destructive flame, and eventually it will consume the planet and turn it to ashes. If I were a religious being, I'd say *our* purpose on this earth is solely to keep *them* in check."

"With rhetoric like that pouring from your mouth, I'd say you long to write as well. It would make an impressive screed on a scroll, wouldn't it?"

"No, I don't think it would. Because, in honesty, who cares to listen to my screed? Not me. It bores me. We live to eat of humankind, not ask ourselves why. You travel as North-man, not poet. Don't you feel shame? Do you not long to live up to the legends the Vikings and their people made? You are magic, North-man, dread hamrammr.* In your lands our tribes take the names of jotunn and troll, aesir and vanir. Names and stories khrissals spoke, and wrote, and carved, because they remember the titanic battles of our tribes before their history. Even in the sleep of their witless egotism they remember. And here you sit and write journals, like a limpid mortal Englishman."

"Limpid Englishmen have written their own tales of gods and blood, and they are no more mortal than Vikings."

"Well said. Tell me something, in honesty. Why do you write?"

---

* Norse term for "shape-changer."

"Why? I write to record, to study. For curiosity. To keep our stories in the worlds beyond our bodies."

He laughs. "Yes, but for whom? A khrissal writes for other khrissals. But who does a shape-shifter write for? Do you think the tribes will read it and champion you as their great scribe? Or do you think khrissals will read your scrolls, your book, and worship you as their benevolent devourer, an Old Testament god-beast come to them bearing a—a what? A new Bible that seeks only to understand their poor benighted souls, and asks only for the occasional blood sacrifice?"

I am chilled by these words, and hope I don't show it.

"I'm not the first of our tribes to keep a journal, Makedon," I say. "No one need read it. You criticize because you're bored. And remember as you do that you haven't read a word I have written."

"Would you like me to read it, then, and give my honest judgment?"

"No."

"Good. As you say, I'm bored, and I've no wish to be further bored."

"Leave him alone, will you? If he wants to write, let him write. You're giving me a headache with your bilious wit," says Gévaudan. He is still wearing around his shoulders a banded serpent that he throttled to death this morning, when it bit his ankle. "The pup speaks. Bilious indeed. Our prey was too steeped in bitterness. An unhappy fool practically begging to be killed, blundering along the countryside with not so much as a weapon to protect from bandits. His spleen has infected me with a distemper."

I see a fury run across Gévaudan's soft face, and wonder at this passion.

"Why try so hard to strip this man of dignity in death? Have you abandoned your ideas about khrissals and their destructive Promethean fire now?" I ask Makedon.

He laughs without humor. "I find it difficult to believe that he cares if I mock him, in his current state as slurry in our bowels and pieces in our fardels."

"You may have lived longer than I, but do not underestimate man and his ingenuity, nor the growing venom of his fear for things beyond his ken," I say.

"Shall I not underestimate woman also? No, for man and woman both are equally succulent, and fear's venom flavors them all the better by stirring the iron in their veins."

"We should give thanks now to the man who feeds us and strengthens our souls," I say, yearning for quiet.

"How about we give tribute to the whelp whose skin you write on, North-man? He had many lives within him yet, none of them ripened when we took him," Makedon says, now playful.

"And one of those lives was that of an orphaned beggar, wandering in misery on the streets of Lahore. Would he have liked to live that one?" Gévaudan asks.

Makedon laughs again, this time more genuine. "He's got your back, this one."

Gévaudan whispers tribute to our prey, touching the earth and blowing the clinging crumbs of soil into the air from his fingertips. I stroke the damp earth and do the same. Makedon removes the dark curls waving in front of his face, looking up at the stars. He gets up.

"Where are you going?" I ask.

Makedon walks a few feet from us and begins to shed his furs and raiment. "I'm going to hunt," he replies, tossing his clothes on the ground. His eyes seem to glow already with fervor, the green of their orbs waking with reflections.

"Again? We have remains in our fardels," I say.

"Then I'll hunt to kill. What is one less worker out of the twenty thousand over there? In fact, why settle for a worker? I will bring you the head of the emperor himself come sunrise," says Makedon, his smile as bright as his eyes.

Gévaudan sits up. "Would you like to bet on that? I could do with some coin. Buy myself a fancy new blade from the next blacksmith I happen upon. And if I lose the bet, at least we'll have the head of an emperor, and we can sell it to his subjects for riches."

Makedon snorts. "What's so unbelievable about it, Gévaudan?" He pulls off his boots and stands tall and proud and naked on his bare feet, taking his hardening penis in his hands and pissing a steaming circle around his clothes. The rising smell of his waters fills my nostrils, pungent, clinging to the winter air as the ground melts to frothing mud. He stares at the mausoleum rising out of the ground. The many

bone trophies sewn and burned into his skin writhe with his movements, the rib shards down his back bristling like the nubs of worn
skeletal wings. He looks at me.

"Write all you want of their giant baubles to dead mates and gods,
North-man. Write it down, all the details. Your text matters as little as
these cities and temples and palaces. They'll all be gone in time. Ours
is the true power. Let even the great Shah Jahan see what I can become,
and see if he doesn't shit himself. Let them provide our words: djinn,
devil, or werewolf, though I never saw a wolf that looked like my second self. We'll take all of them. What's in a name? By any name we are
greater than human. I can slaughter his whole imperial guard in one
night, and swallow him whole as the final course. The Shah Jahan is a
man, and as easily killed as any of those poor fools building his wife's
tomb or guarding his body, should he folly to challenge a shape-
shifter." Makedon turns toward the Yamuna, raising his arms to the air,
the sour musk of excitement falling from his lean and muscled body
and riding on the wind, raising the hairs on my neck.

"Well, then. Be careful," says Gévaudan. Makedon turns his back to
us and sprints toward the river in a crouch. "And good hunting,"
Gévaudan adds, crossing himself as the Christians do. When Makedon
is very far, I think I see him shift, his run changing to a bounding lope
before he vanishes into the river.

On the other side of the Indus, before I made this scroll:

By the shores of the Kabul, which flows into that other great river, we
came across a group of shape-shifters in a dance around a bonfire.
Sunset skirted the hills and turned the tree-clad slopes dark and blue,
the shoulders of giants shrugging flame to the sky. We could smell the
dancers across the water, their scent rising on the bonfire's heat. We
breathed deep that breeze glimmering the air, breathed their tarry
musk that raised our hackles even in our first selves.

In winter light we saw the dancers' faces gaunt but arms thick with wattles of pale fat hanging like loose raiment, their eyes black as oil when not lit by their second selves. They soon emanated their second selves uncaring of humans should they be anywhere near, uncaring of us, and in those mighty shapes they danced and shook the ground. Dust rose to curtain the falling sunlight, and the din of their dance sent watering rhinoceroses fleeing down the bank on their rocky hooves.

We watched as the soil of the river's bank ran wet with their blood— they had met to flay one another in their second selves, as some tribes do in the winters. They did this with their teeth and claws, forming a ring and tearing the hides from one another's backs and limbs for what seemed a long and painful time. Their lowing and growling hummed in our ears.

Once the flaying was done, they hung the bristling pennants of their skins on branches. Their pelts dripping above them, they feasted on the pile of human bodies they had danced around, to heal them- selves when they changed back to their khrissal forms. From their scent, their ritual, we guessed that they were of the tribe of the vukod- laks. Though they were probably migrating east from the realms of the Ottoman sultan, it is not the Turks but the Slavic peoples who carry the stories their tribe favors. We were surprised to see them so far from their native lands. But the great migrations bring diverse tribes to dif- ferent lands every passing century, and this one all the greater for the witch hunts that have plagued the western realms.

We observed the vukodlaks, ready to reveal our own second selves should theirs attack. Their skinned backs glistened in twilight as they turned the pile of corpses to bones and scraps, dark streams draining from the gutted bodies to the river. In the fire, the clothes of the men and women they had killed. At least a dozen khrissals tangled in death. I wondered how many villages and farms the vukodlaks had raided, or whether they had gathered the corpses by stealth, taking travelers off the road one by one and dragging them under the moon to this spot. In one village we passed, I remember a toothless farmer, lungs heavy with snot, telling us that his son and his wife had gone missing, and imploring us to help him. We ate of him soon after, I relieved to end his grief. My companions complained of his age. I insisted.

The vukodlaks noticed us three watching their ritual, but did nothing.

We kept our distance until they were done feeding. Their old skins had gathered crows and other birds that wheeled around them in the trees, mazed by the taste of something not quite of their world. By this time it had darkened to night, and the water fed a thin mist. In that firelit haze the vukodlaks shifted to their first selves.

They caked their bloody backs in poultices and walked on their shadows, away from the bonfire. Their white bellies swung full of human meat as they squatted on their thin legs, and their bony cheeks were flushed. We watched as they threw the bones of their prey in the river, their eyes shining on the other shore. Some watched us, too, their black, straight hair stroking the water when they squatted. Others took down their skins and hunched over them, and I saw smoke curl up from between their fingers, and flickers of light.

One waded across. His voice was deep and his chin hard though hairless, and he had small breasts whorled with tattoos. He had wrapped himself in a wet cloak, so I couldn't see between his legs. He called to us, speaking in amalgam. Gévaudan and Makedon ignored him, sitting in silence. I greeted him, separating from my companions. Like my companions and myself, he wore bones in his skin, but otherwise he looked nothing like those of us who travel among humans. His nails were grown long like claws, and bone splinters pierced the corners of his mouth to mimic the fangs of his second self. It is likely they keep to themselves, except when they hunt.

"Viking-eater," he greeted me, and held out a bloody pelt, its fur wet and sleek, heavy with yellow fat that clung to the pink tissues of its underside. So thick and real, and yet. "A gift, because you watched our dance. It will return to anima. Burn it before it does. If you don't, I will know your scent as vile, and I will mark you for death. It is the pelt of my second self. Next I emanate, I am new, my second self, new."

I took the gift and thanked him.

"A kveldulf of the Viking-eaters, a son of Lycaon, and a loup-garou,"*

* Lycaon is a mythological Greek king who was turned into a wolf, while *loup-garou* is a French word for "werewolf." *Kveldulf* is Old Norse for "evening wolf." *Vukodlak* is a Serbian word that refers to a type of folkloric ghoul that can have shape-shifting abilities. It, too, can apparently mean "werewolf."

he said, gesturing to me and my companions. "An odd trinity. Omen? I will ask for the blessing of the hags. Farewell." With that, he, or she, left across the water to rejoin the rest. I was quite startled by the vukodlak's divination of all our tribal origins, since the three of us traveled dressed similarly, and kept our tattoos hidden. Perhaps they are good at such things.

I looked underneath the fur of the pelt and saw letters, words burned into the fat in amalgam:

> *In hinterland of Raska wanders*
> *A boy with a cunt,*
> *Hounded from home, now parents dead,*
> *   this one revealed by love:*
> *Branded abomination with bruise and burn,*
> *Ugly with pain.*
> *I watch, follow, eat whole this*
> *Child, sweet.*
> *Now I am abomination, their fear*
> *Returned, I grow my nails and weigh my wattles*
> *   with stone in skin, chisel my teeth*
> *So they see their abomination*
> *Better before I eat them in second self.*
> *And so I am judged beautiful by pack hag.*

It was, I think, the story of the human whose shape the vukodlak now wears as its first self. A fine gift indeed. I felt something, something strange, as I read these words etched into the sloughed fat and skin of a shape-shifter's second self. I felt an urge, to take a burning twig and sear my own words into it, to preserve that moment. I brought the gift to my companions, who scorned it, suspicious. They were fine with me burning it. I didn't show them the words beneath it. We made a fire and threw the pelt in. The fat bubbled away hissing and steaming, taking with it the words of the vukodlak burning in my eyes and casting tears to the ground. I found in this a freedom, to let a sorrow out and ache all over my body, because they could not see, Makedon and Gévaudan could not see, cannot see, their eyes burning as well. By

the time the fire had died out, the pelt was gone, and only ashes remained in the charcoal.

Across the river, the hanging pelts had rotted to dust and cobwebs
on the branches above the vukodlaks. These remnants they tore from
the trees and threw in their fire, turning the flames to flashing white in
the gloom. We moved on. It was growing to dawn.

Weeks later, a child, a dead infant, a dead mother.

And so, now: I write.

Gévaudan licks the knotted white string of scar that runs down the
side of my face. The perfume of his boyish arousal when Makedon
stripped came to me quick, and their combined musk, Makedon's lingering still, makes me ache to shift into my second self. The last time
Gévaudan and I fucked, it was upon the bed of the Indus, our second
selves silted yellow, reddening the water as fang and claw pierced holes
in hide and mud.

It has been a while. The days when three of us courted on hunts,
each to each. Rare are the days now when we drag the carcasses of man
and woman in scented trails through desert and forest, through snow
and mountain rock, bringing one or both companions to frenzy.

Perhaps it is simply that we have been too small a pack for too long.

"Not now," I tell Gévaudan. He thrusts his hand between my thighs,
but I grab his wrist, grinding the bones under his skin. His grimace
turns to a smile, and he bares his blunt teeth at me, a pearl of spittle
falling off his flushed lip. A blow to the neck sends him to the ground.
The flesh is soft under the jaw and his cough guttural, but barely a
breath is missed before he leaps on me again and pushes me down on
my back, his hands on my throat, his mouth on mine, biting the ten-
der of my lip. I ram my fingers into his side, and he springs back from
me and staggers wincing. "Not now, Gévaudan," I say, panting. He
charges but I am faster, grabbing his attacking arm and pulling his
body close so that my free fist hits his face, the crack of stone striking
tree bark. Gévaudan tumbles to the soft ground. There is a familiar
sharpness emanating from him, like old peaches.

He laughs and spits red strings into the soil. I am just exciting him, so I draw my Pesh-kabz, taken from the belt of a brave Pashtun we hunted when crossing the land of the Afghans. Gévaudan remembers the blade's bite, no doubt, for in that warrior's hand it had sliced a full five inches of his arm.

This message he takes, and sits licking those bloody lips. He is quiet. No curses, no protest. This makes me uneasy. Still, I sheathe the blade.

"I'm in no mood for it, that's all," I tell him.

"Go back to your writing, then," he growls. Suddenly I wonder whether he'll try to hurt me in my sleep, or challenge me later. "Might as well hang up your fucking pelt like those witch-faced vukodlaks and declare yourself a khrissal," he adds.

"Gévaudan." I shake my head. "You blame me for acting the khrissal. Yet you cross yourself, and show the signs of jealousy, like a human wed to a mate."

"Because I've eaten many Christians, and many jealous husbands and wives. What's your excuse? Did you eat a poet while I wasn't looking?"

I smile. "Not everything humans write is poetry."

"I'm a shape-shifter, not illiterate. I have read their books. As many as you have, I'm sure. Maybe more. The holy ones. The romances. The poems."

"And what is your opinion on human literature, Gévaudan?"

"All the same. Litanies of arrogance."

I nod, and laugh. But there remains a glamour of malevolence around him. He is not happy that our fight ended with no catharsis, one way or the other. I would be worried, but there are other things on my mind.

Now night lingers around me:

And I can only think of you in that courtyard, in the afternoon sun yesterday. And then I think of you by moonlight last night, so different.

I am sick with fear, should Gévaudan or Makedon find what I'm writing. I take the lock of your hair on my necklace, press it to my mouth. I look at what I wrote after returning from the bazaars of Mumtazabad, after I first saw you. I barely thought of it at the time, but it is as a letter, to you. A letter that is also a lie, though it came so easily and so true. Such is the nefarious magic of this human art.

When I saw you, I did not wish you were not human, as I wrote then.

When I saw you, I saw also the face of that mother outside Lahore, her face gemmed with flies, the created life she'd held inside her wasted. I remembered the urge I had to kiss that corpse on its open mouth.

But it occurs to me that I have the answer to Makedon's question. I could never tell him that, but I do. You: hunted, uneaten, spared. You are the one I write for now. If this knowledge gladdens me, I cannot tell.

A hunt, yes. But it was not to devour.

INTERVAL

As commanded, or hired, to do, I type out the stranger's hand-written manuscript relating the arrival of three European shape-shifters in seventeenth-century Mumtazabad. After I type out each section, I print it out, fearing that my computer will crash and the stranger's notebook manuscript vanish, leaving me without any sign of this strange episode. It's been a slow process, carefully deciphering his sometimes unruly handwriting and remaining faithful to it. I've also added my own footnotes to the journal, to keep my own thoughts about the whole thing straight.

I often wonder why I'm doing this. I keep teaching my classes, go about my life as if nothing is happening. I tell no one about the stranger. I don't hear back from him, either. Sometimes I'll see an item in the papers about gruesome human remains found in the river, or in the marshy lands amid the city's coagulated sprawl—an unidentified torso, a head, a rotting body eaten away by what's presumed to be feral ani-mals. Nothing too surprising in and around a city, terror and loneliness bleached to mundanity in newsprint, dulled by repetition. But I'll see these headlines, and I'll entertain the odd fantasy that it's the stranger's handiwork, that these are leftovers from his prey. That he's left them to be found just for me to read about over cups of tea, burnt toast, and poached eggs in the morning.

I have very few friends, and I don't much get along with my family anymore. No one I truly confide in. So there aren't a lot of people I can tell about the stranger and the job he's given me, really. All the same, I

keep this secret close to me like a bounty, not even sharing it with Gitanjali, the one professor in my department I meet socially and actually
get along with to some degree. I want to tell her, but I'm afraid she'll
think I'm being stupid, or in danger, befriending and accepting jobs
from random strangers with outrageous claims. Gitanjali and I sit in
the College Street Coffee House exchanging faculty gossip after we're
done with classes, and I feel like an anthropologist who has made an
astounding discovery, but is unable to divulge his findings to the
world. I grasp my cup in both hands, wanting to flirt vaguely with her
like I used to. But I'm unable to. I look at this thirty-something divor-
cée opposite me, her dark lipstick dissolving in acrid coffee, and I find
myself perplexed by my own existence, by the echoing confines of the
place we are sitting in, by the civilization around us. I think about the
thoughts of those mad souls roaming the streets of Kolkata. I think of
the beasts out there beyond the city limits. When I return home after
coffee with Gitanjali, I pick up the manuscript and read it again and
again, closing my eyes after each page to will myself into a trance.
Then, with a glass of whiskey handy, I start typing again from wherever I last stopped. I often wonder about the tale in the manuscript—
whether the stranger or someone else has written it. Whether it was
first written by an impostor, or a man living a supremely confident
delusion, or an actual shape-shifter during the seventeenth century.

Whatever the truth, it matters little now.

SECOND FRAGMENT
Makedon returns:

Out of the water in his first self, emerging naked and washed by the Yamuna. He holds in one hand the severed head of his prey, water trickling from its open mouth. Makedon tosses the head on the ground, where the sallow pearls of its retreated eyes look at nothing.

He walks to me. His body is bronzed in water, long hair clinging in sinuous tattoos to his shoulders and neck. I can smell the recent carnage on him, sticking to his skin. It makes my mouth water, even though we fed well today. It is unease, as my second self speaks to me in hunger, tells me that I need my strength for something.

"Stop staring," Makedon says, sitting on the ground. He doesn't bother wearing his clothes. "Gévaudan sleeps like a babe in a crib. If you need to, you could probably fuck him twice and he wouldn't stir," he says with a sneer.

I say nothing.

"I can smell you pining. If I didn't know better I'd think you've taken me for a permanent mate."

"Don't flatter yourself. How was your hunt? Am I mistaken in thinking that this is not Shah Jahan's head?" I ask.

"I'll leave that a mystery. Now that Gévaudan is asleep, we can talk."

"About what?"

"About your hunt, yesterday. The one you went on alone," he says.

"What about it?"

"Tell me again about your prey," he says.

"I told you already."

"Tell me. Again," he says.

"A woman I took off the street. In Mumtazabad. Why?"

"Don't play innocent," he says and smiles at me. He doesn't blink. His teeth are black from the kill.

"What was it like?" he whispers.

"What?"

"Raping a human woman."

"I didn't rape her." The words fall from me before I can stop them.

"If a farmer should in boredom and loneliness fuck a dumb calf fat for his plate, would your khrissal poets call it lovemaking? The calf is his prey, and below him, and a carnal act with it is vulgar," he says.

"We spring from the human soul. She's no dumb calf, nor is any human. No more than you and I."

"Ever the romantic. Clothing your perversions in language. Gévaudan might be too young or dense to use his senses properly, but I could smell your desire for that female from the moment we walked into the caravanserai yesterday. You can't hide something like that from me. You think yourself old. I ate of sacrificial children on the altars of Arcadia before even Europe came to be, before that tricksy carpenter of Bethlehem died to conjure a new god for the nations to come. The sons of Lycaon himself split my soul in two long before this shape you wear was spewed into existence."

"Did you follow me yesterday night?" I ask.

"No, you fool. Are you and Gévaudan so dulled by the human world that you've forgotten that your first selves aren't wet clay of human flesh? No, North-*man*. I can still smell that khrissal on you. I can taste her sex on you, in the air."

"What do you want?" I ask.

He backs away, hitting his chest once. The heavy thump of flesh and bone. "I have you," he says, his voice low. "Do you even realize? What you've done is forbidden by the tribes."

"The tribes. You know as well as I that you don't care about the tribes. How can you even claim to know what tenets the tribes here, or farther east, or north or south, follow? We can't just scrabble out the meanings of our existence from the stories of humans, and assume that others of our kind do the same in places we've never even seen."

"I'm not interested in speeches and debating again, North-man. I'm not interested in pretending we have culture when we don't need it. Leave that to the khrissals. I'm interested in your penance, for repeatedly bringing up this fucking nonsense, and committing an aberration in its name."

I know that he's right. I am only delaying the inevitable. "I was always a solitary, Makedon. I'm fine with not seeing any of my tribe, when I never truly belonged to any single one. Tell me what *you* want from me."

"What could I want? I could demand slavery, make you my mate and servant for the rest of your years, to follow my bidding in return for my silence. I've no use for such a slave, miserable and subservient, waiting to kill me in my sleep. No." He turns away, looking at the moon and shaking his head. He looks beautiful in his sudden calm, his profile traced in a bejeweled line of silver as water drips down his face.

"No. I don't want that, and you certainly don't want that. What I want is for you to give your life. You've mingled with our prey. I won't travel with a khrissal-fucking betrayer. Sacrifice yourself. That's what I ask," he says.

I flinch as he takes one of my hands in his. I don't resist, letting him lift my palm and press it against his slick chest. "For your honor and for ours. Strip yourself, cut yourself from ear to ear, let your lifeblood fall upon your lap and your hands so you can wash yourself of this deed. Let me feast on your remains. It will be a noble death. You will live on in me."

"You talk of my perversions, and you would eat carrion of your own kind?"

"To feast on a betrayer is no forbidden thing. You've exiled yourself."

I can feel his heart beat under my hand. I can feel it split, two drummers beating the cage of his chest. Two hearts separating. Under the slippery cold of water, his skin and muscles burn with fever.

"I see through you, Makedon. You fear what I've done, you loathe it. But you also desire it. You would feast on my flesh, my life, my soul. You'd seek out the stain of a human heart against mine even as you bit into it. You want to feel what I've felt, in union with a human woman."

He smiles at me. "Maybe I do. It doesn't change anything," he says.

I pull my hand out of his and return it to my own lap, not wanting to betray my trembling. I don't know how old Makedon truly is, but I have hunted with him. I don't know if I could defeat him in his second self. I can already feel it coming, the energies of his recent prey burning like coals in the furnace of his human shape, blazing in his souls. This is why he went on a hunt, to feed his second self an entire khrissal alone, instead of a communal meal in his first. To give himself strength. It is coming, and I feel nothing. I feel no desire to emanate my second self even though I need to, because all that envelops me is fear and weakness. My second self abhors such things.

"I'll leave and travel on my own. You'd never see me again," I tell Makedon.

"We're going to the same place."

"I won't go east. The Mughal Empire is vaster even than the Holy Roman Empire. I'll travel, avoid the tribes. I'm willing to live in exile."

"No. Too easy."

"Then what? Will you fight me? Is that what you want?"

"Not unless you want to."

"Then what stops me from leaving right now?" I ask.

"If you leave, I'll return to Mumtazabad. I'll tear your lovely little human woman apart limb from limb."

"I'll kill you. I'll kill you before you go near her." Even as I say it, I know, at that moment, I've lost already.

"You are welcome to try," he says, shaking his head. "But if you fall under my tooth and claw, you'll still forfeit the lives of your khrissal mate and her unborn child, if you've left one in her womb."

"Don't. You'll never see me again. I swear to you. Aren't we companions, joined under the tribes?"

"Oh, now we're joined under the tribes. Now the tribes matter," he says.

"We've traveled far together. We've been a pack, shared the ghost fires. Do this for me," I plead, repulsed by my own desperation.

"What's going on?" Gévaudan asks, clambering up, mud caking his furs. I can't tell if he's been listening for long, but he seems wide awake, gripping the serpentine corpse around his neck and shoulders. His sudden awakening is almost comical, though the circumstances prevent me from appreciating this.

Makedon's fingers are around my neck. I ram my fists into his sides. His ribs crack under my knuckles. The pain only feeds his desire to emanate, his grip getting stronger. Gévaudan grabs his shoulders and pulls him off me but is elbowed back. "Stop, you two," he wheezes. I get up, also coughing.

"Mewling boy-cunt." Makedon strikes Gévaudan on the chest, shoving him back.

"Makedon, stop," Gévaudan says.

"He's challenged me, Gévaudan. Let him be," I say, rubbing my throat. I begin to strip. Makedon turns away from our companion. He starts pulling his bone trophies, stretching his skin as if it were a garment he was itching to tear off. He squats. The rib shards burned into his back move as he flexes his shoulders.

"You choose battle, then," he says.

"Yes," I tell him.

"Don't do this. We're a pack," says Gévaudan:

I take off the layers of animal skin that cover me, leaving only the one that mimics a human. I am flaccid, shivering even in this weak winter. Makedon strangles his flushed cock, grown stiff in his hand. He will enjoy this battle. Gévaudan walks toward him, hesitant.

"Step back, whelp," Makedon says to Gévaudan, his voice grating and inhuman. I feel a pang of regret for rejecting Gévaudan earlier. I wonder how these two will travel without me. They probably won't. I take off my boots, and am naked like Makedon. The earth is soft and startlingly cold under my feet. I dig my toes in.

Then Gévaudan steps lightly behind Makedon and pushes him. Startled, Makedon stumbles forward, his legs buckling. There is a knife handle sticking out of his spine like an ornament. Gévaudan removes the serpent from his shoulders and whips it around Makedon's neck with resigned grace. Our young companion is fast. He tightens the mordant noose. I see Makedon's eyes bulge in their sockets, even as he tries to free the blade in his back.

In this moment, what is Gévaudan but utterly human, hairless and worm white in skins peeled from other animals. His soft face twisted not in savagery but calm, premeditated malice. There is no majestic beast rearing behind Makedon clothed only in the tangled mane of its own fur. There is no clash of two titans, no revel in the glory of spilling blood, blood of second selves rich with the memories of thousands upon thousands of human prey.

No, there is just the white hand and its brittle fingers, curled around the handle of a knife. He pulls it out of Makedon only to return it to his quarry's neck. The blade slides through tendon and artery, above the choking coils of the serpent. I watch as Gévaudan cuts and cuts through the steam of escaping breath, slicing deep to release the ruby sheets now draping Makedon's naked form.

Makedon pulls Gévaudan's hand away from his slashed neck and bites it. The oldest of us tears free and falls to the mud, trying to free himself of the deadweight of the serpent. Gévaudan kneels over him and slams the knife into his spine again. I hear a crack of metal pushing between bones. Drooling, he pulls the blade out and holds Makedon's head by the hair. Makedon claws into the mud. Knee against broken spine, knife between teeth, Gévaudan ties Makedon's arms behind his back with his lifeless reptilian familiar.

There is a fury in Makedon's wide eyes. Centuries, millennia of lived life bulging against darkening irises. I feel a dread witnessing this— this ugly killing, none of us three in our second selves as it should be, our mate trussed and butchered like a human being murdered by one of his own. Our companion, our pack-mate, his voice drowned. This is my fault. He spits, recognizing the inevitable end of his age-long life, but not accepting it, burying his toes into the ground rigid till the very moment Gévaudan cuts his head off.

Sick with gratitude, I close my eyes in the red rain.

And as I do, I think of you, of the moment of my shame and your despair:

The caravanserai was silent at night, except for the soft snuffling of camels in stalls, sitting by their sleeping owners in dolorous gratitude for their shed burdens. A few of the stalls surrounding the courtyard still glimmered with the weak light of tapers behind curtains. In my hand I held the piece of you that you gave to me. It guided me through the empty courtyard, showing me the tracery of your wake coiling in the air amid the vapor of camel shit and dirty fur.

The knot of your hair a circular rune in my outstretched palm, I watched my shadow stride across the stone, my boots silent as a panther's paws. I came to your stall and parted the curtain. A whisper of disturbed fabric against the floor. You were ready for me, your intruder. Moonlight drifted on the dust and fell into the blade in your hand. I could hear you breathing, lungs heavy with fear.

"I'll kill you if you come one step closer," you said with admirable fervor. What was I to you at that moment, with the moon at my back, setting the pelt on my shoulders ablaze with blue fire, my wild braids a mane for my head, face dark but for the pinpricks of reflection in my wet eyes, my great shadow yawning cold upon your body? Was I a beast in human form?

"I won't hurt you," I said, soft as I could.

"It's you," you said, after a moment of silence.

"Yes," I said, and entered the stall. You backed away like a cornered animal, and I felt the pangs of pity. Fear was not my intent, though inevitable.

"Please, don't be afraid. If you scream, I'll kill you as swiftly as a tiger on a weakling calf. There's no need for that. It would hurt me to do that."

"What do you want?" you asked.

"What's your name?"

Perhaps you knew that I meant what I had said, so you answered, "Cyrah." I thought it as wonderful a name as I had ever heard.

"Cyrah. Are you scared?"

"Yes. You may think by my size that I've no chance of fighting you off, white man, but know this. If you hurt me, I'll hurt you back. Even if you leave me dead, I'll leave you blind and a eunuch if I have to."

"It wouldn't do much lasting good to do either to me, but fairly said. Then I'll make this promise to you: If you don't hurt me tonight, I won't hurt you."

"I don't hurt people unless they give me cause," you said.

"Unless you see the very trade you live on as cause for hurting me, I will give you none tonight. I don't want to harm you."

"It's not a trade. It's something I do to survive in this land run by men, as a woman, and one without a husband at that. I told you, no harem protects me."

"You're beautiful, Cyrah."

"You must be joking. And you're a lurking pig-fucker. Why didn't you give me custom today at noon, when you met me, when I asked you? Why have you come here at night like a criminal, if not to hurt me?" you asked me with a sincerity that brought tears to my eyes. Despite your bold words, you were terrified.

"I've never slept with a human woman," I said.

You were silent, before you asked me, "So what?"

"It's against the tenets of my tribe to lie with a human woman. I couldn't buy your company in front of my companions."

"Again, with these white man's lies. I'm not a child, I won't believe these fancies. How do you beget children in your tribe?"

I shed my pelt and raiment.

"Stop," you said.

I took off my leggings and boots.

"Fucking stop," you said.

"We don't bear children in our tribe, Cyrah," I said, and walked forward naked as a newborn.

"Don't come closer," you said. I came closer, without weapons. You held out your blade.

"We have our mates, who come and go. But we have no love. We are forbidden from making love, from fucking in our first selves, our human shapes. We've forgotten, but we all came from human wombs, before we were initiated into the tribes, before we were born again, and freed our second selves." You must have thought me insane, a terror. And yet I spoke on, like a confessor, eager to let my words fall on human ears.

"My companion Makedon says the first of our kind was a king named Lycaon, who believed himself transformed by a god he called Zeus. But the human is the only creature on this planet that can manifest the demiurgic instinct, and this Zeus, I believe, was at first merely a powerful man, one who could hold sway over other humans and help them transcend their humanity."

"Stop it. I don't understand what you're saying . . ."

"Listen, Cyrah, and you will. You will understand why I must do this, why my kind and yours are connected. Lycaon was just one king. There are stories of our tribes in many forms. In Europe we are oft made wolves, the devil's children, but in the arid lands between the Bosporus and the Indus, where you came from, the tribes of our kind take the name of djinn, from stories the Khorassians wove of beings who can change shape, created by your Allah from a smokeless fire. In the African plains, perhaps our unknown kinsmen take the second selves of great hyenas laughing under a blood-red moon, slack-tongued lions stalking the savanna. In the flesh of sailors who hailed from beyond the Red Sea, I've tasted rumors of jackal-jawed cenobites of Anapa roaming the dead cities of the pharaohs. And what are we here, in Hindustan? Perhaps here our other selves are chimerical tigers burning bright in the Asiatic jungle, not so far from here."

You were stunned by this ungainly history vomited from my mouth. I walked over to you and winced as your dull blade found a path across my forearm, parting my skin. You sprang away nimbly, but I have strength and speed to beat any khrissal, and grabbed you by the arms. You held the blade still in your fist as I stayed your hands, and you stared me in the eyes. I could hear your teeth grinding together. My face was close to yours.

Panting, you said, "I suppose you want me to spit on your face in fury. I'm not going to, you smear of pig shit. I'm not giving you any more parts of myself."

Your anger hurt me, but I went on.

"I don't know how we came to be," I told you, hoping, hoping to entrance you without magic's aid. "But none of those tales, none of our history is hidden from your kind. None of it recorded by our own tribes. It is all written and told by humans, not us. Look to the tales of ancient Greece, and you will find the history of Lycaon and his fifty impious sons. Perhaps we only steal your history to make of it ours, just as we steal your lives to extend our own. We call ourselves hunters, but we are scavengers."

In black drops my blood fell on you from the wound you made, painting a trail of crimson blossoms from your hurriedly worn headscarf to your plain blouse.

I took both your wrists in one of my hands. With my other hand I reached out and touched your face, illuminated by the scents that emerged from your cheeks and lips and neck and eyes, the different elixirs of the body shimmering around your bones—sweat, tears, oils, spit, turning with the fevered heat of fear.

"Do you see now, fragile Cyrah? Like thieves we snatch babes from their cribs, children from their parents, and perform the rites on them, and they become our kin, shape-shifters. Like murderous bandits we attack men and women, wound them with our teeth and claws, and tear their souls into two so that they may join us. We cannot bear offspring—only creatures bound to one shape can hold a life in the womb. To give birth means banishment to the weaker self for nine months, and that is abomination enough to be exiled from the tribes. Our second selves are hermaphroditic, so we shift, and mate among one another, though no offspring is born. We are the devouring, not the creative. That is humanity's province, and we've gone beyond human. So now I seek a human. Do you see?"

I pushed my thumb against the warm crevice of your mouth, as if to free the words from your coiled form. You uttered a guttural, animal sound as your entire body hardened. "Please don't be afraid," I told you. "I think our time is waning. I only want to create." I could feel the tears streaking your face, salt lines crawling under my fingertips. The slick stones of your teeth. Behind them, your tongue moved, and you said, the words humming against my thumb, "Allah curse you, bastard." You turned your face away, grimacing, each movement cutting me as sure as your blade did. No, you were not entranced, and spat my thumb from your mouth.

"Cyrah, I will kill you if you try and fight," I said again, though it pained me.

"You really mean that, don't you," you said.

"This is important to me. I will slaughter everyone in this caravanserai if they get in my way."

Your eyes glistened with rage, or fear, or both. "The world is yours to take, you loathsome child, you white boy," you whispered.

I was shocked to find myself shaking, like you. I didn't want to kill you, but it seemed like you were testing me, like you were pushing me to that. But you said instead,

"Fine. Let me go. I'm no fool, I won't try and fight. I've no dying wish." No words could give me sweeter relief. I let go of your wrists. Slowly you put down the knife and took two steps back, your eyes always on me. "Listen to me, white man. You've no right to buy your way into a woman's bed with nothing to barter with but fear. If you will not stay your hand, I want my fucking payment."

"I gave you coins."

"For my hair. Not this. Not this," you said through closed teeth.

"I will pay you, then."

You wiped your eyes and nodded. I saw the muscles tie their graceful knots under the skin that covers your jaw. "Do not think that this will in any way repay the debt you've incurred tonight. For that you must barter with your own god or devil in whatever hell they send you to," you added.

"If I have any god or devil it is myself, unfortunately."

"The blade stays by my side," you told me, pointing to your blade with one shaking hand. I nodded.

"Do what you will, you mad fucking son of a bitch, and stop telling me your stupid stories."

She-wolf you, Cyrah, moon-shone maiden, I kissed you on your lips, licking the aphrodisiac of your burning anger. My second self struggled to emerge like the latent orgasm but I held it back, you in my arms. As if human-to-human, I came into you. Silent my child came to be, in you, unformed, a seed in the soil, a thousand tales untold.

Gévaudan's pelts are stained from the kill:

Hands and dagger as one with red. A devil's hands. I can taste Makedon's blood on my lips. His headless body lies stretched out on the ground, neck stump spewing steam like a doused torch, limbs bound in the banded coils of Gévaudan's serpent. From across the trees near the bank, and across the river, jackals cry out in the dawn stillness.

We sit in silence until Gévaudan picks up our companion's severed head by a tuft of curls. He places it next to Makedon's final prey. The two heads sit side by side, brothers in death. Like two humans. Gévaudan sheathes his knife, after wiping it on his already stained clothes. With sticky fingers he uncoils his serpent from the corpse and throws it on the ground. Then he sits by me.

"You've made a coward of me," he tells me, and waits for a response. I give him none.

"Makedon's second self could have easily defeated mine in combat. I attacked him unchallenged, unheralded, without warning. I killed him in his weaker self, and I used my weaker self to do it. Like a soft khrissal assassin," he tells me, crouching next to me but avoiding looking at me.

"You saved my life," I say.

"A traitor's life."

"You didn't have to," I say.

"Yes. I did."

"Why?"

"Because I've broken the tenets, the same as you," he tells me.

Gévaudan wipes his damp face, leaving a swath of crimson across it like war paint. There is a half-moon of torn flesh on his hand where Makedon bit him. Because of our years of travel and companionship, I feel an instinctual urge to take the hand and lick it, suck the wound and aid its healing. I stop myself. The howling of the jackals in the trees turns to sharp barking. Gévaudan picks up the head of Makedon's final prey. With a snarl, he hurls it into the air, sending it far into the trees. We hear it crash into the distant undergrowth, and the cries of the restless animals are stilled for a moment. He turns back to me grimacing.

"In France I would see young human lovers frolicking in the woods during summer and spring, and my hackles would rise with envy. I would shed their blood, eat their bodies, so perfumed with the stink of their love. But it is you who've finally turned me into one of *them*," he says. It disgusts me how much his words sound like mine, like the words I've written on this very scroll.

I shake my head, utterly exhausted. "What reason have I ever given you to. To love me."

Several yards away, the sound of snapping and growling as the jackals find the head.

Gévaudan laughs. "What reason is there for love? The curse of the Apollonian soul. Makedon's words, not mine. There was reason for our tribes to slice it from our existence. Still, yours is another aberration entirely. I thought Makedon was the one you wanted, when all the while your eyes were straying to khrissals."

He still does not look at me, turning his head to the mausoleum. To the east, the horizon warms. "If this misery is love, it's no wonder humans have their poets to pine about its mysteries, and palaces to tell the stories of their dead mates," he says.

"I'm sorry, Gévaudan. I can't help you."

"Nor I you," he says. He finally looks at me with a resentful longing that transcends carnal desire. I want to recoil from this. I wonder if you felt the same way as I held you. No, that is a lie. I know you did.

"I can seek solace in the fact that your khrissal bitch doesn't want you. Nor will she ever. I'm right about that. Aren't I," he sneers, wrinkling his nose to make a feral echo of his second self.

"You are."

Gévaudan claps his sticky hands together, rubbing them as if to rid them of the drying blood. The bite wound, though deep, doesn't seem to bother him. "Then we'll be united in our sorrows, at the very least. We'll be human together, and atone for our sins like their goddamn papists."

"Where will you go?" I ask him.

"Perhaps one day I'll return to France, to the province where I took my name. To hunt the lovely lads and lasses of Langogne and Les Hubacs again, as they sing on heath and hill in their bliss of spring copulation. Who needs a pack? I will go alone. But for now, a whole empire awaits." He stops, laughter dissolving as he draws a deep breath. "And you? You'll go begging at the feet of your forced khrissal mate, like a pet dog?"

"She said something to me, afterward."

"What did she say?" he asks me. I see his bitter amusement, that I should be so shaken by a khrissal female. But he is also curious.

"She said planting my seed and trying to create new young doesn't make me any more human than a mangy dog fucking an unhappy bitch amid the feet of the bazaar-goers."

Gévaudan throws his head back and laughs loud and cruel, echoes barking across the lapping river water.

"I could have torn her apart then, Gévaudan." I look down at my hands. They are trembling in my lap.

"But you didn't," he says, and spits snot.

I shake my head.

"Because no matter what your khrissal whore says, you're more like her than you are your own kind."

"I have lived a long time. I have known love, Gévaudan. I have kept it locked away, but I have felt it. I believe others of our kind feel it, have felt it, but hide it as well. You. You know this. There is more than anima* and lust in me, in all of us. But that is all she saw in me. A creature less than both animal and human."

---

* It's worth noticing that the shape-shifters appear to use the term *anima* to refer to a primal aspect of their "second selves" rather than the more conventional meaning of the Latin *anima*, "soul" or "inner personality." It isn't too far from that meaning, but they seem to use it quite specifically to refer to the "beasts" they carry within them.

"An *honest* creature. You stupid old fool. You've never let humanity go, like your kin. Like Makedon. Like me."

"I fear that in trying to become more like them, I have become less so in her eyes."

"What does it matter what she sees?" Gévaudan asks. I can hear his teeth creak as he grits them. "*I* see your humanity with my eyes, be they a devil's."

"Yes, you do." I laugh. "And you despise humanity. I can see nothing in me for you to love."

His cheek twitches. "And you can see something in a khrissal you met once and decided to rape instead of eat? You're a funny one. When it comes to love, we're both blind maggots squirming in the mud. Maybe that's why. Maybe that's why."

I remain silent.

"Then go, run away somewhere," Gévaudan snaps.

"I can't come with you, Gévaudan. Our pack is broken. We should respect that."

His one eye burns against the blood smear on his face. I wait for him to attack, bringing my thumb to the metal wolf head of my Pesh-kabz handle. But Gévaudan gets up, his bone trinkets chiming. He bends down over me. I flinch. But all he does is press his mouth to my forehead and turn to walk away. His kiss burns in the misty air. I want to say something, to bid him farewell, but I cannot bring myself to. I watch him walk away and vanish into the trees by the river. A terrible howl sounds, heralding his departure. The death of a jackal, or two. I turn away, look across the river. Marble and water throw back the light of the sun, setting the river and the mausoleum on fire. I write.

One bloody jackal, golden in the dawn, sprints out of the shadows and across the mud of the bank. In her fangs a tuft of hair and skin, scalp torn from a hurled skull. She peers at me with wary black eyes, wandering far down the bank and sitting on her haunches to tear the tissue from the hair.

I will pause here.

* * *

I bury Makedon's body and head so that he may return to the earth. The jackal watches as she eats her scrap of human. Monkeys emerge from the treetops, dancing as morning becomes itself. Furred minstrels of the earth, uncaring of the quarrels of shape-shifters and of jackals. They prance across the mud and throw stones at the jackal, which snaps and bares her teeth. I dig.

As I put my pack-mate in the ground, surrounded by waking animals in their kingdom, these creatures barely aware of an empire of humans around them, I think of the dust-clad second selves of the djinn tribes, hunched and lapping the ruddy peaks of a charnel ground in the Sindh. Perched like sphinxes on those rocks, victorious and languid in the sun, haunches coiled, their great claws sunken in trophy bodies of dead humans, tongues snaking between razored teeth to clean blood-wet cakes of dirt clinging to their long faces. Their second selves were shaped in ways foreign to me, some with arches of bone growing from their muscled shoulders, feathered with plumage to resemble great flightless wings. The dust they cloaked themselves in to deceive and blind foes sifted across the baleful sun, stirred by their false wings. They had seemed to me like that human fancy, angels of death. I wonder how human eyes see my second self, or Makedon's, what nightmares and demons we may represent in your folklores. Here I bury a terror to all of your kind, and no one knows or cares. Only you will know, if you ever read this, and yet Makedon has done nothing to you. I am the monster in your tale.

When I'm done burying Makedon,
I pack mud over the grave and piss on it:

The jackal sniffs the air and runs back into the trees, chasing monkeys away. The grave is unmarked, hidden. Makedon's clothes remain on the soft banks of the Yamuna, for someone to weave a tale out of. I can still smell the circle he pissed around them. His fardels I loot, to fill my own. The possessions I find no use for, I throw into the river. I wash my raiment and cloak, which have been stained by Makedon's murder. They are already dyed dark with years of dried remnants from fights. A little more will do nothing. I take Gévaudan's dead serpent and hurl it into the river.

Across the river the long line of workmen returns to the mausoleum site. I get up and walk away from Mumtazabad, the last of the pack that set out from Europe. When we dispersed and left the muddy gates of Nürnberg, we gathered again in the countryside at least twenty-five strong, with a twin pack of another twenty shadowing us. By the time we crossed the borders of the Mughal Empire, we were reduced to three. Infighting, tribal battles, others who chose to remain in the many different empires and kingdoms we passed through. One day I might write of that great migration, of the events that shaped this pack down to me. Me leaving the far-off tomb of Mumtaz Mahal behind me, leaving the unmarked grave of Makedon of Greece behind me like the grave of any murdered mortal man. Perhaps I will write of that exodus when I find a new reader, because why would you want to hear more of my tale? I have asked enough of you.

I wonder if I will ever see any of my kind again. I wonder if the other packs that joined the migration are somewhere in this empire. Trickling into the vast populace of this new land after the long journey they have undertaken to see the fresh hunting grounds of the eastern realms. I am an exile now.

A shape-shifter's love means nothing, but I give it to you and to our child, a gift, like the knot of hair on my necklace. I ask of you only one thing: that you not silence the little heart that beats with yours, marking time's passage under the smooth brown sheath of your navel-notched belly. It deserves not the wrath of the devouring wolf, but the love of the prolific mother.

I wonder if I will see you again.

Part Four

OF HISTORIES

1

It takes me several weeks to finish the transcription.

Months after I've finished, the stranger calls on my landline, asking to meet so that I can give him the typed version. He takes long enough that I figured I'd never see him again. I ask him how he found my number, and he answers simply: It's in the phone book. Of course it is.

The handover happens at the Indian Museum, over the stale wrappings of its resident Egyptian mummy. Perhaps he finds that amusing, in a Hammer-horror kind of way. A half werewolf, a mummy, and a human meet at a museum, et cetera. I watch flies peck at the glass of the display case, trying to get to the long-desiccated corpse within, while the stranger flips through the stapled sheets of the typed transcript. He has grown an ungroomed beard, so I don't even recognize him. His tapering jaws hidden by hair, he takes on the look of a sunroasted prophet. Thankfully, he remembers what I look like. He seems delighted at my work. We leave the museum and walk up Chowringhee, drinking milky sweet street chai from little clay cups despite the steaming heat of the summer afternoon.

He points at the baking green expanse of the Maidan, across the sun-reflecting river of traffic oozing down Jawaharlal Nehru Road.

"I remember when that park was nothing but swamp and jungle, and a few hovels huddling around the dirt road to Halishar. Our pack, we'd pick prey off that road so often—travelers without a clue. Oh, don't look at me like that. If we didn't, bandits would have, or tigers, sometimes even the odd mazed elephant. We usually left the villagers alone, though."

"When did you finally give in and move into the city?"

"The city? The city didn't happen for a long time. And who said I live in the city now?"

"Don't you?"

He ignores my question, of course. "The British messed it all up. Built their City of Palaces here, built Fort William. Everything changed after Plassey. It was something, though."

"What was?"

"The first day they turned on the lights over Chowringhee. Gas lamps. It was a summer evening; July, I think. July of 1857? I forget the year. I only read about it later. Didn't much keep track back then. I watched from the wilderness. They didn't even have bloody pavements yet, but they switched on the lights. A string of fireballs in the dark, unceasing. Quite something. When I saw them flicker to life, I had this gut-wrenching feeling. I knew things were changing faster than we'd ever expected."

I look past the dirty metal pillars of the flyover that bisects Jawaharlal Nehru Road, and at the fenced-off Maidan. A kite drifts above the trees that jostle the pointed spears of the wrought-iron fence. We keep walking.

He is no longer putting up the pretense that the first story he told me at the baul mela wasn't about him. He is admitting to having a somewhat abnormal life span, and to the admittedly unusual activity of hunting humans. It makes me smile, though I don't know myself if it's a smile of patronizing skepticism or just relief at gaining a bit more of his confidence. After all, if the stranger's stories are real, I'm faced with carrying a truth too enormous and terrifying to contemplate.

"So tell me truthfully. Did you write the story in the notebook you gave me?" I ask.

"It's more than a story. It's a confession, a journal, an apology."

"Right. To the poor woman in it. Cyrah. The one woman in it, I might add."

"Yes, to her. And no, I didn't write it, obviously. I just translated it. Like I said, do I look blond and blue-eyed?"

"Then who did?" I ask.

"The narrator wrote it."

"Don't get meta on me. You know what I mean," I say. "Well, anyway, it's probably a good thing you're claiming not to have written it, because your 'narrator' is an awful man—"

"Not a man . . ." The stranger smiles.

"Yes, yes, shape-shifter, not a man. Poor, benighted soul, raped a woman, and I'm supposed to cry for him because he wanted to 'create'? Both this story and the one you told me, they're supposed to be somewhat sad, right?" I almost stop because I remember exactly how melancholic the stranger's narration had been, when he told the story that hypnotized me at the mela. I become a bit nervous that he might get offended, but I see that he's waiting placidly for me to continue. I go on. "But even ignoring the whole human-hunting thing, they're from the point of view of a kidnapper, and then a rapist, and both times there's a woman who only exists in their story to suffer for their strange needs. And whether or not they're not human, they look and act, for all intents and purposes, like human men. I mean, am I supposed to be sad for the narrator here?"

I become even more nervous when he doesn't say anything.

"I'm not, am I? That's ridiculous. I hope he's not supposed to be sympathetic. Is he?"

"You'd have to ask him that, now, wouldn't you? Will you just relax for one moment, Professor? Just relax, take a breath, enjoy this bright summer day. You ask so many questions, I hardly know which ones to answer. Do you want some jhaal moori?"

"No, I'm okay."

He drinks the last of his chai and tosses the clay cup into one of the piles of garbage that punctuate the hawkers' stalls lining the pavements of Chowringhee. Walking to one of the vendors with their metal carts, he buys himself a paper bag of jhaal moori. Pouring out even handfuls of the spicy puffed rice in his palm and tossing them into his mouth, he speaks between munches.

"Thank you. For typing that out. I told you I'd pay you for your services, and I will," he says, stopping to savor the moori. His thick beard moves up and down over his slender neck. I see the green bulge of a prominent vein snake up that long trunk of sinew and skin, and avert my eyes from it.

"Okay, what's my payment? I'm intrigued," I ask, clearing my throat.

"Have you ever been to the Sundarbans?" he asks, sniffing the myriad scents in the air. To me, everything is overwhelmed by the stink of pollution from heavy traffic just a few feet away from us.

"The Sundarbans? No, why?" I ask.

"It's a pity that most people in this city barely even realize that one of the largest delta forests in the world lies just hours south of here."

"Well, I'm aware of it. I just haven't gone."

"I'm paying you in travel, Professor. You can thank me later. I've booked a trip to the Sundarbans," he says, lapsing back into familiar presumption. He smiles, small flecks of puffed rice crumbs sticking to his lips and black beard. "I'll pay you in money, too, in case you're worried. Think of this as a bonus."

"You want me to visit the Sundarbans. With you."

"Unless you don't want your bonus. It's nothing to me." He shrugs, rolling oily peanuts around his palm with his thumb.

"Why the Sundarbans?" I ask.

"It's close. And I want to show you where I grew up," he says. The peanuts and stray rice disappear, crunching loudly between his teeth.

"You grew up in the Sundarbans?"

"I just said so. You really must stop with these incessant questions, Professor. Come with me and I'll tell you about it. This is neither the time nor the place."

"I'm just a little surprised. It's not every day people ask me on trips into jungles. Or anywhere, for that matter. I barely even know you."

He munches his moori, squinting, placid. A sheen of sweat shines on his high forehead, catching the burning sunlight.

"Can I think about it?" I ask.

"Of course. Should you decide to accept payment, I also want to continue our arrangement. Professional or not, you're just fine at the job, Alok. You should give yourself more credit once in a while," he says.

"There is more to the story, then?"

"Quite a bit more." He nods and unzips his worn backpack. He hands me a mustard-yellow manila envelope, just like the first time. This time, it has loose sheets instead of a notebook, but filled with the same handwriting as before. "Another manuscript," he says. "If you can call it that. Another journal of sorts, translated. You might be interested in it. You seem most concerned, after all, about the woman in the previous journal. Compile this one and type it out, like before. If you're willing. Again, payment will be arranged. Simple money, if you like."

I think about this. I know he might well be barking mad, but then again—if he is, so am I. He made me see things, see stories even as he spoke their words. I still don't know what's happened between the two of us, whether he drugged me into accepting some hallucinatory reality of his own the first night I met him. But if I'm dancing with a trickster, I'm nothing if not awed by each step, each move. He's leading, with skill.

And if everything he says is real, I don't even know. I don't know what that means. It means I'm to be a historian like no other, my lack of ambition be damned.

So I take his second manuscript and agree to be his unqualified contracted transcriber once more, if only to give us a reason to keep meeting, to wear away my remaining rational impulses to stop all of this and never contact him again.

I won't say I'm not scared. I am. But being afraid rouses me, in a way. It makes me interested in what's to come in the world. In my world. I haven't felt that for so long. Not during meetings with Gitanjali at the coffeehouse, eating greasy chicken cutlets and trying to figure out whether we really want each other (or whether I want her, to avoid presumption on my part). Not during endless classes and lectures, or writing and editing textbook drafts. Not during nights alone drinking whiskey and wondering what my parents, my family, are doing, my inflamed love for them in absentia only matched by my hatred at them for disowning me.

At the end of our walk, I also agree to go on the trip to the Sundarbans with him. I don't know if I actually will, but it seems the best thing to say for now. He doesn't react in any significant way, but he seems happy at my decision. He also hands me a thick envelope of thousand-rupee bills, as additional payment for the first transcription. He says we'll meet again, but once more doesn't say when or where. It has been six months since our first conversation at the baul mela, yet here we are, shaking hands and saying goodbye with the confidence of common acquaintances, at least. And he does shake my hand, I'm not making that up. As if we were business partners, and I'd just sold him something more substantial than my ability to type out handwritten documents. It is a strange and uncharacteristic gesture, but he is the one who initiates it. His grip is warm, very firm. My own limp academic's hand slides out of his, tingling with the shock of touch. We part at the red-brick façade of New Market: he vanishing into the pungent-aired warehouse at its center, filled with animals and carcasses, glistening, clucking, braying under bare bulbs; I wandering off to buy brownies at Nahoum's.

2

Several months pass us by with no mention of the trip to the Sundarbans that the stranger promised, so I assume he was lying about having booked it when he first told me about it. I don't mind. I might even be relieved, since I'm still not sure I'm going to go with him. We start meeting often. I hand over portions of the typed manuscript every time, over coffee or cool bottles of Kingfisher beer. When monsoon rolls around, it's whiskey doubles over fibrous beefsteak at Oly Pub. On the days it isn't raining, we pick apart cheap chili chicken under the violet night sky on the Lindsay Hotel's rooftop bar, surrounded by white tourists smoking cigarettes and gazing out at the lights of Kolkata (by now, the new law has kicked in, and this is one of the few bars where you can smoke at a table, because it's outdoors). He is utterly delighted, always, by the various ways humans prepare food and drink, and the various venues in which they partake of it.

We talk. I'd try to put down every conversation we have here, but they wouldn't all be interesting to a reader, which may be surprising, considering the unusual nature of our relationship. But many of these talks we have in the interim are actually genuinely uninteresting in a way that shocks me, and also gives me a lot of pleasure. At times, it feels like talking to an old friend—that's how normal it all is. He spends a lot of time asking me about my life, and I indulge him, to a sensible degree at first, and then with a complete lack of restraint. He's a far better listener than I would have expected of such a consummate storyteller. An excellent one, in fact, never interrupting, and always completely rapt in even my most boring recollections.

I tell him about my engagement to Shayani, a fellow history student

I met while doing my master's at Presidency College. About our long and blissful courtship in classrooms and hole-in-the-wall eateries, spooning soggy momos into each other's mouths in dim Tibetan restaurants. Sheer relief after long hours lulled by professorial droning. The quick kisses in the hallways between classes, the bliss of ending those eternal summer days by fucking beside the open windows of my little apartment in Jodhpur Park. I tell him about my quiet proposal in bed, taking the ring from the bedside drawer while the sun rose outside. Shayani's calm, clear-eyed delight, the ring a cold new hardness on her finger when her hand wandered down between my legs, spit on palm, and she kissed me till I came. I tell him about my parents' approval of Shayani being a pretty Bengali girl, and the various elaborate lunches and dinners and receptions over which our two families bonded and became one, using our romance as an excuse. About the collapse of all our plans and the cancellation of our impending betrothal—a tortuous, mutual decision to respect the beauty of our courtship and not have it be rotted away by the boredom we felt after our relationship became a performance for our families. About the rift between my family and me that followed—my rejection of their hysterical reaction to this breakup. The inverse of Romeo and Juliet: two families so eager to be one that the star-crossed lovers can't stand it anymore. He especially enjoys that last comparison, laughing as I tell him about my farcical tragedy.

I don't, however, tell him other, more complicated reasons that provoked the end of my engagement to Shayani, and exacerbated my parents' unhappiness with me.

I don't tell him about the men I slept with on occasion before Shayani, usually fellow students during my undergraduate days, sometimes strangers. I suppose this is because he is, at least going by appearances, a man, and I don't want to draw attention to the fact that we're meeting alone. Despite this concealment, I'm more candid with him than with anyone else in my life. It feels reckless and wonderful, as if pouring out the details of my past intimacies to him might make them new again. I wonder sometimes if he is as hypnotized by these stories of my unspectacular human life as I was by his tale telling at the baul mela. If this is what he craves—the memories of an unremarkable man.

Anyway, the point being we talk, like human beings. Like two nor-mal human beings, whether or not he is one.

He almost never talks about himself. When he does mention him-self, it is always an offhand remark taking us back in time. He might wave at the grumbling blue flickers of lightning on the horizon as we sit on the roof of Lindsay Hotel, telling me how they remind him of the flashes of musket fire from skirmishes between French and British co-lonials, back when they were still vying for domination of the area. How the chaos and confusion of battle made for exciting hunting. He might ruminate in the now cleaner-aired Oly Pub on the smoking ban in bars and restaurants, mentioning his forays into the dank opium dens of North Calcutta once the nineteenth century rolled around and the city was a thing that could no longer be avoided. I take these mor-sels, and the pages he gives me, grateful for them in the absence of whatever magic he worked on our first night together. He doesn't seem willing to demonstrate that again, and I don't push him.

It becomes clear over the passing months that he has a taste for nostalgia. I listen, always, captivated, letting him speak more and more. He never mentions the baul girl he might have rescued (kid-napped), or his exile from the alleged tribes. He never goes into too much detail about his present or past life, lives, or those of his fellow hunters of the swampland that became Kolkata, only giving fragments. I wait, not pushing, not commenting, letting him talk. I ask nothing of him. I doubt nothing to his face.

He seems to enjoy my company.

Part Five

The Second Scroll

The Second Scroll

(To Rakh'narokh)

In Mumtazabad I first saw him, that rapist, that coward monster, that filthy dog-man, that self-pitying deceiver, your father.[*]

His Pashto was flawless, and that wasn't even the start of it. I had never come across foreigners who seemed so utterly foreign before. Three white men (though one of them was brown enough to pass for one of Shah Jahan's subjects) walking through the caravanserai so casually, like wolves stalking through a den of tigers without a care in the world, was something to see. We had seen white men in the town before, more in Mumtazabad and Akbarabad than anywhere else I'd been in the empire, but certainly none of them had looked or walked like these three (who walked alone, instead of with the vast retinues that white folk usually had following them everywhere).

The courtyard of the caravanserai was cleaner than the streets outside—but there was still foot-stirred dust to clog the nostrils, and pats of camel shit simmering in the sun, and squirts of piss left on the walls by dogs and mischievous children with full bladders. And yet I could smell them from twenty feet away, your father and his companions, as they strolled in behind the camels of a merchant.

Your father was the one who lingered in the courtyard when his two fellows disappeared inside to bathe or rest. He was the one who came up to me, without a word, sniffing as if taking in the rank air he carried with him like an invisible cloak.

---

[*] The narrator in this scroll is Cyrah, who has appeared earlier in the translations as the survivor of Fenrir's sexual assault. She is a young Muslim woman, homeless and poor enough that she chooses a transient lifestyle. A woman of her means in the Mughal Empire would probably be illiterate. Perhaps this was orally transcribed at some point?

He was an ugly man: huge and covered in the crudest clothes I had ever seen, stitched from animal pelts, leather, and some kind of coarse cloth. Necklaces of trinkets and bones, some brown with age and others white and fresh as ivory, hung from him and sang a constant clicking song. Slung from his back were great fardels, swollen with weight and carrying who-knows-what, the kind you would expect hung from between the humps of a camel or on the back of a mule, not hanging off a man. The hair that covered his great head was knotted with dirt, braided into thick coils like dusty snakes—it might have once been the wheat gold of those men from the far northern reaches of Europe, but was now a copper brown. His face was monstrous, one eye blue, the other gray and speared by a thick scar that ran from socket to corner of lip, skin the ruddy leather of a white man gone too long under the sun.

He was like no man I'd ever seen, really. I couldn't tell where he was from, or what his calling was. I guessed that he was some northern tribal man from the mountains or that far Arctic land some wanderers call the Rus, or a traveler from one of the European settlements on either shore of Hindustan, now come to see the great tomb that was being built for Shah Jahan's dead wife.

When I began to cool in his shadow, and it became clear his eyes were not simply passing me by, I asked him what he wanted in Pashto, just to see if he would talk to me in some clumsy language from Europe. Not that I could have asked him in very many other languages, as I spoke only a few.

"As a foreigner, I want to talk to one who isn't foreign to this land," were the first words he said to me, answering my question. I remember them so clearly because the last thing I expected him to do was speak Pashto, let alone Pashto so clear the words poured from his mouth like springwater.

I admit, right then, I was enchanted. Not in love, or in lust. But I couldn't have turned away from him even if I had wanted do. So I let him talk to me, and gave him a lock of my hair for a few coins from Europe.

Trading words with him had a strange magic that I'd never felt before, because he gave no regard to custom. I spoke with him in ways I wouldn't dare in any moment outside of that one, as a commoner and an unwed woman, a woman with no family or harem to fall back on. It didn't matter who I was talking to, foreign or not, woman or man. I just wouldn't, the way I did with him.

I felt like a woman from another time, another world.

It was this that kept me from taking my leave of this smelly, ugly man, that led me to accept his strange and unclean request, even though I regretted that the moment I did it. Still, I was definitely grateful for his blasphemously unconventional company. I should have left Mumtazabad right then and there, ran and not come back, but then I wouldn't be writing this for you, and should I regret that? I don't know.

The white man dressed like a beast came to me that night in the caravanserai, and he raped me. Though he was far from pleasing to my eye, I would have fucked him if he'd asked and given me some money for the favor. That is how I often paid my way in life, after all, and I'm not ashamed to say it, though most asking for such favors do so in a most shameful manner, and mistake the favor for ownership. But this one didn't ask, instead getting between my legs by the most convoluted conversation I've ever had. He took what he wanted, with no regard for my opinion on the matter.

Anyway, if I can say one good thing about him, it is that he promised not to hurt me that night, and he didn't. Not in body, anyway. He was as gentle as a virgin boy, and as clumsy and unsure as one, too, though he loomed like a giant above me, and I nearly drowned in the stinking drizzle of his copious sweat. If you ever venture into the world of men, they will sometimes tell you that some women all but ask to be raped, that women complain to make the lives of the opposite sex hard, that it is all just a game to drive men crazy. I'm your mother, and I can swear to you on your life and mine that I found nothing but fear and regret on the night of your conception. As ever, I say this not to hurt you but to make of you something more than your father.

He talked a lot. I can't even remember most of the many things he said to me as he fucked me, but they were the ramblings of a madman. Or so I thought at the time. Brevity and clarity weren't his best talents. Though considering the circumstances, he could have been the best storyteller in the world and I'd still have hated every word. He told me about a Grecian king who was turned into a wolf a long time ago by some god or the other, and he told me about his tribe and how they don't think of themselves as humans, and how they have two selves and kidnap babies and are forbidden to bear children, and he even cried a bit. He did catch my attention when he said there were others like him who called themselves djinns, a word I grew up with, listening to folktales told to me by my mother. It felt awful to hear that familiar word, which reminded me so of happier times, in that situation, coming from the mouth of a man about to violate me.

Mostly, he made a big show of wanting to conceive a child, because his people couldn't create.

I thought he was a broken man, but I felt no pity whatsoever. If he'd told me such stories in the courtyard where we met, I'd have thought him curious—a giant child. But there in that cramped stall, demanding my body, he was a scared animal. A huge, strong, desperate animal. I'd have screamed or tried to fight harder, if I didn't think he was capable of snapping my neck like a twig before I could spend half the breath in my lungs.

He looked like he had nothing left to lose, and everything to gain by claiming me as his prize.

When he finished, he was wise enough not to lie by my side, instead getting off me and gathering his clothes. I could feel what he'd left of himself inside me, his seed like tallow down my thighs, hotter than that of any other man who'd ever been in my cunt. Though the taper was out, I saw the webbing of scars all across his naked back by the moonlight coming in through the curtains. I didn't get up, for fear of pushing him into some other action that I couldn't comprehend. I just lay still and waited for him to leave. He turned to me and for a moment I thought his eyes glowed green, the flicker of sunset on swamp water.

"You're upset. I am sorry," he said.

"Are you?"

"I truly am."

"Then why did you go ahead and fuck me?" I asked. My throat was trembling like a plucked string, much to my disgust. I cleared it, to steady my voice.

"I didn't expect that you would resist me so strongly," he said.

"You thought I'd be pleased, then. Do you know nothing of being human?" I asked.

"No. Not much. It's been so long since I was human. And though I have many human lives within me, they all fade like dreams, as does their meaning. That's why I did this. To create. To be human. I thought you'd *want* to help me."

He looked at me like the dumb brute he couldn't have been, not if he was able to talk to me with such ease in a language not his own. I shook my head.

"Do you want guilt from me now? Is that how this works in your tribe?" I said in a harsh whisper, just about remembering not to shout and wake the entire caravanserai.

"I have ways of glamouring humans into docility, methods that would have made you calmer prey, should I have wanted it. I didn't use them on you. Because I didn't want to think of you in the way I think of my normal prey. I never intended that."

I laughed, truly amazed then. "What tricks could a white man of Europe possibly have over Muslims and Hindus, I wonder, to make an unwanted fuck something to be desired? How lucky the women there must be, to have such a privilege. And to be thought of as prey."

I heard him take a big breath, his massive lungs sucking in a breeze that rattled in his throat like a terrible growl. "I'm not a man. Not as such, though it is one aspect of me. You don't seem to understand this. But how can I expect you to, without showing you? Regardless, I didn't mean to hurt you. That isn't why I came here tonight."

"I've been raped before." His head jerked up at the mention of rape, as if in surprise. Perhaps he was about to say something, but I didn't let him. "It's a risk I've long been familiar with, being a woman with no family, in a land ruled by men. Not everyone cares to pay for what they want. I managed to hurt two who tried to force themselves on me, and quickly left their company while they suffered. One I submitted to because he was much stronger than me and better armed. Three men, all different from one another. None of those worthless swine pretended to be sorry about what they were doing."

"I'm not pretending, Cyrah."

"Don't use my name."

"As you wish. I thought wrong when I came here, I admit. I've often been wrong about humans. But if it makes you feel any better, you've done nothing tonight to lessen my respect for your kind."

"That is cause for celebration."

Perhaps he had the capacity to detect the irony in my voice, perhaps he didn't. But once again, he gave no evidence of either.

"What's your name? Or are you so cowardly that you won't let me have even that?"

"You. You can call me Fenrir."

"Well, you should know something, Fen-eer," I said, struggling to form this strange name between my lips. "Planting your seed and making new young doesn't make you any more human than a stray dog fucking a mangy bitch at the feet of the bazaar-goers."

He didn't flinch, not that I could see, but then it was dark. I was afraid he might break his promise and hurt me, but I went on.

"It's not just your raiment that lends you the disposition of a beast. It's what you are."

He actually laughed a little at that, or I thought he did. It sounded like the chuffling snort a caravan tiger gives to his trainer through the bars of his cage, to show affection. Despite the strangely friendly sound of it, for a moment I was afraid I'd gone too far, that I'd pushed him beyond his apparent shame and into some cruel amusement at me. That swaggering confidence he had shown that afternoon in the courtyard seemed to come back, just from that one exhalation. But then he just kept putting on his clothes and necklaces, and only said, "You don't know how right you are."

"I really think I do. Go now, unless you would break your promise."

Fully dressed in his fur raiment again, he stared at me. He stood with his back to the moonlight coming in from the parting in the curtains, as he'd done when he first came in. I imagine he considered at that moment whether he should break his promise. I imagine I was very close to death. I don't remember whether I realized this. But when he looked at me then I was once again as terrified as I'd been when he first parted the curtains.

"Listen," he said, his voice low. "Think of a child sleeping in your lap a year from now, warm and real—a living, breathing creature born out of your body." Though I was completely awake because of the fear coursing through me, as Fenrir said these words the stall around me seemed to dim and fade away, and my limbs felt heavy.

"You've not seen, as I have, a thousand upon thousand mothers holding their young to them by firelight as the howling nights closed in. It is that incandescent light kindled in the womb, this love between human mother and human child, that so often kept the darkness away from them, burning brighter than any flame. It kept the beast at bay. It kept—me, from them, from my prey, over and over again, when I hunted alone."

Fenrir's eyes glowed like windows in the dark of some foreign landscape, where the winds of winters past blew cold against my skin. Against my will, I was pulled closer to those flickering windows until I saw within them clear by firelight those myriad mothers, holding their children close as the wind shuddered against their shelters. I realized I was seeing them as Fenrir had seen them, lurking hidden like the predator he was. Like dancing shadows they changed in the light, so that I saw many different mothers with their children. Women and children from places I'd never been to, dressed in clothes I'd never seen before. Some with pale skin, some dark. Some alone, some with families, men, other women, around them. Some terrified, some fierce; some holding weapons, some armed with nothing but fortitude; some huddled around campfires, others in tents, in huts, in houses.

"When you hold a child to you a year from now, and it is your offspring, perhaps you will forgive me," came Fenrir's voice from somewhere far away.

I don't know when this vision ended and turned to a deep sleep, in which I dreamed of my own mother and wept in her arms. When I woke up, I was drenched in sweat, and Fenrir was gone. His vision, though, lingered stronger than any dream I'd ever had, a memory left fresh as if I'd truly walked across the centuries and seen those distant mothers and their sons and daughters.

His smell, too, lingered long, both in my bedroll and on my skin, bringing me back to the unclean truth of where I was and what had happened to me.

It was only once Fenrir was gone that I wanted him back. It wasn't because your mother was some weak-willed fool with a secret need to wed a rapist. No. It was because of the vision he'd left me. I was never one given easily to superstition, but how could I ignore such a thing? Not only had he violated me in flesh, he'd violated my mind like some infernal djinn out of the stories. He'd even mentioned that some of his kind called themselves djinns, after all. Suddenly his wild tales seemed a little more possible, if not true.

It was only in that dead, moonlit silence that I emerged from shock of all this strangeness and began to truly think of the consequences of Fenrir's actions. I checked my entire body for wounds, to make sure he'd kept his promise that he wouldn't hurt me. He'd kept the other promise he'd made me as well, and left a leather purse full of coins by my bedroll. It was little relief to me then.

As I'd planned when I realized that there was no escaping sex with him, I took one of the browning lemons that I always carry in my belongings (I had just two left), and sliced it in half with my bloodstained knife. I licked it, to wake me from the dullness of anger and confusion. Usually, I'd use half the hollowed skin to block my womb if the man let me (and if he was drunk or fool enough, even if he didn't), and at other times I used various ointments or tinctures that my mother taught me to make, depending on ingredients I could find. Fenrir, of course, wouldn't have allowed any of that, because he fancied himself a creator of children. This time it was too late.

I squeezed the stinging juice between my legs all the same, and rubbed his come off my hair and thighs with it and some water. While I sat there smelling of lemon with my cunt feeling like sweet-scented fire, one thought ran through my head again and again: This sad devil Fenrir might have made me a mother, and if there is one thing a woman cannot be in this empire all by herself, it is that. I wanted no child, let alone one forced into my womb by a mad white soothsayer I didn't know or love in any way. Fenrir's strange beliefs, the unavoidable proof of sorcery that he'd left me with, made me dread the possibility of a child given to me by him even more than any other man who'd ever fucked me.

Without thinking I ran after him into the night, wrapped in my shawl, bare feet throbbing on the cold tamped ground of the caravan-serai courtyard. I would have shouted his strange name if not for the risk of waking the whole town, silent then in sleep. I ran as far as the chauk outside the gate, but there was no one around. I parted my shawl and flapped it, pushed heavy breaths from my throat into the air, as if my scent might bring him back like a dog. But he was gone.

I don't know what I expected of him. But if he had the power to put such visions in my head, to weave a prophet's poetry from so base a thing as rape, perhaps he had the power to erase that prophecy as well.

My eyes were wide open when the first rays of morning drenched the curtains like a sop rag. I might have dozed while sitting on my bed, blade in hand, but I got no real sleep. I was up all night waiting, hoping Fenrir would return, and also dreading that he would. My head hurt, and my ass and back ached like a hag's from sitting in one place for so long. My entire body was stiff. I heard the sounds of the new day spreading through Katra Jogidas, the sellers taking their places in their stalls and shouting at their sleep-muzzled errand boys, the camels beginning their snorting and groaning, the guests of the caravanserai parting their curtains to join in the rough chorus of coughing and blowing to clear their throats and noses of the winter night's mucus. As I heard these things, it was as if I came awake, despite having had no sleep. I couldn't stay inside forever, waiting for Fenrir to return and right this wrong he had done to me. That was like waiting in bed to see if a dream you just had might replace what was real around you.

If he still lingered in Mumtazabad, as unlikely as that was, I couldn't spot him by sitting in bed all day. I looked at the dull blade of my knife, a farmer's blade that I'd never before used for violence. The edge was darkened with a thin sliver of Fenrir's dried blood. There were also dark crimson spots on my dupatta and choli. I decided I would wash neither. I don't know quite what compelled me to keep these souvenirs of that night. Perhaps it was something to do with his odd way of preparing for what he was going to do by asking me for my hair. I felt a symmetry in doing the same, cutting a portion, however minuscule, of him out of his body and keeping it. Somehow I felt that keeping a part of him, aside from what he'd left inside me, might yet give me some power over him.

Eyelids throbbing from lack of sleep, body shaking from the cold of dawn and the shock of the last night, I got up to get dressed.

The first thing I did was visit one of the merchants and exchange the European coins Fenrir gave me for rupiyas I could use, so that I didn't have to take any suitors for a while. I could find some work in the bazaars or helping at the construction sites if I ran out of coins, being able-bodied and young. But Fenrir had been generous in that, at least, and there would be no need, not for a while at least. The merchant looked at me with suspicion, surprised at the value of the coins, especially since I was an uncovered woman and thus marked as poor. But what could he say? Nothing. He was just glad to get his hands on them. I probably let him rip me off. My heart wasn't in the haggling.

This done, I began my search, wandering every caravanserai and bazaar in Mumtazabad till my feet ached. I felt no joy at my sudden wealth, since I was still the same woman in the same world, where no amount of money could make me a noblewoman safely ensconced in a palanquin. I didn't even have an appetite to waste coins on food. Fenrir and his companions were nowhere to be seen. I returned to Katra Jogidas at sunset, tired and upset, and finally gave in to sleep.

I spent the next day wandering the chauks and bazaars of Mumtaz-abad in a trance like a witless beggar-girl. I didn't need money, so I took no suitors, didn't look for any other work. I slept little, though I spent many hours every morning in bed trying to will away this new life I didn't want. I was on the verge of deciding if it was time to move on, to leave Mumtazabad for the great cities of Akbarabad or Shahja-hanabad and see if I could just start anew there while I still had Fenrir's money. I've never stayed anywhere for very long, after all, and I've rarely had more reason to keep moving, lest my mind stagnate in ill-fated Mumtazabad like a muck pond that breeds disease. I wanted no diseases of the mind, and it felt like I was well on the way to festering a few into existence in my aching, sleep-addled skull.

Then, on the third morning following the night Fenrir came to me, I saw him. I happened upon him wandering the scented bazaars of Katra Fulel.* Well, I thought it was him, at least, at first glance, because of a flash of fur and bone trinkets. But it wasn't Fenrir, but one of his companions—the palest one. The youngest one, whose skin color was most suited to the description of a white man. His clothes were very similar (and similarly ugly and crude) to those of Fenrir and the other one, except that he had a longer and finer cloak that hid most of his animalistic accoutrements. Fenrir had swaggered about showing them proudly. This one wasn't ashamed, exactly, but a little wary of flashing his bone necklaces and fur raiment. He also looked quite a bit younger than Fenrir. When I spotted him he was strolling leisurely past the stalls, his face empty of feeling—looking dazed and rather alone without the other two by his side. The sick, flowered air of the bazaar seemed to suit him, his nostrils flaring but face calm.

Obviously, I was surprised to see him. But I was far more surprised, and frightened, when his eyes met mine, and he started striding toward me through the crowd. I wondered whether to run—I admit I felt a strong urge to do so, but they tell you never to flee from a wild dog unless you want to enrage or excite it even further. Thinking him not unlike Fenrir, I stood still and waited for him, telling myself that he could do no harm to me in the middle of a bazaar, that he would be beaten by the men on the street if he tried anything.

He stopped a foot from me, staring as if unsure of what he was seeing. A frown knotted his otherwise smooth and boyish face as he looked me up and down, making gooseflesh prickle against my clothes.

"You . . ."

Though I suppose I should have expected it, it surprised me again that he, too, spoke Pashto.

---

* The Perfume Market.

"Yes?" I asked, heart pounding. I wanted to speak, but he seemed to be about to say something.

"You smell familiar," he said. His accent was very different from Fenrir's, like that of a lisping but deep-voiced child who has just learned to speak.

"I don't know why you would say that," I told him, trying to sound forceful, and feeling at least a hint of an advantage because of my more lucid speech. "But do you know Fen-eer?"

His eyes widened. "Fenrir? Who told you that name?" he said, his voice dropping lower till it sounded near inhuman. I felt his hand grasp my arm and I whipped it out of his reach, stepping back.

"Don't!" I whispered. "Don't you dare touch me, if you value your own life. Don't you realize where we are?"

He didn't seem to care where we were, but lucky for him no one seemed to have seen him grab me, or didn't care enough yet, considering his somewhat imposing looks (despite the face of a boy just growing into a man). But he didn't try to touch me again, instead nodding to himself.

"I knew it. I was right. It is you. His beloved bitch."

"Beloved? Who the fuck do you think you're calling a bitch?"

He gave me a wide grin, a little startled. He licked his teeth.

"Force of habit. Fenrir's not his name, but I know who you're talking about, little girl."

"You came in with him, to the caravanserai. In Katra Jogidas."

"Yes. He was talking to you. I didn't quite remember what you looked like. But your smell, yes. It stands out even here. It was on Fenrir, almost, became part of his scent. I couldn't understand it at first, fool that I am."

I ignored these comments, though they only sharpened the urge to move away from him, as far as I could, to never see any of these three men from what ungodly parts of Europe I don't know, these three men who had suddenly come into my life and broken it. I cleared my throat.

"What's his name, if not Fen-eer?"

"I don't know. He never told us."

"In your journeys he never told you his name?"

"He told us a name. He doesn't know my name, either. He just knows a name. Trust him to tell you his name's Fenrir. Fancies himself a god. At least I think that was a god. From one of his stories about his old land. Nostalgic till the end, with his moping."

"You don't seem to like him very much, for one who's traveled so far with him."

His entire body flinched for a second and I thought he was about to hit me, but his arms didn't move from his sides. I stepped back, keeping my eyes on his now livid face. To my shock, there seemed tears about to spill from his eyes.

"What insight is this, coming from a human whore who fucked him once?"

"I didn't. I didn't do that," I said in a broken voice, cursing myself for sounding so like the little girl he repeatedly called me.

"That's not what he said. Are you calling him a liar, little whore?" I felt the spray of his spit on my face as he said *whore,* and I clenched my jaw in revulsion, going against all my instincts and not walking very fast in the opposite direction. I knew that would be the best way to weaken myself in front of this man.

"He's many things, that cowardly cunt, but he's not a liar. Not to me, anyway," he said with a petulance that startled me, though he seemed less angry now that I'd stood my ground. I let myself speak as he panted.

"I didn't *choose* to lie with him. That's what I meant. And please lower your voice, unless you want to be at the sorry end of a mob."

"I could rip any of these people apart one at a time or all together, if it came to that, so don't worry about me," he said, his eyes still watery, but his mouth smiling. I felt goose bumps crawl under my clothes. "Tell me something, little bitch. Why do you still stand here listening to me? You don't like me very much, I can tell."

"I'm looking for your friend, whatever his name is. That is the only reason I'm standing here. You're no more pleasant than he was, if a little more honest about how base you are. Whatever tribe you both belong to, it is a shameful one."

"I don't know what he told you, but we don't come from the same tribe."

"He didn't tell me anything that made sense."

"That sounds like him, to be sure. Shall we go somewhere we can talk properly? Where do you take the men?"

"I'm not going anywhere. Do you think me such a fool, even after what your friend did?"

He laughed at this, shaking his head. "Just because Fenrir had a hard-on for you doesn't mean everyone else does, too. Trust me. I have no desire to fuck you or any other human. The very thought sickens me."

I stifled a sudden rage that blossomed in me, making me blush. I knew that he probably took that to be shame. But it was anger at this notion, that I thought myself desirable to all and sundry because his friend deigned to rape me. I felt like whipping out my blade and stabbing him, but I didn't. Doing so would probably end with me executed for a mad whore. Or disarmed and gutted by this boyish-looking but undoubtedly dangerous white man.

"Well, little boy," I said through my teeth, giving myself no time to regret my sharper tone, since I was already quite scared. "Your older friend has shown me that trust isn't something I should be handing out to savage-looking white men, so forgive me for not taking your word that you don't take after his habits. There's no need to go anywhere. Just tell me where he is and we can part ways."

I saw his jaw jump. Again, he began panting, soft and quick. It was such a wrong thing, to see a man do that standing in one place, without physical exertion to tire him to heavy breathing. I could feel my palms sweating, eager for the handle of my blade. He opened his mouth, spoke in a language I couldn't understand, paused, and then spoke again in Pashto, so low that I almost couldn't hear him.

"Why do you seek Fenrir? Do you love him?"

"No," I snapped, not only because I certainly didn't feel anything approaching even the nether regions of love or like for Fenrir, but also because, for whatever reason, it was clearly the safest thing for me to let this man know this.

The panting ceased. He looked relieved. I, too, was relieved.

"He's not a coward, you know. I didn't mean to say that," he said, taking a deep breath and shaking his head. *Next you're going to say he's not a cunt, either,* I felt like saying, but I didn't push my luck. "He is afraid of many, many things, little one. But he is not a coward."

"You make as little sense as he does. Perhaps it's your dead men's Pashto that makes you all sound like madmen to me."

He narrowed his eyes. "He told you a few things, did he?"

"As I said, nothing that made any sense to me." I decided not to tell him about the vision Fenrir had given me.

"Fenrir isn't mad, as you seem to think he is. He may have some madness in him, as may we all. But the things he told you can be explained. And I can track him, so you may talk to him about whatever it is."

"So you can help me find your friend. What do *you* want from me, if not what Fenrir wanted."

He squinted. "Fenrir has left Mumtazabad. We didn't part on the best of terms. I shouldn't have let him leave. I have my own reasons, and I'm going after him. You can either come with me or not. I don't want anything in return."

"You expect me to believe that you're doing me a kindness?"

"I expect nothing. To be honest, I didn't even expect to find you. I wasn't looking for you. But I can help you find Fenrir. I find his interest in you, well, interesting. It is not the way of our tribes to mingle with your kind. I'm curious. I want to *see* him answer to you, in whatever way he may."

"My kind. You're not Christians. But your tribes don't mingle with Muslims?"

"Never mind that. I'm going to set out to look for him tomorrow morning."

"Is that it? Because I'm done talking to you for today." I took a step backward, as if to show him, like a wild dog, that I had no wish to engage with him further.

He peered at me from under a frown and spit copiously at my feet. Then, suddenly, he crossed himself. "I'm sorry if I have frightened you on this day."

I had to stop myself from laughing in surprise at this shocking change, and the odd gesture. "You haven't," I lied, despite the fact that he looked, in that moment, so very young and soft, so confused, with his long hair and large, moist eyes.

"You've got spunk, for a little human girl. I can see that's why Fenrir chose you. If you want to settle whatever debts or matters you have with Fenrir, then be at the Northern Gate tomorrow. If you're not there by the time dawn becomes morning, I leave. You'll never see me again, nor Fenrir. You have the night to make your choice. Does that sound fair?"

I nodded. He sniffed, returned my nod, and turned away with a swirl of his cloak, raising a cloud of dust that made my nostrils itch. Even through the perfumes of the bazaar, his smell clung to the wake of dust, and I felt a clammy sweat form under my headscarf as I remembered Fenrir's stench.

Now, I know you'll judge me for actually going to the Northern Gate at dawn the next day, my possessions gathered and my will strong. It seems the most stupid and reckless thing I could have chosen to do. And it was. But you have to understand, the possibility that Fenrir's child was growing inside me horrified me more than the possibility of being attacked by his fellow devil from Europe. I had my knife, and I decided when I set out into the crisp cold of this new day that if this one tried what Fenrir had, I'd rather die defending myself than give myself to his whims. If my last breaths were taken while cutting a rapist open, I might just allow myself to slip into death content. I know that times have changed since, that this might seem rather extreme, that people might value their lives a little more now than they did back then.

To be clear, it's not that I wanted to die. I didn't, especially not violently at the hands of a mad white prophet, and that not even a Christian one (I don't know if I ever had a conception of white men who weren't Christians before I met Fenrir). At least that would have made some sense, what with the stories of the Crusades and all that. No. I didn't want to die, but I was *prepared* to. I had no one to look to or leave behind—no family left, and no friends or companions. I was used to living day-to-day, surviving by myself and myself only. I'd done so for years. I simply decided, that morning, that if I found myself with no more days to have to survive by myself, it wouldn't be the worst thing that could happen to me. It would be quite terrible, but not the worst.

Was I scared? Of course I was. But I was ready to see this through to its end, though I had no idea what that end was. I was compelled by Fenrir's prophecy. Compelled not to accept it, but to chase him to the ends of the earth, and demand that he use whatever ungodly power he had to take back this new destiny he'd written into my body and mind, to erase it from me like ink from parchment. If he was truly anything like a djinn—like the ones the Fisherman and Al' ad-Din met and bargained with—there was a chance he could take back the woe he'd given me. And if he couldn't—then I didn't know. I could always demand more money from his endless fardels. Or his life, even if it meant ending my own.

Most important, I would face him prepared this time.

So it came, the time to leave Mumtazabad, with the companion of my rapist.

"So I know you and your lot don't seem to give much worth to names, but if we're to travel with each other I need to call you something."

"Hm. Gévaudan. Call me that."

"Jevah-dan?"

"As you wish. And what's your name?"

"Cyrah."

I tightened my scarf and shawl around me against the morning chill, wishing I had Gévaudan's furs and cloak instead. He was not in a talkative mood, and we had left Mumtazabad in near silence. I'm sure I saw something like relief cross his face when he saw me at the gate, though. It made me uneasy to see that—he *did* care whether or not I accompanied him, and I didn't know why.

"So how does this work, Jevah-dan? I'm not just going to follow you blindly, you know. Where are we going? How do you intend to find Fen-eer?"

"I told you, I'm good at tracking. We all are. So I'm going to the place where I last saw him, and I'm going to pick up his scent from there. Depending on how careful he's been, it might work. It hasn't rained, and the weather's been cool, so his spoor should linger."

I remembered how Fenrir had taken my hair and come back at night.

"Wait. Would a bit of his blood help? I spilled some, on my dupatta." I decided not to tell him about the stained knife.

"You spilled Fenrir's blood?"

"Yes."

"That's pathetic. Pathetic." He thought about this for a while, grimacing all the while. Then, becoming aware that I was watching him, he nodded.

"Yes, that would help. Give it to me."

"Right now?"

"Yes."

I hesitated, then turned away from him to loosen the bundle I had slung on my shoulder, and pulled out the dupatta. I didn't want to just hand him a piece of my clothing, since I was wearing the only other dupatta I had to live with, so I bent over and cut a bloodstained portion of the cloth out with my blade. I heard him pacing about, but he didn't ask what I was doing. It left a ragged hole in the dupatta, and that hurt a bit. But I could mend it later.

I put the blade away and turned back to Gévaudan, holding out the stained piece of fabric. He glowered at me and took it.

"Are you angry that I cut him because he's your friend?"

"No," he grunted, looking at the dark-brown spots on the rag. Then he held it up to his face as if he were blowing his nose into it, and began taking deep breaths with his eyes closed. I looked away quickly, feeling as if I'd happened upon something private and vulgar. He did this for an entire minute or so before shoving the rag somewhere under his cloak.

"Let's go," he said, and strode forward.

We passed through the gardens that Shah Jahan had planted around the banks of the Yamuna to delight the eyes of visitors to his wondrous wife's tomb. I was only just able to keep up with Gévaudan as he wove in and out of the morning mist, which the numerous fruit and cypress trees had gathered under their eaves like a damp bounty. I trampled many a rose and daffodil on the way, which I admit gave me some pleasure despite my trepidation (as a child I used to love running through flowers, snapping crisp green stems and kicking petals into the air). I was also very nervous we would get caught, as I didn't know if we were even allowed in the gardens. I had never been in them before. It was an impressive sight to pass through, though Mumtaz Mahal's incomplete tomb wasn't visible because of the mist. I've heard that these emperors' charbaghs* are meant to give us an idea of what Paradise looks like, and though this one wasn't finished it already looked like it could be a nice enough place to spend a while in, if not an eternity.

I could hear the faraway calls of the workmen from beyond the trees, and each time I did, I would duck low, wondering if we'd be caught as trespassers. Once or twice I fell straight into the great mounds of cold earth dug up between the trees (for more trees and flower beds, I assume). To my surprise, Gévaudan came running back whenever this happened to help me up with such strength and speed that I barely had enough time to shrug him off and tell him I needed no help.

By the time the sun was two fingers above the mist-smudged horizon (we had left Mumtazabad before it emerged) and burning bright enough to call the day a day, the tomb was visible beyond the foliage, looking half there in the wet and sunlit air. Indeed, it was only half there, its ivory-white façades and minarets gaping and toothless, yet to be finished. The scaffolding was already crawling with workers.

As I followed Gévaudan, I thought we were heading straight for the tomb. But we were heading northeast, as I realized when the ghostly vision of the mausoleum in the distance began orienting itself to our left. By the time we reached the banks of the Yamuna I was feeling warm under my shawl. The sun had crawled up another inch and set the mist aflame across the dark line of the earth, so that it looked like there was a fire blazing all across the distant horizon. The tomb was a mile or two down the riverbank we stood on. Across the river I could see nothing but muddy flatlands and forested wilderness.

"We have to cross the river," Gévaudan said.

"We can keep going to the next bridge."

"It'll take too long. We're crossing here. The campsite where I was last with Fenrir is a straight line from here, beyond the other bank."

"We can't just cross here. I can't. It's too cold, and deep!"

"I'll carry you on my back. Sit on my shoulders, and I'll swim us across."

* Persian garden divided into four parts.

"That's ridiculous. You can't swim with me on your shoulders. The Yamuna isn't some shallow stream. We'll sink like stones."

"You needn't tell me what I can or can't do, little girl."

"Cyrah. I'm not a little girl."

"Just get on my back, Cyrah. There are lands north of here where it's so cold that this river would be frozen to white ice, and we could just walk over it. So stop your whining. This is weak winter. If I begin to sink you can jump off and swim back to shore. It won't kill you. And I won't sink."

He squatted and patted his shoulders, gazing at me dolefully. Tired already, I decided I couldn't be bothered to argue. There were far worse dangers possible in this journey than taking a dip in the Yamuna.

Grimacing, I sat on his back as if he were a camel, legs on either side of his neck. I flinched when he put his hands around my ankles to steady me as he got up. But they didn't move up any farther. If he was at all bothered by me sitting on his back, he didn't show it. His gait didn't even change, as if my weight made no impression on him. I wasn't the heaviest woman, certainly, but I felt like I was made of nothing but straw and air, sitting on his shoulders.

He waded straight into the Yamuna without hesitating. I gasped as my feet dipped into the water. Gévaudan made no sound, cutting across the water with the ease of a crocodile. There was a gut-lurching moment when his entire body dipped and the water lapped up to my knees, and I swore to say that I'd been right to worry, but it was just the point at which his feet left the riverbed and he began to swim. Though my legs got soaked, he stayed true to his promise and didn't sink us both, somehow managing to swim while still balancing me on his shoulders. I held my breath for no real reason as he carried me over, the world gone quiet as I swayed on this man, his wet hair tickling my thighs. My feet had gone cold and numb in the water even though its ripples glowed in the sunrise as if the Yamuna were a river of liquid fire, like those that run from broken mountains in far-off lands. I don't know how long the crossing took. It felt like hours that I sat on Gévaudan's back, listening to the huff of his breath, my thighs aching to prevent myself from falling off, watching the wheeling patterns of ducks skimming the river before flying off into the haze.

By the time we reached the shore, I was rigid with pain from trying to keep from falling off Gévaudan. But I felt more tranquil during that crossing than I had for all the days since I met Fenrir.

"My feet are numb. How can you not be cold?" I muttered, not really asking him, as we walked away from the river, our feet sinking into the cool mud. He didn't look the least bit bothered despite being soaked. He walked around dripping in the morning chill, his hair clinging to his face and his cloak and furs stinking like the coat of a wet dog.

He turned and bent down in front of me. I stepped back, but he took his cloak in his hands and wiped my ankles with it. The cloak itself was wet, so it did nothing but smear cold water over my skin, but he pried my left foot off the ground and cradled it in his cloak-clad hand as if it were a brittle toy, and wiped it down, and then did the same for my right foot. The coarse cloak left a cool and not unpleasant itching across the soles of my feet. As he let the cloak fall from his hands, I noticed how white and delicate his hands looked, how small compared with his height and bulk. He had long nails, which had blushed a dark purple against his pale cuticles because of the swim. His plump, tapering fingers and smooth knuckles were unlike Fenrir's hands, which had been massive and thick, rough like sandpaper against my skin when he had touched me. Abruptly, Gévaudan got up and squelched ahead, breaking me out of my daze. I would have thanked him for his unsettling, gentle gesture, were he anybody else.

It was a ten-minute walk from the river's edge to the campsite. It didn't look like a campsite. There were no traces of fire, or anything, really, to indicate that anyone had camped there. I wondered if Gévaudan was mistaken.

"Are you sure this is it?"

"Yes," he said with a grunt as he squatted. He got on all fours and peered at the wet ground. To be honest, there were other things on my mind at this point.

"Who are you?" I asked him.

He looked up at me with vague curiosity. "Have you forgotten my name already? I know it's hard for you to say, but you'll have to make some effort here."

"You know what I mean, Jevah-dan. No man can swim across the Yamuna in the dead of winter with another perched on his back, no matter how strong he is."

He spit on the ground and shrugged. "I'm not a man." He said this as if it were the most obvious thing in the world.

"Fenrir would talk like this also. You both keep talking like you're not human. What are you then? What are these tribes you come from?"

"That's a long story, for later."

"Who are you people? Does your madness give you strength? Are you some kind of white faqirs?"*

Gévaudan fished the bloodstained piece of my dupatta out from under his cloak and began smelling it again. I shivered before I could stop myself. He looked like a white man I'd once seen in a caravanserai, snorting a rag soaked in opiates as if it were the only thing keeping him alive.

Then he started digging. He used his hands, which looked even whiter with dark soil on them, the bone-white hands of a ghost. His long fingernails became black as he shoved clods out of the ground and tossed them aside, his face fixed in a frown. I watched mesmerized, wondering what purpose this ritual would serve now, surprised as I was at every turn by him.

He pulled a man's head from the hole he'd made in the ground. Sheathed as it was in a skin of watered mud, I thought it was a rock at first, until I saw the smaller white pebbles of its teeth glittering in the rising sun. They sat in the bubbling hole of the mouth, breathing out the gases that dead flesh produces.

I don't remember if I screamed or gasped, but I do remember that I kept my wits about me. I observed Gévaudan's face, managing to surmise that he wasn't digging up this gruesome trophy to scare me, or to serve as a prelude to violence. In fact, he barely seemed aware of me, wiping the sopping earth from the stiff features of the dead face that stared up at him.

---

* A Muslim Sufi ascetic who has taken a vow of poverty. Faqirs, often incorrectly stereotyped as Hindu ascetics (a popular image of the faqir, or fakir, being that of a turbaned man sitting on a bed of nails), were believed to have developed miraculous abilities and powers from renouncing the material world.

Gévaudan laughed, and then suddenly turned serious again.

"The sentimental bastard. He buried Makedon," he grumbled.

"What. What are you doing?" I stammered. "What is that?" I asked in a weak voice, despite myself. I felt nauseous, though I had eaten only some dry fruit to break my fast since I had woken up.

"Cyrah, meet Makedon. A mutual friend of mine and Fenrir's." He turned the head a bit so it faced me.

It was the third traveler who had walked in the caravanserai along with Fenrir and Gévaudan. I recognized the curly black hair, though it was mired in dirt and clotted blood.

"Why? Why is his head there?"

"I killed him. And Fenrir, idiot that he is, wasted time burying him."

I felt the sour cud of eaten fruit rise up my throat and spatter on to the ground, frothing in the ground by my feet. Retching, I staggered a few steps backward.

"Calm down. He deserved it. And he was about to kill your Fenrir."

Even light-headed with nausea I reacted to that, spitting the bile from my mouth so I could speak. "He's not *my* Fen—whatever his bastard name is! He's your friend, and he's fucked things up for me and run off, all right? Which is the only reason I'm following you around while you dig up heads and Allah knows what else. He's not my anything, your wretch of a friend."

Gévaudan gazed at me, steady-eyed, head in his hands. "Right. Well. Anyway."

"Anyway," I confirmed, wiping my mouth.

"We had a fight," he said, looking at the head like he was talking to Makedon and not me. "That's why we all split up. Well, Fenrir and I. Not this one, obviously. Things got ugly. Makedon was about to kill Fenrir, so I had to cut his throat."

"What were you all fighting about?"

Gévaudan smiled, running his thumbs across Makedon's blackened lips. "You."

"What do you mean, me?"

"Well, I wasn't involved, not directly. But Makedon had a problem with Fenrir going out and doing what he did, with you."

I swallowed another wave of sickness, feeling faint.

"Makedon wasn't a moral creature. He wasn't worried about you, if that's what you're thinking. It's just that Fenrir, what he did, it's forbidden. Like if you fucked a pig. Makedon wanted him to atone by giving his life."

"You're mad, you people. Allah forgive me for talking to your friend, and to you. Allah forgive me for not turning away when I could."

"When all's said and done, I'm sure your god will forgive you, if he's the sensitive sort. Not your fault, is it? You're just lambs, you people. What Fenrir did to you was wrong. He preyed on you, hunted you, but he left you alive. It's unnatural."

"It's you and he that are unnatural. And you know nothing about my god. You are a godless people, I can tell."

"Oh, I wouldn't say that. Many of our tribes worship the same gods you humans do, or at least recognize them as gods; some don't do either; some even claim to be your precious gods, and others your devils. Many among your kind think we *are* such, believe it or not. But honestly, we've no need for gods or devils ourselves. That's what I think."

I sat down, not caring if I soiled my shawl on the earth. Pushing my hands against my face, I shook my head.

"I don't think your own god much favors women whoring themselves to men out of wedlock, no? I'm pretty sure it's all there in his holy book. So I wouldn't take too much of a stand against my godlessness if I were you, lest hypocrisy also be considered a sin under your religion." He laughed softly.

I gritted my teeth and closed my eyes. I could say nothing, and didn't want to admit that I'd never read the Quran. My mother had told me about it, and recited from it, but I knew little of what was actually in it. I tried not to think about it, telling myself Allah would forgive the way I had to make my living because I'd had so little choice since I was born.

I wiped my eyes, not wanting to start that debate in my head again. "Fen-eer told me what you said, that it was forbidden among your tribes. To lie with a human. I thought he was just talking nonsense," I said.

"Not nonsense. It was foolish of him to do what he did to you. He can be most cruel. Though he scarcely knows it."

"Foolish," I repeated, and laughed. "And are you not cruel, Jevahdan? What are you doing, holding your so-called friend's head in your hands? Bury it and let him be. Has he not been punished enough by being killed? Let him be, for God's sake, and let us leave his resting place."

"You want to keep going?"

"Yes, I want to keep going. What did you think? The petty fights of your people are of no concern to me. I don't want to know about your friend Makedon and how you two killed him, or what you fought about. I want to leave this desecrated grave and find Fen-eer like you told me you would. I have words for him, and I will say them no matter what. He can't run from me."

Gévaudan smiled and dropped Makedon's head in its hole. It landed with a horrible slap. "Spoken like one of us," he said. I don't know if he meant for me to hear that. He probably did. Why else would he say it in my language?

Night fell quickly, a cloak draped across Shah Jahan's lands. The day had passed like an eternity, with me not talking to my fellow traveler, though he felt like no fellow of mine at all. I kept remembering Fenrir telling me he was a foreigner in all the lands he traveled in because he didn't know where he had been born. I didn't believe him when he had said that, and I still don't believe it, but it made a stupid kind of sense. I'd never met anyone who felt as foreign to me as Fenrir and Gévaudan, even though they spoke my language as well as I did. There were a thousand questions brimming at my lips, but I kept them sealed as we traveled along the tangled wilderness that clings to the edges of the Yamuna, using the river as a path. I wondered if Gévaudan was staying close to the shore for my benefit, or whether he was following Fenrir's trail. He always kept his friend's blood close, tying the rag around his right hand and occasionally raising it to his mouth. I couldn't see properly, but he might even have licked it, for all I knew.

On the other side of the river, I could still see a few lights from Mumtazabad in the distance. I felt no fear to be out there in the dark and the wild with this unknowable man. I only felt a deep, sickening excitement, which distracted me from my fatigue and hunger (I had finished all the dried fruit and nuts I had carried with me).

Finally, Gévaudan decided to stop and camp for the night, probably realizing that I was tiring. It was too dark to tell anything from his face, not that I could fathom much from it anyway.

"Has Fenrir been traveling this way? Are you following him?"

He nodded, shrouded in shadow. "I wouldn't worry about it if I were you."

"I'm not worrying, just asking."

I sat down, pebbles and moisture attacking my rear through the shawl that I had wrapped around myself.

"Can we make a fire? It's cold."

"No. A fire can be seen from miles away," he said, gruff, and took off his cloak. I wondered why that mattered—who he thought might be watching. He walked behind me and draped his cloak across my back, his hands firm on my shoulders through the coarse fabric. I took the edges and pulled it around me. It was very thick and very warm, un-like anything I'd worn before. I assumed it was so heavy (like some great animal's skin had sloughed off on top of me) because Europe has colder winters that make rivers freeze. He tramped around me and walked away, facing the river.

"Thank you. I can barely see anything, though," I said, shivering in the sudden warmth. The cloak smelled of dirty hair, and I wondered if it had lice. It probably did, but I didn't much care at that point.

"There's nothing you need to see. I can see everything for us," he said. I wondered what he meant by that. *Everything*.

"I'm going to go get you some food."

"In the dark? Don't you have food in those big bags?"

"I do, but nothing you'd want to eat, trust me. And like I said, I can see just fine. I'll be back soon. Don't move, don't make a fire. Just stay here."

It felt wrong to feel afraid. I should have felt afraid to be around Gévaudan, not afraid that he was leaving me alone. It made me feel ashamed, disgusted at myself. I said nothing, not daring to give myself away.

"I'm going to undress," he said bluntly, whipping off his clothes and pelts. The bone trinkets clattered in protest. His fardels fell heavily to the ground.

"Why? Why are you doing that?" I asked, alarmed.

"It's how I hunt."

"It's cold, why on earth . . ."

"Will you stop going on about the cold? It doesn't bother me. I'm not asking you to strip, am I? This is how I hunt," he said, firm, harsh. His voice sounded hoarser.

He peeled off his boots. I was thankful for the darkness, though his naked body was so pale I could see enough even in the dark, making me realize that I was still looking at him. I turned away quickly, looking at the far-off lights of human life instead.

I heard the patter of his piss hitting the ground, and I gritted my teeth, wondering if I should even bother to ask. I held the cloak over my mouth and nose as a burning smell clawed its way into my head.

"Don't touch my things unless you want to die. I'll know, trust me," he said. And I heard the slap of his bare feet on the ground recede, become faster, until it sounded like he was running on all fours. I kept looking away until I could no longer hear him.

I dreamed that something came to me while I lay there between river and forest. A slouching thing that crept until it was close, and pushed its long fingers into my hair, scraped with one dirty claw so that a line was drawn through my scalp, beaded with blood. Its breath like scalding desert air against the back of my neck, its tongue a swamp snake hot with life, slithering between my salt-smeared roots until its blind head was at the thin wound. I felt it taste the cut, tongue-snake squirming its way across the line of my blood and swallowing the scent of my scalp, felt the crown of the beast's great fangs quiver around my head. I felt tiny, as if the beast grew in size with each passing moment, until it loomed like a mountain over the river, blotting out the night sky. I crouched on the ground under its cavernous maw. Its tongue-serpent was huge and engorged, sliding across my face and through my hair.

I couldn't move, through any of it. I felt something pass between my body and that of the beast, slow, almost imperceptible. My life, perhaps; it could be I was dying at that moment, that it was licking away my will to live from that thin little wound. I couldn't tell. I drifted off into a (second?) sleep until that sleep gave way to my awakening.

I bolted upright into the insect-torn air, the pests colliding with my skin as they hummed around my head, ants crawling all over my skin, somehow having found their way under my clothes. My scalp was burning, my face sticky. I stuck my fingers in my hair and felt the narrow, rough tissue of a long cut underneath it. I looked at my fingertips, coughing at the stench of something pungent on them. No blood, as far as I could tell. Just a scratch—I wondered if an animal had clambered out of the forest and clawed me, or if I'd just cut my head on a pebble or rock as I slept.

The darkness had thickened, clouds obscuring most of the stars and the moon. It felt like I was in some limbo, especially because I had no idea how long I'd slept.

I could smell him.

"Jevah-dan?"

"I'm here," he said. My eyes adjusting, I could tell that he was sitting about five feet away from me. As far as I could tell, he wasn't naked anymore.

"Did you sleep?" he asked.

"I, yes, I did. Not very well."

"Come closer and eat."

I waved away the insects stinging at my face, raising the cowl of the cloak and tucking it close under my throat. Holding the cloak tight to me, I clambered closer to him in the dark, feeling completely at a loss.

"What did you find?"

"A couple of rabbits. I hope you eat meat."

"I do. But we need a fire now, don't we? To roast them?"

"We don't. Your ancestors ate flesh raw, and so can you."

"What? I can't do that."

"So you think. It's all in your mind."

"I can't eat a rabbit raw, even if you can. It's unclean. It will sicken me."

Gévaudan didn't say anything. He was entirely a thing of shadow and dream in that dead light from the covered moon, reflected off the sleeping world. I saw the shape of the rabbits, one hanging limp from his hand, another on the ground.

"You need to eat."

"I'll be fine. I'll find some berries or nuts tomorrow. Or make a fire during the day."

My stomach rebelled at the thought, growling. I hoped that Gévaudan hadn't heard it over the deafening chirping of the insects and the lapping of the Yamuna not too far from us.

"You'll eat now. You've barely eaten all day. I can't have a sick and starving human straggling along with me. I'm not going to take care of you."

"And you'll not tell me what to do. You offered to help me find Fen-eer, not the other way around. I don't need to be taken care of by any-one, let alone you. I've lived in these lands longer than you have and I've gone far longer than a day without anything in my belly."

I heard his heavy breathing as he dragged the rabbit's legs through the ground, playful. I looked again across the river at Mumtazabad's lights, now almost gone, feeling agitated and sick. I could easily go back, if I wanted. We weren't that far away yet. Then I heard a sound like the tearing of a cloth, followed by dripping on the ground. I real-ized that Gévaudan had just twisted the head off the rabbit in his hands.

I heard more crunching and squelching for several minutes as he skinned and gutted the animals, maybe even with his fingers and teeth. I looked away throughout, light-headed and on the verge of retching once more.

I jerked away, startled, when he approached me.

"Here," he grumbled. I felt him take my hand in his, and put some-thing warm and wet in my palm.

"Just eat it. You won't get sick." He waited a few seconds, before adding, "I promise."

I put the meat in my mouth, too tired to argue. It was soft pulp, tasting of metal and salt. As I held this wad of flesh between teeth and tongue, I knew that Gévaudan had chewed on it already so that it wouldn't be completely raw. When I realized this I didn't spit it out for some reason. Perhaps I needed to eat more desperately than I had thought, though it was true that I had gone days without any real food on several occasions. The flesh was hot, as if it had been stewed in a pot of simmering water for a minute, though the taste of it belied any illusions of such a thing.

I swallowed and waited what seemed a long time with my jaw clenched tight as a vise to keep it from coming back up.

I could hear Gévaudan crunching bone and meat, feeding on the carcasses all the while.

"See?" he said, smacking through wet lips.

He handed me another, larger lump of ragged chewed meat. I took it and ate it, choking back the urge to throw it up, unable to understand why I was doing so. My hunger didn't seem a good enough reason.

"Your teeth are sharp stones, dulled by civilization," said Gévaudan.

His pale face glowed in the dark, his mouth a black smear where the rabbit's blood had painted him like a courtesan's colors. The flies and other flying insects hovered around my mouth and crawled across my chin, my palms, and my fingers, tickling my skin as they tried to get to the raw juice of the dead animal on me.

"What are you and Fen-eer? You don't look alike at all, and yet you speak of the same tribes, and have the same madness in you."

He grunted. I could hear the bubble of blood between his lips as he breathed out, and spoke.

"Fenrir's from somewhere else. Some land far north of where I come from."

"Where do you come from?"

"A kingdom called France."

"I've heard of it. I've never heard of people like you and Fenrir, though."

"You have. They must have tribes of our kind here as well, with names in the languages of these lands. Where Fenrir and I came from, humans are killing one another for fear that we are among them—they burn one another, hang one another, flay one another to check for fur underneath, as if it's that simple. They tell one another stories—that we turn into wolves at night and live as humans during the day, that we are beholden to Satan, the devil of the Christians. Occasionally, they even catch us. I suppose that's why we left. Or I did, anyway." He paused. The moist rustle of his tongue running across his lips.

"On the outer edges of this empire, past the Indus and beyond, in Khorasan, the land of the Afghans, the tribes of our kind call themselves djinn. They are numerous. There is the tribe of the ifreets, who shape their second selves with great flightless wings, which they flap to make storms of desert dunes, who strike fear in the hearts of their enemies by setting their oily hides on fire. There is the tribe of ghuls, who stalk their prey with stealth, and enjoy mingling often with khrissals in cities to lure prey to death, and sometimes take the hyena as a totem for their second selves." As I listened, I felt again the ache in my chest, to hear these familiar words—*djinn, ifreet, ghul*—in a voice not my mother's. He went on.

"We lived among these tribes for a while, in the wilds of the mountains and deserts. They didn't much take to us, though. There were battles. Terrible ones. We brought strife to their land, because we were followed by another European tribe—the Theissians, the Hounds of God, who worship the Christian god. True to their name, they hounded us across the Black Sea to the Khorasan. They think shape-shifters of other tribes are demons, that the power to change shapes is given either by the father-god of Christ or by his fallen angel, the devil. In their eyes, to deny their religion as shape-shifter is to brand oneself as witch and demon. In the Khorasan, the Hounds went from chasing us to chasing the djinn tribes. So in a way, the djinn saved us. I hope they killed every last one of those self-righteous fools, who would betray their own to scrabble at the feet of a khrissal god."

"My mother told me stories of the djinn when I was a child. Fen-eer mentioned them also, when he was babbling. Is that truly what your people believe you are?"

"Believe? Are you not listening? I don't need to believe anything. Do you need to believe that you are a human? I simply am what I am. I don't call myself djinn, ghul, or ifreet, demon or witch or wer-wolf, but these are words that might be used to describe me."

"So. You and Fen-eer think you are not human." It wasn't a question. I thought of us crossing the Yamuna, how it had struck me that no man could have carried me on his back while swimming, like Gévaudan had. I thought, of course, of Fenrir and his vision.

"We aren't. And I don't know what Fenrir thinks. He certainly acts like a human when the whim takes him," he said, low in his throat. Silence, and then once again I heard brittle bone snap, the slurp of spit and gristle disappearing into his mouth.

I moved my tongue through my mouth, ushering the bloody bits of rabbit toward my throat as something swelled inside me, making me dizzy. I burped a foul breath of carrion.

"He raped me."

In the gloaming, Gévaudan looked up, and even with no light to reflect in them I thought his eyes gleamed gem green as he moved his head. Like Fenrir's eyes.

"I know," he said. "Like I said. Human."

The insects observed our conversation, an invisible congregation as vast as the emperor's audience. The flies crawled on my lips, trying with desperation to enter my mouth.

"What am I to you, then, Jevah-dan? To your kind. If not something to use, to fuck. You look at me sometimes like that is exactly what I am."

As if to oblige me, to demonstrate, he looked at me. I couldn't see his expression, but I knew it, I could see it in my head, even after just a day of traveling by his side. I heard the peeling of his stained lips.

"To me, to my kind. You are prey. Not something to fuck. Something to kill, and sustain us."

"You are cannibals, then."

"No. We do not eat our own kind. We eat you, little Cyrah. You keep forgetting—we are not human."

We are the devouring, not the creative.

"One of the things Fen-eer told me was that your kind can change shapes. What shape can you take, other than this one?"

"We have our second selves, yes, that we may turn into, should the time be right. And those second selves may change in time, or use the arts to guise themselves in nature. We may change our first selves as well, though it is difficult and dangerous to molt so."

"Can you"—I touched my mouth, stifling nausea—"turn to smoke and fit in a lamp, so I could carry you around like a trinket?" I tried to make myself smile at such a thought but couldn't.

If he found this funny, he gave no sign, either. "It is rumored that there were tribes, and still are in some parts of the world, who have many selves. That their souls are not merely bifurcated, but multifarious things that enable them to change shapes until each of them is legion in itself."

"Show me, then. If all of this is truth and not madness, as I thought when Fen-eer told me of it, then all you need do to convince me is show me your second self."

"And why would I care to convince you? My second self is sacred. If a human wishes to see it, that human must be willing to give himself to certain death, or to the joining of our tribes."

"Then why are you even telling me all this? What pleasure does it give you to recount your own existence as if it were something new? You want to tell me. You want to show me what you are, like my suitors pride themselves on disrobing, as if it were some heroic thing that they were born with cocks between their legs, which they all thrust out in front of themselves like so many monkeys. So show me, right now, this sacred and holy second self. Reveal it. Take off this human you wear."

I heard him breathing, panting like he had before. The strange sound of a man behaving like a beast.

"You've never actually talked to a . . . a human, about any of this, have you. Just like Fen-eer. You were blabbering. You can't help yourselves. Stop talking. Stop boasting about your superior race and show me."

"Stop this now."

"I said show me."

"Fuck you."

"Show me, Jevah-dan. I know you want to."

I heard the rabbit carcass fall, heard him stand up. The bone trinkets clattered, the giggling of infant skeletons. My heart thundered so loud that the insects and their continuous song were finally silenced by the sound of my own blood flooding my head in fear.

I felt myself whipped off the ground like I weighed nothing, so hard I heard a crack in my neck as my head was jerked back. He had lunged at me so fast I barely had time to see him cover the few feet of darkness between us. My body felt like lifeless mud and straw. I wondered if he had broken my neck. My feet left the ground, my legs dangling. A livid rain wet my face, and I thought the clouds had broken but it was his spit. His face was inches from mine, hot stinking breath burning the tears from my eyes. I heard a hissing and crackling, like stones grinding together. His teeth.

I flexed my fingers, then my hands, and felt the fur of his pelts, grasped at them in tufts as if it might hurt him. I could still move. I held on to that thought. My neck wasn't broken. He wasn't actually holding me by the neck at all, but by the knot of his cloak (which I wore), right below my throat. I felt the cloth push tight against my neck and begin to choke me.

Even inches away from my eyes, I couldn't see his face in the dark. I was glad, because I could feel enough of the ugly, hideous mask of anger that I had brought forth to cover his boyish face. Somewhere, buried deep beneath panic and terror and pain, I felt pride. Just as I felt my throat close off completely because of the tightening knot of the cloak, I fell from his hands.

I coughed and gasped, the wind gone from my lungs, pain spiking my neck each time I tried to look up. I gave up and just lay there on the ground, curling myself into Gévaudan's cloak as he stalked away. The earth was cool and soothing against my cheek. I could smell it, too—an odor that I imagined was what clouds might smell like at that moment. I breathed it in, to drive the fleshy smell of Gévaudan's mouth from my head.

He was still panting, maybe ten paces away from me. He was staying away.

"You're a coward. Just like Fen-eer," I murmured and tried to laugh. Instead, I coughed until my body shook. Even after it stopped, the shaking wouldn't go away, leaving me trembling on the ground, cloak drawn tight like a caul around me.

He said nothing. Once again I heard the ripping of meat and skin, the frenzied twig-cracks of bones being chewed. I doubted he was even eating that poor rabbit anymore. My teeth clicking together, shaky gouts of breath returning through the fevered shuddering, I marveled. Whatever he was, I had scared him. I had scared mighty Gévaudan, whether djinn of France or white cannibal with syphilitic madness. I had scared him. That made two of them now.

* * *

I know it sounds strange, but I think Gévaudan trusted me more after that incident, and I him. He had, after all, not killed me yet. When I goaded him into attacking, I thought I'd pushed too far, that he would at least hit me, or do something to leave me bleeding. But no, he didn't. Not a drop of my blood was shed. I didn't know why, but I knew that I wasn't merely prey to him. I was hurt, that night—I couldn't move my neck without pain after that for days, but I know I should have ended up dead or worse, facing off against such a man, or thing. I don't know what I believed at that point, or maybe I just don't remember. But we said no words that night after he hurled me to the ground. Aching, giddy from the rush of my bitter victory (if you will allow me to call it that), I just stayed curled up in his cloak, as safe and warm as I could get ten paces from that man or monster who had just nearly choked me to death, and decided not to.

When the sun showered its light over the Yamuna again, splintering it straight into my eyes, I woke to see Gévaudan bent low over the bitten bones of those two accursed rabbits, hands and mouth still encrusted in dry blood. The dawn light tickled his green eyes (I never could tell whether his or Fenrir's eyes were actually green—it was only at times that they appeared so) and turned them pale as his head snapped up at the sound of my stirring.

I hissed and put my head back on the ground, my neck seizing with pain as I looked up. I immediately regretted showing him this weakness.

He laughed, showing his teeth, gone brown with the uncleaned offal. "I have hurt you, little one. Haven't I? Have I crippled you?"

I clenched my jaw, closed my eyes, and sat upright, wincing against the pain.

"No, you have not crippled me, despite your best efforts."

"You're a fool, girl. You've no idea," he said, and turned serious, his soft white face slackening. I saw the glaring light of the sunrise illuminate the fringe of fur around his red mouth, his swollen lips. He looked at the bones.

"If these were the bones of a human child, they would tell me things, and I could wear them on me to sing in the breeze. Sing you awake, Cyrah. Rabbit bones tell me nothing. They break, too, most easily. But so would yours, I imagine."

"What do you want from me, Jevah-dan? Just tell me now. Why did you bring me with you? I've had enough of these games."

"You're the one playing games. You gambled with your life last night."

"My life is my own to gamble. Tell me what your stake is here. Take off my blindfold. If we're to play a game, let us play it together at the very least."

He ran a finger across his bulbous lower lip, smiling. "Play," he repeated like a child.

I stood up. He cocked his head like a curious dog.

"All right, little girl," he said, voice thick. "I brought you as bait. I think Fenrir will be more willing to see me, talk to me again, if I have you with me." There had to be more to his plan than that, but this was a start.

"I thought as much. You intend to stand by and watch him rape me again? Then settle your quarrels over my corpse?"

"How dramatic. Did you fathom nothing of Fenrir's ways? He'd rather die than take you by force again." He tossed a little bone idly over his shoulder.

"Is that so."

"He thinks he loves you, for fuck's sake. He knows nothing of love. Neither do I, for that matter. It's quite clear to me that it is entirely a thing of weakness, and turns the brain to runny porridge." Rubbing my neck with one hand, I approached him, though not with the caution one might expect. Nor was he startled or surprised by this lack of caution. He looked at me as if he expected this, as I closed the gap until I was standing over him and his mangled bones.

"You're human. You're a woman. What do you know of it?" he asked me.

"Of what?"

"Love."

"I loved my mother. I don't think I've known any other love. I've only heard stories, and poems."

He looked comically disappointed, squatting at my feet. I felt like slapping him, kicking him down, and grinding his face into the mud.

"You never loved any of your suitors?" he asked.

"Don't be stupid."

"Never met any man, or woman, who lit a flame under your heart?"

"No."

He nodded, mulling over this.

"You hurt me," I said, as forcefully as I could be.

"Yes, as I said. So?"

"I can't travel with someone who's going to hurt me."

He shrugged. "Then don't. Leave. What do I care?"

"You obviously do care. You just said so. You need me as bait."

"I don't need you. It would make it easier for us to find Fenrir if you're with me. That is all."

"Then you need me to make things easier."

"So?"

"So I'm going to keep going with you. And you must promise not to hurt me again."

"No. I owe you no promises, khrissal."

I laughed, my gut coiling like a snake with fear. "Then show me your second self. Why not? You're going to hurt me anyway."

"It is sacred." He bared his teeth and gums like a dog enraged, spitting the words. I held my ground. I saw in his darting eyes something other than simple anger—a fear that betrayed his curiosity. "You don't have any idea what you're asking, you stupid little bitch. Do you want to die?"

"I'm not afraid of dying."

"What you're saying is, you want me to kill you. I'm not your personal hound, here to do a job you're too cowardly to do yourself."

I smiled, though I felt nothing if not a fiery emptiness within my chest. "What I want is to see that you're not a liar, nor Fenrir. Whether you kill me is your decision. But do not call me coward when you can't muster the courage to show me the greatness, the magic, that you say is within you and your friend, that so justifies your hatred for us mere humans."

That curiosity, still kindling in his eyes. Whatever tribe they were from, he and Fenrir were not beings to ignore a challenge. His mouth twitched. "Not hatred. Hunger. We are the greater predator, just as you are a better predator than other animals on this earth. My second self yearns only to hunt you and your kind, and I yearn only to help it do so."

"Until I see your second self, these words of yours will remain cowardly lies that veil an empty hatred."

He shook his head, a half smile on his twitching lips, revealing bloody canines. "You really don't care. You want to meet something that could slaughter you in an instant, just to prove that I'm not lying?"

"I watched my mother die in my arms, shitting herself because of some sickness that fate slipped into her food or water—fate, too, can be a coward. Since she went, I've met no one who has left me wanting to stay in this world. No, I don't want to die. But I'm not afraid of it."

Gévaudan stared at me in amazement and shook his head. "What sad, pathetic little lives you humans lead."

"Then show me, Jevah-dan of France, what lives of worth and beauty *you* live, you and your precious sacred self."

Gévaudan got up, towering over me, though not as much as Fenrir. He looked as if he were about to say something, not in anger, maybe even in admiration. I could be mistaken, though I don't think I am. But he closed his mouth, turned away to pick up his fardels and sling them over his shoulders. He shrugged, that half smile turning dark.

"If you can walk, and you seem still able to, follow. We've wasted enough time."

And so I followed, again.

If you were anyone but my son, this is where you would wonder if this is my true tale or some fable conjured from my imagination, such as those Scheherazade wove to save her life. Perhaps this *is* a fable, even though it is true; perhaps this world I stumbled into when I met your father and his companions is the place where fables come from.

Let us return to the telling.

I followed Gévaudan of France into the forest, only to see him shed his clothes and pelts once again in the midst of the verdant sals and khairs, and he turned to me glowering like a man possessed, eyes so green they seemed filled with the sap of the forest that surrounded us. He snarled at me, and this is not a fanciful use of the word—he actually snarled the words, and I was filled with a holy terror as I realized that he had bowed down to me. He stood upright, panting, taller and stronger and greater than I, but I knew right then that he had submitted to my demands.

"Your wish. Is my fucking command." He laughed and laughed until it turned into the barking of a jungle cat or a monstrous dog, or both. A stream of piss fell from him, and he walked a circle around his clothes, spraying the golden liquid all over the ground, his legs, his feet.

Trembling, I asked him, "Is this your second self, then, Jevah-dan? You as your mother saw you first? You, unclothed and bare, pissing yourself?"

"I've no mother," he leered. Giving off a powerful stink, he whipped the piece of my dupatta with Fenrir's blood on it off his hand. His body

was horribly white and writ with tattoos, the tangled knots of hair
between his legs and in his armpits a jarring contrast, the color of rust.
I realized that many of the bone trinkets that hung off him were actually sewn into his body, hanging off his chest and stomach. I could see
his cock growing and hardening, and I grasped the handle of my knife
in one sweaty palm.

"It is sacred!" he snapped again, peeling back his lips. "No human
may lay eyes upon it except as prey, or one of us. But without your
eyes. Blind, you can see it blind." Would he pluck out my eyes? I wondered. He laughed again, his own eyes spinning wild as he took in the
world in this sudden frenzy, taking in ground and bark and leaves and
sky as if he were just seeing them. He tossed me the dirty, blood-
browned rag. I snatched it out of the air, fumbled and dropped it because of my tremors. I picked it up.

"Wear it. For me to open your eyes, you must blindfold yourself."

I looked at him, lungs hitching with the ghosts of questions.

"Now, for fuck's sake. Now! Blindfold yourself. Trust me. You will
die if you don't. Quick!"

I did. I tied that bloody rag around my head, fingers barely able to
tie the knot amid the grime-thickened tangle of my unwashed hair. I
trusted him, trusted madness itself, because I had come inches away
from death's door in his hands last night, and I had been pulled back
by those same hands. In that unreal moment, it felt like I had known
him for an eternity instead of two days.

"Good girl," he panted as my quivering fingers completed the knot.

The day was bursting into brightness at that very moment, a rain of
light through the leaves and the damp ground-mist rising and turning
back into air. My fingers went back to the knife at my waist, clutching
it tight.

"I see the knife. Draw it," he told me, and I did, without hesitation.

"Do you trust me? You asked for this. Do you?"

I nodded.

"Cut your arm, let the blood run."

I swallowed hard. "Trust me! Fucking do it now!" he shouted.

I did. I felt the cold line I drew across my skin with the blade turn warm as the wound welled up, from the crook of my elbow to near my wrist. It dripped down to my palm, gathering there, sticky.

"Good girl," he growled, again.

I heard him pacing, feet stamping the dew-damp ground, loud slaps as the pacing became faster. I heard the thump of fist on tree trunk, the bone-breaking splintering of wood, and it felt like the whole forest shook with each crash, the treetops swaying and the leaves hushing, the birds bursting from their roosts and screeching above us. I heard his growls grow deeper until it sounded like he was vomiting out his very soul. I heard the sound of sap spilled and bark torn from the trees, raked with what sounded like blades but could not be.

And then, silence.

How can I describe what came to my senses, in that silence? Even the birds stopped their screaming, the insects their singing. The smell of it was overpowering. It smelled like birth, the birth of god or demon, raw and animal and steaming in the morning air. Sweet and musk, like frankincense and myrrh; heavy and pungent, like the juice of living things, blood and piss, sweat and spit; rancid and fecund, like waste, shit, and earth. It stank of both life and death, both so intoxicating I found myself flushed with my own blood, my heart aching. I could hear it, feel it breathing, the rumbling of a mountain slumbering through centuries slivered to seconds. It walked to me, twigs snapping sharp under its great hands and feet, soil squelching under its enormous, impossible weight. It was on all fours, or so its steps told me, and yet I could feel its boiling breath, a hot and humid wind on my face as it approached. Even crouched, it was as tall as me.

"Come," I whispered to it, and it was as if I could feel it smiling, inhuman, fangs bared. I let go of the blade and held out my hands, palms itching with its heat. The rumbling of its breath grew louder. It was a foot away from me. I stepped forward, and my breath hitched as my fingers met fur and skin, thick and coarse. I have touched wolves and tigers cautiously, through the bars of caravan cages, and their heat was nothing compared with what I felt when I touched this beast. It felt like desert earth rumbling, warming my cold palms. I ran my hands across it, feeling its vibrations hum in my own flesh. My fingers caught on the bone trinkets sewn deep into the skin, a constant between the two shapes of human and beast. The beast rose and fell, and I wondered if I was touching its chest. I felt sweat roll down my face as it breathed its hot, rank life into me.

"Jevah-dan," I said. Its fur bristled into stiffness at the name spoken, like spines, pricking my palms and drawing blood. I breathed out, a feather-light gasp, the thin air of my lungs meeting with the heavy humor of the beast's. I laughed. Something wet slid across my arm, wiping the blood from the wound I had made. Once, twice, thrice. Its tongue like a swamp snake, slithering blind. It tasted me. The wound tingled as the beast lapped at it. It stopped.

It said nothing, didn't bark or spit or growl, only continued to rumble under my fingers, filling me with an ecstasy I cannot express to this day. Tears ran down my cheeks from under the rag, and I felt a throb deep in my chest. I felt like weeping, wailing like one bereaved, sobbing with my entire self like I had when my mother drew in her last rattling breath while I held her.

It said nothing.

I don't remember if I heard words in my head, or just felt it, but I knew it was waiting. I knew it wanted me to climb onto it.

"Show me how," I said through my tears, my voice shaking. The blindfold grew damp as it soaked in my tears. I felt the beast move, felt it lower itself into a hunch, my hands following its movements.

I knew I couldn't hurt it in any way, felt it let me know this.

I walked around it, its great head following me, I knew, its eyes burning against me. I climbed onto its back, feet and hands digging into its sides, clinging to its spiny fur as it bristled and cut new wounds into my skin, like clambering across a slope knotted with bramble. I sat at the ridged peak of its spine, fur sharp as pins against my legs and buttocks and forearms as I clung to it. It stood again on all fours, lurching up, my entire world quaking.

I knew I had to hold on tight, very tight. I couldn't hope to hurt it, no matter how tight I held it.

With me on its back, it ran.

It felt like it ran faster than any animal I have ever seen, and yet it seemed to restrain its power, perhaps only for my sake. Its muscles moved under my body like thick ropes, melting and re-forming every second, burning the skin of my arms and thighs with the scathing speed of their rippling. Each pounding step it laid on the ground I felt. I clung to the beast until I was sure I would fly off, until I was sure its fur would be torn from its skin because of my grip. My toes and fingers dug into it until its scorching blood pooled under my nails. My hair unwound itself, my tears dried themselves, and the thick cloak whipped out behind me as if it were light silk. I felt branches whip at me, tearing hair from my scalp and scratching skin off my muscles. I felt the open air of the river's mudflats rip into my face and fill my lungs, heavy with the scent of clay. I felt the spray of the Yamuna as the beast galloped along the river's silvered flank, heard the feathery beating of wings as flocks of waterbirds took to the air in its wake, felt its fur grow dangerously slick in my grasp.

I felt the impact of the beast colliding into something, and I struggled not to be thrown off. I heard its rolling growl erupt into a roar that hurt my ears, felt it contort under me as something brayed in fear and agony. I held on as it shook with abandon, the warm spatter of fresh blood mingling with the cold spray of the Yamuna as I heard the rip and crack of meat and bone giving way under its jaws and teeth, a strange familiar sound now, like Gévaudan chewing on his rabbits but much louder. The thunderous crash of the animal going down under the beast's force. Each clench of its claws on the captured prey flickered across the cabled muscles of its entire body like lightning, twitching under my legs and arms so that I felt every moment that culminated in its kill.

I laughed and I laughed and I screamed, louder than I ever had before, not caring who or what heard me, my tears lost to water and blood and wind even as they escaped my blindfold, my body shaking as it purged all the sorrows of my life in one howl that rode with us.

I washed my wounds as best I could in the waters of the Yamuna.
Every part of me ached. My neck hurt terribly. I lapped the icy water
over the wounds I could reach, rubbing them clear of grime. I didn't
want to take off my clothes for fear of Gévaudan seeing me naked, and
I couldn't bathe with them on because it was too cold, though I was
already soaked from before. So I washed with care, reaching under my
clothes and rubbing the slashes on my thighs and calves where I had
sat on the beast, on my hands and arms where I had clung to it, the
bleeding cuts on my head where branches had struck me.

I was still shaking, as I now realize I was wont to do often in those
days of discovery. I felt drunk and high, as if I'd swilled an entire
pitcher of bhang.* Gévaudan was making a fire for the glistening red
swaths of meat that lay on the ground, painted with dirt and grit. From
the fringes of golden-brown fur with white spots still visible on the
pelt, it looked like the prey had been a chital. I assumed the beast had
carried the animal in its mouth after the kill, when it brought me back
to the place where we had left our belongings. The smell of Gévaudan's
piss still hung in the air.

I wanted to thank him, but decided not to. I couldn't tell what he
might construe from such a gesture. It was strange to be back in his
presence, rather than that of the beast I rode along the Yamuna. Yet I
couldn't stop smiling like the little girl he always called me, so I kept
my face away from him, watching the cranes dip their long white
necks in the river on the other side.

* Ground cannabis, usually in a drink made with sour milk.

"I have never done that," he said. The flames snapped to life, look-ing weak in the bright morning sunlight. We hadn't said a word to each other since I had removed the blindfold and seen only Gévaudan, not the thing that had carried me through forest and riverside.

I kept smiling to myself.

"Shown a human, that is. Shown a human my second self, and left that human still alive, or still human. You should be well and dead, lying here by this fire instead of this deer."

I wondered again if I should thank him, and thought again, no.

"I saw nothing, Jevah-dan. Do not worry yourself."

He drove one of the ragged chunks of meat onto a spit he had fash-ioned from some branches hacked off a sal. There was a sizzle of sparks as the flames met wood and flesh, and blood steamed in the heat.

"You're . . . clever. Yes. A clever one," he said, staring into the fire. His hair dripped water, coiling again as the flames began to dry it. I felt a thrill of delight at this compliment.

"You can bathe, if you wish. I will look away," he said, as if he had read my mind.

"No. I can't do that, not in front of you."

"Then come and dry yourself by the fire. You're shivering."

I did, because I was very cold. I wrapped the damp cloak around myself and huddled close to the fire, which was growing as it fed on the pile of brush and branches. The meat began to darken. Gévaudan tore into the other raw piece with his teeth.

He looked as shaken as I was, his eyes not meeting mine.

"Are you all right?" I asked him.

"Yes."

"Were you afraid, to show your second self?"

"No. But it wasn't something I've done before. It took great will . . ."

"What did?"

He hesitated. "To keep from tearing you apart."

"But it didn't tear me apart." He said nothing.

"I don't know about you, Jevah-dan of France. But your second self, it is a wild and wondrous thing. And I sensed in it a purity—no, an honesty—that I have never seen before in any man or woman. I am glad to have been in its company," I told him through chattering teeth.

He might have been offended by the way I phrased this, but if he was he showed no sign of it. He looked happier than I had seen him until then, his shoulders rising in pride and his brows creasing in a frown to cover his joy. He said nothing. At no point did he look more like a boy than at that moment, despite his size and formidable pelts. He glanced at me and obviously noticed me shivering.

"You will catch a chill. Humans are frail, in that way."

"Does your kind not feel cold, then?" I asked, sniffling at the river water and snot dribbling from my nose.

"Oh, we do. In the depths of a northern winter, perhaps, hunting during a blizzard with not a stitch on us. Then we may feel a slight chill cut us."

"What's a bliz-urd?"

He got up, and walked to me. His smell was different, placid in a way it had not been before—perhaps it was the Yamuna on him. I gasped as he sat down and pulled me to him, wrapping his arms around my shoulders. It was much warmer in his embrace, if it can be called that. I thought I would protest, but I didn't. Without recourse to taking off my wet clothes as they chilled me to the bone in the winter air, I let him warm me with the unnatural heat of his body.

"Jevah-dan," I said.

"Yes?" His voice hummed through me.

"If you try anything, I'll stab you. I found my blade on the ground where I dropped it." The chattering of my teeth was lessening, but still there.

"I know. If you weren't ready to stab me, I wouldn't be doing this." His voice was tight and subdued. Perhaps it was with disgust? Not quite. But it was clear that he wasn't comfortable being so close to me, not in this shape, anyway. Nor I him.

The meat lay on the ground uneaten, and on the spit, also uneaten, fat oozing off it like yellow tears, sputtering as they landed in the fire. The Yamuna glistened as the sun rose higher. Gévaudan's heat spread through me in waves, lessening the clinging discomfort of my wet clothes, the itching wounds that covered me all over. I started in his embrace, on the verge of sleep.

"Jevah-dan. I recognized it. When it licked the wound." Once again, he said nothing.

"I had a dream, last night, when you were gone to hunt. Something came and scratched my head." The cut on my scalp from last night, forgotten amid the many others I had now, came alive at this mention, in my mind at least. "It licked the blood from the wound."

There was only silence.

"Your second self. Its tongue felt familiar. It felt the same. It wasn't a dream."

Still he said nothing. I felt drowsy.

"Why did you do that?" I asked.

He grunted and took a deep breath. "I needed to taste you. You are prey. It's difficult to resist." Something felt wrong about the way he said it. He wasn't lying, exactly, but he was still hiding something. I didn't think it was because he felt ashamed in any way about his intrusion while I slept.

"Is that why you made me cut my arm?"

He nodded. "My second self would have overcome any restraint on my part. It would have ripped you limb from limb, if it didn't see that you were willing to give something."

I nodded, watching the cranes, their bright red heads mesmerizing as they bobbed up and down, their long legs sending ripples across the shallow waters where they waded. Closer to us, at the fringe of the forest, I could see the ghost shapes of jackals as they crackled through the undergrowth, tempted by the smell of the meat lying in the open. Occasionally I'd see a small pink mouth open in a hiss of aggression, ringed with needle-like white teeth. They never came close, though. I knew they wouldn't, not with Gévaudan around.

"What did you taste? In my blood," I asked him, drowsy.

He moved against me, taking a large breath. I felt it leave him in a soft growl. "You are with child."

I sat up, my heavy lids snapping open.

"What?"

"You heard."

"Are you sure?"

"Quite sure, yes."

"What is quite sure? What do you mean? Are you sure or not?"

"I am sure."

I closed my eyes and clenched my jaw. I thought of what had happened to me this past day, thought of how nothing could ever be the same. Thought of how this child in me was insignificant compared with that. But I couldn't make it so. I'd kept the hope alive that Fenrir's seed might have lain fallow in me. And now that hope was gone. My new companion's word was hardly the certainty of a bump against my belly, but after that morning, I trusted that Gévaudan was telling the truth, that he could taste the alchemy of a new life in my blood. Still, I tried to make my peace with it at that moment. I am sorry that you must see how painful the thought of your conception was to me, but I must be truthful, or not tell this story at all.

"Allah damn that fucking bastard to hell," I whispered.

Gévaudan nodded, something inside him shifting. "You want Fenrir to take it back. To destroy it, somehow."

I said nothing.

"He can perform that task for you no better than any human being can with the basest of tools. No better than I could, for that matter, if you had the courage to ask me instead. But I can't, nor can he. There is no power in our kind to take back the planting of one's seed in the womb."

I felt on the verge of spilling tears onto my cheeks, Gévaudan, the river and forest around us blurring. I don't think I actually cried. I don't even remember how hopeful I was at that point that Fenrir could somehow take back what he had done to me. After what I'd just witnessed with Gévaudan—was it that impossible to hope for such a thing? When my rapist was a creature of myth, given to changing shape at will and imparting visions? It hit hard to hear Gévaudan make certain my helplessness, and even harder because he could see what I wanted from Fenrir.

"I am sorry," he said, and I had to breathe hard to keep the tears back, pushing his warm body away from me. It felt so very wrong to hear Gévaudan say those words, strange and hurtful. I nodded, a silent laugh behind my lips.

"Why? Why are you sorry, Jevah-dan?"

Gévaudan said nothing, the knot of his jaw jumping.

"That's right. Don't tell me you're sorry. You don't know what that is, really. To be sorry for something. At least, I don't think you do, nor do any of your kind. Except maybe Fen-eer. I think he has learned."

He turned away from me.

"I will teach him, if he hasn't," I said. "I will teach him. I will make him more sorry still." How I planned to do this, of course, remained completely unclear to me.

Gévaudan nodded, realizing that I was telling him that I wasn't going anywhere, that this was the course I had taken, and that this was the one I would stay faithful to until we found Fenrir. I couldn't tell what he was thinking. Perhaps he found it amusing that I, a young human woman, thought I could make a being like Fenrir sorry for anything. Or perhaps he wasn't surprised at all, having seen with his own eyes that Fenrir was capable of remorse, or at least some mimicry of it. Or perhaps he remained silent because he thought that Fenrir's time for remorse was long over. That the next time we met him, we would find only wrath.

"You're still shivering," he said, and put his arms around me again. I didn't push him away, though every cord in my body tensed up.

I knew there *was* one way to destroy the child, that Fenrir himself had told me before he raped me. A being that changes shapes can bear no offspring. But Gévaudan was right. I didn't have the courage to ask him, nor to ask myself, truly. So I let him hold me, and dreamed of the great beast that lived within him, and of you, the little child that now lived within me.

Gévaudan held me and said nothing more, as if he were human.

It was late morning when we left the campsite by the river, emerging from the trees to travel on a well-worn road. Gévaudan had made quick work of what was left of the chital, cutting the pieces, salting them, and storing them in his fardels. I was warmer by then, if still snot-nosed and heavy-headed. My clothes were surprisingly dry, perhaps from Gévaudan's heat against me.

Walking along the road, we saw in the distance a cloud rising off the sunlit horizon like steam off a heated blade, dust pounded into the air by a nobleman's hunting party, the rumble of horses' hooves driving the bristling shapes of wild boars out of the groves and darting across the grasses, their yellow tusks flashing. And I could only think to my-self how I'd ridden upon a steed like no other at dawn—a creature that fed on my kind as prey, just as those humans on their horses would butcher and eat the boars they ran their spears and swords through.

As we watched the hunting party in the distance, I turned to Gévau-dan.

"Will you promise me something?" I asked.

"No," he whispered, squinting into the sun, eyes set on the tangled shape of the hunting procession, banners twisting in the dust.

"Can I ask you something, then," I said.

"Yes," he said.

"Can I ask that your second self kill no human being while we travel together."

He spit on the ground and said to me: "My second self does only what it wills, No one commands it but I, and no one commands me but myself."

I asked no more.

So we walked the roads of the empire, as white man and brown woman.

It wasn't long before we found the body of a man, naked and im-paled through the chest, by the trodden dirt of the road. The sharp-ened branch run through him shimmered black with flies drinking bloody bark. I'd never seen such a thing by the roads, but had heard of the more cruel among lords and noblemen punishing criminals by impalement, and then displaying the bodies in public. I told Gévau-dan so. He seemed especially interested in the gruesome sight, but I asked him if we could leave it behind with haste, and so we did.

When the sun rested at noon we passed a group of resting dervishes under the greened shade of a chinar tree, turbaned heads bobbing in a drugged stupor from drinking bhang, and I wondered whether I, too, had been drugged into a trance days long. I felt fevered, whether from the strangeness of these days or simply from catching a cold I couldn't say. The holy men basked in winter light falling through the leaves, their reddened eyes rolling to watch us pass them by, their fingers soiled from crushing the buds and leaves they put into their potions. I wanted to ask them: *Can you see this bone-white man walking beside me, dressed in pelts and hauling fardels? Can you see the thing he can become? Have you spied it at night, galloping across the land?* Gévaudan peered at them with hungry eyes, and the air sang with silence.

Then one of them called out to me, as if answering my thoughts. Startled, I went a little closer. He clambered up and came to the side of the road to meet me. The dervish raised a hand and said: "I've seen your face, in a dream."

"I think you're mistaken, holy man. I've no interest in portents," I said.

He smiled under his graying beard, waving away flies, and he said, "It was not my dream, but one given to me by a wild white man."

I felt a chill run through me. Fenrir. It had to be. Gévaudan was on the right trail after all.

"He came to us last night when we lit our fire, his eyes aflood with tears, speaking our language as if he'd spent all his life in these lands," the dervish went on, a rhythm to his slurred words, as if he were reciting poetry.

"He called himself Mangy Dog, an odd name, but well suited to him. Perhaps that was meant to be a joke. I laughed, I don't know if my brothers did," the dervish said, looking around. The others were looking at him, listening, but too far gone into their stupor to join in. Or they didn't care to. One of them snored softly. The dervish went on, ignoring the lack of response from his companions. "He wasn't a funny man, despite his funny name. Not at all. There are not many things that will frighten me easily at this age, with my brothers at my side and food in my belly. But this man did. That Mangy Dog gave us all a dream, a dream wrapped in a story of his lost love who spurned him. He showed us her face in this vision, and the face he showed us was the face of a Mughal woman." He pointed at me again. "Your face."

"Well. I. Thank you, for telling me that."

He nodded, scratching his beard. "Yes. Sister, I don't know why you are traveling with that boy over there, but he wears the same look as that Mangy Dog. I give no portents, only advice. You should leave these white folk behind. They are wild and not of this world, a different evil from the traders in their companies. I do not think the man who calls himself Mangy Dog has taken well to being spurned by you, if that is indeed the true tale, and I do not think that white boy you travel with can save you from him."

"I don't know who you met, and I don't think it was me you saw in your dream, but thank you. For the caution," I said. The dervish watched with glazed eyes as I backed away. I turned and saw him raise a hand to his forehead in farewell.

As I walked away, he went back to his perch under the tree.

"Beware the Mangy Dog," he called out in his singsong way, and leaned against the trunk to return to his afternoon doze.

I quickly went back to the road where Gévaudan stood in wait. He was still staring intently at the dervishes. "Fenrir and his stories. Always telling stories," he muttered. He shook his head and walked ahead.

"You heard all that?"

"Of course I heard. And I've heard that so-called story he told those drunkards."

"They're not drunkards. They're holy men."

"I don't care what the fuck they are. Fenrir already told me his sick story about how he worships you, right before we parted. And now he tells it to every half-wit khrissal on the road he walks. He is not a man, has he forgotten that he is not a *man*, to behave like one with no shame, like a common fool husband spurned by a harlot wife? To give himself the totem of a creature as lowly as a sick dog." He spit his words, drool sliding down his chin. I saw his fist clenching and unclenching, inches away from his sheathed knife.

"Why are you getting so angry?" I asked.

"I'm going to kill those men," he said calmly, not bothering to wipe his chin. "To save his dignity, and yours."

"No," I breathed, swallowing hard. "Please no. I beg you, don't. My dignity is mine alone to save." I didn't mention Fenrir's dignity, nor whose duty it was to save.

Gévaudan looked at me for what seemed an eternity, his panting slowly dying down. Abruptly, he walked on. I could hear each step as he drove his boots into the ground to raise a trail of dust behind him. My heart a drum to accompany his steps, I followed. The dervishes began singing a sleepy song that drifted behind us like a lonesome bird.

When among the long shadows of late afternoon we saw a group of women carrying heavy pitchers of water from well to village, their arms thick and feet caked with damp dust from treading on the spilled droplets of their burden, I wondered if Gévaudan's leering gaze as they passed us by held any hint of carnal desire, or whether it was pure hunger. The women didn't cease their loud singing, and ignored us as they tramped past. I watched them pass as well, envious of their simple lives, though I knew nothing of them.

When in the droning air of red evening we saw a falconer traipsing by the road, ringed by a variety of colored birds seated upon the hoop hanging around his shoulders, calming them with song from the flute at his lips, I wondered if I was like those birds, soothed by an invisible song, following an inscrutable being that might well barter me off to another even worse, or devour me. The falconer passed us by, trailing the nervous flutter of brittle wings.

The day died like fire in the leaves. Gévaudan looked up at the sound of a howl in the distance, squinting at the sky as if it were parchment burned dark by a sun gone out, the stars emerging like the leftover embers of scorched letters. He said nothing, and if he read anything in the stars he didn't say. I couldn't tell what animal made that distant, sad sound, which made me sure what it was.

Gévaudan stared at the moon, wiping his face. His smell was strong, sweet like ripening fruit, making me hock up the snot from my nose. The howl came again, and I didn't know whether it was closer but it felt so. "It's time," Gévaudan said, grabbing my arm and pulling me off the road toward a field of scraggly winter millet through the trees. The stalks were silver under a moon cut in half by the night sky, right along the middle like a sliced cantaloupe.

I hissed at him, pulling my arm away. We stumbled into the feathery stalks of millet. After a day numbed by wonderment, I felt terror claw its way back into my chest. "Time for what?" I snapped at him, panting, head heavy and stuffed.

"To move faster. You must get on my back."

"You want me to ride upon the back of your second self. Again?" He wiped his face again, slender fingers catching in his long hair.

He looked to the dark of the forests bordering the field. "Perhaps it would be easier. For me, and for you. If you were better acquainted with it. In my wildest dreams I wouldn't have thought it possible, but you seemed strangely at ease in its presence. It might lessen the danger to your life if you continued to show it—show me—that."

In my wildest dreams. Such a familiar and mundane phrase, one I wouldn't expect from a creature living a dream. I found myself moved.

"We're in danger right now, aren't we? You've found Fen-eer. Or he's found us. That was him we just heard."

"Yes," he said, and spat. He explained no more, which didn't surprise me.

We weren't following Fenrir anymore. I was certain of it. I was witness to some strange dance of aggression that unfolded on the breeze, with neither player in sight of the other. No, there was only burning musk left under fallen leaves, piss on bark, a dead body uneaten and left by the road impaled—not the work of a nobleman but of Fenrir, of the Mangy Dog that roamed ahead of us, telling his stories.

Gévaudan started shrugging off his belongings. His fardels crashed to the ground like stones.

"Fuck all this. I've had enough of dragging the weight of twenty pointless lives around. I'll leave all this," he said and looked straight into my eyes in the gloom. I clutched the edge of his heavy cloak, which had kept me warm for two days and still did so. "Listen to me. I need to let it out right now, Cyrah. It has met you once, and let you live. I don't know whether it'll spare you a second time. *Help* me keep you alive," he said to me.

I was shocked by the strength of his words. Despite willfully bringing me into this ritual between him and Fenrir, swinging me between the two of them like a glittering bauble, he truly meant those words in that moment.

"What does it matter to you whether I live or die by your hand, or mauled by your second self? Just another meal," I said, my voice strangely calm even as anticipation churned me sick. He walked close enough that I could smell his carrion breath, his fists crushing the stalks tickling our elbows. The sweet smell coming off him in waves, making me cough again.

"Fenrir has wronged me," he said, grimacing. "He's made a fool of me. A pathetic thing, like—him. We were a pack, and he sundered us. We shared kill, we ate of the same men and women and children, bathed in their fluids, and shared the blessings of the ghost fires. We were bound, and still he sundered us. He has wronged you as well, as his prey. He should have killed you, not left you so, with . . ."

"With child," I said. The howl came again from beyond the forest, sounding across the millet like a wind.

"Yes. It was a perverse act. If I deserve a chance to set things right with him, so do you."

"Of course. And I'm to hop on the back of your second self so you can usher me like a morsel to your friend. So he can finish the hunt, instead of leaving me—so perversely—with child." I touched my forehead lightly.

I wanted to keep backing away to the road, flee from this wild white man.

I wanted to embrace him, to greet what was waiting under Gévaudan's skin, climb onto its bristling, mountainous back again.

Where was there to flee? Only into moonlit dark, into the arms of the Mangy Dog.

"Please," he said, shocking me with that word. "We've idled along this human road long enough. He's near. I'm weak in this shape. I need to emanate."

"All right," I said, feeling very tired, taken aback by how vulnerable he was, not bothering to deny my accusations. He seemed so forlorn, trying in some way to communicate with me, to bring the two of us closer, as incomprehensible as that was. And for what? It made my chest heavy. I couldn't understand myself, nor him, nor the world, at that moment. But it seemed he couldn't, either. I realized then how much he *wanted* me on the back of his second self. That it was forbidden, thrilling to him in a way fucking me was exciting to Fenrir. Some part of Gévaudan, of his second self, had been taken by surprise, had liked the feeling of a human being, of prey, small hands, legs, clinging to its back without fear. With trust.

I was tired. I wanted it, too, I knew I did.

"You must carry my clothes and my blade. The rest of my things I'll leave. None of it matters," said Gévaudan.

I felt some regret at leaving behind all the meat in his fardels from the chital he'd—we'd—killed that morning, but I let it go. I couldn't eat anything right then anyway, hunger the last thing on my mind despite my stomach growling like a cub. I burst into coughing again because of the fever all over my limbs and lungs, the thickness in my head waiting to loosen. After the stillness of traveling with Gévaudan as human and human, there was a tensing in my arms and legs, my thighs and calves tightening at the memory of sharp fur and spines and clinging to something too fast to hold on to. I stopped myself from giddy laughter, I was so overwhelmed by what was happening. Finally, it was approaching—a reminder that magic was real, that the morning's ride through the mudflats and the river actually happened.

I watched Gévaudan strip. As if we were adulterers hiding among the millet, out for an illicit night of moonlit romance. I watched him just like I'd watched so many strangers, all men, strip in anticipation of my body. Like I'd watched Fenrir strip as he prepared to squirt his own idea of fate into me.

I told myself that Gévaudan was disrobing for *me,* that this being of raw magic was stripping down to its true self just for me. That I was the rider and keeper of what lived within his naked body. I saw again what looked like a young man leave himself utterly bare. And this time he looked to me like little else—a lean boy, healthy but so very vulnerable despite the fearsome bones and scars sewn into his skin. His skin milky with moonlight and sweat.

I wanted to go up to Gévaudan, hold his face in my hands and pull open those blushing cheeks, take out my blade and cut that skin off him to help free what hid beneath. He bared his teeth—a movement of his lips and face so familiar to me now—and shoved his clothes and boots and knife into one of his fardels. He handed me this bag of his possessions. It was very heavy, and the straps hurt against my shoulders. Gévaudan took a rope from the thrown fardels at his feet, uncoiled it in haste, and wrapped it around his neck.

I wondered if he was about to throttle himself in front of me, full as these shape-changers' lives were with strange ritual. Though honestly, I think humans are no less bound.

He slipped his fingers under the noose he had tied, testing it. He then threw the rope to me. I caught it instinctively.

"The knot is loose," said Gévaudan. "When I emanate, the noose will widen but hold. Let the rope guide you to my second self. When you are upon its back, tighten the rope and don't let go. The rope will help you stay on. Tie it around your waist, so we're—" He seemed to lose his breath, wiping his mouth. *So we're bound.*

I looked at the rope in my hands, pale under the moonlight.

A leash, I didn't say. "Thank you," I said. I tied the rope around my waist with both hands as he walked away, letting the coils fall beneath the stalks and disappear. An umbilicus also, I thought, seeing the rough hemp trail away right below my navel.

Gévaudan stood in the millet rubbing his genitals, the rope hanging from his neck. I should have felt horror at this sight. But wearing this man's possessions on my back, having seen this once before, I knew it wasn't a desire for my body that heated his blood and stiffened his cock. It was a desire for emanation, for his second self, for what was about to happen. But despite the glow in his eyes, he was scared like he hadn't been when he changed this morning.

And there was also the rope around his neck, in my sweaty palms, around my hips.

"The blindfold," he said.

The ritual was little different from the first time—the blindfolding, the cutting of my arm, the wait. The rebirth—the tapestry of the universe itself torn and woven again twenty paces from me. The rope whipped through my grasp as the noose expanded.

My blood against the stalks, an offering taken rustling, serpent-tongue licking my arm.

The smell of the thing filled my lungs and cleared my heavy head, banishing the trembling in my limbs. So overwhelming it made me gag, flushed me with new energy, new spit in my mouth.

Somewhere, Fenrir answered the newborn—reborn—creature's roar with a lowing that stirred the earth and caught in the treetops, emptied them of birds awoken from their roosts. I only heard their wings from under the blindfold as they burst into the night sky. With the rope in my hands I climbed on my companion's second self, carrying my belongings and the belongings of its first self. Feeling for the rocky blades of its spine under hide and mane, I straddled that ridge and pulled hard on the rope to leash this mighty djinn to my hands. An illusion, perhaps—but a powerful one.

The djinn that lived in Gévaudan didn't maul me. It didn't devour me. For the second time it accepted me as its passenger, its rider. One soul, upon two.

Cold wind hit my blindfolded face, pushing out tears that dried quickly on my cheeks. There was nothing like that release, and it was only after I had it again that I knew how much I craved it. Darkness, yet freedom from everything, from life, from the growing child in my belly, from thought and worry. It was a waking dream, like flying across the earth as I did in my sleep. So freed that I couldn't think of anything but the wind against me, the animal miracle holding my body up—a blessing. The fur underneath the only thing keeping me tethered to my real, easily broken flesh. A cloak of insects followed us, caught in the thundering djinn's fur. Their wings and legs flickered all over me, tickling my skin and eyes and mouth. The rope taut in my hands and around my waist as I held on for life, my thighs locked and cramping against the shifting crags of sinew and spine, warmed by strange fire raging in the heart that pounded below me. I wished it would run even faster so that I'd fly off it like a bird and come crashing to the earth, the breath of my child-to-be driven from my body by the impact.

Always I was aware of the other presence behind us, so near that I wondered if the beast under me was running or being chased.

Yet on Gévaudan's heart-locked djinn I could feel little fear of what followed us, or anything, really. I let go of the rope and clung to the beast's back as if I were its offspring, clutching its thick mane with my hands and pushing my face and chest into sharp fur and muscle, not caring that my chafed palms were getting cut. With my fingers and toes in the tangle of its hide, the crags became warm earth, and the wind that swept over us felt like time slipping away from me.

Under that blindfold the fur in my fists became wild grass on a late-summer night, and next to me on the dewy earth was my mother sitting on her side, and above us were the same stars we rode under, Gévaudan's second self and I, but much clearer without winter's mist to fade them. I lay on a djinn, and I also lay on the ground on my belly, safe and warm, a small fire of twigs crackling next to us. My mother patiently held her blade to the flames till it glowed like a slice of orange peel. Squinting against the sparks, she dropped a bead of hashish on the blade and huffed the milky smoke that sprang out. Her eyes were amber in the glow. "Careful. And go easy, child," she said, voice heavy as she exhaled and I leaned in. We shared the sweet smoke and let gobbets swim from our mouths to the night sky. Just the two of us on a little broken island of the past, hurtling across a river of time, carried on the back of the djinn that swam it. Somewhere else, the Bazigars we traveled with washed their hands and feet in a river of water, not time, performing ablutions after supper. My mother spit on the blade and drove it in the ground to cool. A tarnished but valued tool, bartered off a farmer for some of our food, to be carried by me if, when, she died. She had, as far as I knew, never used that old blade for violence.

"Hold on tight, Mama," I said to her. "This ground, it's carried on the back of a great djinn who hides within a white man. It's running as it carries us on its back, years from this moment. It runs fast, very fast, so hold on tight."

My mother's eyes rolled in pleasure as she leaned her head back, hair spilling out of her dupatta and falling to the ground. "You're stoned as a goat with a bellyful of ganja, sweetheart," she said, her laughter coarse from the hot smoke. I nudged her arm lightly. Her skin was cool against my knuckles. "Shh. Goats have cooler heads than you or I. They don't get high from eating ganja trees," I said, though I had no idea what goats did or didn't.

She looked at me and smiled. "Always took after Scheherazade, you. Night after night, finishing every story I told by yourself, outdoing the queen herself."

"You're here," I said.

She laughed as if I'd made a joke. "I'm here," she said, taking my hand in her rough fingers and blowing on my knuckles. Her breath raised goose bumps on my hand. I stared at the little hairs blossoming under my mother's breath, until I remembered to grab hold of the grass so I wouldn't fall off the world.

A storm loomed in the distance, a thundercloud blotting the stars above that island in time, lightning showing the form of a ravening dog—a great wolf humbled to terrible rage. Tusk and claw unseen, spit a hissing rain on the leaves.

INTERVAL

Before I know it summer's gone like the blink of a firefly's abdomen, and it's puja season. The stranger and I walk around the city in the midst of festive crowds, taking in the illuminated drawings that decorate the streets—tableaux made out of strings of Christmas lights, twisted with pagan irony into designs and animals against bamboo banners and arches to celebrate Durga Puja.

We visit a few pandals. Inside, the stranger smiles at the idols of Durga, wrapped in human-woven sarees and garlands and bedecked in human-made jewelry, holding cheaply fashioned but shiny human-made weapons, towering over slain asura Mahishasura, also given modesty in the moment of his death by a human-woven loincloth. Of course, their flesh was also shaped and given the color of life by human hands. The blood pouring from Mahishasura's wounds paint mixed and applied by brush. The stranger looks at these deities incarnated in dried earth and made to represent good and evil, and he tells me they are iconic human representations of witnessed shape-shifter battles from millennia ago. That the devi and her monstrous asura foe were from different tribes of the race he belongs to.

In the pandal at Maddox Square, he points to the lion, the vahana by Durga's side, her animal vehicle, and tells me it is either a representation of one of Durga's non-human selves or a fellow shape-shifter in its non-human self. Like a teacher the stranger then points to the fanged human shape of demon god Mahishasura emerging from the lion-mauled carcass of the bull—mahish—that he turned into to trick

Durga, and knowingly comments that it is a stylized way of showing the inexplicable—a shape-shifter transforming from a non-human self to a human one.

"Why does human-shaped Durga have so many arms then? Did she try and turn into a giant spider and fail?" I ask him. He ignores my admittedly weak joke. Though I also meant it as a real question. Who am I to judge the normality of shape-shifters in a remote prehistoric past?

"Maybe that was one of her shapes," he says. "Durga and Mahishasura might not have been restricted to that duality, the first and second self. Apollonian and the Dionysian, as someone once said," he breathes out, stirring the hair that hangs over his forehead.

"Shape-shifters were once more powerful than that," he says loudly, almost shouting in the midst of all the people, but the collective babble inside the pandal is so loud no one even looks up. With a flourish of his hands he makes even the act of wringing sweat from his beard graceful. Wiping his hand on his kurta, he lowers his voice again, leaning in close to me. His breath warm against my ear. "We held in ourselves the multitudes of this planet, the birds and the beasts, the trees, the wind, and the sea. We could be anything, make ourselves in the world's image. We touched the infinite. We *were* the infinite." He puts one arm around my shoulder, fingers grasping, caught in this sermon given under a goddess and a demon that he claims share his origins. We sway with the waves of the crowd ebbing and flowing against us, shoulders and arms damp.

"All your oldest tales show it. Now we have fallen far from the myriads we once held in ourselves, the legions and illusions we could emanate. The beings that humans of this subcontinent memorialized as the goddess Durga and the demon god Mahishasura were more divine, in a classical sense, than I or my kin. Closer to the infinite than anything in this world, this time, could ever dream. Me, I have only myself, and the other. We are powerful, my second self and I, but we cannot be anything, only ourselves. We can change, of course. I can become some*one* else." His fingers slip away from my shoulder, tracing a brief tingle across my back. "But so can any human, with some effort," he says, and it feels like his eyes have fallen on me. I look, and he's staring at Durga and Mahishasura with the ardor of the devout.

I'm fascinated by all this, but ask no more, because it feels like he's sunk once again into one of his unpredictable bouts of melancholy.

"Or maybe the many arms of Durga are just an embellishment," he says, fingers raking through his beard again. "Creative license. Maybe the notion that shape-shifters ever held more than two selves within them is a fabrication based on your stories. Our own myth. Sometimes I think we're just making all this up as we go along, like you." He shrugs.

"Like me? What do you mean?"

"Don't be deliberately obtuse, Alok. I mean humans, obviously," he says and walks out of the pandal. I follow, wondering whether to laugh. I do, a little, but it's just to get rid of the uneasiness in me. Even in my most relaxed moments with him, I cannot, in all honesty, ever get used to him referring to humans as something he isn't.

I feel protective of him as I watch him walk into the throng in the square, as if he might dissolve into it.

I take him to a packed Café Coffee Day nearby, though he hates Kolkata's franchise coffee shops, with their deafening music and blinding lights, their young baristas eternally stunned by their own mandated politeness and their customers' lack thereof. Surely you don't need to be half werewolf to have that original opinion, I tell him, and when he is unmoved I ask him for the first time in our admittedly short relationship if something is wrong.

He seems alarmed that I'd ask him that, and he quickly drinks his coffee to cover up that alarm, that slight blush that touched his face. "No," he says with finality, grimacing at his drip coffee, taken black.

For all the fantasies he's fed me, this seems the most certain and blatant lie I've heard from him.

But I nod along. To ease his mood, I talk about myself, the way he likes. I tell him how much I miss my parents during the puja season, because it reminds me of when they took me pandal-hopping as a child, telling me to pray quietly in front of the idols for a minute before letting me·run around dodging the legs of the other visitors, pretending I was Durga chasing the demon bull through a forest and hacking it to bits so the asura revealed its human form. Then we'd go and eat out somewhere like Mocambo or Peter Cat (there weren't a ton of choices back in the day), followed by a visit to New Market and Nahoum's, where the floors would be muddy from all the puja shoppers walking in out of the rain, and I'd leave my little fingerprints all over the glass panes of display cases asking for this and that, and my parents, basking in my joy, would splurge on multiple boxes of brownies and fruitcake and whatever else I desired.

"Have you tried going back and establishing contact with them again? Just saying hello?" the stranger asks.

"It's not like I stopped seeing them. I went over occasionally, but it's so awkward, so bizarre to talk to the people who created and raised me as if they're acquaintances that I stopped doing that, even. It was too much to take."

"You are the one who cut off contact."

"No. They did, emotionally. I just matched their move."

"All this over a canceled engagement." The stranger raises an eyebrow.

"Well, it's complicated. Families are complicated. History is complicated. You know."

"I certainly do, Alok," he says, looking down at his cup. "So you haven't spoken to your parents since you stopped visiting. Even though you live in the same city."

"On the phone sometimes. Not really."

"You're hoping that if you wait long enough, they will call you and ask you to come over, and the ice will have melted a little."

"I suppose. Yes."

"And the puja season would be a likely time for them to call, considering that they share the same memories of their boy running around pandals and asking for brownies at Nahoum's."

I nod, and give him a weak smile. Without even trying, I seem to have matched the stranger's melancholic mood.

"Your parents haven't obliged this narrative," he says. I shake my head.

"You're their only child. Give it some more time." I shrug.

He is silent.

Then he says, "Did you know that I actually visited Nahoum and Sons bakery when it first opened its doors in New Market, perhaps a decade or so after the twentieth century began. I met the proprietor, a Jewish gentleman from Baghdad, and shook his hand. I was still getting used to mingling into the populace of a human city, so he didn't take to my demeanor, but he served me like everyone else who'd lined up. New Market was actually still new back then, its bricks red as a robin's breast instead of the brown of dried blood."

I laugh. "Now you're just making things up. I'm *sure* you just happened to be at the bakery my parents took me to regularly. When it first opened. In the 1900s."

The stranger smiles. "No way to tell."

"No way to tell," I agree, and sip my mocha.

"Well, we're not in Nahoum's," he says. "But at the very least, let me buy you a brownie this puja season."

"If you insist." I shrug and laugh, though to be honest I feel like crying. How could he say something like that in this moment, something so lacking in his mystique, something so sappy and simple? I'm almost sickened by the sentiment. No commiseration, no telling me about whatever utterly strange family life he might or might not have, and yet his appreciation for my matching of his mood, giving him company, is palpable enough to break me.

I'm very glad when he gets up to buy us both brownies in hot chocolate sauce, and I can hastily use a paper napkin to wipe my eyes and pretend to clean my glasses.

As Durga Puja turns into Diwali the stranger falls silent on our walks, while fire blossoms in the sky and crackers mist the streets with smoke. In his eyes the sparklers of strangers, held out over balconies, showering footpaths with glowing rain. He looks exposed in the light of all this chemical fire. We hide from it all in the windowless shelter of packed bars along Park Street, or walking the narrow alleys of Tangra's depopulating Chinatown. As we eat Hakka cuisine by the pale glow of decorative aquariums, I'm inspired by the surroundings, and try to raise the subject of syncretism within the tribes he and his manuscript have mentioned—with certain overarching belief systems, rituals, and customs (the kindling of the "ghost fires" of prey, the unique shared words, the concepts of multiple selves, the taboo of sex with humans, the notion of the second self as sacred and never to be seen by humans unless they're about to be dead or changed, et cetera) coexisting alongside other disparate tribal systems.

He agrees that it would be one way to describe things, but doesn't engage, ordering gin and tonics instead, flipping through the freshly transcribed pages I've given him. I want to ask him if he learned the habit of gin and tonics from British colonials who invented the drink, with its cocktail of quinine and alcohol to ward off malaria. But I don't want the question to be misconstrued as mockery. I can't imagine that he sipped mixed drinks from glasses much in those days.

But I feel a difference between us on these late-October nights, as if he's distancing himself a little.

When we meet on Park Street on the final night of Diwali, he hails a cab and asks the driver to take us to Prinsep Ghat. There, we cross the Greco-Roman pillars of the monument to the dead Englishman who gave the place its name, cross the hard white fluorescents, silent tracks, and empty platforms of the local railway station, cross an unlit dirt road, and reach the clustered groves that huddle on the waters of the Hooghly.

All so familiar, though I haven't been in a while. It's one of the places where Shayani and I would escape on summer nights. Here on the broken ghat steps leading to the river, we'd sit and talk while sharing melted Cadbury's milk chocolate bars, licking the sweetness from each other's fingers and mouths until mosquitoes, other amorous visitors, or the puritanical patrols of the Kolkata Police drove us away.

I wonder if I'm wrong to be touched that the stranger remembered this spot from our conversations. I wonder what it means that he brought us here, of all places, for solace from the noise and crowds of the pujas. Whether it means anything at all. We watch ripples shimmer quiet under the lights of Vidyasagar Setu, the horizon on the other side of the bridge glowing with occasional fireworks. The moored rowboats used to take tourists on rides during the day bob on reflections, empty now. I sit by the stranger's side as he smokes up, the smell of hash now like a familiar cologne on him. I listen as he remembers the days when imperial boats rocked over that river. As he remembers, in the same conversation, watching *An American Werewolf in London* from the rat-haunted balcony rows of New Empire cinema in the mid-1980s, claiming it was the first werewolf movie he ever watched, and a particularly surreal experience. What his notion of surreality might be, I can only imagine. But something feels off, as if he's doing this, telling his stories, to achieve some kind of symmetry, because it's usually me telling him about my uninteresting life. As if he fears silence between us. But I let him, because it feels like he needs to talk, even if his heart isn't in it.

As we sit, three men walk by behind us on the path above the ghat steps. I know they are three men because of their voices, and because I look behind us to see their dark shapes mottle the unlit tree-lined path. The sky's dull red glow, soaked from the city's light, gives the landscape color enough to see by. As the men pass, they trail a jarring laughter that stinks of drunken, pack-fueled confidence. Then they go silent, their dusty footsteps stopping. Some murmured words.

The stranger and I stop talking.

I hear my own heartbeat quicken my blood. I look behind us again at the shapes of the men, one of their shadowed faces graced with the cyclopean dot of a lit cigarette. They're watching us. I hear a long, soft exhalation from the stranger's lips, blowing out smoke. He doesn't look behind us.

The footsteps begin again. But they don't move away down the path. They come closer, down the ghat steps toward us. "Ah, fuck," I whisper. The stranger says nothing. The footsteps grow louder until they surround us. The scuffing sound of their relaxed gait stops right behind us, replaced by the familiar singsong whistle of a man leering at something he wants power over. His two friends are standing about two feet on either side of us. I don't look up at any of them.

"Are we disturbing you?" asks one of them in Hindi. The ground sparks as a cigarette butt lands right by my feet.

The stranger says nothing. I feel a growing sense of betrayal at this, as the seconds grow long. "No," I say, looking straight ahead at the river and its bobbing boats. I sound very meek to my ears. I remember men occasionally catcalling when I sat here with Shayani. I would do nothing but hold her, and it would be enough. It was never this late, never this abandoned. We'd just leave, and everything would be fine.

I hear flies unzipping in unison on either side of us.

I'm sweating now, despite the cool breeze blowing off the water. I've been afraid of the stranger, but I'm shocked in this moment at how abstract a fear it's become.

What I feel now is like that fear turned bitter. There is no magic here, in being threatened by three bored, ignorant young men with ugly thoughts. Now I *want* the stranger to be fearsome. And he's just a man sitting next to me, and that makes me want to throw up in front of these three other men, also strangers, with their smell of testosterone and alcohol.

"Don't mind us. Go on with your romantic evening," another voice says. The other man, standing nearer the stranger. A cackle behind us. I hear piss hitting the ground and spattering down the steps into mud and water. Then another stream, from another man's penis. Two men, pissing on either side of us, while their friend watches behind us. I keep my eyes straight ahead. We're surrounded.

It goes on forever and ever, until I imagine these rivers of piss flooding the Hooghly in front of us, sloshing and frothing and rising up to drown us. Any moment, I expect to feel it warm and wet against my body instead of the ground. Tears brim in my eyes as they go on pissing right next to us, and the stranger does nothing but smoke his joint.

Then, as suddenly as this moment in time began, it ends. The two men shake off, zip up their flies, and walk away laughing and patting each other on the back, leaving nothing but the wet-soil smell of their urine in the earth. As they vanish into the shadows of the path, their catcalls ring out over the Hooghly, fading with distance. The stranger gets up, throws away his roach. I want to ask him what he was doing sitting there silently, but then, why shouldn't he have been? What else would I ask him? Why he didn't turn into a monster and chase them away or, better, slaughter them right in front of me? The men didn't attack us. They didn't touch us. They didn't threaten to hurt us openly. Perhaps the wisest thing was to remain silent. So I remain silent, now.

I wipe my eyes, shaking with anger and shame.

The stranger laughs a little as he looks over the water, brushing off his butt.

"What the fuck," I say, voice shaking like the rest of me. "What the fuck are you laughing at? We could have gotten hurt."

His tall, slender silhouette is unmoving against the dark-red river and the sparks of city light borne on its waves. The horizon glows again, a thump against the clouds, as if from a distant war on the edge of the city. "Hurt. By those uncouth changras? No, Alok. We couldn't have gotten hurt," he says, and walks a couple of steps to where one of them pissed. He sits on his haunches and runs his fingers through the wet ground, sniffs them. "Them, on the other hand," he says. "They don't even know."

It's my turn to laugh. I get up quickly, viciously hitting myself to shake off the dirt.

"Are you kidding me?" I ask the stranger. "You . . . I *still* don't even know your name, and I'm sitting here with you in the fucking dark in the middle of the night, and we're nearly fucking beaten up by three drunk assholes and you run your hand through some dirty piss on the ground and I'm supposed to be impressed? I'm supposed to be hypnotized into your magical world and think, what, that you're going to remember their scent and hunt them down and kill them very impressively and very conveniently when I'm not around? No. Sorry. That's just fucking disgusting, that's not magical, that's not inspiring. That you just did that in front of me is disgusting."

The stranger looks at me, his face dark like the men now gone, their piss on his fingers.

"Oh, I understand," the stranger says, very calm. "You wanted something different. You wanted . . . fear. Is that it? Did you want me to scare those bad men like they scared you? Did you want *me,* perhaps, my dear Professor, to scare *you* like those bad men scared you?"

The stranger takes his fingers and puts them to his mouth, sucking them clean loudly.

"You want magic, Alok? Stories on the page aren't enough for you? Certainly, then. I'll show you a little magic trick. Real magic." He licks his fingers again, sniffs. "I can tell they drank cheap whiskey tonight. Royal Stag. Your brand, Alok." A little whisper of a laugh.

"One of them has diabetes, and probably won't know it till he dies from it. Are you impressed yet?" He spits.

The shame doesn't go away, but I feel something else uncoil in me, riding the adrenaline in my blood. I don't know why, but I find that I can't bring myself to walk away down that path alone, and whether that's because I don't actually want to leave or because of my fear of the catcalling men I don't know.

The wet ground crunches under his feet as he walks toward me. My mouth floods with salt and saliva, my bladder bulging with piss, like the piss on the ground and on the stranger's fingertips and lips.

"What do you want me to do, Alok? Chase them down? They're not that far. I can still hear them, smell them. Tell me," he says, his voice silken, unfamiliar. "Your wish is my fucking command."

Uncomfortably, horribly, I feel my disturbed blood rushing to my cock, stretching at the crotch of my jeans. I step back, breathing hard. I imagine him hunting those bigots down, his glorious, hulking second self a shadow along the Hooghly, tearing each of those awful young men open from throat to balls, painting the white pillars of Prinsep's monument with blood, hurling their heads onto the street for taxis to send tumbling across the tarmac in bony thumps. All for me.

"I want to go home. Forget tonight. Forget all of what just happened," I say. I take deep breaths, taming the gorge rising up from my gut.

He is silent for a beat, letting the breeze lift the bottom of his kurta so it clings to his long legs.

"Then you'll go home, Alok. You don't need me for that," he says. I

consider the thought of riding with him in a taxi tonight, and it makes
the sweat on me turn cold.

"Yes," I say, still not turning to walk away.

"Are we going to see each other again? Are you abandoning your
job?" he asks. The manuscript, the transcription. I've still got pages
left. I've been going slow deliberately. His voice is sharper, harder. It is,
again, unfamiliar to me—there's a note of panic that I've never heard
before. It only strengthens the unraveling in me. In just one moment,
we're both afraid. We're both afraid now.

"No," I say.

He nods. In the weak light I see his fists unclench. I hadn't noticed
that he'd clenched them. "Remember, you made a promise," he says,
his voice gone even lower.

"I know," I say, barely able to muster the breath. My throat dry. "I'll
finish the job. I just want to go home right now, if that's all right."

"Good," he says. His teeth squeak as they grind against one another,
and I wince at the sound. "Home, yes. That's completely all right. I
advise it. I'm sure you'll find a taxi on the road. If not, just walk till you
do, and don't stop."

"You're . . ."

"Staying here, yes. Leave. It's clearly not safe for you. I don't know
why I brought you here."

"It's all right. I feel, strange, for having said those things. I shouldn't
be angry at you, you're not the one who—"

"I did something disgusting in front of you, remember?"

"Yes." I nod, adjusting my jeans and wiping my face. "You've done
a lot of things that I wouldn't expect. You've shown me things I
wouldn't expect. Amazing things."

"I wasn't apologizing," he says.

"Okay," I say, lowering my chin in a slight nod.

There's a musk coming strong off him, like onions rotting in honey.
Even in the midnight gloaming, his face indistinct, I can feel his smile
from six feet away.

"Go home, Alok. Quickly," he says. "Please."

I waste no more time. Catcallers or not, I walk away, walk on down the dark path and past the harsh blue light of the small Prinsep station and its empty tracks and platforms. Walk on by the lit-up monument and on to the blessedly bright road beyond. I don't look behind me. "Don't hurt them. Don't hurt them," I whisper to myself, like the coward I am. I don't encounter the three men. After several failed attempts I finally find a cab willing to take me, and I go home. It feels like I'm following a command, the stranger's words resounding in my head.

When I'm finally in bed at three in the morning, the adrenaline still hasn't burned away. I'm left watching the streetlights cast shadows on my thin curtains, the pattern of leaves on the tree that crowds my bedroom view. I turn on the geyser, take a shower. I masturbate under the lukewarm water, feverish with arousal. I watch the come wash away under the water as if it never existed, never came out of my warm, blood-beating body. Still unable to sleep, I return to the manuscript in the manila envelope, return to the stranger's calming handwriting. Once again I let myself become the conduit for this story he's given me, a conduit for this woman who's nothing but a ghost in language, if she ever even lived. She, ghost that I quietly carry, is the only one in my life who knows of the people the stranger comes from. The people. Even here in the privacy of my home, I write, *the people*. Shape-shifters. I'm a man of my time, and this is not their time. I cling, I cling to Cyrah, because honestly I don't understand anything that's going on, and I never have. The world makes no more or no less sense with shape-shifters in it.

The stranger exists. This manuscript he gave me exists. The woman in the manuscript exists, if only in words. All this I know. And despite whatever just happened, I can't imagine not seeing the stranger again, can't imagine turning my back on this entirely unexpected phase of my life and just going back to what was there before. Who's to say the stranger would even allow me to walk away? The thought that he might not is actually comforting. This is why I have trouble sleeping.

I keep typing till my eyelids grow heavy, the sky going from dark red to light blue outside.

My dreams, ever faithful, are filled with terrible monsters and skewed, magic-haunted worlds from the past. In them, I often find that I'm a woman.

And so it was. I rode on the back of Gévaudan's djinn a second time and lived to tell the tale.

I don't know how many humans, and especially how many human women, have done such a thing. By the time I slid off its back warm with morning it felt like I was the first in all of history, since time itself began. I fell to the ground soaked in our shared sweat, its fur gone slick and foaming over a night of running. I threw up as soon as my limbs touched ground, to purge its overpowering smell from my throat and nose, empty myself of the tension and exhilaration of the night that had passed. I sat on the ground awhile, listening hard for the sound of a massive animal just vanishing into thin air.

I heard nothing but lapping water and birds greeting the day. When I took off the blindfold the djinn was gone, and Gévaudan crouched naked and steaming twenty paces from me. We were once again by a clear expanse of water into which sunrise poured all its light. The Yamuna again, or perhaps a tributary. The rope hung limp from Gévaudan's shining shoulders, the coils of hemp leading to my belly, to the knot above my navel, still intact. I untied it.

I threw down the heavy fardel with Gévaudan's clothes and blade, not looking at my companion. He remained quiet, panting hard. It had been a long run. I don't think he—they—had stopped even once during the night. I wondered what weight I was to such a being as it ran.

I looked at the blindfold, now dark not just with Fenrir's browned blood but with my tears and sweat and grime. The wound down my wrist was dark, scabbing already. The djinn's spit was a powerful salve. Gévaudan's stinking, muddy cloak hung heavy like a caul congealed on me over the night. I threw it off and went to the river, where I carefully washed my wounds once more. The water was ice-cold and jolted me to the bone. I washed under my clothes, washed away blood and dirt till the thin lines of wounds were bright against clean skin, washed my face till it felt so numb I laughed just to feel my cheeks move. My teeth chattered. There wasn't a speck of fur, hair, or anything at all on me from the creature I'd ridden upon. Behind me somewhere, I heard Gévaudan getting dressed.

I cried out softly when I ran the wintry water over my belly. My gut tightened, and I laid my hand over the hard, flat muscle under my navel. Wet, cold like marble. A hard palace for you, soon to turn soft. I shook my head and spat in the water.

That morning we reached the mud walls of Shahjahanabad, then still newly built by Shah Jahan to replace Akbar's old capital. I had lived in Akbarabad before, and it is a magnificent city. But this was the first time I had seen its replacement. We arrived at the Akbarabad gate, through which runs the southern road that leads to that city. I was by now accustomed to the extravagant architectures that Shah Jahan raised throughout the empire, especially with Mumtaz Mahal's famous tomb always rising up in the distance from Mumtazabad. Cracked and crude in the dry air of winter, the mud walls that surrounded Shahjahanabad looked most shoddy compared with the mighty stone walls of Akbarabad. But once we were inside (Gévaudan had a strange effect on the soldiers and customs officials at the gate, who didn't seem too perturbed to see such a strange-looking white man with a poor Mughal woman), I couldn't help but be awed by the gleaming red sandstone walls of the scaffolded Qila-Mubarak* on the horizon, incomplete but towering over the tumult of the town; the broad avenues swollen like rivers with waves of people; the rows of fresh-planted trees sheltering every thoroughfare; the gilded copper domes of new masjids† rising on all sides to complement the distant edifice of the fortress.

But even as I took in the marvels of this newly built city, something clawed inside me, making me want to leave this glorious settlement, to escape back into the wilderness of the spaces between the cities and towns. I was surprised by how foreign I felt in the midst of all this

---

* The Blessed Fortress, also known as the Red Fort, which still stands in the center of Delhi.

† Mosques.

human life, after just two days outside the walls of civilization with Gévaudan.

I found Gévaudan looking sweaty and out of sorts, and I wondered if he felt the same thing. He had seemed quite at ease being among people in Mumtazabad. As we walked up the wide road that is called Faiz Bazaar, I turned to him. He was silent, inspecting the vaulted arcades of the bazaar rising above the numerous shops on either side of the road.

"Why did you run from him, last night?" I asked gently.

He sniffed sharply as if he'd smelled something bad. "I didn't run. I needed to emanate," he said. He couldn't look me in the eye. "We have followed him. He will have detected this, he's old enough," he said, and wiped his damp face. "Your blood and my musk combined in one. It's a message he won't ignore. He is coming to us, trust me."

"We've found him, then. So why are we here, in the city?"

He bared his teeth, making a guttural exclamation in another language. "Do you do nothing but ask miserable fucking questions? Fenrir might not be very happy to see the two of us together, have you thought of that? He might challenge me in his second self, without preamble, head clouded with what he thinks is love. And I don't know if I can defeat him."

Me riding on the back of his second self, clutching his hide with my human hands. He hadn't expected that. Not one bit. No more than I had. I looked into his wide eyes, saw the beads of sweat trickling down his forehead. How could I stand up to Fenrir if Gévaudan was afraid to?

"I'm sorry," I said. "You're right. We need to be careful." Gévaudan nodded, calming a bit.

"He is more powerful than I. He has lived for many more centuries. I need to talk to him first. He won't challenge me here in these crowds, in the middle of a human city. But he will find us. Very soon."

"Very well. Then let him find us." I touched his hand in reassurance, quick so no one would see, but made confident by now that no one would say anything even if they did. He flinched but said nothing. It was a stupid thing, that. I shouldn't have touched his hand. I wanted to tell him not to be afraid, but I knew not to. The long cut on my forearm throbbed.

What he thinks is love. My stomach churned. I could not smell Fenrir's return like Gévaudan could, but I imagined in that moment that I could feel him in the distance as I had last night, feel him approaching again like a howling monsoon storm. After all, even having been raped by him, I had seen only the calm that came before.

If Fenrir was near, he was also keeping himself hidden.

Gévaudan grew more and more agitated, saying little to me. It felt more and more like traveling with a shy and overgrown boy who'd sunk deep into himself. We wandered Shahjahanabad always looking behind us, though I found welcome distraction in the many sights I saw. The imperial elephants circling in their sandy arena between the waters of the Yamuna and the walls of the Qila-Mubarak, their pebbled skins made glossy with black paint, trunks blushed with vermillion, tusks clattering in the late-morning air. The parrot-pole on one street, where the nobles took turns in shooting at the bright-green bird tied to the top (it survived all the attempts we saw, whether blessed or because the nobles were drunk or secretly fond of it I cannot say). The vaulted mansions of nobility, each the center of a thriving mahalla* filled with the thatched mud-and-brick houses of the people who make the lives of those in the mansions easy. The endless wares under the arcades of bazaars that put Mumtazabad to shame, overflowing with foodstuffs and luxuries from all the corners of the empire and beyond, all overseen by the incessant babbling of merchants—there were bales of finest cotton, perfumes, precious stones; beef and mutton; partridges, ducks, geese, and various other birds raising havoc with their cries as they fluttered among the displayed carcasses of their brethren, as if fanning away the clouds of flies that crawled over their dead; there were raisins and almonds and pistachios in aromatic piles; plantains and pineapples and mangoes and prunes and apricots and

---

* A self-contained district or quarter of a Mughal city.

Allah only knows what else. I'm beginning to sound like a merchant myself, listing off wares like a fool. Aching all over and stomach hollow with hunger, eager to numb the constant sense of having gone utterly mad in the past two days, I gorged on sweetmeats and fruits and nuts till sick.

Gévaudan ate nothing. I became concerned that he wasn't just nervous about Fenrir, but physically craving the flesh of a human being. I had no idea how the appetites of a shape-shifter waxed and waned, and the very thought made me shove it from my mind in fear. I regretted eating as much as I did in front of him, in the bazaars.

I was exhausted by the time the sun began to set, more so than when we had been traveling in the countryside. When it became clear Fenrir would not show himself, Gévaudan and I retired to one of the numerous caravanserais in the city. Like Fenrir, he had plenty of money to dispense with, so I didn't have to spend any of my pointless new wealth. Once again I slept on a mattress instead of hard ground, under roof instead of starry sky. I can't deny that I slept well, but it was but half a relief to be back in a serai chamber dozing off to the flickering light of a taper, as if nothing had changed since Mumtazabad. Less than two weeks had passed since I first met Fenrir, but it felt like years to me, lying there thinking about what I had discovered in these days, thinking about the mysteries on the other side of Shahjahanabad's mud walls. I wished my mother were there to guide me through this, that we could discover this new world together, and protect each other from its unfathomable dangers.

Next morning, I saw Gévaudan talking with an Englishman also at the caravanserai with his retinue. It was strange to see him talk to a fellow white man, because the two standing side by side looked as different as I would standing next to a white woman from France. I recognized the language they spoke as English, and I suppose I shouldn't have been surprised that Gévaudan could speak it, though he sounded most different from the other man.

The Englishman wore the clothes I would expect of a man from a European kingdom, unlike Gévaudan—strange-cut coats and breeches in dull colors, though he sometimes walked around wearing a white shash that looked a little ridiculous wrapped around his puffy pink head, and he also swaddled his shoulders with a cotton dupatta. Always he would carry a sword and dagger at his waist, tucked into a girdle. The man looked like he found Gévaudan's clothes and bearing distasteful. I suppose that shouldn't have surprised me, in that the Englishman shared my own first reaction to my traveling companion and his friends. But the Englishman also seemed very interested in conversing with him, and he often looked at me as if I were an exotic ornament Gévaudan was carrying around, albeit one gilded with poison.

I asked Gévaudan about the Englishman, when we were eating at one of the open-air stalls in the plaza near Akbarabadi-Mahal Masjid. I was basking in the warmth of the smoking iron plates on which the naan baked, taking deep breaths as the stalls filled the air with their comforting burnt-flour smell. We stood by the stall as the bakers handed us the flaps of fresh bread, rubbed with salt and ghee and nestled in pattals, hot against our hands through the leaf. I waved away flies lazily as Gévaudan spoke.

"He is a trader for one of the European trading associations, the British East India Company. His name is Edward Courten," Gévaudan explained, not bothered by the hot naan in his hand.

"Eid-waad Kow-ten," I said.

Gévaudan grinned, something he had not done for a while. He tore a bit of naan with his fingers, tossing it into his mouth, though he didn't seem to like the bread very much.

"Do you take only to raw meat, Jevah-dan?" I asked, a little jaunty, as if I were joking. I was actually genuinely curious.

"No. The things khrissals do with their food interest me. Bread is a useless bit of fluff, invented by the grain-obsessed farmers that preceded all of your modern civilizations and weakened you to the frail and small-mouthed creatures you are now. But I've always favored it as a plaything of the palate. This Khorassian bread, not so much. I prefer the loaf the French make, that they call the baguette. It is fuller and better baked, and more interesting to my tongue."

I noticed how he sometimes talked about humans to me as if I weren't one myself.

"Bah-get." He grinned again as I repeated the French word. I wondered if I would ever get to taste such a thing, though I don't think any kind of bread can be better than naan. I wondered if the Englishman brought his English food with him to this land.

"Well? What are you talking to him so much for, then?" I asked. Gévaudan stared at me as if he hadn't heard.

"The Englishman. I've barely seen you talk to anyone."

"He is a curious man. Like a fly in my ear, buzzing. He wants to know where I'm from, what manner of man I am, what religion I follow. He fancies himself an adventurer, I think. He wondered if I am a white man reformed to the ways of some obscure tribe here."

"And what have you been telling him?"

"That I am a Frenchman and a pagan, that I can speak his language and yours with equal ease. It fascinates him that I am not a Christian. And that too with a Moorish wife. We are a most curious pair of heathens in his eyes."

"A wife?" I raised my eyebrows.

"He has assumed that you are my wife, yes. I didn't deny it. Everyone probably assumes that anyway."

I shook my head. "I don't care what anyone thinks when they see us, as long as you don't think that I'm your wife."

He grunted. "What do you think?" he asked.

"Fine. Never mind that. I understand that this Englishman is curious about you, but what about him fascinates you as well? Have you never seen a fellow white man before?"

He grunted. "He may have his uses. This Courten has a qafila* of many men and animals that he is taking east to Masulipatam, a trading post on the Coromandel Coast. He's willing to let us travel with him in it. I can't stay in this pigsty of a city much longer. Traveling with Courten gives us the option of staying surrounded by people while still moving. Fenrir will not attack in the midst of so many humans, and he will have the opportunity to come forward and intercept us peaceably."

"Pigsty. This city is one of the finest in the empire, probably in all of Europe and Asia taken together."

"You know what I mean. All khrissal cities are pigsties." He looked at me. "To my senses," he added.

"Are we just going east with this Englishman?"

"For now, we will head in that direction. That's where Makedon, Fenrir, and I were originally headed. I don't intend to go all the way to the trading post with this company man, but for now his route will be convenient. North and east of the coast, in the land that is called Bengal, there is said to be a vast jungle at the mouth of the River Ganges, a land between the river and the sea, where many tribes of our kind dwell in solitude. We wanted to see if we could make peace with them, forge an alliance of some sort instead of ending up fighting them like the djinn tribes in Khorasan."

"Tribes . . . like you said before. Like you, but not. Tribes from this land."

"Yes. From here. Several other packs were headed east when the exodus began, hoping to meet the tribes of the Hindustan and find out

* Caravan.

their ways, share new hunting grounds here in this empire. I just want somewhere to take refuge, hunt, and live in peace."

"And what of me, Jevah-dan? I cannot follow you to this place."

"You will go where you please. No one's stopping you."

"And Fen-eer?"

"I told you, Cyrah. He's going to find us, damn it." He quickly lost any hint of good humor. "He's close," he breathed loud, his eyes darting in his still head.

"All right." *You have no idea what we're doing,* I didn't say. That dance between two shape-shifters, still going on.

"Courten's qafila leaves tomorrow, and us with it," he said. "Then perhaps Fenrir will show himself, once we're out of the city. And we can put an end to this."

An end. The end.

I nodded, chewing on my naan and letting myself drift into the noise of the plaza, the shouts of the bakers, the chatter of their other patrons, the whine of flies, perhaps only to distract myself from the ceaseless thoughts clotting my head. Gévaudan sniffed, squinting at the sunlight pouring into the stall from beyond the domes of the masjid and lighting up the smoke and steam. Flies crawled over his pale face, making it look unhealthy, as if sculpted from damp cheese. The naan in my mouth lost its taste as I fought a sudden panic. When I looked again, my breathing fast and vision dampening with blotches, Gévaudan looked almost like a sweet white boy squinting in the sunlight. I looked away quickly.

That evening, Gévaudan and I took a walk to see the new square in the center of the city, which had been given the name Chandni-Chauk.* It wasn't lost to me that we looked like husband and wife—though severely mismatched in appearance—walking together after the sun had set. To be honest, I'd grown accustomed to being looked upon as such. It gave me a sense of safety, of invisibility—a wife (even that of a strange

---

* Moonlit Plaza. One of the main thoroughfares of Shahjahanabad, and now of Old Delhi. The marketplace was established by Princess Jahanara, Shah Jahan's daughter.

white man), after all, is not a bazaar-whore without a harem. That's not to say that we weren't noticed; we certainly were. But they noticed the Mughal wife of a barbaric-looking and unapproachable white man. They didn't notice me.

It was my idea to see the Chandni-Chauk, as I'd heard of its beauty. It surprised me when Gévaudan agreed to accompany me there. He looked a little better than yesterday. The square held a large tank that gathered the waters of the River of Paradise, the canal that runs through the city. The pool reflected perfectly the night sky, which was, to my luck, graced with a crisp, waxing moon. We saw its twin glittering in the ripples of the pool, as the architects of the plaza must have wanted. We walked down the broad western road, under the shade of the trees that sifted the moonlight like flour. We saw the great serai that Jaha-nara Begum, the emperor's eldest daughter, had endowed to the city—the windows in its high two-storied walls winking with the tapers and lamps of only the wealthiest Persian and Uzbek merchants who were allowed beyond its towered boundary, its gates guarded by soldiers. All around us, the flames of the market still danced on the waters of the burbling River of Paradise as the shops and inns began closing down for the night. The distant voice of a muaddin calling out azan from the high minarets of Fatehpuri Masjid gave the air music.

"Do you still think human cities are pigsties?" I asked Gévaudan as we walked along the canal. A light mist hovered over the water, mak-ing the moonbeams under the trees glow.

"You can no more convince me otherwise than I could show you a swine's mud-heap and expect you to be impressed. Here I assume you wouldn't be impressed by a swine's mud-heap. Never know with you all," he says.

I prevented myself from smiling, not even sure if he was jesting.

"Surely this makes some impression on you—the endeavors of men and women, who've created such refuges in the wilderness of this world."

"It is a pretty thing, yes, like a bird's nest, or an anthill, or the sug-ared palaces bees build their queens. I've seen many cities; Paris and London and Constantinople may look different from this place, but they are the same, when you come down to it. Perhaps without the flocks of khrissals wandering their streets such cities would be worth some admiration, as monuments to futility," he says.

"I know you'll say these things. And yet I ask, again and again."

"Then stop asking," he said. I smiled, this time.

"Fenrir is the one who's enamored with such things. He talks like one of your poets when he starts on about the works of your civilizations," he said.

"Again you bring him into it. I have no interest in his opinion on anything."

"You confound me like no human before you. You seek Fenrir like a hound, like no human I've known has ever sought one of our kind, or should. And yet you won't even talk about the one you seek," he said and looked away, his breath heavy, making that awful noise he made when he gritted his teeth.

"What is it, Jevah-dan? What do you want to tell me about Fen-eer? Does it bother you that I hate your friend? Is that it? Have you forgotten what he's done to me? Or is there something else?"

He looked out over the water, shaking his head.

"I know why you stay with me despite everything that tells you not to. What you want from me," he said.

"Ah." I laughed, the back of my throat salty. "I suppose you're going to tell me what it is that I want. Men have a habit of doing that," I said, wiping my nose. "I know, you're not a man," I whispered.

He took a deep breath. "I can't kill him, Cyrah," he said.

I can't be sure, but it was probably that moment when I knew he felt for Fenrir something stronger than friendship, if friendship as humans define it even existed among their kind. I understood why he was following Fenrir.

"I don't want you to," I said. This was, I realized right there and then, not quite true. Maybe this *was* why I was still seeking Fenrir like a hound, as Gévaudan had it. What better chance for vengeance could I ever get than to try to befriend a being powerful enough to destroy the one who had wronged me? It was with a heavy heart that I continued talking.

"After he raped me, Fenrir left me with a vision. A memory, it felt like, or many memories, of him watching mothers with their children.

It felt real. My rapist dared, he dared put me in *his* head, watching women with their young, to teach me a lesson. To make me want this child. I don't think you can imagine what that felt like."

Gévaudan said nothing.

"I will not meet a djinn from Europe, with such magic that we feeble humans can only dream of, only to be slighted by him in the manner of every other vulgar, common *man* I've had to contend with in my life. To let him fade into the night is to become his victim—I will see him again. I will have my reckoning, whatever that may be."

"All well told, and in some universe admirable. But you'd be wise to remain afraid of him. I shouldn't be traveling with you. You are khrissal. It compromises me. I don't know how he'll react."

"Then I am sorry, Jevah-dan, for putting you in this position."

"I've made my own choices, and you yours. You needn't be sorry."

"You are in no way indentured to me, nor I to you. If you want, you can part ways with me at any time."

I heard a guttural sound deep down in his throat, and his body trembled, as if stifling a spasm. I stepped away from him. "You don't tell me that. I know that. I know that," he said through clenched teeth, his eyes turned away from me. The bone trinkets jittery. I tried to calm my fear.

"I just thought that you should hear that from me. I expect nothing," I said, swallowing against a quickening heart.

His throat grated with great gulping breaths. I saw his ear twitch, as if listening to the distant muaddin's lyrical recitations drifting in the air.

He managed a small nod.

"I'm grateful to you for trusting me. For what you've shown me."

"I've shown you nothing. You are still blind, little khrissal."

"Less blind than any other human you've met, I'm sure. I'm still grateful."

"How well you argue for your own demise, Cyrah," he whispered. "I'll admit. I'll admit it. I don't know what I'm doing. Fenrir has exiled himself by fucking you. And yet I run after an exile, a powerful, bitter one, with none other than the khrissal he transgressed with."

"I won't question why you're doing that. But you've been kind, in your own fashion. I thank you for that. I don't stand a chance against you, should you want to kill me and devour me. You are a hunter, after all, like Fen-eer is. A hunter of my kind. But I will fight back, in whatever way I can, should you try."

"I've no doubt about that, little khrissal. None at all." He smiled then, as I knew he would.

We left Shahjahanabad at dawn with Courten's qafila, on camels bought from the Englishman. Before we left, Gévaudan told me something in the courtyard as he brought forward our steeds, his voice low.

"You might hear of this from someone else, so let it be known now. Courten told me that guards found a dead body some streets down from this caravanserai. A woman. Beheaded and torn open. Emptied of her guts, he said. He is suitably horrified."

"Why are you telling me this?" I said.

"You know why, Cyrah," he said, his eyes constantly flicking away from me. "Just more reason to keep moving. I didn't want you to hear it from someone else."

I suddenly felt like forgoing breakfast. A dead body, close to the caravanserai, on streets we had been walking just last evening. This could well have been the work of Fenrir, but I didn't know what Gévaudan was doing after we returned, either. He still looked out of sorts, but better than the previous day. Perhaps he had been unable to resist his hunger. It was clear that Gévaudan was telling me so I wouldn't suspect him. If I heard it from someone else, it wouldn't do him any favors. I tried not to think about this too hard, sweat gathering under my dupatta.

With this ill omen to hound us, we set out.

It was a difficult trip from the start. The Englishman Courten constantly enlisted Gévaudan as a translator so that he could better mediate the constant squabbles between the cameleers, who were Muslim Baluchs, and the ox-drivers, who were Hindu Jats. It became clearer to me that Gévaudan's skill with languages was one of the reasons Courten had agreed to let us travel with his qafila. Out of the walls of Shahjahanabad, I looked constantly to the wilderness around us, expecting that great wolf, that mangy dog to be standing by a tree watching us. In the meanwhile, I remained wary of Gévaudan's clear discomfort.

In the evening, we came across a troupe of Bazigars. They entertained the qafila with their dancing, juggling, and acrobatics. I found out from Gévaudan that in Europe they have people much like the Bazigars, who call themselves Romani. I was delighted by the show, and filled with an abundance of memories that warmed me along with the fire. Though the men of our qafila leered at the dancing women, the Bazigars gyrated without fear of shame, as I'd once done when I, too, traveled with such a troupe. Their arms and faces shone like gold in the firelight from sweat running free down their skin, and their long hair danced with them, leaping around their heads. I saw Courten observing them like a hawk. From the clapping of the Bazigars' palms and the peals of their laughter, the thumping of their bare feet on the ground raising dust to thicken the light of the bonfire, I was moved almost to tears.

After the dancing was done, I went up to one of the Bazigars. She watched me walk up to her, brushing aside the long veil of her hair to get a better look at me. Her locks were so thick they made a waterfall, turning her for a quick second into a giant peering from behind parted water. Strands of silver caught the firelight as it fell into that darkness around her head.

"Hm," she grunted, licking the red sheen of betel juice on her lips. "Not a Hindu, though you dress like one. Your eyes are too light," she said in Hindawi.

I smiled. Such cheap declarations were their way, as they tended to tell fortunes as well. She was right, of course, though I'm sure light-eyed Hindus are not impossible creatures.

"Yes. I hail from the Khorasan, but this is my home."

She shouted something in a dialect I didn't understand, startling me. But it was to one of the other Bazigars some distance away, a man with a long beard who was juggling some apples before stashing them into a sack. He said something back to her, and she laughed.

"Have you come to buy a basket?" she asked, going back to Hindawi.

"No. Just to—" I paused, looking at her hardened arms, the callused thickness of her hands as they danced around knots, tying baskets to her camel. "I don't know." I thought of telling her I'd once traveled with Bazigars, but thought better of it. They have different clans and religions, after all. What did she care who I traveled with, once upon a time?

I looked around, wary. She frowned but said nothing, continuing to tie her knots and chew her betel. I reached under my shawl and into the pouch tied to my hip.

"For your troubles," I said, and held four mohurs out in my palm, looking behind me to make sure no one was watching carefully.

Her thick eyebrows betrayed some surprise at the value of the coins, but she took them without hesitation and vanished them into her person. "I've no troubles that I know of," she said with a smile, "that require others to pay me for them. But thank you. You're a sweet girl. I hope your rich white husband isn't as cruel a young fellow as he looks, or as barbaric as his clothes."

To my surprise, she raised her hand and brushed her fingers across my cheek. I could feel her fingertips rough against my skin.

"You're welcome to come with us, you know. We offer our hospitality to anyone in need. If you have troubles unseen that can't be solved by these coins you carry, and dare to steal away into the night when no one's looking, we'll be on the road heading south, and in no haste." I barely noticed myself touching my cheek where she had, and leaving my fingers there.

"You've no idea how much that means to me," I said. "I'll remember that. And no, he's not even my husband. I made a choice to travel with him."

She nodded. "Barely a minute known, and you're already a mystery. Good."

"Farewell, and peace be with you," I told her, and hurried away. I saw her smile and nod as she got on her steed. As the troupe left in the opposite direction as the caravan, I watched them with a leaden heart.

By the time the sun had set on the second day, one of the carts had already broken in two, and the entire qafila was uneasy from the distant, dreadful howling that had plagued us all night. Some of the workmen swore they also heard the guttural belching of a larger creature than a wolf or a jackal, and that a lion or a wandering tiger from the heartlands of Hindustan was stalking us. The more superstitious said the journey was cursed with a more supernatural hunter.

Courten cared little for any of these murmurs, having lost a cart. Several fardels of his saltpeter and indigo lay mired in the ground under a cold winter rain, turning the puddles blue with seepage, much to the Englishman's anger and dismay. I assumed he much regretted his decision to take a longer course so that he could see the abandoned imperial city of Fatehpur Sikri before turning east. The hired Jats and Baluchs salvaged what they could, pulling the extra fardels onto their oxen, their corded arms shining from rain and exertion under the lanterns. I watched Courten bark in broken Hindawi to the yeomen as they toiled, and watched the yeomen pay no regard to him. Soon enough, the Baluchs and the Jats were fighting again.

"What are they shouting about now?" I asked Gévaudan, pulling my cloak tighter around me, rainwater trickling past my cowl and dampening the shawl underneath.

"What?" Gévaudan mumbled, looking dazed.

"Never mind," I said. I don't know why I asked, really. No, I do. It was because his anxiety had only increased since we left the gates of Shahjahanabad. He was always peering beyond the bustle of the caravan and into the distance, always sweating despite the cold, always brooding and silent. I just wanted him to speak, to relieve my own tension at seeing him this way.

"One of the camel drivers is missing," Gévaudan said, as if finally hearing my question. "They suspect the Hindu ox-drivers of murdering him last night and leaving him somewhere beyond the road."

"The Englishman knows?"

"Of course he knows. He cares little. He thinks the missing camel-
eer simply deserted his duties and ran back to town."

"Do you think the missing man ran away?"

"I don't care."

"He was killed, wasn't he? But not by the Jats. You would be able to
smell something like that. If someone's blood was spilled last night. He
was killed, and taken. You know."

"There are many humans and animals in this qafila. I smell nothing
but their shit and dirt, all the time."

And Fenrir. I knew he could smell Fenrir as well, following us.

I heard the slap of fists on flesh as two men came to blows. Under
the wildly swinging lanterns I saw the two men churning the muddy
ground with their limbs, others trying to pull them apart. I saw the
glimmer of red mouths and wet beards as the men spit their blood on
each other, their arms a blur of motion, cracking as they hit each other.

"Aren't you going to help the Englishman talk to them?" I asked
Gévaudan.

"I've had enough translating. Courten can deal with his own men.
It's his fault they're fighting. Overworks them so they blame one another, then ignores them when one of their own goes missing," he said,
sullen.

"It was kind of you to give what help you could."

"Kindness has nothing to do with it," he snapped.

"Then why?"

The smell of his sweat came through despite the rain that washed
his furs and face. He wore no cowl since I wore his cloak, so his hair
stuck to his face. He didn't answer me, glaring instead at the violence
unfolding fifteen paces away as if it mesmerized him.

The two men were finally tugged apart by their respective allies,
who continued to shout at each other, while Courten and some other
white men tried to overcome them all with the volume of their own
shouting. The blood of the two men glowed bright under the flame-lit
rain. Gévaudan sniffed the air.

"Worms in ash. Maybe this was a mistake," he said, so soft I almost
didn't hear him. But he said it, nonetheless, in Pashto, not any other
language.

After the skirmish between the cameleers and the ox-drivers, Courten called for the qafila to make a maqam[*] because of the turmoil and the weather. The hundreds in the caravan spread out for what seemed a mile, many lying under blankets in the open rain. There were many tents pitched as well, glowing like serried cloth lamps in the darkness, the shadows of their occupants flapping against them, trapped moths.

Gévaudan and I sat in the rain next to our resting camels, having no tent to pitch. It wasn't long before a gruff Armenian (one of the white stragglers Courten had in the qafila) came up to us and told Gévaudan in English that Courten had invited us to his tent. We followed the man through the camp, past the lowing camels and oxen, miserable in the rain, past tents and knots of people huddled together against the chill, looking up at Gévaudan and me with suspicion. But they were more wary of one another than this strange-looking white man and his commoner wife. In any other circumstances we would probably have been the center of attention amid such a mix of people, but the caravan had already reached a boiling point just two days out, and the Baluchs and Jats had set up invisible walls between each other, always on the watch for sneak attacks from either side. I had been in caravans before, and severe wounding, even murder, was not unheard of when men in them began to fight.

I looked longingly beyond the tents and the people at the pitch-black night, wishing I could be out there instead. How I had looked

---

[*] Daily camp/assembly on a journey.

with fear at the wilderness, at the threats it presented to one who is always alone, and how quickly this had changed. That was, of course, the least of what had changed for me in recent times.

We arrived at Courten's large tent, steam and smoke escaping from the open flap, lit from within. The Armenian gestured and walked away. Gévaudan and I ducked inside. At the very least, I was grateful to be out of the rain. It smelled of wood smoke, damp clothes, and lentils inside.

The Englishman was sitting on a little wooden stool with its legs sunken into the soft ground. He was hunched over a little fire that made the air inside the tent gritty. My eyes watered. A lantern also guttered with its own flame, next to the stool. The shash was off Courten's head so his chestnut curls glistened, damp like everything in the camp. He looked tired but glad to see us, or probably just Gévaudan: someone who could speak his language well.

He gestured us inside. I was surprised by how cheerful he seemed, despite the turmoil in his camp.

He started talking too fast for me to remember any words of what he said, but he gestured to the tin pot over the fire. Clay bowls were passed around, into which we took the khichri bubbling in the pot, and he gave us some stiff pieces of naan to dip in it. The supper was quite bland, as there seemed to be no spices but salt in the pot, but it was good of Courten to share his food, and I wasn't about to complain.

"You are strange, for a wife of this land," Courten said to me, in crude Hindawi. I assumed he meant that I had a strange choice of husband.

"You, too, are strange to me, Englishman," I replied in the same language. Gévaudan sat and watched us both, impassive.

"There is more, behind you both, I can't see it. There is more," he said, his words slow to come out of his mouth, which was glistening with the soup of the khichri. Though it was clear he had trouble speaking Hindawi, this manner of speaking made him sound sinister to my ears.

"Isn't there always," I muttered, filling my mouth with naan in the hope he would stop talking to me. He grinned, his teeth looking very yellow, perhaps because of how pale his skin was.

"You are Muslim?" he asked me. Gévaudan looked at me.

"Yes, I am."

"You are not, eh, covering yourself," he said, waving his hand over his face.

"My husband does not ask me to, so I don't."

"Your husband is not one for Allah, I see. Yes?"

"That is his business. He is my lord, and I do not question his beliefs."

"And what are they?" he asked.

"It is not my place to say."

"No, no. Of course it is not. Would it interest you, lady, to know that I do not see anybody like your husband where I'm coming from? He is a very interesting man."

Courten smiled, and flinched a little when Gévaudan shifted in his seat, clearing his throat. The Englishman had a wild look to him, his watery gray eyes wide open. I admired his fierce curiosity in the face of all the obstacles he had encountered, alone and mired in a foreign land. He was clearly fascinated by Gévaudan and me. This scared me, of course, but I too was curious to be so close to an Englishman, and to be inside his private space.

We ate, the small space of the tent filled with the sounds of loud slurping and chewing from the men. To clear the air, Courten offered Gévaudan something that looked like wine, from a corked glass bottle. I wasn't offered any, though this was unsurprising. Perhaps he knew that Muslims are not meant to partake of spirits, or perhaps he just thought it uncouth for a woman to drink wine. I don't know the customs of his people, after all. It was unusual enough that I'd been invited inside the tent. Courten and Gévaudan began to talk in English while I marveled at the clutter in his tent—it was so filled with various possessions that it felt more like a permanent room than a transient habitation. His swords and daggers gleamed in the shadows, stacked right next to a musket. There were chests and saddlebags piled together like bricks for the walls of the tent. Next to his unfurled bedroll was a fat book made in the European fashion, upon which was a silver necklace with the Christian emblem they call the crucifix.

* * *

I excused myself after I was done eating, as Courten and Gévaudan were talking in English and I couldn't understand. Gévaudan gave me a small glance that might have been concern, but I ignored it and stepped back outside. I waited in the rain until the supper was done.

"He presses me," Gévaudan said, sitting outside with me afterward. "About how I came to marry you. Where I'm from, where I'm going. He's starting to irritate me. He doesn't know how close he's coming to death."

"Don't say that. We're surrounded by humans. Don't kill him. Please."

"I'm not stupid. Of course I won't kill him. He's beginning to annoy me, that's all. And if I did kill him, it would be an easy thing to escape. We can leave this wretched qafila anytime we want."

"Maybe we should, then."

He grunted, and licked rainwater into his mouth as it trickled down his face.

"What did you tell the Englishman?" I asked.

"I tell him nothing. Fancies. I tell him I believe in nothing like his Jesus and one God, that I follow only nature, and want only to wander this land. He sees the bones hanging off me, my raiment. He thinks I'm a warlock on the run from Europe. And that's true, in some way, I suppose. But he has no belief in magic, except that of his religion."

"He won't have you arrested or killed, will he?"

"It wouldn't be so easy to do either to me, but no. He doesn't care to. It seems in England their fear of our kind is receding, as Fenrir sometimes predicted. It's been several years since I talked to a human from Europe for any length of time. This Courten, he thinks I'm a man with delusional beliefs in a pagan religion. That's all. It doesn't even pass his mind that I could be something more than human." Gévaudan seemed quite surprised by this as he told me.

"It's been a while since you set out on the migration?" I asked.

"Yes. A while."

"There must be a reason he's pressing you like this. He wants something."

"Courten wants me to lead him to some lost tribe of escaped witches and warlocks from Europe, hiding here in Hindustan. He thinks that's where I'm headed, to a gathering of exiled heathens. He thinks it will be a great discovery and, recorded in his journals, will make him a prosperous and famous man in England when he returns."

"He wants to write about you?" I asked, somewhat alarmed on Gévaudan's behalf.

"I don't care if he does. I've told him nothing. Though he has no idea how close his theory is to a truth. He would thank me, if he knew what meeting the tribes would lead to for him."

"He's a clever man, isn't he? To have guessed so much just by look-ing at you."

Gévaudan looked at me, breath white as it escaped his mouth. I could barely see his face, but his eyes caught what light came to us from the tents and lanterns around the camp.

"Courten's cleverness means nothing. He's arrogant. He believes I'm a man, and nothing more. He believes in his one Christian God, and no other. He believes in his empire and its ways, and no other. If he were truly clever, clever enough to believe what I am, he'd end up no more than a pile of shit between my legs, all the endeavors of his little life a morsel dream in my head, his tailbone an ivory bauble to hang from my skin to remind me that khrissals are little more than monkeys that forgot how to swing from the trees."

I felt a strange pain at the vicious bite he put into his words, spitting them into the rain-slashed air. I felt as if this sudden revulsion were directed at me. I may not have been English or Christian like Courten, but I was after all a human, though it was so easy to forget that in those days, living in the twilight between humanity and these shape-changers. I didn't show this hurt, of course. I could also see that Gévaudan was in a way shaken by Courten's manner, his lack of super-stition. Why this should be, I couldn't tell, since it appeared to me that he had left Europe because of the superstitions of man, and the perse-cutions that spread from them.

I searched and searched for something, anything, to say that would diffuse that deep, animal loathing for me that underlined everything Gévaudan did and said. Even in the moments when he seemed most human, it was as if he were pushing that instinct away for a moment, not overcoming it. I knew it wasn't me he was reacting against, but my whole race; man or woman, young or old, pale or dark, Christian or Muslim or Hindu, we were all khrissals. He saw me as meat to sink his teeth into, to chew up and swallow and shit out. When I talked to him, conversed with him as if he were a true companion, when I shared with him the aspects of my one and singular self, it evoked some form of visceral disgust or anger that I couldn't begin to understand.

The rain pattered down on us without respite, dripping off the cowl of my cloak. I searched and I searched, and I said it.

"You were once human, Jevah-dan. Isn't that right? Fen-eer told me so. You all were, once." Even as I said it my heart hammered in my ears, pushing the sound of rain into a faint hiss beyond my cowled head.

He didn't offer any reaction, let alone violence or anger. He seemed to think about it, for an endless moment.

"Yes," he said.

I exhaled, my relief overpowering. I waited to regain my breath, and asked him, "Do you remember that?"

"In a way. Like a dream. It's for you . . ." He drifted back into silence.

"What is? What's for me?" I urged him.

"It's for you that I say I was human. So that you may understand. But that was something else. *I* was born the moment my soul was bifurcated. The human that existed before is just an aspect of me now. It never was me. His life exists in my head like a dream, like the dream-lives of all the khrissals I've devoured in my life. But dreams fade until they have little meaning that resembles their origin. In my own way I've lived the lives of many humans, but I cannot know what it means to be human any more than you can truly understand what the worlds of your dreams mean."

"And what do you dream of, then, Gévaudan, when you sleep?"

"Many things. The lives. The lives I've eaten."

"How old were you when—how old was the human, when you were born?"

"He was a young man. I was birthed by a tribe in Paris, who lived amid the cemeteries and underground quarries of that city, and hunted the streets at night. And they still do, I've no doubt."

"Was that a long time ago?" I asked.

"For you, yes. For the tribes, I am very young still."

"You look like a young man. Your kind does not age."

"We do. Much slower than khrissals. In your estimation we can, perhaps, live forever." He paused and looked around. There was no one in earshot, though maybe he was looking beyond the camp, rather than in it. I could see he wasn't done, so I let him speak.

"I remember my first human kill. That is the moment the first self stops aging, after the first ritual killing and devouring of a human. If one's soul is split when he is just a little babe, his first self is allowed to age somewhat like a khrissal would, though faster than a khrissal child. He goes through the phases of childhood, eating only animals or human flesh procured by his elders, until he comes of age and hunts his first khrissal prey. For me, I didn't have long to wait, since my first self already held the shape of a matured man."

You're blabbering again, I thought in wonder, and I could only be grateful. I shivered as he continued, his words soft, distant though he was right next to me. Whether this was out of caution or simply because he was transported back to a different time in his head, I couldn't tell.

"It was days after I was born, after the injuries done to tear that man's soul in two to create . . . me, after those injuries had healed. My imakhr and his pack chased a man from the midnight streets, hounding him into the yards of the Cimetière des Saints-Innocents, where the Parisians piled their dead, and where my tribe scavenged when they were not hunting. There under a full moon, among the heaped dead, I slew him in my second self, fresh-sprung, while my imakhr watched, and there I acquired the insight to transcend the mortality of my prey, and truly be one among the tribes."

I waited for him. He said nothing more. I had no idea what this Paris would look like, but just his words, the way he pronounced them, evoked something in me, as if his entire body exuded the essence of his memory, as if I could smell and feel what he had back then.

"This . . . This ima . . . That word you said. That was your parent?"

"We have no mother or father. He was my imakhr. I suppose to a khrissal that would be a parent, but it is not. He was my guide. He was many times my mate also. When one's soul is torn in two, one is . . ." He paused to give a very quick laugh, an innocent curl of the lip that betrayed some fleeting joy in that young face, for just a moment before returning it to its recent dour expression.

"Overwhelmed, by the new birth. The imakhr fucks the new shape-shifter, to ease its delirium, control its wonder."

"He was a man."

"His first self was a man, at that time."

"Why didn't he come with you on the migration?"

"Maybe he did. I left Paris a while ago, to explore the rest of Europe. What he has done since is not for me to know."

"Do you miss him?" I asked.

"I don't miss anyone. That is the province of those who love, and love is a folly of khrissals."

I clenched my teeth. That had been an obvious mistake to make, far too obvious. Somehow I thought he'd be tricked by the question, miss the implications of it, though I hadn't consciously tried to trick him. But the rote recitation of his words blatantly betrayed his guilt. I don't know if he ever loved his imakhr, but I knew, by now I knew that he loved Fenrir. And I knew, for him and Fenrir, love was a sin.

You love Fenrir, I wanted to tell him. I let the words form on my tongue, tried to free them from my lips, but couldn't.

"You said your mother died. Was that long ago?" he asked.

I sat there shocked for a moment. I couldn't believe that he was asking me something, instead of the other way around. Something personal, something about my life as a human. It was, as far as I could remember, the first time. Perhaps he knew what I was thinking, wanted to steer my mind back to myself.

"She— Not that long ago. I haven't been alive that long. Especially compared with you, I'd think. She was a young woman still when she died. People would often mistake us for sisters: she the elder, I the younger."

"She was very young when she bore you."

"Barely more than a child." I took a deep breath. "She didn't expect me. She was very poor, and she was raped, too."

The rain fell over his head, endless, making me almost angry that he didn't cover his head. He was soaked, unmoved. A statue. I wondered if he felt any sympathy. Why was he even performing this pretense of humanity, this interest in my affairs? Why was he mimicking what I had done moments earlier, when I asked about his past?

"She left Kandahar when she found out she was with child, and a merchant traveling to Lahore took pity on her. She never was very clear about what that meant, but I think he just kidnapped her on the way, and used her as he willed. But how much of that is just my own bitterness, tainting her life?"

I felt that familiar ache of rage rise up inside me, only stoked by Gévaudan's lack of reaction. But I went on. He had asked, and I would tell. I had listened, and he would, too. Certainly we deserved that, after he had bared a part of his soul forbidden to my eyes, and I had let my blood for his tongue.

"Still, whatever it was, he took her in, and didn't care that she was a mother. In Lahore he had her trained as a tawaif, educated in song and dance and lore. He had her taught to read and write. I remember that city, though not well. Growing up in the mansion of the zamindar, playing in his gardens. Once I grew older, we left his house. Again, I'm not sure what happened, whether he got nervous and kicked us out, or whether my mother got sick of living there, or what. My mother headed east to Akbarabad, where the imperial court was, with the money he'd given her. He said she'd be a fine courtesan in the imperial harem. She never got close. She danced and whored herself out in caravans and serais, but she was no courtesan. We traveled for a time with the Bazigars, who were kind to us, and we pretended we were like them—nomads, entertainers. But friendly as they were, we could never be one of them, either, as they have their own clans. But we went with them on the roads when we could. My mother taught me what she could, what she knew. Then she died of a wretched disease."

I heard the patter of rain on our bodies and the ground. The sounds of the camp had died down. Light still flickered in some of the tents. Many of the hired men were still awake, but they talked in hushed tones that I couldn't hear over the rain. Gévaudan's jaw was clenched. The anger bubbling in me had simmered down to a painful throb that pushed tears out of my eyes. I rubbed them away and stanched them, taking deep breaths of the cold air, heavy with the smell of wet earth. My cowl dripped on, cold drops on my nose.

Gévaudan's head snapped up. He looked past me, toward the edge of the camp.

"What?"

He said nothing, staring, his ears twitching through his soggy curls.

The sounds came to my ears as well. Shouts at the edge of camp, a wave of activity spreading outward from the distance as more people were roused from their state of rest. The blossoming lights of new lanterns and firebrands lit.

"They're dead," Gévaudan said.

"Who is?"

"The men Courten sent back to buy a cart, and more camels. They've been killed. One got away."

"How . . ."

"I can hear what they're saying. Not bandits." He paused, listening.

"An animal. A beast. Rakshasa, he calls it."

"Demon," I whispered. I had heard the word used before by the Hindus.

"He's here," said Gévaudan.

I can't describe the rest of that night to you. I will try, but the terror that overcame me was like nothing I'd ever experienced before—it was the inverse of what I had felt riding across the world on the spiny back of Gévaudan's second self. That night, I was reminded that Iblis[*] was of the djinn, a shape-shifter like the man sitting next to me, like the man out there beyond the firelight of the maqam. I saw how our ancestors saw their race in the shadows and wrote the legends we now know.

Courten had sent four men back to Akbarabad; one came back, covered in blood from head to toe, foaming at the mouth from frenzied fear, struck with the immovable belief that he had witnessed something not of nature, a dread miracle, a man changing into an awful, gigantic animal. The survivor was a Jat, and for him the beast of supernature that he saw killing his companions was a rakshasa. For the Baluchs who looked on fearfully it was, perhaps, a djinn, a wandering ghul brought on a fell wind from the northeastern deserts. For Courten it was a large animal that had turned man-eater—a great wolf, a tiger, a lion. The survivor wept, and said their attacker was greater than all those animals.

Courten scoffed at these claims, but I saw him rubbing his crucifix in one hand.

* * *

[*] The devil, in Islam.

It didn't matter what anyone thought, in the end.

Fenrir's roar split the black sky like a bolt of unseen lightning, so loud it felt impossible, heralding his approach. Gévaudan took my hand, unheeding of his own strength.

A chorus of terrible screams rose up all around us, and for a moment I was frozen with horror, thinking that something inexplicable was happening, that the roar we had heard had overturned nature itself, made the dead rise from the ground in pain. It took me a moment to realize it was the lowing of the oxen and camels as they stirred awake throughout the camp, all woken by the unearthly cry of our intruder.

I cried out as I felt my hand crushed in Gévaudan's grip. He didn't even notice, his eyes wide. "We need to get out of here," he said.

He began pulling me through the crowd.

I grimaced through the pain in my hand, which I was unable to free from Gévaudan's. "Maybe it's just an animal, Jevah-dan," I gasped, hoping that he would say yes, it probably was.

"It's Fenrir. He has spoken. He has spoken. To me."

"What did he say?"

"I . . . I can't put it into your words."

"Please, you're hurting me." He let go, holding my wrist instead, lighter this time. My hand was numb.

I couldn't believe what I had done. In one moment, I lost all my desire to see Fenrir again, to have him make amends for what he'd done to me and take away his child from my belly. I felt like a coward, a betrayer of my own soul. I felt like a miserable little girl, cold and wet and afraid in the rain.

Another roar rumbled across the camp like thunder, turning to a bitter howl that seemed to last forever, drawing all the eyes of a woken camp to the outer edges of darkness that surrounded us. Gévaudan winced and shook his head.

"What is he saying? Please tell me."

Gévaudan ignored me, stumbling to his knees as we reached the pile of our belongings, next to the agitated camels. The animals had stood up in a panic and were trying to escape the pull of their tethers.

I grabbed the bundle that held my few meager things, slung it on my shoulder.

"I didn't think he'd do this. The city, we should have stayed in the city," Gévaudan said.

"What are we going to do? Run? We can't, he'll just outrun us!" Screams rang through the camp. They were human. Gévaudan squinted in their direction. I looked. People were running in all directions now, some grabbing their animals, a mob forming as panic spread. Fenrir had breached the camp.

I saw flashes glisten through sheets of rain as tents collapsed in the wake of something huge, lanterns exploding and setting new fires in the night. There were splintering crashes as carts tilted to the ground and spilled their freight, some toppled by fleeing animals, others hurled aside by the advancing intruder. Rippling flags of flame sprung from the fabric of fallen tents, marking out the path of the beast in the darkness. I saw something bright leave the ground in the distance and fly through the air in an arc toward us, like a falling star in the shape of a man. It *was* a man, his clothes and flesh burning, hurled into the air with inhuman strength. I watched him soar and return to the earth, crashing into the fleeing crowd, knocking several of them down into the muck. I heard the sound of all his bones breaking even through the tumult surrounding us.

"Come on," said Gévaudan, holding my wrist again. We left the camels (he hacked their tethers) and his fardels.

As I looked back, I heard the sharp pop of a musket, saw its muzzle light glittering in the rain. Courten, or one of his men. The beast responded. A roar burst across the crumbling camp, so deafening it hurt my ears, and I feared the rain trickling down the sides of my neck was blood. Gévaudan's fingers tightened on my wrist again, and then remembered how frail the bones of a human were.

"Get on my back," he said, bending low. "I can run much faster."

He sounded calm now, but his eyes were glazed like an opium-eater's. I fell on his broad back, covered in the coarse damp fur of his pelt-raiment, and put my arms on his shoulders, my hands locking around his neck. He lifted me off the ground and ran, knocking the breath from my gut. My legs flapped limp behind his, feet kicking at his thick calves. He didn't run as fast as his second self, but he did run faster than any man could. Several times fleeing men came in the way, and I heard the crack of their bones snapping or the slap of their flesh opening as he rammed into them and sent them sprawling. I closed my eyes tight through it, feeling sick. I had brought this upon them, these poor, hapless humans. My fellow humans. I had brought this upon them by seeking Fenrir, by following Gévaudan, by hoping to use the being under me to deliver penance to his friend.

Gévaudan didn't stop running till we were in the darkness beyond the camp, his legs working through the mud. If anyone saw us, they weren't following. Most of the qafila was fleeing on the road we had made maqam around, pouring down it in a tangled wave of animals and men. Their raw cries of confusion and horror; the spit and crackle echoes of the East India Company's few muskets; the firelit slivers of arrows let loose by those hired men who tried to fight back; the sparking bonfires and boiling steam of burning tents; all of this made it seem like some manic parade churning in the rain to welcome this dark and terrible djinn from a bitter land none of us had ever seen.

And there amid the despairing flock, there he was, Fenrir of the north.

The beast I'd imagined when he appeared at my curtain steeped in moonlight and fur, now sprung free from his human form. There it was, looming huge over everything, the eye of the storm pausing to observe the swirling chaos it had created. Surrounding it were corpses of men, oxen, camels opened to the rain, running with reddened rainwater. The beast was like no animal I'd ever seen on this earth. Glowing red in the flickering light of rain-swathed fires, with its war paint of blood and tattered flesh, which hung like ragged pennants off its spines and slicked fur, it was rakshasa of the Hindus, it was asura, lord among their demons. It was glowing, infernal ifreet of the djinn, it was Iblis made incarnate, rising from cold wet earth instead of the arid sand of the desert. It was a towering impostor god of Europe resurrected in this empty stretch of Shah Jahan's empire and worshipped with fire and violence.

I let go of Gévaudan, tumbling to the ground, the cloak clinging to me like a skin of slime now in the mud and the rain. "We have to go back. He'll kill them all. What are we doing? We must go back, Jevah-dan. It's us he's looking for."

"He'll kill you. At least I have a chance. He'll kill you, Cyrah."

"He won't. He thinks he loves me. He would have killed me in Mumtazabad if he wanted to."

"This is his second self. It won't hesitate like his first did. He'll rip you apart, and devour you and your soul."

"Why do you care?" I screamed, and I actually meant it. I wanted to know why.

He was stumped by the question, but another roar from the road broke the brief stupor.

"I can't. I can't do this," I whimpered, and my skin prickled as I felt the beast, a hundred yards away, turn its head and look at us. Or maybe it didn't, but that's what I felt. I turned, and even through rain and fire and smoke, I saw its eyes blaze like far-off suns. It howled again, making even the rain shiver in a wave that spattered my face, as if the sound were a baleful wind from this monster's dismal country.

I saw Gévaudan buckle to his knees, holding his ears. Spittle drooled in strings from his mouth, and he was saying words in a language I couldn't understand.

I started to scrabble toward the road again, blinking the rain from my eyes. I could see some of the men climbing onto the beast and plunging sharp weapons into it, and I applauded their bravery, but they looked like children clinging to a trembling giant. It plucked them from its sleeked wet fur with idle ease, using its jaws and tusked fangs, and it tossed them into the sea of bodies that swirled past it. It seemed to revel in whatever pain it received from the human weapons thrown against it. It moved slowly and then rippled with sudden speed, cleaving an ox in half with one swipe, the divided body crushing several men.

Gévaudan grabbed my cloak and pulled me back, sending me splashing back to the ground.

"Don't look at it," he shouted.

"It wants—he wants *me,*" I said, clambering up again. "Let me go to him. How can I run now? After all this? This is what I wanted. Those people are dying because of me."

"No, no," Gévaudan snarled, and returned to the babble of different languages he had sometimes dipped into, as if arguing with himself, his eyes darting in their sockets. He looked like he had when he was about to change shapes.

The beast had changed direction, tearing through the humans and oxen and camels, the stinging stampede writhing at its legs. It was leaving the road. It was coming toward us.

I got up, my heart hurting, swollen with terror. I would meet it. This was what I had traveled with its kin for. To meet the devil again. I ran toward it, but Gévaudan grabbed me.

Gévaudan's hand lashed out so quickly I didn't see it. But I felt his hand slap my neck, just by the throat. I heard it in my head like a thunderclap, and for a moment I couldn't breathe and I felt spit gush into my mouth and I felt my gut coil and I thought I had to vomit and I felt my heart stop its frightened drumming in my ears and the whine of silence flooded them instead. And then the world vanished, and darkness burst in like a great tide released by that approaching monster.

The rest I felt as if in a dream, rising in and out of darkness. I felt Gévaudan carry me in the arms of his second self (for the first time), felt the speed of his flight across the rainswept plains, the winds lashing at both of us as Fenrir remained always at the horizon behind us, a following storm; the ground shaking with the galloping of these two beasts, the burning caravan receding to a wavering line. I was paralyzed, whether by the blow or by some infernal glamour I didn't know. I felt Gévaudan slit my arm open with one long claw, lapping and sucking at me as Fenrir approached from afar.

They stopped then, far from the caravan.

I hung from Gévaudan's arms like one dead, he poised over me leechlike, his mouth daubed in my blood, which dripped in ruby lines down the slit in my arm. I don't know which shape he stayed in when he stopped to face his pursuer. Fenrir slouched in the distance, wary, the mud around him steaming with his heat, the rain boiling off his back. In the distance, the sounds of the fleeing survivors, the white men under Courten emptying the last of their gunpowder into the night air in panic, small lightning in the distance.

Did they both change back into their first selves? I can't say. But one way or the other, Fenrir said to Gévaudan, his eyes flooded with tears of rage: <<What have you done, you traitor?>>

<<I have done nothing. Come no closer.>>

<<Leave her be, or die like those khrissals back there.>>

<<So you can kill her, feast upon her, and have her for yourself, because she'll never come to you of her own accord?>>

<<You've sullied her, haven't you? In your jealous fit, you've done what I did.>>

And Fenrir's tears landed on the ground sizzling and spitting, and his claws dug into his palms to raise blood, his growl rolling across Gévaudan in a fearsome wave.

<<No. I've done no such thing.>>

And Fenrir looked at him and saw the truth. His tears ceased, and his growling slowed.

<<I see you. Makedon called you whelp, and whelp you are. I see you drink her blood, suck from her soul the memories of her night with me. You pretend to be her companion, but you just want what lies in her. You care nothing for the flesh itself, or the person it holds.>>

<<As you care only for the idea of a human lover, and for the idea of the child she carries.>>

<<You're so young. I see right through you, whelp. You wanted to devour Cyrah, and undertake the long sleep of ekh'du, to shape your first self into her form. That's why you took her with you on this journey—you were preparing to molt. You wanted to *be* her, so that I might love you back. You wanted to give Cyrah to me, in you, so that I might love her, and you.>>

And Gévaudan said nothing.

<<A bold idea and a beautiful sentiment, Gévaudan. If you'd had the courage to actually do it instead of merely wanting to, I might even have come with you. I might have seen past your betrayal and loved the shards of Cyrah's soul made manifest in yours, and in so doing nurtured your own sickly love. But you wouldn't have held a child for me. You wouldn't have sacrificed your second self for nine months.

And that alone would reveal the falsity of your new flesh. Even if it looked like Cyrah, it wouldn't have been.>>

<<You are the mightiest of all hypocrites in this world, Fenrir. How dare you lecture me, as if you were not the one who started this great fucking drama? *You* are the one who claimed to love a khrissal, and raped one. I had no great bond with Makedon, but we were a pack, Fenrir. We shared the ghost fires, and we ate of man and woman together. He was one of us. And it is because of you that he is dead, and by my forced hand.>>

Fenrir pounded the bubbling ground around him in fury, bellowing: <<I *created,* like the gods of humankind!>>

<<I *created,* like the lowliest khrissal can, and we cannot. I usher in a new age for us all, rather than calling the empty mating of our own kind by a human word. I have created progeny. You have created nothing. You couldn't even steal Cyrah's shape to create a new self of your own, let alone fashion something from the blood-loam of the womb.>>

So saying, Fenrir walked forward toward Gévaudan.

Gévaudan said: <<I will destroy your progeny and your human love with it, if you come closer.>>

And Fenrir smiled as a devil would.

<<Boy-whelp, you have tasted love, and instead of ridding yourself of it, you've languished in it, and now it infects your soul like a canker. It casts your world anew, and sickly pale, you see your love for me bleed across the chasm between your two souls, and you *understand.* You understand how one of our kind may love a khrissal, a small, fragile, beautiful human being.>>

And he roared so loud the clouds stilled their weeping, and he lunged at Gévaudan. And as Fenrir had foretold, Gévaudan spared my life, threw me aside so that I wasn't caught between these two unrighteous beings as they fought. Fenrir, flushed and engorged from his feast of humans, oxen, and camels from the ambush on the road, filled with power; Gévaudan, weakened from his abstinence from hunting for several days because of the company of humans, because, though I didn't know it for all those days, of a promise to me that he never even truly agreed to. Overpowered, his genitals crushed under Fenrir's knee, throat gripped in Fenrir's huge scarred hand, Fenrir's spittle running down his face and Fenrir's piss streaked over his chest and caved, empty belly, Gévaudan submitted to the challenge. And it was agreed that they would do battle.

In their first selves they returned to the site of the massacre, I slung senseless in Gévaudan's arms, and together they retrieved their fardels and clothes. There were no living beings left at the site, only carrion and guttering fires, fallen tents and upturned carts. All else was fled. In a moment of strange regret, Gévaudan searched the sea of bodies for Edward Courten, but could not find him. Of course, the maqam had stretched far across the road, and it's possible he simply missed Courten* if he lay dead somewhere. But Gévaudan chose to assume that the Englishman had escaped.

Fenrir allowed Gévaudan to feed from a body, though not very much, because there wasn't much time. Other travelers could come upon them, and it wouldn't be long before the survivors called for soldiers and formed a new caravan to return to the site of the attack and recover the dead. The two of them hacked limbs from some of the bodies with their blades, salted them, and wrapped them in waxed cloth to keep for later.

And so it was that I was lashed to Gévaudan's back along with his carrion-filled fardels, as if I were no more than a possession for these two creatures to fight over, and they traveled ahead to their decided arena, the ghost city of Fatehpur Sikri, which had been Courten's next destination. They traveled fast, even in their first selves, not stopping once throughout the night. By the time the sky began to lighten with the blue of early dawn, they had reached the rocky ridge upon which

---

* According to my research, Edward Courten of the British East India Company did actually visit India as a factor (a trader), and broke his contract by prematurely booking a passage back to England via the western port of Surat (in Gujarat), after he claimed his qafila was attacked and destroyed three days out from Akbarabad, near Fatehpur Sikri. His journals were never published, and he burned them on his return before changing his mind and saving what he could. The salvaged pages were said to describe the caravan's ambush by a "demon" that the "Hindoos call rakshasa," and even go so far as to identify the "rakshasa" as "Kali," the apocalyptic demon who is a herald of Kali Yuga, the Age of Vice. In his testimony, Courten was said to conflate the Hindu Kali (not to be confused with the goddess Kali, also a figure in Hinduism) with the Christian figure of Satan. His service was terminated, and he was judged mentally unfit and incarcerated at Bethlehem Royal Hospital (also known as Bedlam) of London in 1650, where it is presumed he died.

the walled city sat—a craggy arm of the hills of Vindhya, which the Hindus say once grew so high they would block the path of the passing sun.

How my abductors (and they were such, as I had no say in this journey) kept me in the half death of that sleep I don't know; but they had their ways. Though I dreamed of things similar, I experienced none of this awake, dangling helpless from Gévaudan's back as he climbed up the ridge with Fenrir, and they entered the quiet privacy of that empty place. For those scarce, anxious hours before their duel, Gévaudan and Fenrir became traveling companions once more, as they had been for the years of their journey from Europe, and as if in respect for those years, they entered the city in silence. Only once did Gévaudan speak, to ask: <<What will happen to Cyrah if I lose?>> And to that Fenrir only shrugged and said, perhaps truthfully: <<I don't know.>>

Then and now, no one lived or lives in Fatehpur Sikri, the "City of Victory" that Emperor Akbar built to honor the spot where a Sufi foretold the birth of his first son. It's said that it was a thriving and magnificent place when Akbar first unveiled it to his empire. But once the water tanks grew fetid and diseased in the summers, growing parched on the high rocks of that ridge, Akbar's new city became rife with illness and death, and its people left and never came back. And so Fatehpur Sikri itself died, still young.

I remember opening my eyes and thinking that I was dreaming of flight, so high above the world was I, with no ground beneath my hanging feet or roof above my windblown hair. I was tied to Gévaudan with my back against his, so Shah Jahan's empire lay sprawled below me like a painted map feathered with dark forest and threaded with road, stretched across the rocky table of the earth. The lamp of the sun was still hidden behind the edge of that table, though its light had begun to creep up the vaulted tent of the heavens, weakening the pinholes of the stars. The cobweb clots of clouds had torn apart after the rain, and hung threadbare in the dawn. My body lurching with every movement Gévaudan made, I smiled, giving little thought to where I was and why. I raised my hand to the horizon as if to leap away into the open air. The cool of an early-morning breeze tickled my arm and trickled through my fingers.

With effort I looked to my side and saw the wall of Fatehpur Sikri, and the dark stealthy shape of Fenrir moving up its sheer side like some giant bat in the gloom. My arm turned leaden and fell back. A human hand stuck out of Fenrir's bulging fardels, having escaped its wrappings. Its rigid fingers reached for freedom. The bony chiming of Gévaudan and Fenrir's trinkets a soft dawn song. I felt a brief fear of falling when I realized I was not afloat but lashed to Gévaudan, and I wondered if the creaking harness would hold. But my head felt heavy and my eyes shut again.

The ruins of Fatehpur Sikri are overgrown with wild grass and indigo, the bright flowers always dancing amid the broken buildings. Weeds and other plants now live in the crumbled remains of entire neighborhoods. In the distance, the imperial palace still stands tall over all else, its minarets and walls untouched by time, a reminder of the city's former glory. I saw this ghostly place through eyes veiled with the visions of dreams—and I wondered if Allah had emptied this once glorious city just to make of it a quiet monument for pilgrims escaping the stench and hardships of real life. I remembered Gévaudan telling me at Chandni-Chauk that he might appreciate a human city if it was empty of humans, and wondered if it pleased him to be in this one. I wondered if this was what Akbarabad and Shahjahanabad would look like in a century.

Sunlight burned the edges of the clouds in the sky, and dark birds began to wheel through them, and my thoughts turned to death, and the impression I had that I was somehow already halfway to its door, held there by my godlike abductors.

I tried to wake, struggling in the bonds that tied me to a beast in human shape. He and Fenrir walked through the endless broken streets. The wind whistling through the shattered city began to rise, or so I thought, and the indigo flowers danced everywhere as if to mock my helplessness. The wound on my arm hurt.

Gévaudan laid me down and licked my arm, the tip of his tongue flicking against the scabbing edges of the slit. His breath smelled terrible, of some unknowable poison. Fenrir loomed over us, watching. I felt the scalding drip of Gévaudan's spit fall in a white string on my arm, and he rubbed it into the wound with his fingers. Wild grass lay crushed under me, a soft and fragrant bed. I asked him to wake me up.

He said: <<You cannot be awake for this, Cyrah. You will sleep now. Fenrir and I must fight.>>

Fenrir watched, and I could feel his brooding thoughts like a sweltering cloud over us three. Gévaudan hesitated, but said it, to me: <<I am sorry. For everything.>>

I wanted to say: *Fuck you. Fuck you and Fenrir. I can trust no one, human or djinn, angel or devil.*

But I could only moan like a sick child, and tears flooded my eyes and splashed down my face.

Gévaudan said: <<Goodbye, Cyrah.>>

Did they fight over me, or over their tattering of the tangled webs of their tribal laws? Who can say, really? But they did fight, and it was a battle to be seen, though I didn't see it. But I dreamed it, so caught was I in the poisonous glamours the two had cast over me to keep me unconscious during their duel. Glamours that were, I imagine, strongly tied to them, making their violence mine. Or perhaps I just dreamed a dream, which was nothing like the actual battle.

What I do know is that they fought for a day and a night in the arena of deserted Fatehpur Sikri. They shed their clothes and fardels next to my sleeping form, which they had placed in the cavern of a fallen building, and they each pissed a circle around their belongings. They lifted up my head, and poured water from one of their gourds into my dry mouth till my stomach was full. Then they covered my face in my cloak, so that I could see nothing of their contest even if my eyes opened—leaving me like a shrouded corpse. Naked they walked into streets now flooding with golden morning light, and changed into their second selves. And they began.

Even in the dream I was far away, high above their battle. Drifting like an invisible bird, I saw them wrestle in the broken city of their prey, slow and languid like lovers, their sunlit fur iridescent in the dawn. Lances of light flashed upward into the sky from them, and I could scarcely believe how beautiful they were. Gévaudan shone in the growing day with streaks of bright orange and crimson against black like plumage, while Fenrir, the larger of the two, seemed a thing of shimmering darkness, pulsing with dark grays and bitter blues, the black of a raven sky at night. Their spines bristled in waves, shattered

by the caress of their clawed hands as they grappled. Their long shadows fell across the fields of indigo that now painted the avenues and
roads.

As they tangled into one beast in that blazing winter morning, I
observed their dance, and I marveled that these were beings that didn't
know love. Then again, they were fighting because they had, each in
their own way, found the same—and their violence was, perhaps, to
purge their disgust at that stray human emotion.

As the sun rose higher, the two beasts drifted apart and circled each
other, exploring the ruins but always facing each other, even if miles
apart. They licked their wounds and regrew their spines, sealed the
ragged tears in their skin with spit, snatched small animals from the
undergrowth and devoured them.

And then, when the sun was at its zenith, they ran to meet each
other again.

I swooped down on a sudden wind to see them leap miles across
the city, two monstrous celestial bodies casting their hurtling shadows
across the shivering ghost city. The very air shook as they met high
above the ruins, and I was sent flying away as they clashed in the rays
of the sun and tumbled toward the earth as one, a demon meteor that
hung for too long above Fatehpur. When they crashed down to earth,
the impact sent the stones of many ruins cascading into dust, gathering in a cloud that hung over them. Their roaring made avalanches
tumble down the hills of Vindhya. Their huge clawed feet dug deep
trenches into the earth, tore plants and grass to shreds, left deep worms
wriggling in the open so that birds lunged down to catch them, only
to be thrown from the air and trampled under the fury of the two fight-
ers.

When the dust settled, paling their giant forms, the sun had begun
to set. Streams of their blood had made new gutters for the deserted
and overgrown streets, bubbling and hissing and destroying what
plant life grew nearby. Their fight had slowed again. They were caught
in a fierce embrace, their massive claws swiping bloody swaths through
each other's flesh. Steam robed them as hot piss and blood fell down
their legs and pooled in their deep footprints, and clumps of shit fell
from between their rippling legs, containing what decayed matter of

human souls I don't know. As night fell I saw one of the two finally fall, though it was too dark to see which. And I saw the other take the hackles of the fallen one's neck in its jaws and gallop through the city dragging its opponent across the ground.

When this gauntlet ended, the fallen moved no longer. The victorious beast pounded the fallen into the earth as if to bury him, and the earth shook my grounded body, making me falter from my dream—heavy coarse cloak suffocating my face—only to fall back into it. I rose higher and higher, till Fatehpur Sikri was a miniature sandalwood city, until the clouds dampened my vision, until I vanished into the endless black.

I woke to see Fenrir crouched over me. Gévaudan lay some yards away on the ground with his back to me, motionless. Both were naked. Fenrir's bone trophies clattered. They were both red from head to toe. Blood. My hand was crusted in it, too, though the wound had scabbed over. I tried to get up, but my head ached so much that I turned and threw up.

Fenrir sniffed. "I see my child. It lives in you," he said. Once again I was struck by the smooth beauty of his Pashto, as opposed to the rough, if fluent, speech of Gévaudan. "I wasn't sure. That it would grow," he whispered, the burning reflections in his eyes lighting his tears.

"Get away," I managed before starting to cough. He flinched, as though just realizing that I was awake.

Though weak, I crawled away from him. He didn't give chase. A cold crescent of moon floated above the dark shapes of the ruins around us, casting a glow that lingered among the rustling indigo and grass. I staggered to my feet, still coughing. I wanted to run, but where would I run? How could I outrun such a being?

Instead, I faced him, trying to stand as straight and upright as I could in my condition. I was afraid, and I'm not ashamed to admit that—but truthfully, my fear was tempered by the fact that I was no longer mired in that strange sleep I'd been trapped in for more than a day. I had returned to my body and my own will. Fenrir barely seemed to notice what I was doing, instead going on speaking, like a mullah reciting, face hard-set now.

"Do you know, Cyrah, that your new companion lapped at your blood like a fool shroud-eater, an undignified upir,* because he couldn't muster the courage to kill you and eat of you? Gévaudan wanted to devour you and take your shape. So I would love him as he loves me, the fool whelp. When I look at him, I almost understand your disgust at me."

He looked at me with his mismatched eyes, his glistening scar showing through the blood his face was painted in.

"I know he loves you," I said, my voice broken and sore. "I just can't see why. Or maybe it's entirely clear. You're both monsters." I was relieved to find my mother's gifted blade still in the sheath tucked into the saree knotted at my waist, a weight against my hip. I gripped the handle. It gave me some measure of strength.

"You're lying," he said. "I can smell it in the blood on your arm, in your sweat. You don't think Gévaudan is a monster. Perhaps you thought him no different from me when you first met him. But you've changed your mind. In fact, you're wondering if he's alive right now."

I kept still, as if he might not be able to read my mind if I did so. My cloak—Gévaudan's cloak—hung heavy with dried mud. I held my breath and didn't ask the question on my mind. The puddles that Gévaudan lay in were crimson, and I could see gashes torn into his body. The lips of wounds slashed across his thighs and buttocks were so deep they were rimmed with the ghastly yellow of fat. I felt so very tired.

Fenrir looked at him. "He's not dead." He breathed deep. "I think he likes you, in some way. Perhaps in mimicry of me."

"He's not like you. He didn't force himself on me," I said.

"He did worse," he said. "He tasted you but made no consummation. I didn't want to hurt you. All I wanted was to create, like the human that died to birth me so long ago I can't even remember."

"You raped me. That's not being human. It's an unnatural thing, punished by our laws and religions," I said, and spat on the ground.

"And yet you yourself were beget by rape," he said, and I flinched at this violation, this intimate knowledge that he'd somehow taken

---

* A possible etymological root of the word *vampire,* present in several Slavic languages.

from me. He shook his head and smiled, blood and tears and dirt running across his face. "Yet I see khrissal men take their women all the time, with no regard for whether they want it or not, in every kingdom and empire I travel through. Women create. Men inflict violence on you, envious and fearful, desperate to share in that ability. And it is this hateful battle that keeps your kind extant. You have taught me that your race's love is just a beautifully woven veil, to make pretty shadows out of a brutal war. This, too, is a terrible art. But I don't know anymore if it is an art worth emulating. I see now that your kind and mine are not so different. We are to you khrissals what human men are to human women. You are prey, Cyrah, no matter how you look at it." He grinned at me.

Palm sweaty around the handle, I drew my blunt old blade from its sheath. "I look at it like this. Your only human act was the lowest, most cowardly of our crimes. So congratulations on your success," I said, fighting my fear to walk closer to him.

Fenrir growled, deep in his throat, baring his reddened teeth. He got up, unfurling like a giant. "What I committed was not your ugly khrissal crime of rape, it was a gift. In Ragnarök, there must be violence before renewal. The great wolf must attack before his bloodlust is dimmed," he said, each word barked as he loomed tall over me. But I walked closer still, until there was a foot between us, and I looked straight up at him, blade held at my side.

"You talk of humanity and how it fears and loathes its women, Feneer, as if your kind are faultless as you walk and hunt among us," I said. "But I see none of you wearing the shape of human woman. Three of you I've met, and all big, strong men. Or maybe you are just the scared little boys among your race, each hiding under the armor of a man's body. Maybe that's why you are all without pack or tribe."

He seemed to consider this for a moment, and crouched again over Gévaudan's body. "Gévaudan told me you want to kill the child in you."

"I don't believe he would tell you such a thing."

"Don't presume to know our ways simply because Gévaudan allowed you to ride on the back of his second self. Even as we gouge the flesh from each other's bones, our blood speaks when spilled."

Fenrir plunged his fingers into one of Gévaudan's wounds. Gévaudan convulsed but made no sound.

"Stop that!" I shouted, pointing my blade toward Fenrir's face. He ignored the metal poised inches from his face, and pulled his glistening fingers from the wound to examine them. "It is not common for us to eat each other. But what is it, between two traitors among the tribes, to break just one more tenet?" Fenrir reached under Gévaudan's torso and picked him up, cradling him like a dying brother in his arms. The puddles underneath them sloshed and rippled. Fenrir leaned close to Gévaudan's bloodied face, his neck, like a holy man embracing a sick one to kiss his forehead.

Eyes on me and my weapon, Fenrir bit into the flesh of his friend's neck. I heard the sound of his teeth pierce skin with a squelch.

"Don't," I pleaded, lowering my blade. "Don't do that. What do you want?" I couldn't hope to do battle with this feral thing. I knew I didn't stand a chance.

Fenrir looked up, stared at me like some repugnant dog.

"Do you love him?" he asked, his face a mask devoid of hope or happiness.

"What is it with you two and love?" I shouted, the echoes bursting through the crumbled chasms of the city. I got on my knees next to this false man, not caring that my legs were steeped in cold blood and mud. "You rage against it constantly, but think of nothing else in the human world. I don't love anyone on this earth but my dead mother. Is that good enough for you?" I asked.

"Then why should I not kill him right now?" he asked, slack lips dripping.

"Allah damn you to hell, Fen-eer. He has trusted me, and I him. In ways no one else has since my mother died. I will not leave him for dead. Whatever he may have planned, he resisted it against all the manifestations of his instinct. I will respect that. I have nothing left."

Fenrir sighed, his heavy breath a coil of smoke in the air. "I could spare his life, but how do I know you won't do something to my child later?"

"It's *my* child, too, you son of a bitch," I said. I know it seems strange and sudden that I would say that, having described how I didn't want the child, but I did say it. The words jumped out of my mouth as if they were a living thing, or an exclamation spoken by none other than the creature growing in me, or by the sinews and spaces of my own body. I shook my head, and held the handle of my blade in both hands. I turned the point of it to rest between my navel and my crotch, against my womb. My body woke with an invisible fire, raising every last hair on my skin. The point felt clean and sharp against my belly, even though the knife was blunt and tarnished. Fenrir's eyes widened, shoulders snapping tight like ropes.

"*Only* my child," I said. "Mine. You lost your claim as a father when you forced yourself on me. This child deserved the love of a kind and gentle man, a true father. It deserved a mother that wanted it. You woke it before its time and gave it the life of a bastard-child, in a world that you yourself have observed is full of bastard-begetting men, who brand their own children outcasts after fathering them with women they spit on and call whore after raping them."

"I can be kind and gentle, just as any human man can be savage and cruel," Fenrir said, his fingers clenching, twitching around Gévaudan's body as if to demonstrate his capacity for affection. For the first time, his voice wavered. "If you had let me, I would have stayed by your side and learned the love that you say belongs only to a human father."

I clenched and unclenched my hands around the handle of the knife, mimicking his fingers. I pushed lightly against myself with the blade, the pinpoint flaring with pain as it opened skin, freeing a tiny bead of blood. Fenrir sniffed sharply, smelling this new wound.

"As you said, Fen-eer, I shouldn't presume to know the ways of your kind. But I know the ways of my own kind, and I know that any man who rapes a woman is unfit to be a father by my side, even if he is capable of kindness."

Panic in his eyes, Fenrir let Gévaudan's body slide out of his arms, putting him gently on the ground. "If you will spare your child's life, I will spare Gévaudan's. I swear to you," he said. *Your child.*

I removed the point of my blade from my skin. It left a small burning, a pinhead of pain. I sheathed the knife and nodded.

"Do you promise?" he asked, voice low with fear. His one creation, inside me.

"I do," I said, and I reached out against my disgust and touched Fenrir's face, let my palm and fingers rest gentle against his jaw and wet cheek because I knew how much this would hurt him. He sat petrified as I did this. I let my hand rest there a moment, absorbing the raging heat under his skin, and I let it fall away.

We sat on the ground, the two of us, our fallen companion between us.

"You have hurt him badly. You can't leave him like this. He saved your life, Fen-eer. Have you so quickly forgotten that? He killed for you."

"That is our way," he said, voice different, lower. He made no eye contact as he looked at Gévaudan, removing the clotted hair from his opponent's forehead. "He has written no poetry, painted no grand pictures, made no promises, built no palaces. He's as much an impostor as I am. I am grateful for what he did, but I don't want his love."

"You want mine."

He didn't answer for a moment. "Yes."

"You'll never have it. You will never know the love of a human."

Fenrir ran his fingers through the grass and indigo flowers milling around him. He walked to his clothes and began putting them on, disregarding the blood that covered him from head to toe. I said nothing more, letting him dress in silence. For a moment, just a small moment, I felt sad for him.

"A long time ago, before either you or Gévaudan was ever alive, I once came as near death as I've ever been," he said, turning to me.

"Not because of a fellow shape-shifter, but a human, wearing the skin of a wolf. He surprised me with his ferocity. His passion. I was much younger, my second self much less powerful, and I hadn't eaten of a human being for weeks. I killed him, but I was left like Gévaudan here, laid waste. In one night I healed myself, by eating his body. It was the bond that I made with my prey that helped me survive. I saw the fiery anima within his soul, waiting to be freed. He would have made a fine shape-shifter. But he was dead, so I used that anima to heal my own selves. It was powerful enough that I molted overnight, and took his shape as my first self."

"I'm not going to kill myself for Gévaudan, if that's what you're saying," I said.

"Gévaudan has a powerful bond with you, one that he has never experienced with a human before. He was, after all, trying to become you, in a way. You shared yourself willingly. If you give him your blood, he'll remember the taste."

"That'll heal him?" I asked.

"No. But it'll help. I'll do the rest."

So I cut open my wrist once again, wincing at the bolts of pain it sent up my forearm, an old wound woken and given no purchase to heal. If it weren't for Gévaudan's spit, I expect it would have festered by then.

Fenrir had dragged Gévaudan inside the shelter of the broken building where I'd slept during the duel. In the gloom, I lowered my arm to rasping Gévaudan, whose breath was weak and slow, tickling the fresh cut skin on my arm. But as if by instinct, his mouth closed around the bleeding slit, his body sucking for him even though he wasn't awake. I gritted my teeth and refused to cry, though it hurt. Gévaudan himself looked like some prostrate red monster, his boyish face now grotesque and swollen. His plump lips were even more so now, bruised and blushed into fat leeches that embraced my wound. I could feel my blood leave my body in a surge, rushing into his to nourish his twinned souls. I felt very cold and very weak; I hadn't eaten in more than a day now, and had been trapped in a stupor for most of that time. I swayed and watched Fenrir, shadowy black against the moonlit opening in the wall of the crumbling room we were in. He sat with a crude carved wooden bowl, emptying blood into it from his own wrist. My blood and his blood, to nourish both souls encased in Gévaudan's broken form. He spat in the bowl, mingling the two fluids with his fingers. The white threads of spittle glittered in the moonlight pouring in behind him, diamond strings falling from his mouth. He placed the bowl at his feet when he was done, licking his wrist. He looked at me. I couldn't see his expression, his face dark.

"You are prey, and he is predator. And yet you let him drink the life from your own body, as if he were your child," Fenrir said, his voice hoarse.

"Don't say that. Don't say things like that," I said through gritted teeth, feeling sick. My throat was dry. In the dim light, my head swimming, Gévaudan became just that: a giant infant by my side, wet and crimson and suckling at my wrist instead of at my breast, blood instead of milk, half dead but eagerly drawing from me, sprawled and helpless.

"You will be a good mother," said Fenrir.

I swallowed to keep myself from throwing up, though there was nothing left in my stomach. I burped, and coughed as a retch escaped with it. I could feel sweat gluing my hair to my face and forehead, even though I was shivering with cold. I felt faint. I heard Fenrir get up and walk up to me. My neck prickled.

His callused hand on my shoulder. He pulled me back, plucking my wrist from Gévaudan's mouth. The wound burned as if it were a brand across my forearm.

"That's enough," said Fenrir, and grasped my shoulders, helping me stand up. I realized I had almost passed out. "You can't let that bleed out. You could die like that," he said. I was so tired I let him lean down and lick my wrist, several times, his tongue sliding up and down my wound. I looked away, not wanting to see what pleasure he took from it. I felt him tie a piece of cloth around my forearm. "There," he said. I staggered away from Fenrir, who bent down to Gévaudan and tilted the wooden bowl to his lips. I sat down on the weeds, which made a tangled carpet on the rough floor. With a slurping noise, the bowl emptied into Gévaudan, a single dark tear leaking from the corner of his mouth. Fenrir wiped it away with a thumb, leaving a pale smudge in his dark-stained face. He then loosened one of the fardels and unwrapped the salted pieces of dead men the two of them had carried with them. Taking a severed hand, Fenrir bit into it. I heard the little bones crunch loud between his teeth, and my body shook. I was so hungry, and yet so ill, listening to him bite into that dead hand. He chewed for a while and touched his mouth to Gévaudan's, slipping the flesh into his defeated companion like a bird feeding its chick. In the dim of the room, it looked like a gentle kiss. But I heard the sticky sound of carrion passing between them, and heard Fenrir grunt soft and grind his lips against Gévaudan's as he used his tongue to push the food down the throat. Chilled sweat dripped down my neck, pasted

hair to my temples. Fenrir stopped, and slapped Gévaudan's face—
a meaty, thick thud instead of a sharp sound. I flinched at it. He slapped
him again, held his chin and tilted Gévaudan's head. I heard a low
gurgle as Gévaudan swallowed. Fenrir picked up the severed hand
again and plucked the thumb and forefinger off it with his teeth, like
fruit from a bush. He began chewing again.

I ran outside.

The moon shone down bright on the dead city. The wild grass tickled my palms, and the flowery arms of the tall indigo plants trailed
across my face, feathery and cool. I cried till I was on my knees shaking, watching piss flow away from between my legs in a little stream.
If you asked me why I cried then, I couldn't say. I felt so many things
then that it seemed the only sane thing I could do. My grubby face
streaming with tears, I walked the empty streets of Fatehpur Sikri as if
it were my home. I climbed the stepped remnants of a ruin, scraping
my knees bloody and not caring, opening old wounds left on my legs
by the rough hide of Gévaudan's second self, and I sat on top of a broken rooftop, looking over the fields and tangled gardens that had once
been streets, looking beyond the city and to the land that I had lived
in as a human for so long. A cold wind blew into me, drying my tears,
but the caked cloak of Gévaudan kept me warm enough. I could see
no lights anywhere for miles, and I felt like I was the only human left
in the world.

After the life I had led, I was not one given to dwelling within self-pity, or wandering and getting lost in ruins while weeping. Having pissed among the indigo and dried my tears entirely, I made my way back to our camp (I say "our camp" still, even though I had basically been their prisoner for two days). Gévaudan lay still, wrapped in the same shrouds that had been used to contain the dismembered corpses. Fenrir had made a small fire, over which he was roasting the carcasses of some small animals, obviously for me. Starving as I was, I ate quickly, not noticing whether or not they tasted any good.

When I was done, I threw the little bones in the fire, and I admit, I asked Fenrir to turn me into a shape-shifter.

"No," he said, terrible and gentle, as he so often was. "It would kill the child. You made a promise."

"I have no obligations to fulfill promises to you, who've wronged me so terribly."

"You are not so callous, Cyrah. You made the promise for your child, and for Gévaudan, not for me. And I know you won't break it. You don't want to."

"Don't tell me what I want. Again and again, men, shape-shifters, all of you, you cursed things, telling me what I want and don't want. Nothing about this is fair. How can I be expected to keep living my life as a human, as a woman, after everything I have seen since you and Jevah-dan strolled into Mumtazabad?"

He shook his head.

Even though it was impossible that early, I felt the life, the child in me. I felt you. I felt you kick from the inside, and a hum filled my head and tingled in my limbs as if a thousand insects had replaced my blood. I walked to where Gévaudan lay sleeping, and I tore two strips from the shrouds covering him. I tied the strips around my knuckles, tight as I could. I faced Fenrir, coming close, standing right over him.

"I know you want to hurt me. I can see it in your eyes every time you look at me," I said. He looked up at me, his face calm. Staring straight into my eyes with his, blue and gray.

I struck him with the back of my hand across his scarred cheek, feeling for the first time since being raped the solidity of this creature's flesh and bone. The sound of it was loud, shocking. He didn't even blink as my knuckles glanced off his cheekbone, which felt like a knot of wood under the leather of his skin.

"Hurt me," I said.

This time he looked down, averting his eyes. His hair fell, hanging over his forehead. I curled my hand into a fist, raised it, and hit his face. I saw him close his eyes before my knuckles smashed into him. It hurt, a lot, and I clenched my teeth at the thud. I grabbed my hand and breathed hard to push the pain down into myself. I saw the small blush on his cheek where my knuckles fell.

"Hurt me like you want to, Fen-eer. Let that djinn monster out," I said, lungs heaving though I wasn't tired. I was filled with lightning, with heat, sick to my stomach. I swung my fist into his face again, into one of his eyes, yielding amid the hardness of his face. This time his head moved a little, and I heard a soft huff of breath.

"Kill me. Tear my soul in two," I said. Again he said nothing. He kept his eyes closed. He was a statue, a wooden, painted totem. I hit him again, with all the strength I had. I heard his nose snap under the weight of my fist, and I pulled back quickly and hit with the other, hissing through my teeth to ignore the jagged pain in my hands. Streams tumbled down the crags of his face, deepening the red of his already stained mouth, dripping off his chin.

He said nothing, did nothing, breathing loud through his now broken nose. So I hit him again. And again. And again, again, till my fists could take no more pain, and I felt like I'd broken them. The rags I'd tied around my hands were wet. Fenrir's face was awash in blood, his features swelling. I swept away tears of pain with my aching hands, stood over him and let the rhythm of air entering and leaving my body calm me.

He opened his eyes. One of them had turned a dark and gleaming red around the pale gray of his iris, as if to mark him as a monster. He coughed just a little, a spurt of blackened snot and bloody spit falling from his mouth and nostrils.

"I will not," he said.

I nodded slowly, wiping the sweat from my brow. Unwrapped my knuckles and looked at them. They looked swollen, and some had opened. I cared little about this. I stepped back, sat down a few feet away from Fenrir, light-headed.

I shook my head. "I can't do this. I don't know how to live as a human woman anymore."

Fenrir breathed deep. He didn't wipe his face, or even touch it. Red lines were crawling down his neck, little ruby beads falling off his chin. "I have something for you," he said, his voice rough.

I looked up. "Don't you fucking get in my head. Don't you dare get in my head and show me your visions. You don't get to show me how to be a human woman."

"I'm sorry for that presumption. I'd thought, that night, that my memories would help heal the hurt I'd done, and help you want the child. I thought wrong, again. This is no vision I want to give you, though it also contains within it my memory." He reached into one of his fardels and took out a tied bundle of brown parchment. It had writing on it.

"This is an account of some of my travels from when we met. It's for you," he said.

"I can't read. And that looks like a very long account."

"You'll find a way. Keep it with you. Stories are valuable."

I took the scroll, heavy and coarse to the touch, a little smudged with Fenrir's recent bloody fingerprints. The words scrawled on the parchment were beautiful and curved, an intricate linking of symbols. Some of it was a language and symbols I'd never seen before. But as I unfolded the scroll, I saw that the language turned at some point into something more familiar—Arabic script, which I could recognize.

Throughout the scroll, woven through the language, were tiny draw-ings, intricate miniatures of bodies and designs in motion, telling the story in between the words and letters. I know now, of course, that the part Fenrir wrote after he met me was written in Pashto so that I would be able to read it in my own language, if I ever learned to read it. I had never seen parchment like this before.

It was a gorgeous thing, so splendid it made me feel miserable at that moment, so utterly miserable.

"You wrote me a story." I laughed, shaking my head. "You wrote me a damn story. You want so badly to become human again, Fen-eer. So why don't you? Why don't you just stay in your first shape and be human?" I asked.

"You know why," he said, his nose whistling. He raised a hand, held it. I winced at the crack as he pushed the broken bone back into place and sniffed sharply, spitting blood on the ground. "Nothing is as sim-ple as it seems. Would you abandon all the raiment of civilization and society to live like an animal?" he asked, his face glistening like a mask of raw meat in the firelight.

"I've wanted to, many times," I said, rubbing my hands. Some of the knuckles were welling up, crying little tears of blood.

"It's not so easy, is it," he said.

We sat in silence.

"I have ended a multitude of stories in the past few days, for no reason other than anger and jealousy," he said. "I have wasted so many human lives, killing them without respect or thought, consuming nei-ther their flesh nor souls, leaving their bodies to rot on a road, and their stories to evaporate into the void. But that one, that one inside you, it can survive this. It can survive this terrible mistake I've made."

I said nothing, but he didn't press me further.

So Fenrir left. And there I was, human guardian of a fallen djinn. A djinn, or war-ulf, wih-ich, still alive because the one who defeated him wanted to show me he was capable of some aspect of humanity. For days I guarded Gévaudan's body as it healed. He looked for all the world like a broken human, and not the beast that had planned to devour me and steal my shape, to use me as a key to unlocking the heart of the one he loved. But that was not the beast that I knew, the beast that I had ridden upon blind, the beast that could have easily destroyed me at any time but didn't. It had chosen not to. He had chosen not to. And so I stayed by his side. I stayed, to honor that. I stayed, because I could not return to that teeming mass of humanity waiting below Fatehpur Sikri without Gévaudan as my companion, without some link to this new world I had walked into.

There was an easier way, of course. I could jump off the high walls of Fatehpur and shatter my body and soul on the hillsides of Vindhya. But I had always had that option, and had always refused it. Now I had even less reason to take it. Why would I make myself food for worms when I could exchange my human life for another one—that of a djinn, an asura, a shape-changer, as fearsome and beautiful and unshackled as a tigress in the jungle? I could not imagine killing another human being, but I had faith that would change if I transcended humanity and became something else entirely, just as I'd always had faith that Allah exists in some way even though I couldn't see him or feel his presence through the daily struggles of my life. I didn't know whether I still believed this in the same way after everything I'd been through, but I believed in a god more than ever before.

Gévaudan did recover, slowly but surely, whether because of Fenrir's blood magic or simply because of his own resilience, I don't know. I won't tell you the first words we shared when he woke from his deep sleep of half death, because those are between he and me alone. But he spoke again, and walked again, and grew back the strength of both his souls, and soon we rode from that broken city and once again into the empire of Shah Jahan, into the world of men. Of humans, I should say. We did so as new beings both, I'm sure.

Eventually, I rode upon the back of Gévaudan's second self again.

Eventually, Gévaudan allowed me, human, khrissal, to look upon his second self without a blindfold. I did, and I survived.

Just as Fenrir's second self had been terrible like nothing in this world, Gévaudan's was beautiful like nothing in this world.

But I should tell you of Fenrir's departure, and of his last words to me.

Before he left, I told him: "Fen-eer. Those things you said before, about my kind. That human men and women only war and rape. The worst thing about you is that you almost make me want to agree with you, with everything you say about my kind. But you're not human. You've no right to say such things. I do. But I'll never say those things. I am one woman. I am not all women. Do you hear me, you fucking, sad, sad thing? You bring out the bitterness in me, Fen-eer. You bring it out like a fountain. All you do is make me remember rape and agony and hatred, and forget every other moment in my entire life, in which I loved, in which I loved my dear mother and laughed with her and marveled at her courage, at how much she cared for me, in which I danced and told stories with the Bazigars, in which I listened to their songs under the stars, stoned off my ass on their hashish, listened to their throats and tongues just make music like nothing else on this earth and I cried with happiness and not hatred and sorrow and fear. I've never loved a man in my life, but I'm not fool enough to think that there are no men and women in this world who truly love each other, and love their children together, and did not conceive them through violence and pain. I will not be your human idol, your little goddess of suffering. I am *not* all human women, Fen-eer, and you'd do well to remember that while you devour and rape and preach and lament that humans will never love you. You—you *are* what all women fear in this world. This is why I am here by your companion's side, and not yours."

He looked at me for what seemed an eternity before saying to me:

"I don't know what it bodes for the new age to come, that a human looks a shape-shifter in the eye and speaks her wrath, that a human guards a fallen shape-shifter, but I will never forget such a sight. Human though you are, Cyrah, you are also wal-khiri, brave and powerful. Just as my nemesis centuries past was human but also ul-fedh-nar. Again, after so many lifetimes, I am laid low. Your child will be proud." With those words, Fenrir took his fardels and he left my life, still crusted in the blood from his great battle, still marked by my own hands, but otherwise the same as he had looked when he walked into it.

Here ends the tale of how you came to exist in me. For it was not till that moment when Fenrir walked away that you became truly alive and not the ghost of a possibility. That sad devil knew from the moment he met me that I am not one to break a promise.

I remember the moment you were born, in the country of the eighteen tides. Your cries pierced the wet air, drifting across the tidal waters of the river-jungle. I remember the belching growls of tigers prowling under the mangroves, drawn by the scent of blood spilling from between my legs. I remember my screams, and how I imagined them to drift out of my mouth and mingle with the moonlight hanging in the sky. I remember Gévaudan hunched between my legs, feet in the salt water of one of the jungle's many sea-rivers, his lips red from my blood, tongue flicking between his teeth as he struggled to keep from changing his shape, sweat dripping off his scarred face and matted hair to speckle my thighs. I remember the dark, the lack of a light, because Gévaudan could see by night. I remember how his eyes were like green candle flames hovering in his face. I remember his repulsion and wonder at seeing this act of creation forbidden to his kind, the terrible washes of his affection and concern. I remember the lukewarm water brimming around my ankles, the mud under me. I remember the silent green bumps of crocodiles slicing through the calm surface of the river behind Gévaudan.

But most of all, I remember you, tiny, larval human curled red in Gévaudan's hands. Your crying a trumpet to herald a new age.

The story's over. Cyrah's life, or what part of it I was allowed to re-live, is over.

I wait for the stranger to take my seemingly pointless typed version of that life from me.

Winter returns to Kolkata, slow and hesitant, the shadows of my apartment growing cool enough to banish the whir of the ceiling fan. Outside, during the day, the city looks the same, if a little less sweaty, the more thin-skinned among its populace wrapped in monkey caps, shawls, and scarves. Bereft of the damp of summer and monsoon, the air begins to smell rich and smoky. At night, the streetlights wear thin wedding veils of mist.

I lay down this work.

When the sun is folded up, and when the stars scatter, and when the mountains are set in motion, and when the ten-month pregnant she-camels are left untended, and when the beasts are gathered together, and when the oceans are set ablaze, and when the souls are reunited (with their bodies), and when the infant girl buried alive, is asked for what crime she was slain, and when the records are unfolded, and when the veil of heaven is removed, and when Hell is set blazing, and when Paradise is brought near, then each person shall know what he has brought with him.

SURAT AT-TAKWIR 81:1–14
THE QURAN

Part Six

SUNDARBANS
(Fenrisyuga)

1

I buy a daab off a little boy, who hacks the top off the unripe green coconut with a rusty machete and sticks a plastic straw in the top. He charges me twenty rupees for this, which I decide is too much, but then I stop to wonder how much twenty rupees really is to a boy living on the fringes of the largest metropolitan area in West Bengal and selling coconut water to tourists sailing off into the Gangetic delta. Probably enough to keep him from going hungry for an entire day. I hand him a crumpled note, feeling manipulated. He flashes me a grin and leaps off the boat, quick and nimble, just as its diesel engine coughs to life and sends it drifting downstream. I've been dreading being seasick (the last time I was on a boat was when I was a toddler), but the motor makes sure the boat cuts smoothly through the gray water without any swaying or tilting. Thirsty after the three-hour drive from Kolkata to this little rural dock, I suck the coconut shell empty in very little time.

The stranger stands at the bow, wrapped in a shawl and staring out at the mist-clad river, looking for all the world like an ancient masthead to our semi-modern motor launch. His thick, tangled beard makes his face look even thinner than before, matching his long, untied hair. He looks like a wild river deity carved out of wood.

I feel predictably like Conrad's Marlow about to journey down the Congo River. And the stranger, whose name I still don't know after a year—he could be my Kurtz, I suppose. But he's already on the boat. Best not think too deep on that. Still, over-obvious allusions aside, I have no idea what he intends to show me on this trip into the Sundarbans. I can scarcely believe it's actually happening, after all this time, after that night at Prinsep Ghat. But this has been the rhythm of our correspondence since I met him.

When he called a week ago to say that this trip was booked, his tone was quick, impatient. I barely had time to think before agreeing to come along. Thankfully, I have some time off from teaching for winter. The rented car, the rented boat, lodging, the full itinerary—I try to imagine the stranger making travel plans, and I can't.

This morning was the first time we've seen each other since that night. He's acted like nothing happened. Warm, but distant.

In my satchel, as requested, is my transcription of Cyrah's journal, finally complete. He hasn't yet asked about it.

Looking over the edge of the bright-blue launch, I see a world turned gray—the sky is blotted out by the mist hugging the land, and the water we travel over is just a darker shade of that haze. At the edges of the broad channel, children skitter and wave their tiny penises and buttocks at us, spots of color on the steeped gray mudbanks. The launch gains speed, skimming through the occasional shadows of concrete bridges that span the width of the tributary.

I don't feel like I'm in a delta forest. I ask one of the crew about that (this being a private launch, the stranger and I are the only "tourists" on board), and he says we aren't in the forest yet, and won't be for a while. So I sit on one of the plastic chairs set out under the wooden canopy in the center of the launch, which crowns the cabin and its cozy beds. I let the purring of the motor lull me into a waking sleep.

I watch the stranger's rigid back. He doesn't move. Standing there, tall and slim, an arrowhead pointing south to the mouth of the Ganges, he becomes our boat's engine, pulling us across the tidal waters with his growling will alone.

When I wake, everything has changed. The gray world gleams with sunlight, and the dull earth around has sprung to green life. On either side of the rippling silver sheet of the river is the mangrove forest. The ends of their roots stick up out of the muddy banks like groves of little stakes, waiting patiently for high tide to cover them with water so they can breathe again. Pale, pink-faced rhesus monkeys frolic among these stretches of vegetative fingertips as if they were fields of tall grass. The forest shimmers surreal and bright, the short mangroves hugging the edges of the banks and allowing no glimpses into the swampy forest beyond. Immediately I start looking for tigers amid the trees.

The stranger still stands at the tip of the boat, apparently unmoved from when I last saw him. As if sensing that I'm awake, he turns around and smiles. We are in the Sundarbans.

2

We spend the whole day traveling the waterways of the delta forest before we reach the island-village of Sajpur, where our guesthouse is. The channels are as varied as the forest is uniform and impenetrable. Some of them are narrow streams, others broad rivers, others vast confluences of water that stretch out to the horizon like great lakes bordered by dim land in the distance. Sometimes gaudy red-and-white tour boats pass us by, packed with people bending eagerly over the rails to catch a sight of all the wildlife the boats drive away with the sound of their engines, making me thankful for our own private launch. I spend the day out on deck or inside the cramped cabins, sprawled on the hard beds looking over my transcriptions of the stranger's manuscripts. The sea-smell of the salty delta water drifts in through the windows of the cabin, a natural incense to relax my mind.

The stranger spends all his time looking out to the forests as they pass us by. Sometimes he points out the odd bit of fauna to me. A great estuarine crocodile basking in the sun-warmed mud, skin studded with emerald scales glittering in the afternoon, slithering into the water with lethal ease as our boat drifts by it (motor off, so that we can observe). A gray monitor lizard tasting the air with pink tongue at the edge of the forest. A brown-and-white hawk with ruffled feathers, its beak a yellow hook, perched on the watchtower of a bare branch sticking up out of the forest canopy. Sometimes I hear a rustling along the tree line when the boat travels close to the shore and the motor is off, and I imagine it to be the sound of great paws treading on the undergrowth, bright patterned sinews brushing against the mangroves and low palm leaves.

In the evening, the sun snared behind the mangroves, our boat stops to refuel at an estuary whose shores act as a docking area, filled with boats in transit. All of us wandering the arteries of the delta, drawn here to form a glittering human scab on the water. The stranger and I sit in the captain's cabin and play cards to pass the time, a plastic plate of flaking samosas and ketchup between us.

Beyond the windows of the cramped wooden cabin (a felt hanging of a tiger above the hard bed), this ephemeral city of boats bobs in the twilight, air heavy with the smell of diesel and the growling of generators. The stranger has little interest in half-shod blackjack as he observes the brief settlement outside, an apparition of civilization in this wilderness, marked by Venus glowing in the soft sky above it.

His memories drift off him on the curling fumes of his sweat, igniting my imagination. The flaccid sails of Portuguese pirate ships soaked in the last rays of sunset, stippled with shadows of mangroves and palms, torches wavering over the water. Human blood spraying like dark wine across wooden decks, ships groaning and swaying under the heavy feet and hands of monsters disgorged from the jungle. The stinking fear of these seafaring bandits and merchants: fear of this strange yet lucrative land so far from their home, of crocodiles and tigers beyond the water. All overwhelmed by their terror at the beasts that have boarded them, nimble as humans, quick and silent like nothing on this planet—beasts that can walk upright, garlanded with bones, dwarfing even the mightiest of Bengal's cats, monsters of unimaginable beauty and ferocity. Screams ringing across the delta waters as animals watch from the forest, tigers panting jealous of the massacre taking place, confused and afraid of the beings that cause it.

I breathe it all in, now leaning over the damp edge of the boat, watching cigarette smoke leave the stranger's mouth in a white tendril. I'm shaking, and I try to hide it. The stranger hands me his cigarette, and I take it with gratitude. It's damp against my lips, from his mouth. I inhale deep, imagine cinders in my lungs, hope the nicotine will help with my sudden headache. My visions of the past linger in that ache, and I touch my mouth, as if to feel the traces of his saliva on it, from the cigarette. His smell, his sweat, his spit. I wonder if I'm beginning to hallucinate, queasy with excitement. He hasn't made me see his stories since the night at the baul mela. Maybe after all this time, something is changing.

"Alok," the stranger says. I'm afraid to speak, because my teeth might chatter.

"Y-yes," I say. His cigarette burns like a firebrand, scorching the air and painting the stranger's face, and I'm back in the baul mela for a fleeting second, the first moment I looked at him. The glow of a match against the shadows of his cheekbones.

Cigarette between his teeth, he takes off his own shawl and puts it on my shoulders. His hands firm on my shoulders, fingertips briefly pushing against my muscles through fabric, through the wool of my sweater.

"Thank you," I say, swallowing my tremors. His hands slide off me, smoke tracing their path.

"Listen. The last time we saw each other," he says. There we are. It had to come up. "At Prinsep Ghat."

"Alok, don't even. It's fine. It's ancient history," I say.

"My name isn't Alok. It's yours," he says, smiling in the dying light.

"Shit. Sorry, slipped out. It's difficult, talking to someone without a name. I just wanted to put a name where one's missing, and that one was the closest."

"Indeed," he whispers, and looks at me. I shudder again, shaking my head to throw the headache.

"That night, I didn't intend to offend you. To truly offend you," he says.

"Don't say things like that. It makes you sound like someone else, someone I don't know at all."

"I am a stranger, no?"

"In name," I say.

He nods, taking another drag. "Ancient history, then."

"That's right."

He nods and clears his throat. "Do you have the complete transcription?"

"I do," I say, reaching into my satchel and handing him the manila envelope full of my printed version of Cyrah's tale. I look around and feel silly. It's not like I'm handing him a bag full of drugs. His long fingers close around the package, cigarette propped in between the knuckles. "Thank you, Alok. This is a fine work you've done for me," he says. The envelope crackles as he tucks it under his armpit. His eyes glow as he draws on the cigarette, looking intently at me, his transcriber. No longer. What am I to him now?

"Feels like you just took pity on a bored and lonely college professor and gave him some money and something to do, but you're welcome."

His eyes don't move from me.

"What?" I ask him.

"Nothing. Are you still cold?"

"I'm fine. Thank you."

Just like that, my job for this man, this so-called stranger, is over. The shivering vanishes abruptly, as if something has drained out of me.

The boat coughs to life again, the crew shouting warnings to the other vessels that surround us. They guide it out of the little city of boats with rapid ease, and the cluster of life floats away from us like an illusion. Soon we are in the rivers again, traveling in the settled gloaming between the trees. Despite my headache, I feel a calm words can't describe, a light breeze brushing past the stranger to jostle my hair. When he's done with his cigarette, he doesn't throw the butt in the water, instead licking it damp and making it disappear into his kurta. We're moving fast now, the water rippling after us like oil in the sunset.

It's dark by the time we moor at the little docking area of the village, the stars gleaming fierce in a rich blue sky. I can see no lights anywhere except for the lanterns on our boat. We cross over to land on an unsteady plank that rests in the mud of the shore. The guesthouse itself is very close to the riverbank, reachable by a brick path laid down in mud, crossing through a narrow fringe of forest separating village from river, and running alongside broad, fallow fields that adjoin the plot of land the tourist lodge occupies. At the edge of the fields, the moonlit mist pales the black, thick line of the forest. The sound of thousands of insects screaming always with us. A pack of friendly dogs, which look like the same mongrels that wander the streets of Kolkata, follow us eagerly, though never coming close. They never do, when the stranger is around. There are no lights to help us see during the walk. The stars and moon are bright enough, casting shadows. The village is asleep.

As we enter the lodge, a whitewashed two-storied building surrounded by smaller cabins, I can make out a courtyard-garden through which the brick path winds. It's all illuminated in the glow of moonlight reflecting off earth and forest, glistening off damp leaves and grass, with not a single visible flare of electric light to aid it.

The electricity has been shut off for the night to save power, except for the dim blue fluorescents in the dining room downstairs, where we eat a home-cooked dinner of large-grained rice, dal, and chicken curry, having kept my bags in our room on the second floor. The cook nods at us, toothy grin in her round face, her midriff swelling bare from under her saree and sweater-blouse, solid as a baobab trunk. We thank her, and she retreats into the kitchen. The rice is so fresh I can feel the grit of chaff between the grains, the chicken soft and wet under a fat sheath of goose-bumped skin. Our host is the overseer of the travel lodge: Shankar-babu, an amiable and overeager man wrapped in shawl, sweater, and woolen cap, squinting at us through bottle-thick glasses that enlarge his watery eyes. He tells us the bird we are eating was killed hours ago, brought in from the village. He regales us with tales of life in the Sundarbans (talking in Bengali, and allowing me to hear the stranger speak in it for the first time, in an erudite accent that far outshines my own grasp of my mother-tongue). Shankar-babu shows us a newspaper cutting in a plastic folder he brings to us, which tells of tiger attacks just a few weeks ago in this very village. He tells of the recent injury of a fisherman whose leg was snapped up by a crocodile. I look at the darkness outside the windows, nervous. A large brown spider darts its way across the whitewashed wall next to the barred window. The stranger tells me it is called a huntsman.

3

Our room is spacious and clean, sparsely furnished with two beds and a hurricane lamp to see by. The mattresses are thin but comfortable. There is an adjoining bathroom with a toilet and a shower. Two windows look out onto the fields behind the lodge, and the forest beyond that.

"Well, this is quite nice," I tell the stranger. "I wouldn't have expected you of all people to be a champion of gentrified forest tourism."

He smiles, sitting on the bed, looking dazed. I wonder why. "I can hardly lead a civilized man of the city into the wilderness without taking a road well worn and comfortable," he says.

"Fair enough." I return the smile.

He continues sitting. He has brought no luggage except his now familiar, dirty backpack. It lies on his bed. I set down my travel bag in the corner. The chilly air feels like a film of oil, a dim yellow spilling from the lamp set on the floor. The flame dances in its glass case, as if to entertain us.

"Are you all right?" I ask him.

He nods. "I am. It's just been a while since I've been here."

"What's a while to you?"

"A long time to you. Let's just say there was no lodge here last time. Actually, there was no village, either."

"Well. Thank you, for bringing me here. It's . . . this is wonderful. I don't think I've ever experienced a place like this. I'm glad I came here."

"As am I," he says, and takes a deep breath. He takes a straight razor with a mother-of-pearl handle out of his jean pocket and unfolds it. I am suddenly petrified. He gets up and walks into the dark bathroom. I sit down on the bed, my heartbeat humming in my ears. After a while, I realize I can hear scraping.

When he emerges, he is changed. His face glossy with water in the jaundiced light, long hair sticking in spirals to his neck. His beard is gone, his tapering chin and jaws smooth as a woman's in the dimness. I am astonished by his beauty.

He sits down on his bed, opposite me, so we are facing each other. The hurricane lamp lies between us on the floor.

"Alok," he says.

"Yes."

"I'm lucky."

I remember him saying I ask too many questions. I think I've asked very few of him since he said that. Still, I just look at him. The lamp casts dark smears of shadows across his face, its light catching on the sharp lines of his skull. Once again, I am reminded of a totem of some sort, a carved idol sitting here in the dark with me. The water glimmers on him, making his skin look fresh-painted, the yellow of an idol of Durga.

"To have found so compassionate and patient a listener," he says. I look away, should he look at me.

"Am I?"

"You are. The most, perhaps."

"There've been others."

"In so long a life as mine, it would be difficult to assume otherwise."

There is silence. I feel like I've interrupted something.

"Well, thank you. For saying so. I've done nothing, really. You've been an interesting companion, to say the least. You must know that about yourself. You do, I can tell," I say.

"Can you?"

I laugh and clear my throat, nervous. The bed creaks under me.

"Yes, I think I can. You were different when I first met you. It felt like you were trying, somehow. To be interesting. But you don't need to try. Of all the people I've ever met, you don't need to," I tell him.

The bed creaks under him, his hands grasping the edge. I decide to meet his eyes, and am filled with a churning, intoxicating fear as I do.

I don't know what's happening. I can't tell what will happen. His smile isn't defensive—it's boyish, shocking. His mouth glistening and soft, not the jagged maw of a monster. My throat dries out. The room is tight, cold.

"I'd keep listening," I tell him. "I'd be glad to. For however long you wanted."

"Would you?" That smile, a thing of terror, unknown to me in that face. It's been so long since I saw his features without the beard. A drop of water falls off his chin. I think I can hear the minute pat of it hitting the cold stone floor.

"Are you . . ." I feel breathless. "Are you angry?"

A sound emerges from his throat. A cough, a laugh. He gets up, the bed rattling as chilled wood pops and groans, and I straighten up. In a second he's right in front of me, bending down, and I feel his lips against my own. My hands remain at my side. He pries my mouth open with his, slides his curried tongue against mine, and I exhale into him, feel my weaker breath against the scalding desert wind that rushes from his throat. Our heartbeats clash in our mouths. Water beads off his face and onto mine as I let him bend my head back, his long-fingered hands grasping the back of my neck, thumbs caressing the curve of my jaw, nails feather-light daggers against the arteries nestled under skin.

I close my eyes and remember the first time I kissed someone. Swapan, a boy my age, twelve at the time. A family friend and next-door neighbor whom I flew kites and played catch with on the rooftop of my family's house in summer, the grainy stone floor scorching under our bare feet. We pressed our mouths to each other, salty with sweat, surrounded by the low rooftops of Ballygunge Place, watched only by the beady eyes of voyeuristic crows. I remember the last time I kissed someone. Shayani, tear-stained lips warm after fucking, both of us aware that we were done being engaged.

It has been years. It has been even longer since I've had sex with a man. But it all comes back in an instant, the yearning, the ache for immediate intimacy, immediate consummation.

I've never been so physically close to anyone whom I trust could kill me with ease. His thumbs could press down and squash my arteries till I spasm into an endless sleep. He could throttle me, use his jaws and shining teeth to rip out my throat. But it is all potential energy, made all the more powerful by how gentle his hands are, rising across my neck and through my hair, tingling with the promise of carnage. They move down my shoulders, to my chest, and they guide me down. Not a push, a direction. I lie down, legs dangling off the bed. He pulls my jeans and boxers down to my knees, that hidden strength ignoring the buckled belt so that the friction of the pants pulls hairs from my legs. I wince at the pain, the sudden cold air on my bare erection.

He takes off his kurta, takes off his jeans. In his lithe body, the thick waves of hair that gather at his sloping shoulders, his suddenly emerald-green eyes, I see man and woman both, I see a being so human that it becomes inhuman, an animal perfection. War paint of shadow defining the muscles and sinews under his smooth skin, interrupted with long, pale scars. There is a story written on him in small, intricate tattoos, indecipherable symbols and language that crawl along the lines of his body—the ridge of his hip arching out of the dimpled line that demarcates thigh and pelvis, the valleys between biceps and triceps, the slope that turns pectoral to rib. Besides the dark tangle around his erection and clinging to his armpits, he has almost no body hair.

He bends down, folding his tall form with grace, as if performing a dance. I let him take me in his mouth, trust him with my flesh lying inert between his teeth and pushing tongue. The unheated room is cold, and I shiver as he runs spittle-glazed fingers across my torso, sliding them against my hard nipples. His mouth is boiling. I feel consumed, so divinely vulnerable, exposed like a deer in the mud, belly pale and white as it is splayed and ready to be torn and eaten. I lift my head and look in his eyes, which are open, the lamplight hanging in those green irises. He definitely doesn't have green eyes. In them, in his scars and tattoos, the chiseled architecture of hard muscle hiding under lean velvet soft hide, I see Fenrir, gentle and awful as he rapes a young woman, hungry for something he'd never known. His wet hair tickles my thighs and sticks to his face. In those lips, the graceful contours of skin-clad skull, his long black hair struck with silver, that aquiline Persian nose, I see Cyrah, brave and fire-bright.

Not for a moment is he ferocious, even as my bared body burns with the expectation of violence. He licks and kisses, and guides me into his mouth as if I were a fragile, brittle creature. To him, I am. I know this, I believe it. I am human.

I feel the orgasm rip through me like a claw, my jaws clenched to keep from crying out, hands clutching at the sheets of the bed. I feel a part of myself spatter into his mouth liquid and alive. He gasps, barely heard, a sound of satisfaction, of revelation finally delivered. I hear the click of his throat as he swallows that part of me while I soften slowly against his tongue.

4

I feel awkward afterward, lying there in that cold room with the smell of spit and sweat hanging there as a reminder of what has just happened. I don't know what to do, or how to behave. But he doesn't mind the silence, and he pulls the blanket from his bed and climbs into mine, naked. Seeing that I am cold, he drapes the blanket over me, his hard penis brushing against my bare thigh underneath it. He reaches down and douses the lamp, plunging the room into darkness. The smell of kerosene wafts up to mingle with our scents. We lie there together.

"I don't think Shankar-babu would approve of how we've used his room," I tell him after what seems like hours of dozing in and out of consciousness, but is probably just minutes, moonlight from the windows softening the dark.

He laughs, just a little bit. But his whole body shakes, and it is something I've never seen or felt from him. I try to match my breathing with his, and stop myself. I haven't lain next to someone for so long.

We sleep, and we fuck. It feels like a dream, but is not. He wakes me often, kissing my mouth, my neck, my shoulders, pushing into me from behind. He masturbates me using his hand as he fucks me, telling me to say when I'm coming. Every time I do, he makes sure I spill nothing outside of his mouth, ravenously licking any stray droplets from my thighs or stomach. I become accustomed to his pungent carnality—the raw sea-smell lingering in his armpits and hair, the ammonia-and-cinnamon scent of his sweat and saliva, his hunger, the way he gently coaxes me to orgasm after orgasm with his hands and mouth. Continuously, he consumes me.

He never asks to be penetrated or pleasured by me, except by hand. He never comes. I don't ask, not now, not here, not with him. I am grateful. It has been so long.

"Cyrah. She's your mother. And Fenrir is your father," I whisper to him.

"I thought you'd have figured that out earlier," he says, his voice low.

"I did. I just didn't want to ask you."

He turns to me. "I was born here. Right here on this island, though it was shaped differently back then, and didn't have a village on it. It feels very strange, to come back here."

"I can imagine."

"Tourists come here, and they stay in their comfortable rooms and eat their ready-made meals and relax on tour boats. And they have no idea of the things that happened here. There are still shape-shifters living in the forest. I can smell them. And they can smell me. I can see their traces in the air."

I say nothing, but my gut tightens at the thought. It is the first time since the night we met that he has mentioned his fellow shape-shifters as still extant and around us, and it is jarring. I'm lying next to one, if I choose to believe it, and yet him just saying that makes everything so much more real.

"Will they hurt you?"

"I don't think they will. As long as I don't bother them."

"Do they still kill people?"

"Don't be naïve, Alok. There are animals to live off, but the occasional human has to be slain. It is our—their way. To the villagers who live on these islands, they've become indistinguishable from the tigers in the forest now. Avoiding man-eaters has long been a way of life in these parts."

"What happens if they stop eating humans?"

"We start aging faster. Too gradual to notice at first. It might take a very long time, but we'd die out. Or turn to cannibalism."

"And in the cities?" I ask.

"In Kolkata, the occasional missing beggar isn't even noticed, let alone cared about. Most of the people who get picked off the streets are probably glad to be given freedom from their miserable lives."

"Do you need to justify it to yourself like that?"

"No. I don't. I thought you might need me to, though." He sits up, the blanket slipping off his bare legs. The bed rattles. My hand moves to his forearm, the sheen of downy hair on the hard cord of muscle.

"Wait."

"I'm not going anywhere," he says. I can't see his face very well, but I can tell he's smiling. "Don't worry. No one's going to eat you here. Not if I have anything to say about it."

I run my fingers up and down his arm, trying to feel for the symbols of his tattoos.

"You're saving me for yourself, aren't you. The sex is just an appetizer," I say.

Gooseflesh under my fingertips. I wonder if the faint glow in the room is still moonlight or dawn. It has been a long night. I feel a sudden, drowning discomfort and surface from it by asking the first thing that comes to mind.

"Do you want to tell me about your mother? What happened to her?" I ask.

"I was raised by one of the tribes. They worship the Lord of the South, the shape-shifter king Dakkhin Rai, and they have ruled the forest for centuries. I grew up as one of them—a rakshasa. Not a bastard 'werewolf' spawned by an unwilling human and a wayward kveldulf from northern Europe."

"So Cyrah left you behind."

"Not entirely." He looks at the two windows, at the murky blue beyond the stippled glass panes set in the wooden green shutters.

"She stayed in the Sundarbans with Gévaudan, living outside the tribes as exiles. When I was born she gave me to the rakshasas, to raise as one of them. Her life was spared, for the gift."

"So she never let Gévaudan become her . . ."

"Her imakhr. No. But she never rejoined human society, either. In a way, she watched over me."

"Did you know she was your mother?"

"No. I knew that she was a human that lived in the forest. The villagers here would catch glimpses of her riding through the forest and rivers on the back of a great beast, and she became, to them, an incarnation of the divine guardian of the forest, Banbibi. Gévaudan was her vahana, her animal vehicle. We started calling her Banbibi as well."

I've heard of Banbibi, who is worshipped by both Hindus and Muslims in the Sundarbans. On our drive from Kolkata to the launch dock, we had seen a shrine to her on the side of one of the roads—the garlanded idol representing a woman in a saree and a crown, armed with trishul and club, sitting on the back of a tiger, her vahana, with a baby in her lap. The figures were painted in garish colors, housed in a little concrete alcove just a foot from the asphalt of the road. The small size of the shrine against the trees at the side of the road, the simplicity of its art, like a child's crayon drawing made real, made all the more real the human veneration of this deity. To the villagers who live in the tiger-haunted forests of the Sundarbans, she is real, and their only protection against the demon king Dakkhin Rai (whom they also worship) and his minions, be they tigers or rakshasas. The driver of our car had stopped to place some money at the feet of the goddess, as an offering. At the time, I hadn't noticed the stranger's reaction to this shrine.

Somewhere beyond the lodge, something howls. The dogs we saw earlier, probably. The sound makes me shiver.

"I'm sorry," I say. "That she was so distant. That you didn't get a mother and a father."

"Don't be sentimental. It's—" He paused. "—sweet of you. To be sorry. But why should you be? I grew up proud and strong, a shapeshifter. I needed no parents. I wanted none. I had an imakhr, a tribe. That was all I needed."

"But Cyrah abandoned you. In her writing she seemed so protective of you, by the end."

"She spared me the misery of a human life," he says, curt. I regret saying what I did. "She spared me the misery of being torn between two worlds, trying to claw my way back to my so-called roots, like Fenrir and his pathetic scrabbling to be human as his first self once was. I was rakshasa, hunter, man-eater. She gave me that." He pronounces each sentence like an ultimatum. My hand slips off his forearm as he moves it. I wait.

"Until she gave you the journals that she and Fenrir wrote," I ask, or tell him softly, perhaps in some false hope he won't hear me.

The monotonous shriek of insects beyond the windows. Another howl turning into low barks in the distance.

"Yes. Until that." I hear the sigh of expelled breath. He lies down again, breath sour and close.

I think of Cyrah, illiterate young woman, impossibly writing out her tale on a scroll. There are answers yet to be given.

"Go to sleep," he says, and kisses me on the cheek. I don't want to go to sleep. I have so many more questions. But my eyes begin to droop as soon as he says those words, and I begin to fall away from wakefulness as words trickle from his lips and into my ears.

I am an infant, taking my first steps, tottering on young, chubby legs, miniature feet sinking into the warm mud of the forest. My imakhr smiles, her teeth red with carrion. She looms over me, a giant, naked and brown, caked with forest and gristle, dead deer at her feet. I cough small giggles as she waggles her long red tongue at me. My quivering legs fail me, and I topple into the mud. Pondering whether to cry, I watch my imakhr stoop over the carcass on all fours, dipping her head into the crimson cavern where the deer's chest has recently been opened by her second self. She comes up trailing tendrils of blood from her chin, cheeks swollen. Her powerful hands pluck me off the ground like a fallen fruit, lifting me up into the air, making me dizzy, making me forget to cry, making me burp in delight. My legs pinion, feet coming to rest on her muddy bare breasts, where bone necklaces draw fresh lines in her clothing of dirt. She lifts me to her face, carefully parting my tiny mouth with her lips. The deer's blood rushes into me, warm, bubbling, dripping off that snake-sharp tongue and into my growing belly. I suckle, legs and arms twitching as my food splatters down my body in comforting rivulets.

* * *

I am a boy, dragging the slick, heavy shape of a beaked turtle out of the delta water, its flippers and neck trapped in barbed vine. A fellow whelp wades out of the water, dripping white foam from his mouth in excitement, his taut body glistening in the moonlight. He holds a blade fashioned from hewn stone, and punches a dark gash into the shell. I join him, with my own blade, which cracks open the pale moonlit belly, freeing the fish-scent of the turtle's guts. With a shriek, I bite into the turtle's tough, leathery throat, tearing the blood free so that it bubbles in the mud. Its flippers twitch and thrash. Small silver fish glint and leap around us like inverted rain, thrown to the shore by our hunt. I bite into the turtle, succulent cold skin, warm flesh, the contrast making my entire body shudder with pleasure. It tastes water-filled but fat; it tastes of the sea beyond our forest home. I plunder its corpse, digging into the ripped hole in its underside, fingers closing around the soft orbs of its eggs while my hunt-mate hacks at a flipper to sever it. The mangroves whistle in a sudden wet night breeze, and I know from the clatter of bones that our imakhr watches from the trees, squatting somewhere in between the branches, her eyes green stars poked into the dark between the leaves. I know she is proud, I can smell it, carried in the breeze like incense.

I am a man, grown tall and muscled from climbing the mangroves, from running across the mudflats and swimming in the delta rivers, from leaping into the air to catch seabirds in flight and snap their brittle bodies into fresh meat between my teeth.

I feel the second part of my soul clawing upward from deep within my chest, disengaging from its sticky embrace with the first, ripping away and turning me inside out. The rakshasas bark in the trees, howl in the undergrowth, clawed hands and feet pounding the mud. The human honey-gatherer runs to a freedom he knows is lost. The world expands, I expand, the scents that I grew up with filling my head with mad potency. The touch of trees, of soil under me, of leaves slithering off my back, or feet tearing through stiff roots, all so intense that the mere chase becomes orgasmic, the wind against my naked, beast-bent body a blanket of voices. I scream and it is a grating howl that wakes the forest into terror. My roar bursts out across the country of eighteen tides, becoming one with the chorus of baying rakshasas, a thousand green flames in the foliage watching me. We mark the realm of our king Dakkhin Rai with this war cry, remind the animals and the humans that the deep forest is our land. The villager tumbles to the ground and I am upon him in an instant, my speed closing the twenty-foot gap between us in a second. For the first time, I truly know my second self. It has waited long to be sprung.

I make my first kill of khrissal. I am rakshasa, man-eater. My tusks sinking into the man's back, I taste him. He tastes of his life, his stomach spilling the warm slush of rice he has eaten every day since he could eat solid food; his liver soft with liquor to drown the burden of poverty; his sinews tough and burning with years of gamy resilience, of escaping death in the forest; his blood tinged wine-bitter with sorrow at leaving his wife a widow and his son fatherless; his love for them meaty and thick in the saturated ventricles of his tough heart. I am a god, swallowing his life whole, using it to strengthen my two souls. For an infinite moment, I am him. Beyond the blood-haze, my imakhr paces in her second self, her spined tail whipping the ground, waiting for a bite of the young one's first human prey. Her growl of approval a rattlesnake whisper that makes my fur bristle with delight.

I am a shape-shifter.

I watch her. The human we do not kill, for reasons unknown to me. She is distant, on the silver-blue sheet of a moonlit mudflat stretching away for miles from the forest. She sits atop her vahana, a beast that looks both similar and different from our second selves, from the shapes we know. It is clear that it has grown itself in another land. I cannot look away from its rider because she is both human and unafraid, her legs shaped strong from clinging to the sides of the great monster. Her hair flows long, pouring down her back to her buttocks, down her shoulders and to her thighs in curtains of black that clothe her, tangled amid the flapping pennants of the torn cloak she wears over her saree of white cloth. A leathery flutter of bats speckles the glowing night sky above them. I have never thought that I could find a khrissal beautiful, but she is. I know she can see me, too, lurking here among the trees. I have always found humans to be weak, sad creatures; I have feasted on that sadness, thanked them for it, reveled in my freedom from it. But this one's sadness gives her a power that makes me frightened, that fills me with unease. The beast bristles, as if holding back an urge to gallop over the flats and attack me. I know it is far older and stronger than me, that it can easily kill me. I also know that she wouldn't let it. I know she is watching me, too. I don't know why I cannot look away.

5

When I wake with him still next to me, arms around me, I turn and ask him, because I have to.

"Why me? I've never understood that."

The sunlight at the windows is dim and muted, inoffensive. A cockerel crows somewhere in the village beyond the lodge.

"Let's go to the roof," he says, and gets up. In the morning light, the delicate lines of tattoos still weave across the contours of his naked body. The scars, too, linger. I didn't dream them by lamplight. He gets dressed, brushes his teeth—a shocking revelation—all in silence that isn't uncomfortable as such. It feels somehow appropriate, after my night of visions, of his whispered words soothing me into a different time as I slept, lending me fragments of his life. It is a sacred silence, in this chamber where we've declared our intimacy. I perform the same mundane rituals of waking, and together we make our way to the roof. It is just six in the morning by my watch, but I feel awake despite the little sleep I've gotten. From the roof, we can't see beyond the courtyard garden. Everything is submerged in the haze of dawn. The sun, filtered by this milky cloud, hangs low like a perfect orange droplet of magma glistening in the ash-gray sky.

"Will you answer my question?" I ask him, my breath emerging to blend with the mist.

"Yes, Alok. I chose you for no good reason at all."

"There are millions of people—"

"I know. But there you were. You smelled of loneliness. So I came to you, like a wolf to lonesome prey. Or a tiger. A man. What else can I say? It's the truth. I'm not dictated by currents of fate or any other mystical force, just because I'm a thing of magic. I make choices like anyone else."

"I smelled of loneliness."

"You did."

I laugh, without humor. "I don't think I can deny that, though I don't know what loneliness smells like."

He looks at me. His eyes are dark, earth brown in the morning.

"It's not something to be ashamed of, Alok. It's something we have in common."

"I've known you for—a while now. And I don't. I don't know. Will you at least tell me your name?"

He sighs. "I don't have one, Alok. Not in the way you're thinking. We have many names, or none, sometimes. This body, this face; it's the one I was born with, the one that Cyrah and Fenrir gave me. But I can change it, if I will it, though after so long it would be difficult. But I can. Just like I can change my second self as well, if the circumstances are right. Identity doesn't mean the same thing to us as it does to you. Names are arbitrary in such an existence. I didn't leave one out just to sound mysterious."

I nod, looking at the treetops of the garden, half there in the moist air.

"It was part of it, though, wasn't it?" I ask.

"What?"

"The reason you didn't give me a name. It was partly to sound mysterious," I tell him.

He smiles.

"When we first met. At the baul mela. Why did you introduce yourself as a werewolf if that's not what you identify as?"

"Half werewolf," he corrects me, as he has so many times before. "Though I suppose that's not correct, either. The simple fact is that the werewolf is more easily identifiable, iconic. Recognizable." His mouth twists as he chews the inside of his cheek. "And I have actually called myself that, in the past. Werewolf. I've used that word to shape my second self in ways rakshasas don't. When I left the Sundarbans, I thought of myself as more werewolf than rakshasa, though I didn't know the word then. It was because I knew I came from Fenrir and a human; I saw myself as different. For better or for worse, those stories changed my life. I formed a splinter pack. Some of them even mimicked my ways. The first werewolves of Hindustan. We traveled up the delta and came to the swamp jungle that would be Kolkata. We made that our hunting ground, our land."

"Were you sad to leave your imakhr? The home you grew up in?"

He smiles, squinting into the brightening orb of the sun as it thins the mist with patient persistence. "Cyrah and Gévaudan once had this very conversation," he says.

I remember reading that conversation even as he says this. I remember typing it out.

"I don't know," he says. "I don't think I knew sadness as an emotion I could really feel, then. It was something we tasted in humans, not something we experienced."

The shrill brassy noise of a bell rings through the air from downstairs, setting the dogs in the garden barking in curiosity.

"That's breakfast. Shankar-babu will start wondering where we are. Let's go," he says, touching my arm as he turns to walk to the doorway that leads to the stairs.

6

We have a quick breakfast of onion pakoras, biscuits, and sweet milk tea in the dining room, listening to Shankar-babu talk about his family and his plans to one day move to Kolkata, while squares of sunlight brighten the floors, shifting with the hours.

Afterward, the stranger and I set out for a walk beyond the lodge and into the village. Shankar-babu tries to insist on the guide coming with us, but the stranger is persuasive enough to convince him this isn't required.

The garden is jeweled with dew, catching the light of the sunrise. Everything glows, spider silk tracing ghost lines between plants and trees, leaves and flowers blinding and hyper-real to eyes weakened by lack of sleep. I squint at it all, again feeling caught in a dream as the stranger walks by me, his ubiquitous backpack slung over his shoulders. It makes him look youthful, not immortal, and this gladdens me. I realize that I prefer it when his hair is down instead of tied into a ponytail.

We see the first glimpse of other guests at the lodge—a couple sitting on the swinging wicker chairs set up in one of the grassy patches between the trees. Other than them, we seem to be the only ones staying here. Perhaps it's off season.

The brick path takes us beyond the lodge and turns into a dirt path as we venture into the village. Through the trees bowing over the road, we can see the river shining in the gaps between leaves. Our boat is still moored there. The village is scattered and spaced out, clay and thatch huts clustered into separate cliques under the eaves of the forest. Some of the huts squat next to the water, where men and women both wade knee-deep with nets in the morning chill, trawling for fish and crustaceans, their faded red lungis and sarees ballooning and flattening on the brown waves. We pass shacks by the side of the road that shelter shops selling supplies from civilization, mostly, I assume, for visitors to the island: sachets of supari (same as on Park Street), packets of branded potato chips that are deflated from the journey from there to here, dirty glass bottles of Coca-Cola and Pepsi. Alongside these wares are more exotic local produce—rows of whiskey and rum bottles of different sizes, their labels washed off, filled with the thick amber of honey procured from the forest, right from under the noses of tigers and shape-shifters. Liquid gold from the realm of Dakkhin Rai.

We stop to get a taste, using little wooden ice cream spoons. The honey is thick and grainy with sugar crystals, flecks of wax. It is the best honey I've ever tasted, but that could be just because I know the danger involved in procuring it. It could also be because the only honey I've had all my life is from jars with anthropomorphic cartoon bees on them, bought at grocery stores.

In Bengali I ask the seller, a wiry man in a collar-shirt and lungi, if he believes in Banbibi and Dakkhin Rai. He nods, happy to answer. But it's also obvious that he is used to being asked this. His resigned nod indicates that it is a silly question to him, that belief in those entities is self-evident in this world. I look at the stranger to see what he thinks of the seller's response. He just smiles.

The seller points to a group of men walking down the road, wearing cheap plastic masks of a bearded man on the backs of their heads. Barefoot and in lungis, despite the cold.

"They're going to gather more honey and beeswax," he says. "They'll get in a boat and go downstream into the deep forest."

"Why are they wearing those masks on the backs of their heads?" I ask.

"To trick the tigers. That way the tigers always think that we have our faces to them, that we are always looking at them, even if we aren't. And they stay away because they think they can't sneak up on us."

"Does it work?"

"I'm still alive," he says with a laugh, showing his big teeth, bright against his dark skin. I laugh with him, wondering whether that's because of luck or the masks.

"That is Dakkhin Rai's face," he says, pointing at one of the masks, hanging from a wall behind him. The shape-shifter king. The plastic face of a bearded man, wide eyes and pink skin. He doesn't look too demonic.

"That also helps. If they see their master, they won't attack." He says this with a bit of a smile, as if he doesn't quite buy that the tigers know who their master is. The stranger remains silent throughout.

Even if the masks trick a tiger, I know they wouldn't trick a shape-shifter.

But I don't ask the man about rakshasas. I buy a bottle of honey, which is wrapped in newspaper to keep from getting too gummy. The stranger keeps it in his bag.

We keep walking. By the road, we see fields that seem to have been harvested, and we take a shortcut through one of them, my sneakers sinking through the soft tilled ground and making me unsteady, the dry yellow stalks of whatever crop was grown on it scratching at my jeans. The stranger walks on ahead as if he were treading on pavement, as is to be expected. I wonder if someone will chastise us for walking on their field, but no one does. A black goat watches our progress and decides to distance itself from us, ambling away toward the raised road.

"Where are we going?" I ask, panting a bit.

"I want some privacy. We're going somewhere a bit more isolated."

The forest looms uncomfortably close, looking very dark in contrast with the bright, open field, with its sunlit mist burning away as the temperature rises.

"Wait. We're not going in there, are we?" He says nothing, striding on.

"Are we?" I demand, louder.

"Yes, we are."

I stop walking. He keeps walking. He realizes I'm not following and looks back.

"You can't be serious. We can't go in there," I tell him.

"I am, and we are. It's not exactly the deep forest. There's a village right here."

"There are still tigers in there," I say, incredulous. "Aren't there."

"Yes."

"And—" I pause, peering into the dark tangle of trees and under-growth. "And shape-shifters."

"Yes. There are."

We both stare at each other. The goat brays from afar, giving us its indecipherable opinion. The stranger looks down, nudging the clods of earth that have congealed in the cold with his open-toed sandals.

"I thought you wanted to know more."

"I do, but why do we have to go in there?"

He doesn't answer, instead walking back to me. He stops when he's right next to me, looking in my eyes.

"You're scared," he tells me. I nod.

"I won't let anything hurt you in there," he says.

"Tigers. And shape-shifters."

"Neither will come near us. I promise. I'm an exile, but this is still where I come from. As long as we don't stay in there too long, they'll stay away from us. You won't even see them."

"That's not very comforting to me."

He takes my hand in his. Mine is cold, his warm. As always. The gesture is sudden, and makes me jump. "Alok, I won't let anything hurt you. You'll be safe with me. All right?" He stares into my eyes. If he's crazy, if all of this is a lie, I could be walking straight to a foolish death.

I sigh and nod. "All right."

We walk toward the forest fringe. I don't let go of his hand.

7

The forest is a wall of scent and sound—the constant hiss of leaves, the bone-crackle of branches and dry detritus shifting and warming in the morning, the unending song of insects. The smell of wet earth and shadow-brewed chlorophyll makes it feel like entering the threshold of a new atmosphere, a different world than the one we were just walking in. I twitch and stumble with each tickle of leaf or bug on my skin, my entire body coiled tight in fear. I grip the stranger's hand as if it is a talisman. He gives no reaction, never loosening his hold on me as he marches through the web of roots and shrubs, our palms sealed in sweat, fingers of his other hand scraping the bark of the sundari trees that surround us. It is very dark for the beginning of the day. I trip and fall many times, each time helped up by him. I'm wearing sneakers, but it's near impossible to walk without stumbling because of the overgrown net of roots that overlays the earth. Tiny insects hover in the light hanging from the eaves like living dust. They enter my nostrils, making me sniff and sneeze. Flickering little lizards ghost their way up bark, and pulsing brown globules of earth leap across the ground, only to be discerned as frogs by my confused eyes. I duck in horror at a huge spider suspended between branches, just a foot above my head, the twitching triangle of its body banana yellow and coal black, legs plucking its web for prey.

Already, behind me, the village field we came from is invisible. By the clustered mossy pillars of sundari trunks we stop and sit on the carpet of roots, the mulch of soil and rotted leaves.

"Here," he says, breathing deep, his face calm and eyes glistening, as if he's just smoked a joint. His legs are crossed like a meditating sadhu. "Don't be afraid, Alok. We're not far from our little human en-clave. Don't be afraid."

I can't even speak. I am shaking, wondering what's beyond the tree trunks, in that dazzling profusion of green. Every second I expect the sharp stab of a snake's fangs piercing my jeans. I feel eyes beyond my visibility, in every bead of sunlight that pokes through the ceiling and curtains of foliage that contain this world.

"This," he hisses, and closes his eyes. "This is where I grew up." His mouth is open, cheeks flickering with small spasms. I begin to fear that he will go into some kind of trance, leave me alone and helpless here in the forest where he grew up.

His eyes open. They're the same color as the forest. The green, so intrusive and strange in that brown face. He holds both my trembling hands and kisses me on the mouth, bringing damp to my dry lips. The insects rejoice.

"Talk to me, Alok. Say something. Is it not beautiful?"

I swallow hard. Force myself to form words. "Yes. I've . . . I've never been in a forest. Not like this." His thumbs run over my knuckles.

A speck of gold with legs crawls through the thick waves of his hair. In my daze, I can't tell if it's a wasp or a bee. He doesn't take his eyes off me.

"My mother ended her scroll by addressing me directly. I left that out of the translation."

"What?"

"It said, 'To my son, Izrail.' She never was too sentimental. But that was the name she gave me. If you want one for me, you can have that one. It's a human name."

"Izrail?"

"After the archangel, in Islam. Malak al-Maut, the angel of death."

"Izrail," I whisper. He smiles.

"Thank you," I say.

"You're welcome, Alok." The golden insect leaps from his hair, hov-ers around Izrail's head, and vanishes back into the thick air of the forest. He takes off his backpack and unzips it. The sound slices across my oversaturated mind, making me shiver. He takes something out. It takes me a while to understand what it is—two bundles of brown parchment tied together into fat rolls. The manuscripts. The ones he translated, and I spent the last year editing and typing out. I am finally looking at the source documents.

"You know what this is, Alok. You were patient. You deserve to see what you gave new life."

"I didn't do anything. I just typed them out," I tell him, breathless.

"If you say so. But here they are. The two scrolls. One written by Fenrir, to Cyrah. The other told by Cyrah, for me."

He unties them and hands them over to me. They are heavy, almost like pieces of wood, the scrolls stiffened and leathery. They smell like leather, too. There are no pages—each scroll is made of several pieces of parchment rolled into a fat bundle. I've never seen paper or parchment like it—it's thick and tough, and so dark a shade of brown that I can't make out the inked black script very well. The parchment feels coarse under my fingers.

"This parchment was used by many of the tribes. It's made from the skin of their prey. I assume they fashioned it during their travels through the Middle East, where they had desert sun to treat and dry it. Or perhaps they brought it with them from Europe. I, too, made my own."

I feel no repulsion as I realize that I'm holding scrolls of ancient human skin in my hands, unwrapped and taken from people who lived their lives four centuries ago, inscribed with the stories of their killers. I unroll a bit of one scroll, looking at the script. It looks like nothing I'm familiar with, a scrawl that appears to have symbols from various alphabets and languages, all suspended in a medium of lines and letters that look entirely made up. The first, and shorter, scroll seems to be in Arabic script, though it also has unfamiliar-looking symbols and lines that look incongruous amid the language. The writing is pitted, etched into the skin of the scrolls, as if the ink was acidic. The scrolls are also, to my surprise, illuminated, every inch of space without text filled in with drawings and designs that are sometimes too small to be anything other than an intricate swirl of designs. The drawings on the first scroll are simple yet graceful—like cave paintings looped through the language, showing figures and animals, often in flux. The second scroll's illuminations are more detailed, darker, sometimes filling the borders of the parchment with shaded visions of human faces and bodies that weep across the leather with dark-blooded ink.

"What, what language is it?"

Izrail lets his fingers run across mine, and the scrolls. When he speaks, his voice is slurred. "Fenrir's scroll is mostly in Pashto, so Cyrah could understand. The second scroll, and the earlier parts of the first, are in an amalgam. The language has no name, and parts of it are used by shape-shifters across the continents. It combines all the languages of humanity, cobbled from all our prey. If ever there was a tongue before Babel fell, it was this one. It has spawned words of its own as well. It has its own shifting rules, its own recombinant script."

"It's your language?"

"You could say that. It doesn't have to be."

"Izrail, this is. I don't know what to say."

"Yes, the scrolls. They say enough, don't they?"

"God. How. How did you get these? What happened to Cyrah and Gévaudan?"

I look around, and it wouldn't surprise me too much to see both of them watching us. The forest has become magic itself, burning with filtered sunlight. I am a character in myth, in folklore, and no one even knows it. The villagers are living out their lives just a mile away.

"I'm going to tell you, of course. You deserve to know," says Izrail, his eyelids lazy as they droop over those green irises, unrealistic in their ability to capture the morning light sneaking in through the leaves.

His smile returns, wistful. "You know, I blame them," he breathes.

"I blame my mother and father. So very human of me. It is their blood that runs in me: Fenrir's weak indecision; Cyrah's cloying, over-powering humanity. They made me what I am. I was drawn, always drawn, to my own prey in ways that I shouldn't have been. Even more so after reading, absorbing the stories of my mother and father. It was as inevitable as the doom of this world, as the trumpet call ringing through the cosmos when this orb falls into the bloated sun. I blame them for the decision to rescue that baul girl from my own hunt, that poor girl who hated me for saving her life. I blame them for thinking I had fallen in love, like my father, or like a human. I blame them. I live in the twilight between worlds, like they did. I was born to be an exile. It was decided from the moment Fenrir raped Cyrah."

I don't know what to say, but I say, "Don't—"

His hand goes to my neck, thumb on my throat, stilling my words.

"Don't comfort me, Alok," he whispers. His thumbnail is sharp, and it runs down my neck, waking my entire body with nervous lightning.

"This is where I was going to kill you. In this forest."

I let him say these words, feeling sluggish looking at his drooping eyes and swaying torso. It doesn't even surprise me, doesn't frighten me any more than being in the middle of a forest filled with tigers and shape-shifters. If my heart begins to beat faster it is because I am filled with wonder and curiosity. Tears gather at the corners of my eyes.

"Like the baul girl that you rescued from your own hunt. You killed her."

"Of course I did. Of course I did. I am ever like Fenrir, but she was no Cyrah, even though she reminded me of her, just because I saw the face of a young human female with a strong will, with strength in her. I tried to talk to her, to soothe her with stories. But she hated me. I thought I could do what Fenrir couldn't with my mother, that perhaps I could rewrite that story and make this human creature I rescued from her death love me. A foolish whimsy. She was crippled with terror and grief. What could I do? I gave her respite."

"You killed her, and ate her," I say. The forest swims beyond Izrail's body, its living tapestry rippling as the sun rises higher, somewhere beyond our sight. He nods, a droplet of sweat rolling down the side of his forehead, a glass line.

"Ate her," he murmurs. "And wrote on her skin the story of my mother. Yes. You have so many questions, but you don't ask, because you're kind and you listen to me. So many untold things, inconsistencies and secrets. What human can sit before me and not have questions?"

"And me, Izrail. Will you kill me now?" I remember Cyrah in the forest by the Yamuna, Gévaudan tranced into a frenzy, about to bare his second self. "Are you going to show me your second self?" There is a panic attack roiling inside my body, but I let it envelop me instead of reacting against it, let it thunder in my blood vessels and head like the sea that inundates this delta. I lick my dry lips, feeling their skin split.

His eyes close and open, languid, catlike. "No. I won't. I liked you from the moment I met you, Alok. I remember the things I said to you in our early conversations, and it embarrasses me so deeply. I behaved like a whelp performing the part of a werewolf, the father I never really had, swaggering and telling white lies and acting mysterious. Yes, I liked you from the very beginning. That's why I wanted to bring you here, where I made my first human kill, where I first sprang my second self, where I grew up. I had it all planned out, Alok. Here I would have brought you, and I would have used my knuckles to break your nose, quick, shatter it so you fell to unconsciousness, so you could not cry out or scream. I would have broken your back with my knee to cripple you, and I would have sliced your windpipe with my fingernail to preserve your silence. Then I would have taken off my clothes and let my second self out, drawing my fellow rakshasas from the forest, have them watch me tear your throat out with my teeth, and dismember you, tear you to pieces and eat you, bit by bit, until you were gone, until only the cracked bones of your skeleton remained. They would watch, and they would wait, to see if I dared come deeper into their forest. But this is close to Banbibi's protectorate, to human habitation, and they would allow me this one kill, because it is a fluid place. Because even though I am an exile, I am also Banbibi's son, and that is no ordinary thing. By my scent they would know both these things, and remember the time I was once one of them, remember the change that crept along my musk the day I found out I was bastard son to the human guardian of the forest and a European exile. They would remember how I left with my own pack, and they would sniff out the deep trace of shame that tells of my betrayal of that pack.

"But I am Banbibi's son, and because of this they would leave me be. So I would stay here and dig a deep hole and bury myself naked with your bones, to sleep the molting trance of ekh'du, which centuries ago the Slavs saw the scavenging shape-shifters of their land waking from out of the ground of plague-graves, and so called our kind undead. And in this trance I would digest the life you have lived, live off it as a bear lives off the fat it has gathered on its bones for winter, let my souls absorb it and send its echoes calling through my mind as if it were the longest dream I ever dreamed, and in the womb of the earth I would change and shift as befits my kind, and in a night or a day or a week or a month I would either be dead, or emerge with a new first self— you, my dearest friend, Alok. And you would live in me, as me, or I as you, forever, or until my distant end, whenever that may be."

As I listen to Izrail's confession, I realize that the rhythm of it has hypnotized me, that I am in a waking sleep, even though I hear what he is saying. I feel his fingers touch my eyelids, close them.

I am a shape-shifter, strong, young. It is winter now, the mudflats covered in low mist fanned out of the forest by the trees.

I watch her still. There are now gleaming strands of silver in her black hair. She is wearing an extra fur pelt now over her tattered cloak. As I observe her, she leaps off the beast on her strong legs, feet slapping the soft ground of the mudflat. I retreat deeper into the foliage, shocked by this. She has always seen me watching her, but she has never once left her perch on that great mount.

She walks forward toward me, dimpling the mud with a trail of her footprints. The beast watches, its eyes like the stars above us.

I think of running, returning to my pack. I think of seeing if she will come any closer.

"Come out of the trees, young rakshasa," she says in Bangla when she is twenty feet from me. She says it softly, knowing that I can hear her. It is the first time I have heard her speak. It is strange and frightening to hear the voice of a khrissal so calm and clear while she addresses me. No khrissal has looked me in the eyes and shown anything but fear. Feeling like it would be a sign of weakness to stay hidden, I walk out of the edge of the forest, standing tall in my first self.

I see the beast behind her crouch lower, ready to charge. I tense, ready to shift and flee should I need to.

"Don't be alarmed," she says, bringing my gaze back to her calm face. Her words are lilting like a song, as if she is not used to speaking Bangla. "Jevah-dan will not hurt you. He's just protective."

She looks at me, and I feel ashamed, almost, of my nakedness. It is like nothing I have ever felt before.

"Do you know Pashto?" she asks.

I nod. Though it is not common to do so, I have ranged far enough and hunted enough Mughals to know their languages, and I know even the language of the pirates and smugglers that roam the waterways of the delta forest in their wooden ships from the land they call Portugal, and the languages of other intruders from the far places that fall under the banner of Europe.

She smiles, and my chest hurts. I wonder why. I have never seen a khrissal smile while looking at me, just as I have never seen one look at me and not flee. I feel uneasy to see that she looks proud, almost like my imakhr when I made my first kill.

"That is good," she says, in Pashto this time. "Come closer, child. We must talk."

"I'm not a child." *I could destroy you easier than a tiger swats a mouse dead,* I am about to say, but remember the beast behind her. "Why do you want to talk to me?" I ask.

Her chest rises and falls, a puff of her breath clouding her lips. Her eyes are a crystal gray, almost green in the half-light of the moon. "In your bones, those of your first self, you can perhaps feel it already. You know," she tells me.

The smell of my fear escapes me like a cloud. The shape-shifter bristles behind her, shaking its head and snapping its jaws in loud clashes as it catches the scent.

She smiles again, but it is a sad, terrible smile that makes me want to wither at her knees and beg her to leave me alone.

"You are a child, young rakshasa. To me, you're still a child. In human years, you've just grown beyond boyhood. You're so very young. You'd be on the brink of manhood, mustering the courage to court girls, confused by everything in the world; a sweet and delicate thing."

"I'm no khrissal. What is it you want? Why are you saying these things to me?"

"You're not human, no. But you could have been, so easily." She looks down, the curtain of her hair sweeping past her face as she clutches her fur and cloak closer to her shoulders, and for a moment she is incredible in her fragility. But it is her words that leave me breathless.

"Look at you. Tall and beautiful, so powerful and sure of yourself," she breathes, looking into my eyes. "And yet, I still wonder every night whether I made the right choice."

"What are you—"

"Come closer," she says, her words piercing the damp air with their sharpness. Not aggression, but force. It is the first time she has raised her voice to a normal tenor. I am so startled I obey her, walking up to her so that I am a foot away, so that I can feel her khrissal blood iron-warm in the air, smell her scent of unwashed sweat and skin, beast-musk and forest dirt. Yet I feel no appetite, no urge to rip her open and free that tumult of tastes and odors.

She reaches out with one hand. I flinch, almost pouncing backward into a crouch but suppressing the instinct. *She is a khrissal,* I tell myself. *She cannot hurt me.* Her fingers touch my face, light, grazing the line of my jaw, and her cool palm rests against my cheek.

"I'm sorry, my son. I did what I thought was best."

I keep my eyes locked to hers. She lets her hand fall away. "Who are you?" I demand.

"I'm your mother. I gave birth to you, here in this forest. I nursed you, and held you, and cared for you, for as long as I could allow myself, and I gave you to the tribes."

I stare at her, my breathing now harsh.

"You're not my mother, khrissal. The creature you gave birth to was your son. That is none of my concern. It died when I was born."

The corner of her lip twitches, her eyes darting for a second like those of a frightened deer. I can see the gouges my words make in her. Her face is placid and calm again within moments, but I know that I have hurt her. It is the only thing I can do to keep from fleeing, from never seeing this khrissal goddess and her vahana again. I feel sick. She licks her lips. I see her throat move under the skin as she swallows, and speaks.

"You're cruel, but it's just the way of your kind. I have seen even that overcome, by those who have proven themselves far stronger than the mightiest of beasts natural and magical. But it is as you say," she says. She is so gentle, so unlike anything that I have met, or talked to.

"That . . . creature, that was my son," she continues, looking straight at me without flinching. "He had a father, who was a rakshasa as well, though not like you. A shape-changer, I should say. He came from a different part of the world, and the tribes there do not use the word *rakshasa*, and are different. Jevah-dan was his friend, once."

I say nothing.

"Seeing as how you came from that creature my son, I thought that you had a right to know how that creature came to be. How you came to be. So I give you this. Look at it if you wish."

She reaches under her cloak, bringing out a sackcloth bundle and handing it to me. With that, she stands on her toes and presses her mouth to my cheek. Her lips spark in the winter air like a brand against me, the kiss tingling and evaporating on my scorching skin. She looks at me one last time and strides away, holding her cloak bunched to her hips because it is too long by far for her, her bare mud-spattered calves visible under its torn fringe, the waves of her hair dangling around her like thick black cords from out of her cowl, tangling themselves around her legs and body. I watch her as I always have, watch her return to her companion Jevah-dan, watch them gallop away across the mudflat until they are gone.

I look inside the sackcloth. Nestled inside is a scroll of parchment, made by a shape-shifter.

After reading it, I bury the scroll in the forest, in the center of one of the islands. I mark the spot with nothing but my piss, so anyone digging there will have slighted me.

* * *

The next time I see her, winter has just begun to wane, and she is alone.

I stand at the very edge of the country of eighteen tides, the forest miles behind me. A plain of salt clay stretches before me. It meets the ocean on the horizon, where the falling sun burns and bleeds across the great waters. It is the first time I have seen the open sea, or come this far. I have followed her trail here, through the delta to the end of Hindustan.

Somewhere out there, the cannon-heavy ships of pale-skinned khrissals who call themselves Portuguese, Dutch, French, British, compete on the waves for their futures in this land, occasionally dredging up on the sieve of the Ganga's mouth, where we hunt them and glean their strange stories, so different from those of the delta people. Though I have dreamed their patchwork lives, learned from their flesh and blood and souls the different ways of this world, I have never before seen with my own senses how massive this orb we all make our stories on truly is. What I see in front of me is but a fraction of it, but it looks like eternity itself.

She looks into that vastness, as if she came from it.

I watch her, small against the wide tidal plain, surrounded by shrieking gulls that pick and feed from the wet ground. Crests of foaming water crash in the distance, a constant thunder in the air.

I follow the glare of the setting sun and walk to her. She turns to look at me.

"Your guardian is gone," I say to her.

Her face is wet, flushed not just from the carnal red of sunset but from crying. She smiles.

"Yes. He was never at home here. He was lonely, like I am. Even though we always had each other. I knew that, even if he could never admit it, even if he couldn't face the fact that one way or the other, he couldn't care for me forever. I've never before known loyalty like his."

"If he cared so much for you, why has he fled, leaving you ready prey to his kind?"

She looks disappointed that I would ask such a question, her brow furrowing. The cloak shifts on her shoulders, heavy but stirred by the hurtling damp wind from the ocean. She shakes her head.

"He did not flee, young rakshasa. I told him to leave. I demanded it. It wasn't an easy thing for him to do, but he has respected my wishes. Jevah-dan has journeyed beyond the delta, and, I hope, will one day return to his home of France."

I spit at her feet. "Your friendship is an abomination. You are his prey."

She takes off her cowl, her hair lashing out across her face as if in anger. Then she slaps me, hard, on the cheek. In that second when she raises her arm I see it coming, and am compelled by instinct to grab her limb and snap it like a twig, but something keeps me from doing so. The crack of it echoes in my skull as her nails rake past the edge of my chin. The blow does not hurt me, but the shock of it is tremendous, makes me stagger back. She is still a khrissal, goddess or no.

"I am prey to you all: to your father, to my dearest friend, to you, my son," she says.

I bare my teeth. "You're not my mother."

She bites her lower lip. I see tiny jewels of blood emerge in the seams left by her teeth. "Then kill me. Devour me," she says. I see her shivering in the cold wall of knotted air rushing over the desolate sun-churned sea. Somewhere above the thin dark line of forest far behind us, a half-moon waits.

Piss runs down my thighs, spatters and hisses in the silt. The gulls scream and recoil from us, from the vapors of my spoor. I can feel the change coming, but again, again that doubt congeals the membrane between my souls, stifling their separation, sending a crawling ache deep through my chest.

"I'm your prey. Do what you were born to do. Destroy me," she says.

"Why?" I say between gnashing teeth, spittle spraying against her. She doesn't even blink, doesn't back away as I loom over her, my jaws inches from her forehead.

"Why not? I can't go back to humanity's shores. And I don't belong here, either. If I had kept you as my son, I could have gone back, could have tried to make a life for us both somewhere. But I didn't. I made my choice. I have seen you safely to adulthood, even if it is the adulthood of a creature not human. And I shouldn't regret that. You're far stronger this way."

Still I let her speak, am drawn to her words, want them to keep falling against my ears in that soft, abhorrent, *human* voice.

"What have you done to me, khrissal? Have you cast a spell on me? Are you truly some devi of your people? You . . . you really are Banbibi," I say, my hackles rising, breath blowing the hair from out of her eyes, drying the traces of tears from her cheekbones.

"My dear boy," she says, her eyes widening. Her small hands hold my wrists, tight so I don't shake them off, though I could, easily. But again, I don't. "I've cast nothing on you, nothing at all. I'm no devi. I have no powers. I should have died the moment I met Fenrir, or become a shape-changer myself. And I do not want to become a shape-changer. I thought I did, once. The thoughts of a young woman. But devour me now, and perhaps I'll always be Banbibi, never aging, never seen. I've lived my life like no human, and now I can't die like a human of old age, not alone and mired between worlds."

I retch, drooling slime at her feet. Her hands stroke my arms. Once again, I feel her fingers against my cheek.

"Don't be scared. They're coming. We had a pact, because I gave you to them. Jevah-dan negotiated it. But Jevah-dan is gone now. Our pack of two is gone. They won't abide by the pact anymore. So I'm dead anyway. You'll be the hero of your tribe, the one who slew this human avatar of Banbibi, khrissal who wormed her way into living among the rakshasas in their realm, and helped your tribe's prey escape from them and suffered no consequence for it. Let go, my love. Let your second self out. I'm here, unprotected."

She's right. I can feel it in my guts and in my head, the approach of my pack-mates and my imakhr. They have followed. They are coming. Miles away, I see the forest disgorge dark shapes that speed across the silt plain.

The sun shatters through clouds clinging to the edge of the ocean, its million shining pieces flung across the leagues of water, carried from the crests of surf by wind and thrown to burn in her black hair, turning it bloody gold. From over the far forest, darkness creeps across the wetland, as if brought by the advancing harbingers of my tribe. I can feel the rumble of their clawed feet and lashing of their long tails in the soles of my feet.

Her thumb brushes across my cheekbone. I fall to my knees in front of her like a wretched devotee, as if I am my father the exile, author of that accursed scroll, pitiful rakshasa from Europe who gave himself to a khrissal, who spun off the thread of time that ends here between the sinking sun and the floating moon, the ocean and the land.

They're coming. Her guardian is gone. They will kill her when they arrive. I realize with sudden clarity that I have to be the one to kill her; that I cannot let any of the others touch her or eat of her. I must be the one. I must. I look up into her, and I know she sees this in my eyes.

There is time yet.

She nods, and smiles at me. Blood on her lips, salt water in her eyes. Even though she is shivering, there is no fear in her. I would smell it if there was. I let my second self emerge.

For a moment I don't know where I am, for a moment I still feel an ocean wind in my eyes, still feel the blood of a human demigoddess in my mouth. We're walking across the field by the forest, heading toward the raised dirt road. I stagger and spit copious, bitter saliva into the furrows of the field, almost falling into the hard stalks sticking out of them. Izrail steadies me with his strong hand, and already has a shawl ready to wrap around my shoulders.

I take deep breaths, as he once told me to. Pins and needles prickle across my limbs. I look back at the blackening wall of the forest against the rich pink sky.

"We were in there all day?"

"Don't worry, I told Shankar-babu we'd be gone all day. I convinced him we wouldn't wander off and die. They're not going to send search parties. Not yet, anyway. We should be getting back now."

I stare at him.

He smiles, reassuring. "I know. Come. We'll talk about it later."

I look again at the forest. The setting sun twinkles between the leaves of the uppermost canopy. In the dense dark between the tree trunks, I sense the shape-shifters watch us depart their realm. I can see nothing, hear nothing of them. But they are there, as real as the insects hammering my skin in the dimming dusk air.

I feel Izrail's hand at my wrist. "Come," he says. I look at his eyes. They are dark. There is no green there. He looks weary, and his cheeks, I am shocked to notice, are damp. I nod, and walk alongside him as we return to the road. The forest glowering at our backs, my head spinning from the span of lifetimes I have just lived, I feel like silence is, perhaps, the only conversation for now.

On the road, we see a twinkling line of lanterns in the distance, returning to the village. I hope to myself that it is the honey-gatherers, returned from the deep forest safe and alive.

8

We eat dinner in haste, tolerating Shankar-babu's conversation, giving brief words of explanation about being tired from our long walk around the island. He laughs and asks if we saw any tigers, and we say that we didn't. We are bid good night, and we retreat into the darkness beyond the dining room, the electricity gone again for the night. We hurry upstairs to our room, shut and lock the door with the rattling rusty dead bolt. Izrail unwraps the sticky whiskey bottle full of honey. We both drink from it, and in silence we kiss with our sweetened mouths, hungry, drawn to each other after the day gone by in that dream-filled forest. By the dim glow of the hurricane lamp, we make love, slow and patient. Again he never comes himself, only bringing me to climax, never asking to be fucked by me.

Again he devours me, licking every spilled part of me like a benign monster.

When I kill my mother, I am a shape-shifter, rakshasa, strong and bold, with a second self to make even the bravest of khrissals run from me.

But I am still a child who does not know what it is to have a mother, or a father, and finds that it has both.

Or, in the case of my mother, had. She was khrissal, but she did not run. She did not run from me.

I am slow, sluggish from devouring an entire human body so quickly, with such ravenous desperation. I am surrounded now by my pack, who watch in their first selves. My imakhr leads them.

When she sees me crouched over the stripped bones of Banbibi's human avatar, her brief smile is one of regret. Perhaps she thought she could hide my bastard birth from me all my life, protect me from the curse I carry.

She looks at Cyrah's bones with something approaching fear. The bones of a human goddess. But she approaches despite this, and squats near me, her legs spread wide to let the trinkets hanging from under her thighs show. The baby teeth that fell out of my mouth as I grew faster than any human into the shape of a boy and then a man, burned like tiny pearls into the lines of her imakhr tattoos, shards of tusk and bone and shell hanging off wire and string entwined into scarred bumps, tracing the history of the first animals I ever hunted by myself. I remember clinging to that body as a growing rakshasa in the shape of a human child, hunting with tools as she showed me, yearning for the day I could free my second self, touching and kissing it in mimicry of khrissal sexual ritual right before fucking our second selves when I was grown. Memories poisoned by the khrissal I have just eaten of.

I wait, refuse to react until my imakhr does. Cyrah's remains between us. I want her to embrace me, to comfort me, to give me explication, forgiveness for taking Banbibi's death from our pack, for taking it as my own.

But I know better. I may be Banbibi's devourer, but I am no hero, because I am also Banbibi's son. My imakhr knows me too well. Perhaps she was only waiting for this day, as Banbibi circled our territories on the back of her European vahana, lurking in wait to take back what used to be her son.

I reach out for my imakhr's face, to give her contact, to let her taste Cyrah's blood on my hands. But she grabs my wrist and bites it, quick, and shoves me back. I look at the imprinted half-moon in my flesh. She will have no leftovers. I have kept my tribe from tasting this human goddess, from kindling and sharing her ghost fire.

She gets up. I try to stagger up as well, but she kicks my face and stamps on Cyrah's ribs.

The sound of Cyrah's bones breaking under my imakhr's mud-caked feet.

I leap. My hand cracks against the mouth that fed me as an infant, that kissed me and pleasured me.

My nails have left dark slashes across her cheek. She steps back. Her expression doesn't change. A bead of red oozes from the corner of her mouth. She spits on me. She licks her dark lips, doesn't touch her ripped cheek.

She shakes her head, because she knows. I am changed forever. I have tasted the human life that created the body I wear.

There under the new stars, my imakhr springs her second self. The first falls away a sheath of digested dream. Her second self rises on its hind legs and towers over the beach like a hill thrust out from the sea-damp sand. In that moment it has chosen to bear male and female genitals both, and looming over me it displays the twin rows of flaccid teats running down its massive torso, framed by the embroidery of old bones burned into its skin. A reminder, that I have no mother, no father. Only imakhr. Only pack and tribe. To remind me that I once hung off those swollen teats as a human infant, a pale khrissal maggot stuck to the belly of this gigantic, gorgeous rakshasa, feeding on the oily soma of swallowed souls as it turned me more than human with each suckling breath I took, as it killed that little human being Cyrah gave birth to and began to create what I am now.

I kneel in my imakhr's shadow, desolate. Cyrah's blood dries under the burning breath of the rakshasa that raised me. It lowers its huge head to my torso, a gesture of affection. Its flowing mane snaps in the wind. With its tusks it disembowels me, spilling my entrails on my mother's bones.

Then my imakhr is her first self again. She bends over me as I cradle my own insides, tears and blood drenching my lips. She holds her hand to my bloody mouth, twitches her head toward her wrist. I look into her eyes. She nods. I hold her wrist and bite her flesh, one last time, letting my teeth scrape blood onto my tongue.

In those droplets, my imakhr leaves her first memory of me. Ripening khrissal baby wrapped in palm leaf ripped fresh from the trees and European fabric from a French shape-shifter's fardels. Held out in the hands of Cyrah, her face set rock-hard in resolve but eyes red as a rakshasa's from wiped tears, her companion and negotiator Gévaudan hovering by her shoulder like a ghost. It is a memory my imakhr has never let me experience before, in the innumerable times we have shared our blood, flesh, and humors. The last living moments of the true human being that became me, dappled by sunlight through the leaves, passed from the hands of a mother and into the hands of an imakhr.

I open my eyes and she is walking away down the mudflats, her hair now a sheet of black fire, her feet bare and small on the sand. My imakhr departs with her pack. I used to be a part of that pack. She leaves me to mend myself with my mother's fresh-devoured flesh, to punish me for my betrayal.

I watch her go, crying blood and bile from my mouth. I watch till she is miles away, watch till she walks into the trees naked, letting the verdant tongues of the forest lap her into the dark.

I gather my guts off the ground, the spilled remnants of a life suddenly in the past, already swarming with the insects of the beach. I feel them inside me, crawling and darting in hungry panic. How things change.

I make a torch of broken driftwood and burn the great gash my imakhr left on me, stitching it with string made from my own gut and sealing it with my own weeping fat. Vomiting and pissing, I sink into damp ground and lie on the beach as gulls peck at my body and little leaping crabs explore the earthly legacy of my mother. I feel fallen, human. I don't know what that feels like, and yet I feel it, in this misery of mortal pain and confusion.

I capture the gulls and eat them, wet white feathers clinging to my skin. For days I lie there, Cyrah's life coursing through my agonized human shape, in a fever so scorching that I become in dream's eye a pyre at the edge of the ocean, and see Cyrah's bones glow with a faint green flame at night. The sun rises and sets, dancing with the moon that shifts its shape with shadow and light. Far away, I see the glimmering eyes of my pack-mates watching. But I am alone. I have never known what it is to be alone. I call to my mother, my dead, human mother, like a dying khrissal child, and it is the most pitiful experience I have ever known in my short life.

* * *

When I am able to walk again, I gather Cyrah's bones, stripped clean by salt sea and air, by the days I have lain by them. I choose some of her teeth, and the porous shards of her disconnected fingers, her broken knuckles, and I make them a part of my skin with fire. Newly pierced, fingers still stained with pus, I wash myself in the foam of the tide, snatch the streaks of fish from churning water and eat their silvered flesh with my bare hands.

A smile on my face after what seems an eternity, I piss in the sand and make the ground steam, swallow half my tongue and ululate at the sunrise slicing the horizon. I watch as a wild boar comes to me across the miles of mudflat, galloping with abandon. I pound the ground with my fist, calling it to me with glamour, standing within the yellowed ivory crown of Cyrah's skeleton spread across the sand and silt. It takes it a long time, but it doesn't stop running. I wait.

"I'm sorry, beast," I say as I usher the panting animal to me. As it runs, it showers spit and water behind it in a rage. "You are a low thing, but I should have hunted you. You deserve that much. But I cannot leave these bones. I am sorry," I tell it as it attacks me, charges toward my scarred gut, just healed. I am too quick, and grab its tusks in my hands, whipping its hoofed legs off the ground and snapping its back with the force of its own weight. Landing heavy by me, it drools death into the wetland. The gulls speak their awful language over us.

As always, my pack watches from afar. I know my imakhr will not be among those watching. I eat the boar's flesh, tear off its bloody skin, wash the hide in the sea. I take every bone that once anchored Cyrah's body and soul to this world, and I gather them in the skin of the boar. Knotting this sack in twine from the animal's guts, I sling it from my neck. For a human, the bones would be surprisingly heavy.

I look to the forest I grew up in. My pack, my kin, waiting. Waiting with dread, disgust, curiosity.

Bastard thing, son of Banbibi, eater of Banbibi.

Khrissal-rakshasa.

Khrissal-rakshasa-kveldulf.

I can feel their fear, from far away.

9

I reach over, the wooden bed frame groaning. I touch Izrail's bare back, tracing the furrows of scar tissue that whiplash him from shoulders to buttocks. As if he'd once been mauled by a wild animal. He turns. His body is cold, and damp with sweat or dew. I kiss him, giddy with broken sleep, a teenager again. "How are we still here? It's not morning still," I ask him, and he silences me by licking my mouth. "Sometimes we wake and wake, and one night becomes a thousand, each dream a life lived," he says. Where did his bone trophies go? Centuries of history inscribed on him. I could live with this being beside me for the rest of my life and never tire of him, never know enough. But would I be a historian or a lover to him? He reads my silence, and speaks.

"Don't even listen to me, Alok. I can't believe I'm here, with a human in my bed. It is as much a strange dream for me as it is for you. I'll make this night last," he says, eyes taking in the brittle light from the window. His hair falls against my face, black fire thrown from his head.

And so it is that I leave the country of eighteen tides, my home. Wrapped in a langota, wearing the crown of a tiger's skull, pelt draped across my back and sacks lashed to my shoulders, long hair oiled with coconut and tucked under the teeth of the dead animal, skin cleaned of mud, Cyrah's canines in my earlobes, I venture forth as man.

I am followed by those rakshasas who seek a new life outside the forest, those who want to bear witness to a new age, who want to see what lies beyond the delta with their own eyes and not the memories of their prey. They follow on the trail of my scent, my intent, wearing their first selves of men and women. Curious, willing defectors.

I carry with me the scroll Fenrir handed to my mother, who handed it down to me.

I carry with me my mother's bones.

10

"You didn't want to kill me that night at the baul mela, did you?" I ask Izrail in bed.

"There is easier and less incongruous human prey on the streets of Kolkata than a middle-class college professor."

The room wavers with the light of the hurricane lamp, now lit again. Perhaps because of it, I can hear the insects drumming on the glass panes of the shutters.

"Then why did you bring me here to kill me?"

He turns to look at me. I look at the very small notch of scar bisecting the arch of his right eyebrow, and wonder who gave it to him. Or what. His chest rises and falls. His fingers brush against the pulse in my wrist.

"Humans see through me, Alok. They spend enough time with me and they see a predator, they see something they don't even believe in, and they run as far as they can, hoping never to see me again."

"I saw that, too. I think."

"Yes. And you didn't run. I've had listeners before, but never one who stayed till the end. When you stayed, kept listening, I didn't know what to do."

"You always seemed so in control. So confident."

"It was an act. Smoke and mirrors, to keep you interested. I panicked. When I panic, Alok, my instinct as a hunter is to kill. I thought it might be the only way to preserve what had happened. What has happened. You remind me of Cyrah. You're not afraid of me."

"Like that baul girl by the campfire reminded you of Cyrah."

He shakes his head. "That was delusion, not remembrance. After I devoured Cyrah, I tried to change my first self into her body, by sleeping the trance of ekh'du. To bring her back, in a way, because I had never felt sadness for killing a human before."

"Looking at you now, I'm going to guess it didn't work."

He nods. "My human shape remained as it always was, the body Cyrah and Fenrir gave me. But Cyrah's presence remained, like no other prey before her. I could feel her inside me, as if still alive."

"Like a ghost."

He nods. "What other human has managed to become both devi and ghost, to so leave behind the human without becoming a shapeshifter? Cyrah is the first and only human that I know of who has asked to be killed and eaten by my kind. I think this gave her power over me."

"And you wrote her life down, as her."

"I would write in a trance, and wake to see her story in front of me. I waited for it, every day. And then one day she was finished. She was gone again. Leaving me her tale, as if told by a human woman to her human son."

I touch him, putting my hand on his neck, my thumb on his throat, the most vulnerable part of him, unable to express myself in any other way right then.

"Is she still there in some way, in your head?"

"Every human life I've ever devoured is still there. They're like dreams. I don't remember most of them, but some linger, many taught me much of the world. But no, Cyrah is not there in the way she was when she wrote her story through me."

"Do you wish you'd known her?"

"I know her better than any human son can ever know his mother, Alok."

"You know what I mean."

He purses his lips, runs a hand over his face. "Yes," he says. "Two hundred years ago I would never have admitted that to myself, let alone to someone else."

"Two hundred years ago you wouldn't have been in bed with a human, either."

"Took me long enough," he says, still touching his own face. I wonder what he feels under his fingers, whether it is the face of his mother. "Do you like fucking me?" he asks me, staring at the ceiling.

"Don't tell me you're insecure now. Rakshasa of the Sundarbans."

"Curious. You were engaged to a woman," he says.

"I've had sex with men before."

"I can tell." He smiles. "Do you prefer women?" he asks.

"I don't prefer anything. I'm all right with a human being lying next to me at night."

"I'm not human."

"So you keep telling me, Izrail."

"Does it irritate you that I do that?"

"How could it? You're not supposed to exist. How can that evoke as mundane a reaction as irritation?"

He smiles, and I imagine it is the smile that Cyrah gave him right before he let out his second self and ended her extraordinary life.

"Well. I'm sorry," he says under his breath.

I wonder what exactly he's apologizing for. I wonder if it's the first time I've heard him say sorry to me. I wonder if it's the first time he's ever said sorry to anyone.

"Why did you have me type out the scrolls, Izrail?"

"Alok." He looks at me. "The fact that I'm here, lying next to you, that you're alive. It means that maybe, just maybe, someday I'll stop being a hunter. A rakshasa, man-eater, half werewolf, whatever—the proud thing I was, am. When that happens, I'll start to age slowly, and to forget. To forget the lives I hold in me."

"Isn't that what you want?"

"I don't want those lives to vanish as if they never existed. I wouldn't be here lying next to you, if it weren't for Cyrah and even Fenrir. The Pashto on the scrolls can be read and translated, but the amalgam can't. I want it all in one place before I forget."

"A history," I say, humbled.

"I've been confused a long time, Alok. The hide of my second self is still gray, the snow and shadow of the evening wolf, not the fire and smoke of the rakshasa. But meeting you has made me realize that I didn't give Cyrah enough credit for sacrificing herself to me. I didn't understand that she did it for a reason other than just loneliness. She took a risk. She became a part of me, dormant, until one day she could come back in another time, another world."

"Come back. You think she's going to possess you again?"

"Before I forget this existence and put my second self to rest, I want to try and molt one last time. And when I do, I believe I will rise as Cyrah. Not werewolf, not rakshasa. Human, woman. And that thought, it doesn't scare me."

Someday, I'll stop being a hunter. But not today.

"Well, it scares me. I know Cyrah's stories. I marvel at her, through you. But I don't know her. I know you."

He touches my mouth, fingers drifting down my chin, warm palm on my throat. "There's nothing to be scared of anymore. Someday isn't today, and even shape-shifters know nothing, ultimately. But I know something other shape-shifters don't, because of you."

I smile at him, at the effort he's making.

"You were saying that no one has ever stayed to listen till the end of your story."

"Yes."

"But I have. So, is this the end?"

"For now, yes."

"You're going to leave and disappear, aren't you? Like any worthy mysterious stranger."

"I'm not a stranger anymore." But he doesn't answer my question, instead raising his hands to my face and kissing me.

This time, he guides my hand to his cock until his face softens, his mouth slack with a vulnerability that I've never seen on him. "Alok. Human though you are." He smiles as I clutch him harder, work my hand faster. "I want you to devour me," he says, and though this is a ridiculous thing to say, his words are weighed with the sublimity of all our potential endings, and I smile as I lower my head and eagerly take him in my mouth as he did for me so many times. For the first time, he comes in me and I devour him as he shudders on the creaking bed. It burns in my throat, my gut, like alcohol, like acid, like the blood of some prophet imbued with divine flame. My tongue tingling, I could

kiss him forever on his changed mouth, his face. I do, for mere minutes.

This time, he asks me to fuck him. So I unzip my bag, take out a
squashed cardboard box of Japanese condoms bought at a hawker's
stall on Park Street, and I do. We make love one last time in this country of eighteen tides, his homeland, as somewhere in the darkness the
rakshasas watch the glow of our windows from the sundaris and mangroves, their spiny tails lashing, their eyes fireflies amid the leaves.

As his back arches, ribs and shoulder blades sliding under the
sheath of lamplit muscle and skin, long hair tumbling unruly down
across the valley of his spine, he is again Izrail and Cyrah both, and
this thought makes the lifetimes I have experienced through this creature cascade across me like a tide. My body shudders under his, and I
come into him, crying out like a man speared through the chest.

The storm returns, eventually. That is the way the world turns.

In summer's dusk on the swamplands beyond the delta, the dimming air rains with insects. Grasshoppers, crickets, beetles, moths,
cockroaches, flies, mosquitoes, rippling across the shallows. They
gather on the spined hides of our second selves in rustling cloaks,
many-winged armor that bristles around our bone trophies and pierc-
ings. I sit quiet and let them gather in droves on me as the sun sets,
until I am as a mound of earth amid the brakes of sweet cane grass, the
million legs and fluttering wings over me picking blood and dirt from
my fur as my claws sink into the brackish ground like the heavy roots
of the trees around me.

I become part of the planet, and digest the memories of all the
khrissals I've devoured, feel the vibrations of other lands and kingdoms and empires across the orb of the world, those foreign shores
that Fenrir once wrote of, and hailed from. Across forest and marsh I
see the shapes of my pack crouched in their second selves, dotting the
Bengal plain, meditating by the glimmering ghost fires of their human
prey. In such moments I think I am king of a great court, a king of
wolves in a land of tigers, and Cyrah is goddess and queen, empress of
all these lands, using my two bodies as her palace of bones and meat.

It is a strange rule, but it brings an imperfect peace to my inconstant souls, a temporary calm that has eluded me since Cyrah-Banbibi came to me and gave me her stories on that winter night in the delta.

As the day melts from dusk to night with the stars coming out and the caravans tinkling miles away, I feel something different in the air, sense something I cannot place. Thunder in the distance, though I see no lightning.

I search the horizon. Our hunt is over on this day, and we have raided a caravan. The wisping ghost fires of souls unchained from flesh light the jaws of my pack, presenting the illusion of a khrissal city in the falling dark: a city of the dead. I hear a chital dance through these lights in delight, and hear it fall to tooth and claw thrashing in the oil-black mud and water. I raise my hackles, lift my head to the breeze to cast my senses farther afield to the edge of our territory, where travelers pass, their own earthy fires encased in lanterns, diamonds hung on the threads of their caravans as they weave through Bengal.

The tinkling of bells on their cows and oxen sends me into a trance. I think I hear Cyrah speaking to me from afar, her voice on the wind.

And then my eyes snap open, and I see it.

I see among my land, among my kingdom, an unfamiliar hillock that heaves with the breeze on the horizon, one that begins to reek in my mind under the bright eyes of the Great Bear. I see the shapes of my companions stir with me, but I let them know to keep back as I bound across the marshland toward that strange shape as the sun burns in the trees at world's edge, doused by the milk and water of the rising moon's light. My two hearts pound war drums for Cyrah as I approach the shape amid the cane grass, and I slow down. The hill sways and groans, the grass on its back snapping in the dying sun.

I let my throat open, let the rattle turn into a deep growl, let my spines stand.

The hill changes. Among the fireflies are lit two great lamps of green fire, and they are eyes. Barren stalks and branches wave into bladed spines. It rises out of the mud on four bent pillars, sucking the ground up with it, its grass rippling and changing color in the dimness, fading to dark black and gray. The fireflies rise off it like sparks. It is a shape-shifter in its second self, with skill greater than mine. Though its form has a throat and mouth unsuited to human languages, it opens its maw and lows a single Farsi word, elongated and barely deciphered: <<far-zand.>> It speaks, revealing fangs the size of elephants' tusks, its ragged tongue shedding boiling spit into the ground, its forest of bone trophies sounding among its tangled hide, and it calls me its child.

Without warning I am face-to-face with my father, slouching out of nowhere stinking of me.

We are ringed all around by my pack. But I keep them back. Fenrir attacks me. It is larger and older, but I am quicker, and bound away wearing the stripes of tiger. Somewhere over Bengal the sky opens and washes the land with rain. High winds whirl dervish-like with robes of cloud across the earth in thunder that calls far away. Lightning cracks the edge of the world, rewriting the vanishing sunlight.

It calls me its child and attacks me, and I know from the longing it trails, I know from every bead of musk that clings to the strands of its fur as dew clings to blades of grass. I know it smells Cyrah still burning within me, just as I hear her whispering to me just out of reach, and it knows that I have killed her. It shakes its dark gray mane as if nod-ding, agreeing. A misshapen fool, a monster that wants vengeance for the death of a woman it raped.

I reveal my own fangs, to mirror its display. It tears the earth stomp-ing, its rage shaking the ground. A roar erupts across the marshland, sending a veil of birds to clothe the sky and speckle the storm-flickers to the north. I take my chance at this unnecessary show, lashing across swamp water and grass, soaring to meet Fenrir. My tusked maw closes around the great wolf's singing throat, a vise of cruel bone. I silence its war cry even as the scythes of its clawed hands rake trenches in my hide and meat. Our mingled blood hisses and rains across the swamp water. The panicked birds rush across approaching dark screaming, and the ground hums with the stamping of my pack all around light-ing new night with their eyes. Fenrir and I embrace, just as he and Gévaudan once held each other close, drunk on their own bloodlet-ting in the distant, empty city of Fatehpur Sikri. I ignore the chasms of fire opening across my back under Fenrir's claws, and keep my jaws shut on its thick neck, letting each tooth snag on sinew, tying a knot between me and my father, a bond that cannot be broken. I drink of Fenrir, and Fenrir drinks of me. When the moon has crossed the sky and the sun is lit again in the east, when our shed blood running from Fenrir's throat and my back has cut a crimson stream across the earth of the marshy plain, I let go of Fenrir and let him crash into the dark waves.

Fenrir's second self becomes as a hillock again. Panting, I look at the great wolf fallen, though it looks like no wolf or animal on earth, no more than my second self looks like a tiger though it wears its colors. My pack are phantoms against the rising sun, shades of human man and woman. The insects have returned, drawn by the powerful taste of this opened being, and they crawl over it thick, dying in the breath of its open mouth. Fenrir's maw yawns in pain, and I lower my head to it. Our tusked teeth clatter in the dawn, raising sparks, and our tongues lap our shared blood and spit. Our eyes meet, guttering with sunrise.

Fenrir knows as it looks me in the eye, it knows that Cyrah burns in me by choice, that she asked to be devoured. That she is now forever devi among the rakshasas and khrissals I have left behind in the country of eighteen tides. Pitiful monster, lonesome exile, unasked-for father. Perhaps it feels a gladness in its two hearts for the first time in centuries.

Slowly and painfully it sheds the form of its second self, letting it fall to dream. I look upon the false man who cruelly spared his prey death in Mumtazabad, and thus became father. He does not seem worth the mud on Cyrah's bare feet when she lived. He looks like a defeated, fallen hero from the myths of pale humans from the farthest north. He has been burned by the sun and reddened by our battle, his visage broken and scarred, his long golden hair knotted into shaggy vines. His eyes are different, one grayed by a scar crossing his face, another a blue so bright in his dirty face it becomes iridescent in the early light. He looks at me with these eyes now.

Even as Fenrir's second soul retreats into his khrissal form, the worst wounds of the battle remain, his neck torn to shreds and feeding the red water that licks my ankles. "I had a friend called Makedon once," Fenrir gurgles. He speaks in amalgam. "His throat was cut. I've always wondered what it feels like. It itches." He laughs, convulsing. "He, he told me to let my blood flow, to give my life as penance for. For raping Cyrah. I refused. I refused. He's dead." He coughs. His throat whistles.

As the blood runs off my back and patters off my slick fur, I bend close, the breath of my second self blowing the wet hair off Fenrir's face. He heaves with shuddered gulps, rapt in the scent of my life as it steams off my fangs and tongue.

"Please, show me. The other half," he says.

Growling, I close my eyes, feel the marks Fenrir has made on my back, my life, Cyrah's life. I can feel Cyrah whispering from somewhere within the worlds that nestle between my bones, revealed by Fenrir's claws. I can feel my entire pack watching. Two hearts in me enfold. I open my eyes in the body Cyrah gave birth to, my back flayed by a great wolf, each mark shining in the rising sun. In revulsion and glory I feel Fenrir's mismatched eyes on me as I stand over him. Every cord of muscle under my skin taut as I hold back the victor, for this moment.

He nods, slowly, and gets up even though this should be impossible. He can make it only to his knees. He is barely able to speak. "I've seen. My son," he manages, and smiles with his teeth. Not child this time, but son. I want to deny him, but cannot. I too am monster, after all. I know, as Fenrir stares unfailing into my eyes, that he is speaking to Cyrah as well as me. To Cyrah in me.

"Do it," Fenrir spits. I let my second self return, a drowned man breaking to the surface. In front of my pack, by the light of new day and the death of old night, I devour a shape-shifter for the first time.

It is like death.

A thousand upon thousand deaths and lives burning my self to a husk in that summer morning. I don't know how far my cries carry across Bengal, whether the humans in their villages look to the horizon and wonder if their world is ending, whether my pain echoes the distant nor'wester spending its rage across the forests and sending its winds howling across the swamps. My pack watches, but does not interfere. It is my choice to do this, to eat of a shape-shifter and risk destruction. They are impassive, even repulsed, by this act. But they are also witnesses to my victory over an ancient hunter, and they are my companions. They are, also, curious.

I see Fenrir long in secret for human love over and over again, and forget that he has done so over and over again as he devours these men and women he thought himself in love with. I see Fenrir battle a Norse wolf-man gone berserk, and take from him the body he wore till his death, molting into the warrior's shape over a single night. I see moments older still, memories faded to worn parchment. I see him as woman in dim pasts long lost to him. I see her in ancient tribes, attacked and ostracized by pack-mates for wearing a female first self, until she dwells in barrows alone and drags travelers to their deaths in the sunless days of northern winter. I see her prey, their bloody throats entwined in locks of golden hair that whip away into silvered hide as she springs her second self. I see Fenrir (as him) swallow Fenrir (as her) to nothing over the centuries. I see him live among humans in secret as a Norse mercenary in the Varangian Guard, protecting some long-dead Byzantine emperor, feeding legend by allowing his second self to come free in the battles of human men. I see him marvel at a Thracian woman with the Aegean Sea in her eyes and phoenix-fire in her hair. I see him watch as she runs a spear through one of his human comrades who tried to rape her. I see him fill with pride when his fellow men give her their dead friend's belongings to honor her bravery. I see him kill and devour that very Thracian woman in the throes of what he thinks is love, not daring to recognize that he, too, could rape like the human man he saw shitting out of a hole in his gut for attempting such an act.

I see him leave the yellow-haired men of the Varangian Guard and hunt in the streets of Byzantium, eventually return to the tribes. I see him roam with and without packs, as beast and man, watching human love unfold from the fringes of civilizations, carrying between his two selves an envy as heavy and old as passing history.

Over and over.

And I see him see Cyrah, in time not so far in the past. I feel her uncoil within me.

I vomit into the rich soil, my second self twisting and snapping. Flickers of flame run up and down my body, flashing in the heat of this trance. My pack takes the wet mud in their hands, takes the red water, and runs it over my hide to cool me, splashes it into my gaping maw, my weeping eyes. I purge these lives as Cyrah, somehow, somewhere, helps throw them from me. She crushes the single memory of Fenrir fucking her, throws it out from within me, so it lives only on parchment, and in her own memories that she still keeps from me.

For a day I live as Fenrir and his thousands upon thousands of prey, purging them to stay alive. When I am myself again, I see my reflection in the twilit blood-waters under me, and I see my hide washed of its fire, gone to dark gray and black, to glistering silver that shines with the moon.

I wear now the colors of the great wolf.

* * *

Over the years, I keep on my second self the dark blacks and grays of the wolf and the bear. Some of my pack-mates imitate me in curiosity, though their mimicries look different. Others keep the brighter colors of the rakshasa tribes alive in our pack.

I lead my pack out, farther into Bengal. Into the slowly dying Mughal Empire, where once in a far-off town called Mumtazabad a trio of shape-shifters, each from a different land of Europe, walked past a young Persian woman sitting in the courtyard of a caravanserai.

By the time the Mughal Empire is dead, and Hindustan is under the British Empire, I am alone, an exile with no pack. Cyrah wakes in me, and writes her story as if she still lives and breathes, writes on the skin of a dead baul, a woman I killed. A second scroll.

Then, in a Hindustan now independent, a nation and republic known to the world as India, in a lodge in the Sundarbans, I hold you, warm and real and wrapped in a crumpled blanket. You of one self and one soul.

I am truly my father's son.

And I am truly my mother's son.

*When I came home; on the abyss of the five senses, where a
flat sided steep frowns over the present world. I saw a mighty
Devil folded in black clouds, hovering on the sides of the rock,
with corroding fires he wrote the following sentence now per-
ceived by the minds of men, & read by them on earth.*

*How do you know but ev'ry Bird that cuts the airy way,
Is an immense world of delight, clos'd by your senses five?*

—WILLIAM BLAKE,
The Marriage of Heaven and Hell

Part Seven

AN END

1

I return to civilization alone.

But I urge you not to think of this as a betrayal on Izrail's part. No, it didn't surprise me to wake up on my last morning in the Sundarbans without him by my side, even though I'd wished even in my sleep that it wouldn't happen that way. I didn't go around asking everyone if they'd seen my companion, like some desperate and abandoned lover. No, I knew he'd paid for the trip, knew he'd already informed everyone at the lodge right from the beginning that he'd be returning to Kolkata separately by himself. I don't know if anyone asked how, and it doesn't matter. He has his ways of persuasion, after all.

So I went along with it, said my goodbyes to Shankar-babu and his small staff, and took the boat and the car back to the city I grew up in, as was arranged. It was a strange journey, sitting alone in that cabin under the deck, watching forest eventually give way to concrete bridges again; dozing in the car to waking moments of forest and farmland, small village markets by the road, people haggling over bright heaps of fruit and vegetables; leaving those behind, watching the green and farm-yellow landscape sprouting clusters of suburban buildings and billboards, which then unceremoniously gathered into the sprawl of the Kolkata metropolitan area.

I returned to my apartment tired, so disoriented to be back in the life I once knew, that I was facedown in my bed and asleep before I could even take my shoes off.

I hope, someday, to see him again. Perhaps molted into someone else, perhaps not. I keep my eyes open as I walk through the streets of

Kolkata, as I plow through the crowds on Gariahat and Jadavpur and Park Street and Chowringhee, the places I walked with him.

Maybe one day, among the millions, I will see Izrail, or Izrail molted into a woman I will know, somehow, as Cyrah. Or I will see nothing at all, except the flash of tusk and claw before a sudden death, before I am made one with this being I've shared my life with.

I am alone once again.

I have a new pet—a cat, its cloudy white fur spotted with black. It showed up one day without preamble, slinking in through the grilles of my living room windows and looking at me with expectant green eyes, as if I'd always been the person who feeds it. It looks quite obviously familiar to me, considering how I first met the stranger. It might be my imagination. But I'm glad for its—her—company. I don't name her, calling her variations of Hey, Oi, Aw, and, inevitably, Kitty.

2

I teach my classes. Grade papers. Go for coffee on College Street with ever-dependable Gitanjali, who doesn't deserve as neglectful a friend as me. I even ask her out, finally, in a fit of loneliness over continental breakfast at Flury's, and she puts to rest any doubts about whether she's been meeting me all this time in the hope of a romantic relationship. She hasn't. She nearly brings me to tears by inviting me over to dinner anyway, saying that she's got my back because we're both "scarlet-lettered" in Kolkata because of our failed marriages. She says she'll make vindaloo. I don't actually cry, but in that moment she blazes like a saint in the morning light pouring in through Flury's windows. Scarlet-lettered, indeed. I feel an enduring shame for having asked her out. I haven't taken her up on her offer of dinner yet. I will, or so I tell myself.

I buy books and read them. Watch movies, sometimes about werewolves. There are very few good ones about werewolves, and even fewer about other shape-shifters. I make a point to rent *An American Werewolf in London,* and adore that one, though the ending in particular leaves my chest heavy. I read about mythology and folklore, between the histories that I am used to.

Outside, a storm brews in the cloud-churned sky. Monsoon has arrived again. The curtains billow with damp air like the sails of European ships tumbling on the crests of the Indian Ocean, using monsoon to take them to this far land and its foreign monsters and gods and goddesses. The leaves of the tree by my apartment shimmer in anticipation outside the window, looking in the cloud-twilight like the rustling walls of mangroves.

I like to imagine that Izrail disappeared into that forest from which he once came, to tear away the gray of his hide, hang it on a tree and burn it, to return the fire and smoke of tiger and rakshasa to his fur before whatever comes next.

I sit here typing out the story of his life, his mother's life, his father's life. A part of my life. I do this to keep the promise I made to him—to finish the work I started, or rather, that he started.

I feel an anxiety, a yearning that compels me. This is a history that only I can tell. This is our afterlife, should I die the only human audience for this tale. This is a record of the souls Izrail holds in his body, and one, perhaps, that he holds in his heart. This is what we are left with at the end of Fenrir's Ragnarök, his quest for a new age that culminated in a land far from his own.

At my feet is the dirty blue-and-black JanSport backpack Izrail left in our room at the Sajpur lodge. I looked through every pocket and zipper on it, and found the following: a very stale cellophane-wrapped brownie that is undoubtedly from Nahoum's, a mangled white toothbrush, an envelope containing a wad of thousand-rupee bills, a crushed pack of Gold Flake cigarettes, a depleted pack of rolling papers, one and a crumbled half sticks of aromatic hash wrapped in plastic, a straight razor with a mother-of-pearl handle, a broken pencil, an eraser worn down to a small gray nub, a dog-eared book of the poetry and prose of William Blake.

And, of course, two scrolls of parchment, tied together in twine like mummified stories. There is also a third scroll, separate, by itself.

I could make my career by giving those scrolls up, but I don't, of course.

The third scroll has not been written on except in the script of flesh, the blemishes and scars of the unknown skin it came from, the textures imposed by curing and treating. The scrolls have a powerful, pungent smell that fills the apartment, like leather and soured milk. They lie spread out on my bedroom floor, three uneven swaths of parchment, two burdened with stories, one blank. I don't know whose skin the third one was created from. It could be Fenrir's, stripped from his gutted corpse hundreds of years ago by Izrail.

What happens when you drink the semen of a shape-shifter? Do you give yourself over to wishful thoughts, to dreams of transformation? For all I know, I am not myself, I am dead, consumed by Izrail on that last night in the Sundarbans, resurrected as his new first self. If Fenrir could have molted over one miraculous night under the aurora sloughed off a younger sun, so could Izrail, in one miraculous night sharing the bed of his lifelong prey—maybe that blank scroll is my own skin.

Or perhaps Izrail has already left the world, given his first self over to the ghost of Cyrah, molted into her somewhere in the emerald country of eighteen tides. Perhaps she is the one who waits to return to me, drawn by some distant memory belonging to her son and devourer. This thought makes me terrified, it makes me sad, because if it's true I'll never see Izrail again. But it also gladdens my heart, that such a thing could be true, that I am forever amid the possibility of the impossible, that I might one day meet the woman whose story I lived in these pages.

I don't know. Either way, Izrail is gone, and I am here. I must write.

I grow my hair out, inch by inch till it curls against my shoulders. From Gariahat, I buy a plain white saree, telling the shopkeeper that it's for my wife. When, night after night, I wear the saree, painstakingly relearning how to wrap it around my body from the Internet, of all places, I look at myself in the mirror and take off my glasses to smear its reflection of reality. I have a disgustingly old tube of lipstick in my desk drawer that I've kept since my engagement (and used a few times in between after Shayani left), but I don't use it. I lack the lithe grace of Izrail's body and long limbs, his tapering chin and long neck, but looking at myself in that saree without my glasses, my thankfully still-healthy hair, and clean-shaven face, I pass in my eyes for someone who is not a man, is not merely Alok. No, in those moments, I *am* not merely Alok. Not a second self, but a self, my self, one I've been afraid to let breathe for so long. One who drove my parents to remoteness. One whom Shayani couldn't live with, breaking both our hearts. One I long to be in front of them all one day, their fear be damned. My cat mewls in appreciation at the change, winding her body 'round my legs so the edge of the saree strokes her spine. I feel my shape shift, if ever so slowly, without the magic Izrail's kind knows. But his kiss, his saliva and semen and sweat, lingers in me, in my memory, ignites and strengthens me.

I spend a lot of time looking at myself in those moments, and I feel an inkling of happiness, of some mounting expectation, of pride, a clawing against my heart. I close my eyes and in the darkness tell myself that Izrail is inside me, and so is Cyrah, because I am him, he is me, that he devoured me that night as I devoured him and I am secretly a shape-shifter. Then I open my eyes, and brush away tears.

From Fenrir to Cyrah. From Cyrah to Izrail. From Izrail to me.

And now, from me to you.

Perhaps he just wanted to tell his story, to have people listen till the very end, like I did.

An end, at the very least.

I am Cyrah of Lahore. I am Fenrir of the far Norse lands. I am Izrail of the Sundarbans, son of Cyrah and Fenrir, bastard khrissal-werewolf-rakshasa. I am Alok of Kolkata. I give birth in the swamp waters of the country of eighteen tides, guarded from blood-drawn beasts by my closest companion. I slide out of my mother and into the hands of Banbibi's vahana, in his first self of pale young Frenchman. I am reborn at the end of bitter winter's long night, kneeling by the carcass of an Úlf-héðinn who nearly killed me. I walk beside a djinn from France, and realize that he has become my most loyal friend. I rape the woman I love, the khrissal I love, the prey I think I love. I am not capable of love. I want to love. I am raped by a false man who is in truth a monster. I am born at Woodlands Nursing Home in Calcutta on a sweltering summer day. I become a goddess among my fellow humans. I take a bowl of milk-soaked rice from a chanting villager who holds it out as prasad to me: Banbibi, Bandurga, Bandevi. I run with my imakhr across wetland and marsh, mangrove and river, and we fuck under the moon as villagers wish away the howl-haunted dark with their tapers.

I watch my son change into rakshasa, as I chose for him. I make love to my wife-to-be, huddling close under the blankets to stay the morning light from the windows. I leave the woman I love with my broken pack-mate in the ruins of abandoned Fatehpur Sikri. I leave a human become something else, a khrissal turned Valkyrie, proud and fierce, guarding a fallen warrior. I die at the edge of the Indian Ocean, between land and sea, eaten by my son. I eat my mother down to her bloody bones. I feel Cyrah, my love and prey, consummated and unconsummated, die, not by my hand. I leave lipstick traces on Shayani's mouth as I kiss her, and know that she's only pretending to be comfortable. I stand before my son in the swampland that is his home. I stand before my father, shape-shifter to shape-shifter. I see Cyrah in my son's eyes, and know that it was her own wish to depart the worlds of this earth. I kill my father. I let my son kill me, because I do not remember the human I first sprang from. I kiss a boy named Swapan on a rooftop in Ballygunge Place. I devour my father, my own kind, my own kin, become cannibal, anima-eater, because he is exiled, because I am exiled, because it doesn't matter anymore. I digest centuries of life, anima shaped in different lands. I sleep the trance of ekh'du at the edge of the ocean, buried deep under salt clay. I watch a stranger come up to me and offer me a hash joint at the baul mela. By the grace of Allah I am reborn in my son. I am reborn under a winter moon in Kolkata as a stranger tells me stories of impossible lives. I am Dionysian. I am Apollonian. I am the great wolf at Ragnarök. I tell my son the story of how he came to be, and I tell it by his hand. I write the story of my mother on the skin of a young baul woman I killed, and thought I loved. I am reborn, in language. I listen to stories whispered in my ear as I sleep. I look at the two scrolls, side by side, wrapped in twine. I killed my parents. I am my mother. I am my father. I am a shape-shifter. I am devi. I am deva. I am sura. I am asura. I am male. I am female. I am neither. I am rakshasa. I am djinn. I am werewolf. I am not a khrissal. I was once a human. I want to be a human. I want to love a human. I am a human.

I love you.

Acknowledgments

I'd like to thank a few people personally for their help in bringing this book to fruition. My family; especially my parents, Amajit and Sarmistha, for encouraging my interest in the arts since I was a toddler, and for supporting me when I picked a career that's known for (often) rewarding patience and dedication with penury and obscurity. My brother Abhimanyu, for telling me when I was seventeen to stop talking about writing books in my head and actually try writing one—I did, and unexpectedly found a calling.

My agent, Sally Harding, and her colleagues at the Cooke Agency, all of whom have tirelessly championed this novel, and continue to do so. My editor and publisher in India, Chiki Sarkar, for being open-minded, and agreeing to help turn my bedraggled manuscript into a real-life book. My editor in the United States, Mike Braff, for embracing this uncategorizable novel with such enthusiasm and confidence, for understanding what I was trying to do with it, and for helping me bring it to readers outside India. The many inspiring teachers I've had from school to university, and especially my very first creative writing professor, Nicholas Montemarano, who taught me the most vital aspect of writing—self-criticism. Every workshop classmate I've ever had, for helping me improve my writing.

Every friend I'm lucky enough to have, from school, from college, from university, from life in general—I can't thank all of you in person, but I hope you know who you are. You all give me a reason to get sentimental. I couldn't ask for better people to care about, and to have care about me.

The Brown-Evans family, who without a second thought treated me like a part of their family when I first moved to Canada for university. Thanks to you, I have two families, one for each side of the planet. Your endless generosity and love never fail to move me.

To Les and Neile, and everyone involved with the Clarion West Writers Workshop; to the Carl Brandon Society; to my seven Clarion West instructors; to my seventeen beautiful Clarion West classmates— you all changed my life as a writer and a person. I can ask for no finer community to come home to (and I do, every day, no matter where I am in the world, because you're all *always* there for me and each other). You make being a writer that much easier, and better.

To you, the reader, for making it all the way to this page (perhaps not if you skipped the rest). Thank you. I depend on you.

And finally, a disclaimer. This novel is a work of fiction, and though it's set partly during the Mughal era, it shouldn't be read as history. I've tried to be as thorough as possible in my research, and to show the era as it might have been. But mine is a limited viewpoint. Any inaccuracies are my fault entirely, and should be read as signs that the stories within are set in a world that is somewhat alternate to our own. Similarly, if I've made mistakes in portraying the viewpoints of people who belong to groups I'm not a part of, such as those who've experienced sexual abuse, I'm willing to listen and learn so I can do better next time.

About the Author

INDRA DAS grew up in Kolkata, India, where he wrote his first novel during his late teens before venturing to the United States. There undergraduate creative-writing classes convinced him to keep chasing that writing career. Das is an Octavia E. Butler scholar and a grateful graduate of the 2012 Clarion West Writers Workshop, where he wrote under the tutelage of Kelly Link, George R. R. Martin, and Chuck Palahniuk, among others. He completed his MFA at the University of British Columbia in Vancouver, where he wore many hats, including TV background performer, freelance editor, writing mentor, tutor, minor film critic, occasional illustrator, environmental news writer, pretend patient for med school students, videogame tester, and dog-hotel night-shift attendant. *The Devourers* is his first published novel, though Das has written about books, comics, TV, and film for various publications and has seen his short fiction published in a number of fiction magazines and anthologies. He now divides his time between India and North America and is hard at work on his next novel.

indradas.com
Facebook.com/indrapramit
@IndrapramitDas

About the Type

This book was set in Berkeley, a typeface designed by Tony Stan (1917–88) in the early 1980s. It was inspired by, and is a variation on, University of California Old Style, created in the late 1930s by Frederic William Goudy (1865–1947) for the exclusive use of the University of California at Berkeley. The present face, in fact, bears influences of a number of Goudy's fonts, including Kennerley, Goudy Old Style, and Deepdene. Berkeley is notable for both its legibility and its lightness.